Molly the Maid series

'A glorious read . . . intrigue, heart and humanity by the bucketload. A stunning achievement' LUCY FOLEY

'An escapist pleasure' *SUNDAY TIMES*

'Thrillingly original, and clever, and joyous' CHRIS WHITAKER

'Excellent and totally entertaining…the most interesting (and endearing) main character in a long time' STEPHEN KING

'[Molly's] bravery, kindness and lack of artifice are engaging enough to have you rooting for her all the way' *GUARDIAN*

'Smart, riveting, and deliciously refreshing' LISA JEWELL

'Sparkles with wit and tension' LUCY CLARKE

‘This is cosy crime at its very best – utterly delightful’
Daily Mail

‘A pitch-perfect plot delivered with Nita Prose’s brand of joyful storytelling’ Janice Hallett

‘Witty, joyful and utterly unique’ A J Finn

‘The most winningly off-beat narrator since Eleanor Oliphant. An absolute joy’ Louise Candlish

‘[A] lovable heroine who provides comedy and pangs of sympathy in equal measure’ *Mail on Sunday*

‘Polished to perfection!’ Shari Lapena

‘Thoroughly entertaining, intriguing and utterly compelling’ Liz Nugent

‘Skilfully layered and masterfully told. I loved it’
Santa Montefiore

THE MAID'S *Secret*

NITA PROSE is the bestselling author of *The Maid*, which has sold more than two million copies worldwide, as well as *The Mystery Guest* and *The Mistletoe Mystery*. A *Sunday Times* and *Irish Times* bestseller, and a No.1 *New York Times* bestseller, *The Maid* won the Ned Kelly Award for International Crime Fiction, the Capital Crime Fingerprint Award for Best Debut, and was an Edgar Award finalist for Best Novel. Nita lives in Toronto, Canada, in a house that is only moderately clean. She would love to hear from you at **nitaprose.com** or on Instagram **@NitaProse**.

Also by Nita Prose

The Maid
The Mystery Guest
The Mistletoe Mystery (novella)

THE MAID'S *Secret*

NITA PROSE

HarperCollins*Publishers*

HarperCollins*Publishers* Ltd
1 London Bridge Street,
London SE1 9GF

www.harpercollins.co.uk

HarperCollins*Publishers*
Macken House
39/40 Mayor Street Upper
Dublin 1
D01 C9W8
Ireland

First published in the USA by Ballantine Books, an imprint of Random House,
a division of Penguin Random House LLC, New York

First published in Great Britain by HarperCollins*Publishers* 2025

This paperback edition published 2025
1

A catalogue record for this book is available from the British Library

ISBN: 978-0-00-870858-0 (PB)

Typeset in Adobe Caslon Pro by Palimpsest Book Production Limited, Falkirk, Stirlingshire

Printed and Bound in the UK using 100% Renewable Electricity at CPI Group (UK) Ltd

FSC
www.fsc.org
MIX
Paper | Supporting
responsible forestry
FSC™ C007454

This book contains FSC™ certified paper and other controlled sources
to ensure responsible forest management.

For more information visit: www.harpercollins.co.uk/green

To Dan, my beloved big brother

THE GRAYS

Reginald Gray — Audrey Gray

Flora Gray ···· John Preston

Margaret (Maggie) Gray ···· Fly-by-Night

Molly Gray — Juan Manual Morales

THE PRESTONS

William (Uncle Willy) Preston ⇸ Prudence Preston

Margaret (Maggie) Mead ⇸ Franklin Mead

Mary Preston ⇸ John Preston ···· Flora Gray

Charlotte Preston

Margaret (Maggie) Gray ···· Fly-by-Night

Molly Gray — Juan Manuel Morales

KEY

— Marriage

···· No Marriage

⇸ Widowed

PROLOGUE

My gran loved to tell stories. A maid for most of her life, her best tales featured maids. One of them went like this:

Once upon a time, there was a maid who rued her lot in life. Her clothes were threadbare and worn. Her hands were chapped and dry. Why did she have to toil in servitude instead of living a life of leisure? Why was she fated to work from dawn to dusk for a paltry wage, cleaning a mansion she would never live in herself? She had no family of her own, for they had all forsaken her, but she did know love. Oh yes, she knew it well. There was someone who loved that maid deeply. And just one person's love is enough to keep your soul alive. Anything more is a blessing beyond all measure.

One day, while that maid was toiling in the mansion,

the Lady of the house asked her to clean out a wardrobe containing old footwear. 'There are work boots left behind by a farmhand, slippers forgotten by a young belle, and granny boots that have seen better days,' the Lady explained. 'They're all castoffs – worthless, the lot of them.'

For a moment, the maid wondered: Was Her Ladyship referencing the shoes or those who had once worn them?

'Take any shoes you want,' Her Ladyship offered. 'Get rid of the rest.'

'Yes, ma'am,' replied the maid, holding her curtsy until Her Ladyship left the room.

The maid then got to work cleaning out the wardrobe. Though the work boots were caked with dry muck, they were sturdy. She tried them on, and the moment she did, she was transported into the life of an orphaned stable boy who'd once worked on the estate. She walked a mile in that boy's shoes, cleaning the barn and tending to the horses that provided the only warmth he ever knew. At night, that boy curled up beside a mare on a bed of straw and wished for another life – to be someone else, anyone else but who he was.

Upon feeling the stable boy's keen loneliness, the maid quickly kicked the boots off her feet. She was relieved to find herself delivered back to her own life as a maid. In the wardrobe was another pair of shoes that suited her better anyhow – the beautiful ballroom slippers that had once belonged to a belle. She fastened them to her feet, and as if by magic she was wearing a gorgeous chiffon gown, being twirled around the dance floor by a dashing prince. But without warning, the prince cast her aside for a prettier belle, whom he now kissed right in front of her. She wrestled with the clasps and ripped the slippers off.

Delivered unto herself, the maid eyed the last pair of shoes in the wardrobe – old granny boots. She could not resist. She slipped them on and soon found herself living the life of a wealthy matron who'd once owned the entire estate. Much like a vampire, the matron derived pleasure only from sucking joy from those around her. She had no friends or loved ones, and she pestered her workers ceaselessly, all for her own amusement. The maid removed those boots as fast as she could, relieved to return to her own life.

That night, she reported her strange experience to her beloved, who listened without judgment. When she was done speaking, he had but one question: 'What did you learn?'

'That my life isn't so bad after all,' she replied.

The maid was suddenly overwhelmed with gratitude. By walking a mile in each of those three pairs of shoes, she'd learned a lesson she held close to her heart for the rest of her days: that a life without love is not worth living.

CHAPTER 1

A few years ago, when my gran was alive, she gave me a key. It's a simple skeleton key, tarnished and worn. No amount of polishing has ever made it shine. To this day, I don't know why she gave it to me or what it unlocks.

Gran was ailing when she produced it from under her pillow and pressed it into my hands. I didn't know it at the time, but she had only a few days to live.

'Dear girl, this is for you,' she said as she folded the key into my palm with surprising force.

'What does it open?' I asked.

'My heart,' she replied matter-of-factly.

I sometimes have trouble deciphering the literal from the figurative, but even all those years ago, I knew enough about human anatomy to understand that no key in the world can unlock the human heart.

'If that's a metaphor, I don't grasp it,' I said. 'Precisely what does this key open? A locked box? A drawer? A safe, perhaps?'

'It's the key to everything,' Gran insisted. 'It is all of me. And it is for you.'

Gran was so ill by this point that I assumed her mind was addled from pain. Moreover, I knew it was. There were times during those final days when she'd mutter unintelligibly under her breath – *Birds of a feather* . . . or *A stitch in time* . . . At other moments, she'd suddenly call out to someone she saw in her bedroom when there was no one there but me.

'Gran,' I urged whenever she regained consciousness. 'This key fits a lock. Where's the lock?'

Her eyes fluttered – open, closed, open. She homed in on me as though she'd never seen me before, and yet I'd lived every day of my life by her side.

'You don't know who I am,' she said.

'Of course I do. You're my gran. And I'm your Molly, remember?'

'I remember everything,' she replied.

Then one day Gran asked – begged – to leave this world. I pleaded with her, but to no avail. I wanted so much for her to be well, and yet I always knew she would leave me one day.

'It's time,' she said again and again.

And just like that, she was gone. By gone I do not mean asleep or on holiday or traipsing to the corner store to fetch a jug of milk. What I mean is: she was dead. Yes, dead. There really is no point sugarcoating these things. It was not easy or simple. She died.

My gran taught me to be direct. She also taught me everything else of substance I've learned in this life. For that, and for her, I remain forever grateful.

Today, I can't stop thinking about her. In a cavernous chamber in my mind, her voice echoes, her refrains repeating in a Möbius loop. Perhaps I'm daft, with a mind as soft as unripened cheese, but there are times when I feel her lingering close. It's as if she's trying to tell me something – to warn me of some calamity or unseen danger ahead. I'm used to this, of course – to being the last to know, to understanding too late. What I'm *not* used to are warnings delivered from beyond the grave by someone who is most certainly *very* dead.

'Molly, are you okay? Molly, look at me. Wake up.'

I'm staring into bright lights. Where am I? People crowd around me, shouting and calling my name. Is this an operating room? No, that's not it. The place is familiar, but everything is blurred.

'Molly, listen to me!'

'Open your eyes!'

I know one thing only: something is terribly wrong. Was I in an accident? Am I dying, my soul rising to meet its maker?

Then I hear it, loud and clear – Gran's voice.

All that glitters isn't gold.
Beauty is in the eye of the beholder.

Yes. I remember. I know where I am. I'm in the well-appointed tearoom of the Regency Grand, the five-star hotel where I work as a maid. My beloved fiancé, Juan Manuel, and I arrived early this morning to set up for the day's big occasion – a fine arts and collectibles event with Brown and Beagle, celebrity appraisers and costars of the hit TV show *Hidden Treasures.* I'm not dying, thank goodness, but I'm also not all right. I'm lying on the floor, and all around me are microphones and iPhones and TV cameras and jostling humanity.

This was not supposed to happen. These cameras were never supposed to be focused on me. But moments ago, a revelation was made that was so astonishing, so absurd it feels like a dream. To my utter horror, I'm no longer the invisible maid toiling in the background but the epicenter of attention. An entire room of lookie-loos surrounds me, and they're shouting at me in a desperate frenzy.

'Molly, you're a maid, right? At this hotel?'

'Molly, how does it feel to go from rags to riches in an instant?'

'Molly, can you get up off the floor? You're rich!'

'Molly, *mi amor*? Are you okay?'

The last voice cuts through, bringing me back to myself – Juan Manuel, my love, my life.

Lights and cameras push closer, and I lose sight of him. I try to lift myself, but I lack strength. Stars twinkle in my periphery – *all that glitters isn't gold.* Two men's faces – I know them; I've seen them before, many times – the stars of a popular show.

'Tell our viewers how it feels, Molly. What's it like to be an instant multimillionaire?'

The world tilts sideways and suddenly fades to black.

And then I remember everything: But how? How did it come to this?

'Rise and shine, *mi amor*!' These were the first words I heard as I woke this morning. Through sleepy eyes, I watched as Juan, still in his pajamas, popped out of our bed and pulled the curtains back to let the soft morning light into our room.

I'm not a morning person, but Juan Manuel, just like my gran before him, delights at the dawn of each new day, invigorated with a zest for life, whereas I wrestle my way out from under cobwebs of exhaustion, begging for a few more minutes of slumber. And so it was this morning as it is on most mornings.

'I beg you, press snooze! Please!' I nestled deeper under the covers.

My beloved shuffled into his slippers and like a contented sparrow sang a happy tune as he flitted about our bedroom. A moment later, the mattress shifted as he perched on the edge. I felt his warm hand cajole me from my blanket nest.

'Early to bed, early to rise, makes Molly healthy, wealthy, and wise,' he chimed in his singsong voice.

'Health and wisdom, I already possess,' I muttered. 'As for wealth, that's really asking too much, especially two months before our wedding day.'

He laughed, a sparkling sound, crystalline and pure, like a silver spoon tinkling the edges of a porcelain cup. It's now been over six months since Juan proposed to me in a surprising holiday revelation on the staircase at the Regency Grand. I was happy and relieved to say yes.

'Get up, Molly. Today's a busy day! We have to get to the hotel early. The TV crew will be there at nine A.M. sharp. I'm so excited. We're going to meet the stars of the show!'

We were poised for a huge day at the Regency Grand, where Juan and I both work – he as a chef and I as a maid. Brown and Beagle, the famous appraising couple known for identifying antiquities and long-lost works of art, were bringing their road show to the hotel's Grand Tearoom. It's a shame Gran never got to see their popular reality TV series, *Hidden Treasures,* which debuted two years ago. She would have loved the hosts, owners of the eponymous high-end art auction house, two middle-aged, married men who share a passion for art and antiquities, designer clothes, and each other. The Bees, as they're affectionately known by their legions of adoring fans, delight audiences nationwide with their witty repartee and their historical know-how, all while appraising items brought to the show by everyday collectors spanning the globe.

Most of the items they assess on air turn out to be worthless trinkets or not-so-clever fakes, but devoted viewers – myself and Juan included – watch every week for the gasp-worthy moments when a long-forgotten painting discovered in a dusty attic turns out to be a van Gogh or a wardrobe with a secret drawer bought from a charity shop reveals a hoard of priceless coins.

I felt Juan's hand again, pulling the covers from my face.

A moment later, his lips grazed my cheek as he planted kisses in a perfect garden row.

'If you're not going to rise and shine, *solita,* I may have to resort to extreme measures,' he said playfully as he ducked under the covers and continued his plantation down my bare shoulder.

I wrapped my arms around his warm neck and stared into those beautiful brown eyes, like the turn-down dark chocolates we place on pillows at the hotel, but sweeter and richer because all the love that shines in them is mine.

'*Te amo,*' Juan said. 'And I know just how to wake you up, Molly. I will use Juan Manuel's surefire method – better than all the caffeine in the world.'

And so it was that I was instantly, enticingly awake, kissing my fiancé and tingling with a longing that moments before had not existed in me at all. This is what it's like with us. Each day we spend together is a trove of secret riches. Never in my life did I think such a love could be mine.

We nestled in each other's arms after, and we talked about our wedding, which is only two months away. We're both so excited for our big day. Though it will be a small affair at city hall (Juan and I alongside Angela and my gran-dad), we can't wait to share the moment. Still, it's been stressful managing the costs of getting married on a maid's and a pastry chef's salaries. Mr Snow kindly offered the tearoom at the Regency Grand for a ceremony and reception, but I declined on account of the rental and catering costs, which we could never afford. As for outfits, we most certainly won't be buying new. We looked at rentals, but the price tags added instant wrinkles to Juan's forehead and mine. We still don't have a tuxedo for Juan, and my search for a used wedding dress continues to no avail.

'If I don't find a dress soon,' I said as we lay in bed this morning, 'I'm going to have to make one out of used bedsheets.'

'You could wear a paper bag and you'd still be the most beautiful bride in the world,' Juan replied. '*¡Dios mío!* It's almost seven A.M. We're going to be late. Bust to move, Molly!'

And with that, we both burst out of bed as though the mattress was on fire, and we bustled about our apartment, showering and dressing, and preparing for our star-studded day with two TV celebrities at the Regency Grand.

We were about to head out the door when I remembered. 'Wait! I need a shoebox.'

'*Madre mía,* Molly,' said Juan. 'What for?'

'*Hidden Treasures,*' I replied. 'Mr Snow invited the staff to bring in collectibles for Brown and Beagle to appraise before the shoot. I have a few items that fit the bill.'

'But we don't own any fine art,' Juan said. 'The only treasure in this apartment is you.'

I smiled, then opened the front closet, locating a shoebox, which I brought to the kitchen while Juan reluctantly trailed behind me. I placed Gran's favorite teacup inside the box, the one with an English country cottage scene on it.

'I'll have you know the Bees once appraised a Ming Dynasty teacup at ten thousand dollars. Gran's cup is Royal Standard fine bone china,' I said. 'Maybe it's worth something.'

'Molly, can we go now?' Juan pleaded.

'Soon,' I replied. I rushed to the living room and opened Gran's curio cabinet, which contained all manner of trinkets – her menagerie of Swarovski crystal animals, silver souvenir spoons collected from far-flung locales she never got to see, and one mysterious old key.

'I'm taking some spoons,' I announced, placing the nicest ones in my shoebox. 'And the Swarovski swan, because it was Gran's favorite. And I've always wondered about this old key,' I said as I held it up for Juan to examine. 'Gran claimed it was "the key to her heart," but I've never been able to determine what it opens. Maybe Brown and Beagle can tell me.'

Juan looked at me with a strange expression I could not for the life of me decipher. 'So you're bringing a chipped teacup, a chunk of bird-shaped glass, and an old key . . . but you're not bringing *that*?'

'What?' I asked.

'The golden *huevo*,' he replied. Naturally, I know what a *huevo* is because Juan makes delectable *huevos rancheros* every Wednesday. He was pointing to the top shelf in Gran's curio cabinet, where I keep a bejeweled ornamental egg on its perfectly polished gold pedestal.

'At least bring the egg laid by the magic chicken,' Juan insisted.

'It was not laid by a magic chicken. If only you knew,' I replied.

But he didn't know how I'd come to possess that strange *objet* because I'd told him very little about the time when I was ten years old working alongside my gran in a luxurious mansion owned by a sad and loveless couple. I never went into much detail about what happened to my gran in that mansion or how I came to acquire that golden egg nearly two decades later. Shame is a dangerous emotion. Sometimes it's best left in the past, where it won't contaminate others, spreading like a virulent contagion. I know this firsthand, and my gran knew this, too.

Let sleeping dogs lie.

When I first spotted the egg on the mantel in the Grimthorpe mansion, I was hypnotized. I wondered what it would be like to possess an artifact with such alluring beauty. In a strange twist of fate, long after Gran was fired from her job as a maid there, I met a gardener tasked with cleaning out the property after the deaths of the owners. He remembered me from when I was a child, and he also recalled how much I'd admired the strange, pearlescent egg on the mantel. He said it was a worthless bit of tat and that I could have it. And so instead of going into the trash, that golden egg became mine. Now, it sits in Gran's curio cabinet, a private reminder of what we survived – Gran and me.

'I'm telling you, Juan, that *huevo* is a worthless trinket. But I'm fond of it regardless.'

Juan grabbed the egg, placing it in my shoebox. 'Beauty is in the eye of the beholder,' he said.

It was eerie. He said aloud the very words that had been ringing in my ears all morning. 'I swear,' I said, 'every day that goes by, you remind me more of her.'

'Of who?' he asked.

'My gran.'

CHAPTER

2

My dearest Molly,

If you're reading this, it's because the person to whom I've entrusted this diary has chosen this moment for you to know the truth about me . . . and about yourself, too. My instructions were simple: 'Don't rush it. Wait until the time is right.' And so if your eyes are tracking these words, that time is now.

Oh, how I wish I'd had the chance to convey all of what is written here in person. How I would love to see you with my very own eyes, to enjoy everything you've become, because it was always clear to me, Molly, that you are special in ways you never gave yourself credit for. Despite the trials and travails of your early life, I knew you would blossom into a woman who would make me so proud. My dear girl, remember this if nothing else: you have always been and will always be my precious treasure.

As I write this, my end is nigh. Though I know it has been hard for you to accept, I am very ill, and I will not be getting better. It won't be long now before I leave this world. It's a moment I'm dreading, not for myself but for you. I fear leaving you to navigate life on your own for the very first time. I know you'll manage, and I know it's necessary – the natural order, the older generation making way for the new – but the only inheritance I'm leaving you is grief. Try as I might, there's nothing I can do to spare you from that or from the other slings and arrows this life will aim at you.

But before I convey more, Molly, first, I must issue an apology. It is an unfortunate fact of life that sometimes we grow old before we grow wise, and for my part, I have learned – too late – the error of my ways. A long time ago, I decided to bury my past and hide it from you. When you were young, clever girl that you were, you used to grill me about my personal history, and all I said in response was *Let sleeping dogs lie.*

It was my firm belief at the time that sadness, pain, and loss should be suppressed and buried. I know now that I was wrong to deny you the truth, for my past is not mine alone. It is yours as well.

Do you remember the stories I used to tell you when you were young – fanciful tales of maids and maidens, lords and ladies, paupers and princesses? You'd look up at me with your big round eyes and say, 'Tell me a new one, Gran, a story I haven't heard before.' I was happy to oblige.

My tales started as fantasies, but they never stayed that

way for long. No matter how I tried to keep my life to one side, it wove its way into the fabric of my fiction. Sometimes, the things I made up cleaved so close to my own experience I feared you'd spot the anguish on my face or hear the pained catch in my voice. But you never did – or if you did, I never knew it.

Now, I can't stop thinking about those tall tales I told. Did I do the right thing? Did any of the lessons sink in? Why did I think that veiled fantasies were what you needed when I should have just told you the truth – about myself, about our past, about all that was taken from us? Still, in the end, we lost nothing because love remained. It remains to this day.

My darling Molly, in your short life, you've endured more than your fair share of injustice. Oh, the sticks and stones I've seen hurled at you. I would have done anything to have them strike my being rather than make a mark on yours, but no matter how hard I've tried, I can't protect you from the world's cruelty.

Instead, I created a parallel universe, where we can see ourselves through a glass darkly. I turned our lives into a series of parables with morals I hoped you'd decipher for yourself one day. Perhaps through the legends of a girl or a maid or a princess, you would see who you really are – a uniquely gifted individual whose differences are her greatest strengths. And perhaps over time you'd discover the truth about me, too. For there is always truth in stories, Molly, and herein lies the truth in mine:

Once upon a time, in a kingdom not far away, there was a

young maiden born into a life of unimaginable wealth and privilege. Then she lost everything, or almost everything. Her name was Flora Gray.

Molly, that maiden was me.

CHAPTER

3

'Molly, *mi amor*? Are you okay?'

I know where I am, and I know what's happening all around me. People jostle and push. And then there he is – my beloved Juan Manuel. But they're pulling him away, lights and cameras in his face.

What's happening? My head is spinning. I'm tired and weak. And someone is calling me, not out there, but from beyond.

You are never alone. You always have me.

I follow Gran's voice, closing my eyes and sinking into the cozy darkness, safe and familiar – *home sweet home.*

I remember now, how it came to this. This morning, Juan and I left our apartment and made our way on foot to the Regency Grand Hotel, but once we arrived, a low-voltage jolt in the pit of my stomach made my shoebox tremble in my hands.

'Are you okay?' Juan asked.

'A tad nervous,' I replied. 'I always get this way when we host a big event at the hotel. But all is well,' I said, to convince myself and reassure him.

We both stood for a moment, taking in the splendor of the Regency Grand.

'She's a beauty, isn't she?' Juan said.

'She is,' I replied. The hotel is a timeless treasure. Surrounded by crass billboards and brutalist office towers, it remains an elegant dame, a five-star, Art Deco jewel with red-carpeted steps leading to a gleaming brass portico and shiny revolving doors.

My entire professional life has taken place inside that hotel. I've grown within her walls, learned to be a room maid, and more than that, too. A year ago, our hotel manager, Mr Snow, officially promoted me to a newly expanded role, making an important addendum to my extensive duties. I became Head Maid & Special Events Manager, in charge of private bookings – including today's in the hotel's Grand Tearoom.

I say this at the risk of being stricken down for overweening pride, but even now, after a whole year has passed with me in charge of the tearoom, I puff up a bit every time I think about how far I've come. Me – from Molly the Maid to Molly the Head Maid & Special Events Manager. There are times when my job is demanding and when I get overwhelmed by the workload, but I am happy. And at long last, I belong.

Juan has also climbed the competitive hotel hierarchy. Beginning as a dishwasher, he's earned himself the esteemed role of Head of Pastry in the kitchen downstairs. Beyond overseeing breads, desserts, and baking, he's in charge of high tea, which means not only will we be joined in matrimony in a few weeks' time, but we are conjoined by our job functions, too. I love that man with my whole heart, and I cannot wait to be his wife.

Juan knows just how to put the 'Special' in all 'Special Events.' When the tearoom is full of expectant VIPs, I'll ring the bell, and *voilà* – a tuxedo-clad army of penguin-like waiters marches in single file, carrying in their hands triple-tier tea trays replete with all manner of delicacies made by Juan and his kitchen staff – cucumber finger sandwiches with the crusts removed, heart-shaped macarons in rainbow colors, and Juan's signature marzipan menagerie, one-bite wonders he calls 'marzipanimals.'

'Earth to Molly. Are you sure you're ready for this event?'

I got lost in my memory again, but Juan has always brought me back to the present – the only place where life truly exists.

'Look! It's Mr Preston,' he said.

Standing on the red-carpeted stairs of the hotel, chatting with the new young doorman, was the elderly man who for decades served as the revered doorman of our hotel. But Mr Preston holds another title nearer and dearer to my heart, one that my gran kept a secret from me to the day she died. I was shocked when Mr Preston revealed the truth a few years ago – that he wasn't just a colleague but my flesh-and-blood grandfather.

When Gran and Mr Preston were young, they fell in love, but Gran's family did not approve of the union, even less so when they discovered Gran was pregnant out of wedlock. She had the baby – my mother, now estranged from me – but Gran lost touch with her old beau, Mr Preston. Then they reconnected years later, but by that time, he was happily married to his lovely wife, Mary. According to Mr Preston, Gran and he remained friends to the day she died.

It's strange that I know so little about my gran's past. Sometimes she seems like the biggest mystery of all. Who was her family? How did she grow up? Did she have a loving mother or grandmother, someone who taught her right from wrong? It's a cruel fact of life that wisdom comes with age, which is why I now regret not pressing harder for answers while Gran was still alive. Whenever I asked her about her childhood, she changed the topic. *It's all water under the bridge,* she used to say. *Now let's talk about you.*

This morning, as I watched my gran-dad on the steps of the Regency Grand, it occurred to me that he's the only living link to my past.

Gran-dad spotted Juan and me in front of the hotel and waved. His hair, a bit tousled as always, has turned snowy-owl white.

Juan and I rushed over to greet him, and he threw his arms wide.

'Gran-dad!' I said as he enveloped both Juan and me in a massive hug.

'I'm still not used to seeing you on these stairs without your doorman's greatcoat and cap,' Juan said.

'Retirement has its perks,' he replied, 'but I do miss this place. And I miss seeing you two every day.'

Gran-dad comes to our apartment every Sunday without fail. Juan cooks a delicious meal that we enjoy *en famille,* but I sometimes think Gran-dad might be lonely. He's been a widower for so long – Mary died years before Gran – and his daughter, Charlotte, practices law far away. Lately, after Sunday dinner, the three of us sit on our threadbare sofa and tune in to the latest episode of *Hidden Treasures.* Gran-dad loves the show as much as Juan and I do, and he regularly amazes us with his encyclopedic knowledge of arts and antiquities.

'I'll bet my right arm that's a Tiffany vase,' he said just last week. Lo and behold, Brown proved him right.

'How do you know so much about old things?' Juan inquired.

'Takes one to know one,' he quipped. 'Plus, I wasn't always a boor, you know. As a young man, let's just say I had access to a wealth of experiences.'

My ears pricked up immediately. 'What do you mean?' I asked, but Gran-dad was suddenly riveted by the TV show and did not reply.

As I studied him on the steps of the hotel this morning, I noticed he held a leather-bound book under his arm.

'Is that for Brown and Beagle to appraise?' I asked.

'Indeed. Mr Snow said I could pop by for the day's big event, and I brought an old J. D. Grimthorpe novel, signed. It's not a first edition, but it might be worth something. I see you've brought some goodies, too.'

'I have,' I said as I tapped the lid of my shoebox.

Just then, Speedy, the young doorman Mr Preston had trained to take over his job, bounded down the stairs to greet us. Spindly as a sapling, he somehow manages to heft three or four suitcases at a time though there's barely a muscle on him. When I first met him, I insisted on calling him by his given name, Peter, but he corrected me insistently.

'I'm fly and I'm flash, and I like to dash,' he said. 'Call me Speedy. Everyone does.'

And so, unorthodox though it is, I respect Speedy's wishes. Speedy is always tripping over his greatcoat, which hangs off him, and his cap is so big it threatens to fall right off his head. He certainly does not have Mr Preston's gravitas, but he makes up for it by doing the doorman's job with a surfeit of youthful – if somewhat gangly – enthusiasm.

'Yo, yo!' he said to the three of us this morning as he bobbed in our faces like an eager gopher. 'Bruh and Bagel just got here. Walked right up these steps five minutes ago!'

'Brown and Beagle,' I corrected.

'Like I said, they've arrived. And see that posse? That's the camera crew. There's the gaffer. He shines light on stuff to make it look better than it does in real life.'

Speedy, a tech wizard who loves music and movies, has been taking night classes in video production. He wants to work in the film industry one day, so having a TV shoot at the hotel is a dream come true for him.

'See the long-pole lady?' he said. 'Boom operator. I'm still learning, but one day I'm gonna be a major film asphyxianado.'

'Aficionado,' I said.

'Like I said.'

Keeping up with Speedy's hummingbird pace makes me

dizzy, and there are times when his mouth does not match the pace of his brain, something I'm still learning to forgive.

'We'd better get in there,' I said.

'Lots to do this morning,' Juan added.

The three of us left Speedy and revolved into the busy lobby. Oh, how I adore that lobby, with its tangy scent of lemon polish mixed with a fine mélange of guest perfumes. The grand staircase in the middle of the main floor is an Art Deco *pièce de résistance.* The serpentine brass handrails spiral gracefully to the terrace, where voyeurs can survey the bustling scene below – bellhops and valets crisscrossing the marble floor with luggage in tow, and guests huddled together on the dark emerald settees, their secrets absorbed into the deep plush velvet.

Several months ago, Juan came walking down that very staircase, and in front of the entire staff of the Regency Grand, he proposed to me, slipping onto my finger a ring that once belonged to my gran. A simple gold band with a little heart in the middle held between two tiny hands, that ring is with me always, a reminder not only of my engagement day but of the woman who taught me that love is everything.

'I'm off to the kitchens, *mi amor.* I must check the marzipanimals. I made enough to fill Noah's ark.'

'Will you come back for the preshow appraisal?' Mr Preston asked. 'It starts in fifteen minutes.'

'Wouldn't miss it,' Juan replied. 'Molly's about to learn an important lesson.'

'And what's that?' I asked.

'That sometimes a teacup is just teacup,' he replied with a wink.

'My gran's things will always have value to me,' I said.

'And that's why I love you,' Juan pronounced as he blew me a kiss goodbye. 'See you both in there.'

Juan hurried toward the stairs leading to the dank basement kitchen.

Gran-dad and I took in the lobby, a buzzing hive of activity. The settee area was cordoned off – a makeshift holding pen for the live audience waiting to enter the tearoom. Behind those maroon ropes, hordes of Brown and Beagle groupies – affectionately known as 'Bee-lievers' – milled about with Bee & Bee VIP lanyards strung around their necks, holding in their hands treasures they hoped were real. My dear friend Angela, bartender at the Social, our hotel bar and grill, was attempting to maintain order at the corral's entry point, but if her fiery hair was a barometer of her mood (and it always is), she was losing control entirely.

'Hair in a tizzy means Angela's busy,' Mr Preston whispered, reading my mind.

'Look what the maid dragged in,' Angela said the moment she laid eyes on Mr Preston.

'It's lovely to see you, Angela,' Gran-dad said. 'But why are you manning the lobby?'

'The Social is closed today – Mr Snow's orders – so he's assigned me to crowd control. And it's not going well.'

'So I see,' said Mr Preston as white-haired ladies sans lanyards ducked under the ropes of the exclusive holding area.

'Everyone is excited that Brown and Beagle are here,' I said.

'Molly, these fans are lunatics,' Angela replied. 'See those two?' She pointed to a couple in the crowd. The man held an oversize jar in his hands.

'He claims he's got Napoleon's toilet paper in there.'

'I'm sorry?' Mr Preston exclaimed.

'He swears the fine French lace in that jar was used to wipe the emperor's royal arse. He tried to sell it to me!'

'For how much?' I asked.

'You're missing the point,' Angela replied. 'There's only one authentic thing in that jar.'

'What?' I asked.

'The shite, Molly,' Angela answered.

'How do you know the lace wasn't Napoleon's?' I countered. 'You're not a world-renowned antiquities appraiser.'

'She's right,' said my gran-dad. 'With Brown and Beagle, you never know what might have value.'

'You're as bonkers as they are,' Angela said, pointing a thumb at the throng of Bee-lievers gathered behind her.

'See you in the tearoom?' I said.

'Wouldn't miss it for all the junk in the world,' Angela replied.

'I'll stay here to help Angela,' said Mr Preston.

'Much appreciated,' Angela replied. 'Later, Molly.'

I took my leave and trundled down the long corridor leading to the tearoom. The space was as I left it the night before, each of the forty round tables crisply laid with white linens, a napkin folded into a graceful crane for each place setting, and every bit of Regency Grand silver polished to perfection. What was different was the stage at the front of the room, where the film crew was taping down electrical cords and setting up a display table between three high-backed thrones – on one side, two thrones for the hit show's famous hosts and on the other, a third for the guest.

Mr Snow stood in front of the stage as the lights beat down on him. He was conversing with a man in a rumpled T-shirt who was carrying a clipboard and wearing a baseball cap with a badge on it that said IRONIC in big, yellow letters. Mr Snow, dressed in an elegant three-piece suit, nodded as he listened to instructions.

He spotted me and waved me over. 'Thank goodness you're here, Molly. The TV crew arrived far earlier than expected, and as I think you'll find, they're terrifically eager to begin.'

'But it's only eight A.M. Filming starts at ten,' I said. 'We've got staff appraisals first.'

'Actually, we've already begun filming,' the man in the ironic baseball cap said. 'The best shots are happy accidents.'

'In my experience, accidents are rarely happy,' I replied.

'Molly, this is Steve,' said Mr Snow, 'the showrunner for *Hidden Treasures*.'

'Honored to meet you,' I replied, offering a circumspect curtsy. I fully expected Steve to tip his ball cap, or better yet remove it completely, but I was afforded no such courtesy.

'What do you do here?' Steve asked.

'Head Maid and Special Events Manager, at your service,' I replied. 'Normally, you would not have to ask such a question because I'd be properly attired in my maid uniform, with my name tag pinned adroitly above my heart for ease of identification. But alas, no one was expecting your crew *quite so early* this morning.'

'Right,' said Steve. 'So, can we get the audience and staff in here, split? We're ready to shoot.'

'Wait, you're filming staff appraisals?' I asked.

'Like I said, we film everything,' said Steve. 'All participants need to sign the appearance waiver. You wanna meet the Bees, you gotta sign on the dotted line,' he said as he tapped the stack of waivers on his clipboard.

From the look on Mr Snow's face, I could see he was as surprised as I was by this news. 'Very well,' he said with a sniff. 'Molly, alert the staff downstairs, and I'll tell Angela.'

Steve nodded and left us. I dialed Juan immediately.

'This is Juan, the love of your life,' he answered. 'How can I be of assistance?'

'They're filming now. Tell your staff to come up posthaste.'

'*What?*' he replied. 'We're not ready.'

'I know,' I said. 'But come up anyhow. And, Juan?' I added, 'Can you grab my name tag from my locker?'

'Of course.'

'Thank you. And goodbye.'

No sooner had I slipped my phone into my pocket than a wood-paneled door leading to the greenroom opened beside the stage. Brown and Beagle – *the* Baxley Brown and *the* Thomas Beagle – walked out. The second I laid eyes on the stars, I felt weak in the knees and my heart clapped excitedly in my chest. It was them! It was really, truly them, and in person the celebrity couple was jaw-droppingly magnificent.

They were dressed in their trademark velvet waistcoats – Brown's scarlet, and Beagle's royal blue. Brown was brawny and wide-shouldered, a very tall Prince Charming, with blond locks falling churlishly around his angelic face, a twinkle in his curious blue eyes. He looked even more handsomely chiseled IRL (as Juan would say) than he did on TV. Beagle was his physical opposite, a diminutive man, low to the ground like his canine namesake, but perfectly proportioned and no less dashing than his husband. He had wavy, dark hair and discerning eyes. He reminded me of that pop star who sang about raspberry berets and who changed his name to a symbol, which in my mind is even more perplexing than a man with a name like Peter choosing to go by Speedy.

As Beagle surveyed the room, his eagle-eyed gaze fell on me, and he bowed slightly in my direction. I couldn't believe it. I would have reciprocated with a curtsy, but I feared loosening my knees might bring me to a delirious faint in the middle of the floor.

Familiar faces appeared at the entrance. There was Angela and my gran-dad, and trailing behind them, the VIP studio audience of Bee-lievers, carrying their precious *objets* in hand or wheeling larger items on trolleys. They streamed into the room and took their seats at the white-linened tables.

Next, in came Juan, heading straight for me. He was dressed in clean chef whites and his jaunty chef's cap. 'Your name tag, *mi amor,*' he said. 'May I?' He pinned it on my left side, right above my heart.

'Make sure it's on straight,' I insisted.

'Do you think I don't know you?' he replied. 'Done.'

He then led valets and bellhops, maids and waiters, laundry staff and receptionists, into the room, their treasures in tow. I marched over to my co-workers and asked them to form a neat line that snaked from the stage-right stairs all the way to the back of the room. Various clipboard-toting crew members expedited the signing of waivers with mind-boggling efficiency.

With my shoebox in hand, I headed to the front of the line, where Mr Snow was standing beside Speedy, who was bobbing up and down so much, I felt seasick.

'I'll go up first to quell everyone's nerves,' Mr Snow said. 'Then it's you, Speedy – and please, don't talk over the hosts. After that, it's your turn, Molly. Good?'

I managed a curt nod, but my mouth was suddenly dry.

'Have you ever met a star?' Speedy asked me. 'I've never met a star. We're gonna meet the stars!'

'Quiet on set, everyone!' Steve called out as he loped to the front of the stage. 'Welcome to *Hidden Treasures,* where Brown and Beagle find lost works of art, changing history and lives in a single moment. Cameras are rolling, and this might just be your lucky day. You never know what Brown and Beagle will find on . . . *Hidden Treasures*!'

He started clapping then, coaxing the audience to do the same. Onstage behind him, the two dapper costars blew kisses to the crowd. Then as the applause faded, they seated themselves on their thrones.

'Most of the time, we don't find long-lost treasure,' Steve warned the audience, 'but that's not the point.'

'The point is to take the mystery out of history,' crooned Brown.

'And to dazzle and delight!' Beagle said as he flashed his bejeweled jazz hands, which elicited *oohs* from the crowd. 'Don't be shy up here, folks. Remember, we appraise *you* as much as your treasure.'

'Camera's rolling. First up!' Steve said as he pointed to Mr Snow.

Mr Snow walked up the stage stairs and took his seat across from the two expert appraisers. Under the strong lights, he started melting like soft-serve ice cream in the sun. He mopped his forehead with his pocket square, but the small cloth was insufficient for the task.

'Sir, I think you forgot something,' Brown said.

Mr Snow looked with confusion from one Bee to the other. 'I'm sorry?' he said.

'Your treasure. Or are you so precious you decided not to bring one?'

A hearty chuckle echoed through the crowd.

'My treasure is in my pocket,' Mr Snow said.

'My, my, any takers?' Brown quipped as he sat up straight in his chair, more regal and taller than ever.

The audience laughed, and the hosts waited comfortably, basking in the glow of their witty repartee. As I stood to one side, I couldn't help but feel sorry for Mr Snow. It's no fun to be laughed at. Still, this is what the Bees do on their show – they say outrageous things, and the crowd laps it up every time.

'Pull it out, sir. Let's have a look,' Beagle mused as he rubbed his small hands together with glee.

Mr Snow reached into his breast pocket and removed his pocket watch, a beautiful antique timepiece, pure silver with a crystal face. He detached it from a watch chain that I'd given him for Christmas the year before.

'Ah!' said Brown as he cradled the watch in the palm of his large hand. 'Folks, this here is an American-made timepiece crafted by the Waltham Watch Company.'

'Which is good news and bad,' added Beagle as he leaned in for a closer look. 'The frame is a replacement, but the watch itself is original.'

'And this specimen is in decent shape, only a few scratches,' said Brown. 'However, Waltham was among the first American companies to mass-produce watches.'

'Which means,' said Beagle, 'that this one, even in fine condition, is worth only around two hundred dollars.'

'It was my grandfather's,' said Mr Snow. 'It's an heirloom to me.'

'Sentimental value, but not a treasure,' Brown pronounced. 'Shall we get this man off the stage before he drowns in his own sweat?'

The crowd cackled.

'Next up!' Steve called.

'Here goes nothing,' Speedy said as he bounded up the steps like an adolescent antelope and took a seat on the guest throne. He held out one closed fist, waiting for the Bees to say something.

'What have you got for us, young lad?' asked Brown.

'So my cousin, right?' Speedy began. 'He's like one of those metal detector dudes? He trolls beaches looking for lost gold and crap. Oh crap, I just said "crap"! Am I allowed to say "crap" on TV?'

'Bit late to ask,' Brown drawled, and the crowd chuckled.

'So, my cousin,' said Speedy. 'He finds this coin, right? And it's buried deep in the sand. And he freaks out when he digs it up and shows me. And all these girls in bikinis run over, and now they're all screaming, too, and we're jumping up and down on the beach, and—'

'What's at the sharp end of a pencil?' Beagle asked, interrupting.

Speedy was quietly thinking, perhaps for the first time in his life. 'The point?' he eventually replied.

'Exactly!' said Beagle. 'Now get to yours. We don't have all day.'

'The point is I've got a Roman coin in my hand.' He opened his fist to reveal a round object so tarnished it was hard to make out any features on it until he flipped it over. 'Look. There's one of them emperor dudes.'

He held the blackened coin as the camera zoomed in.

Beagle addressed the crowd. 'What do you think, folks? Hidden treasure or hopeless hoax?'

The image of the coin was blown up on a monitor to the side of the stage. The crowd suddenly burst out laughing.

Brown pointed out what was obvious to everyone watching the screen. 'That's no Roman emperor,' he said. 'That's Queen Elizabeth.'

'And see there?' added Beagle. 'The date might have been your first clue.'

'Oh. Right. 1980. But that's, like, vintage,' Speedy said. 'It's gotta be worth something, no?'

'It is,' said Brown, his eyebrows shooting up.

'Most definitely,' agreed Beagle as he crossed his arms. 'It's worth a penny.'

The crowd heaved with mirth as Speedy was escorted off the stage.

'You're up,' I heard as Steve Ferris-wheeled his arms, prompting me to the stage. My feet were glued to the spot, but I dislodged them and settled myself on the guest throne, legs pressed together, shoebox squarely placed on top. I could hardly breathe as I stared at the two stars – one big, bold, and bright, the other small, dark, and dashing. They twinkled in front of me as their ultra-white smiles caught the glare of the lights.

Sometimes a smile is not a smile.

'So you're Molly the Maid,' said Brown, his apple cheeks curving down to a chiseled jawline.

'How did you know?' I asked.

'Your name tag was my first clue,' Brown replied as the crowd laughed.

'So you're in charge of special events *and* you're a maid here at this hotel?' Beagle inquired.

'That's right. I love my job. My gran always said if you choose the right job, you'll never work a day in your life.'

'So true. I've never worked a day in my life,' Beagle said as he preened his glossy, dark curls.

'Descended from nobility, you're a most regal Beagle,' Brown quipped.

'I've been called worse things,' said Beagle with a shrug.

'Molly, as a hotel maid, you must see so many things behind all those closed doors. Tell us, what treasures have you stumbled across in your time here?' Brown asked.

'Once, I found the diamond wedding ring of a dead tycoon in my vacuum cleaner, and let me assure you, that was quite a surprise. Another time, I stumbled across a guest's snake coiled on a chair in the lobby, but while exotic and valuable, I wouldn't exactly call that serpent a treasure. Oh, and I regularly find untouched turn-down chocolates left behind in guests' rooms, the kind wrapped in gold foil and placed on your pillow? Believe it or not, not everyone likes them.'

'Who doesn't like chocolates?' Brown said.

'Especially when wrapped in gold foil!' Beagle added as he slapped his knee.

Suddenly, the audience's laughter was so shrill I could hardly think. I looked out at a sea of jeering faces and wide-open mouths.

'Are they laughing with me or at me?' I asked the Bees.

'Oh, isn't she just *darling*?' Brown drawled, his blue eyes sparkling.

'*She's* the treasure,' Beagle replied, and suddenly both stars were clapping – for me! The entire audience joined them, and I had no idea why.

'Molly the Magnificent Maid,' Brown said. 'Are you ready to show us the contents of your little ol' shoebox?'

'Yes,' I said. I removed the lid and placed the box on the table in front of me. 'I've brought a few things that belonged to my gran. I wish she could be here today to meet you.'

'Why didn't you bring her?' Beagle asked.

'Because she's dead,' I replied.

Beagle's eyes grew two sizes. 'An excellent excuse,' he concluded.

'There you have it, folks. Molly tells it like it is,' Brown said.

Beagle leaned forward, peering into my shoebox. 'My, my, what do I spy with my appraiser's keen eye . . .'

'Well, well, what have we here?' Brown added as he donned a pair of thick black-rimmed glasses from the breast pocket of his scarlet waistcoat.

'Are you seeing what I'm seeing, Bax?' said Beagle.

'I am, but I'm not quite believing it,' Brown replied as he slowly shook his blond head.

'If you're looking at my gran's favorite teacup, it's fine bone china, Royal Standard, and these are pure silver souvenir spoons, and a Swarovski crystal swan . . .' I explained.

'Yes, all trinkets,' Beagle pronounced with a wave of his delicate, jewel-encrusted hand. 'Worthless.'

'Not to me,' I said. 'I also brought that old skeleton key that I'd love to know more about. My gran claimed it was the key to her heart.'

'The key to her diary is more like it,' said Brown. 'Edwardian-style diaries were often kept under lock and key to protect the secrets of the well-to-do ladies who wrote in them.'

'But my gran was a maid, just like me.'

'Do you have her diary?'

'I don't believe she ever kept one,' I said.

'Then her secrets died with her,' said Brown.

'Yes,' I said. 'They most certainly did.'

'But, Molly,' said Beagle. 'You've managed to point out everything in that box except the one item that's actually caught our eye. Brown, you're seeing this, too, yes?'

'I definitely am,' Brown replied, and as I watched, he covered his mouth with his hand in an expression that, if I'm not mistaken, might best be classified as 'utter disbelief.' Brown reached into the box and gingerly removed the ornamental golden egg sitting on its delicate bow-legged pedestal. He held it carefully in the palm of his hand. The camera zoomed in for a close-up, the lights catching the egg's sparkling jewels and the Bees' rounded eyes.

'My word,' Beagle said as he leaned back in his chair. 'Molly, you have brought us a most unusual item.'

'I didn't mean to waste your time,' I said. 'It was actually my fiancé's idea to bring that silly egg here. It was given to me by a gardener who worked at a mansion my gran used to clean when she was a maid. I've been warned it's a bit of junk, but no matter. It has sentimental value.'

'Good golly, Miss Molly. I wouldn't jump to conclusions so quickly. I'm not so sure that's a bit of junk,' said Brown.

'What do you mean?' I asked.

'Thomas,' said Brown. 'What's your assessment of the jewels?'

Beagle removed a jeweler's loupe from the pocket of his indigo jacket. He held the magnifier over his small right eye, which grew several sizes under the loupe as he examined the egg proffered in his husband's flat palm. 'Jewels intact,' he said. 'Free of inclusions. All cuts and markings characteristic of the period.'

Beagle brought the loupe down and stared meaningfully at his husband, though what exactly that look meant, I could not have said. 'Bax,' said Beagle. 'The gold pedestal.'

'Yes, I know,' said Brown. 'Pure gold, through and through, twenty-four karat, the detailing unmistakable. In all my years as an antiquities appraiser, I never dared to dream I'd see such a thing with my own eyes.'

Both men paused and the audience drew a breath.

'Forgive me,' I said, clearing my throat. I was suddenly aware of the tension in the room. 'I've been told I have a habit of missing obvious clues, but for goodness' sake, will someone please explain exactly what is going on here?'

'Molly,' said Brown as, with exceptional care, he placed the egg on the display table between us. 'I'm afraid Thomas and I are in a bit of a state of shock.'

'We are,' echoed Beagle, his mouth a tight line.

Baxley took off his glasses and returned them to his scarlet breast pocket. 'What you have in that box is a bona fide, jewel-encrusted, one-of-a-kind prototype made by the famed St. Petersburg jewelers who once served the Russian tsars.'

I followed the words, but their meaning was lost on me. It was as though the two men were suddenly Charlie Brown adults blathering in a language I didn't understand.

'Once upon a time, Molly, the Russian royals gave precious Easter eggs as gifts,' said Beagle. 'They hired a very special design house to craft their imperial treasures, and for well over a hundred years, rumors have swirled about the prototype egg that started it all, the only closed egg ever designed, resting on an iconic gold pedestal, the original egg that inspired all those made after it.'

I was certain I was missing something, that as usual I was failing to comprehend the obvious. I decided to voice what was on my mind. '*All that glitters isn't gold.* That's what my gran used to say.'

'And she was right,' said Brown. 'But not when it comes to this egg. Each of the quatrefoils on it are inlaid with the rarest rubies, pearls, emeralds, and rose-cut diamonds.'

'And the pedestal base is pure gold, with cabriolet feet,' added Beagle. 'There's only one house in the world that ever detailed them like that.'

'The House of Fabergé,' Brown said.

'We called the egg the Fabergé – Gran and me. But it was a joke,' I said.

'This is no joke,' Beagle said somberly as he slipped his jeweler's loupe into his blue velvet pocket. 'The specimen of fine art you've brought today is not only rare, it's a hidden treasure, unique in all the world.'

'I would estimate its minimum worth at five million dollars,' Brown added.

Both men's faces blurred in front of me. Gasps and shouts rang through the crowd. Cameras zoomed in on my face, and questions were hurled my way.

'Molly, you're a multimillionaire!'

'Molly, can you hear us?'

'Molly, *mi amor.* Are you okay?'

I couldn't answer. Gold stars unfurled at the edges of my vision. Jewels and quatrefoils danced and jeered.

Then, suddenly, my world faded to black.

CHAPTER 4

My dearest Molly,

It is a great irony that as the curtains close and my life fades to darkness, I begin my story.

There once was a young maiden named Flora Gray, who lived in the lap of luxury. Her house was not a house. It was a glorious, imperial manor with white Roman columns at the entry, a grand oak staircase inside, a ballroom, a library, a conservatory, and so many bedrooms that, try as I might, I can't remember them all. Gray Manor, the country estate was called – a most appropriate name since it described not only its color but its character.

To say it was stately is an understatement. Molly, it was grander than any museum you've ever visited, more austere than a mausoleum, more imposing than a supreme court of law. My father and mother presided not only over the manor house but over the sprawling property as well, which included barns and stables, gardens and glades, a workers' cottage, ponds, and vast hunting grounds.

You may wonder how it came to be that I lived on such a grand estate and never spoke of it, but the secrets I have kept from you will stay that way no longer. This may come as a surprise, but I did not always live a life of penury. Put plainly, I was not always poor. My father, Reginald Gray, was a man of considerable means, descended from a long line of men of considerable means. Not only was he the revered patriarch of the Gray household but he was also the wealthy magnate and CEO of Gray Investments, a company with inestimable holdings all over the world. A man made of money, Papa had never known poverty or the pangs of cold or hunger, nor had he ever suffered the myriad deprivations of the common man. As a child, I was convinced that in lieu of blood, coins jangled in his veins, and where his heart should have been was a cavernous bank vault housing a ruddy cashier who counted bills in a steady rhythm – a beat that would stop only when there was no more cash to count. Oh, Molly, how I revered my father when I was a child.

'What separates a gentleman from the masses is money. Wealth makes the man,' he used to say.

To me, Papa was half man, half deity – commanding his dominion through some divinely ordained force. Like a Greco-Roman god, he was shifty, his moods a storm of unpredictability. Still, when I was young, he showered me with such warmth and generosity . . . at times.

I recall him in my mind's eye before all the troubles began – before the dissolution of assets, the threat of a merger, and the dismissal of servants and staff. I can see him sitting in his office chair – the Capital Throne, my mother called it – handsome and imposing behind his oak desk. A smile breaks out on his face the moment he sees me, his only child, standing in the doorway. I could not have been more than five years old at the time.

He puts down his pen, shoves his adding machine aside, and holds out his strong arms. 'My dear girl,' he says. 'Come.'

I run to him, my black patent shoes click-clacking on the herringbone floor, the baby-blue skirt Mrs Mead dressed me in swishing against my legs. When I reach him, he lifts me into his lap, where I curl like a cat, purring with contentment.

'My little Flora,' he says. 'An exquisite beauty. The moment I laid eyes on you, I knew you were my precious blossom, and so I named you Flora – a delicate flower, a refined and rarefied bloom bringing color to my days.'

I can still smell the scent of him, his imported French cologne, musky and deep, the prickly fabric of his Savile Row suit scratching my tender cheek. But as quickly as Papa showered me with affection, he was equally quick to take it away. This was the era of rock 'n' roll and poodle skirts, and yet in honor of Papa's father and the many hallowed men who'd come before him, my father was running his household like an Edwardian fiefdom, with him as the self-decreed feudal lord. The world around Papa was innovating and modernizing at lightning speed, something he feared and abhorred in equal measure. Papa believed in tradition and continuity, hierarchy and stability. But above all else, he believed in his family's superiority, untouchably above the common man.

My mother, pitiful creature that she was, worshipped Papa. Never did she let me forget how lucky I was to bear the family name. But she'd confessed to me how she'd used her feminine wiles to win Papa, captivating a man of great wealth and stature and, in doing so, making her family proud.

Audrey Gray – Mama – was an ethereal being with raven-black hair and skin so white it was almost blue. She was a much-coveted beauty – or had been, before my birth robbed her not only of her feminine wiles but, according to her, of 'all the joys in life.'

Mama acted as though she was a pedigreed aristocrat when in fact her family's money was more nouveau than Papa's. But marriage had changed everything, legitimizing Mama's family history and changing it forever. This transformation, however, came at a cost. I don't know what my mother feared more – Papa himself, or losing her claim to the Gray family name.

Over time, I have come to realize my mother was a victim of many things, including circumstance, but it took me decades to see her that way. I will not sugarcoat the truth, Molly, and I hope you will understand when I say that both she and Papa lacked the milk of human kindness. Rarely did Mama have a good word for me, consumed as she was with her vanity and flaunting our family's good name.

She would beckon me into her lap when I was a child, holding me close to her heart, but her words offered little warmth. Whenever a lugubrious mood overcame her, which occurred often – meaning every time a younger, more febrile female specimen caught my father's wandering eye – my sad mother would repeat the same refrain: 'Flora, you were born in a bath of my blood, my first child, destined to be my last. And to my colossal disappointment, you were born a girl.'

Born a girl – a fact I was never allowed to forget. Sometimes, it was meant as a boon, but most often, and more so as I grew up, I learned that my gender was a transgression. I could hardly be blamed for it and yet I was. I'd robbed my mother of beauty and a chance to bear other children while at the same time I'd stolen from my father any possibility of getting what he wanted most – a male heir.

It's a sad truth of human experience that repetition dulls the impact of just about anything – but this is especially so in the case of suffering. By the time I was seventeen years of age, I was only dimly aware of the increasing volatility of my family circumstances. Little did I know that the comfortable high life at Gray Manor was coming to an end. Cracks were beginning to show in the veneer of our family's prosperity.

Once upon a time, Gray Manor had teemed with full-time domestics, but the staff had begun to dwindle. I watched, wide-eyed, as one by one my father dismissed loyal, long-suffering servants, making excuses for frog-marching them out the door. 'That stupid maid used a monogrammed silver spoon as a shoehorn,' or 'I never liked the look of that chap.'

The workers dwindled to a skeleton staff, but my father could not dismiss everyone. The two very best remained. They were closer to me than my own kith and kin, a fact that both galled and mystified my parents. Closest of all was Mrs Mead, my beloved nursemaid, who'd raised me as her own from the time I was born. Ruddy-faced and portly, she had a special smell, like a warm loaf of bread fresh from the oven, and the kindest eyes you ever saw, one blue and one green. When she looked my way, it was like the sun shone on me and me alone. I loved her with all my might, trusted her with my whole heart. When I scraped my knee or elbow, she'd console me, then dress the wound with a bandage.

'There, there. They stumble who run too fast.'

If a visiting child tried to take a toy from me, Mrs Mead ensured I got it back. It was at her kitchen table that I did my homework. And when I came down with the curse in my fourteenth year, it wasn't to my mother I ran but to dear Mrs Mead. She taught me to stanch the flow, both of the blood blotting my skirts and of my deeper, blooming shame.

'Chin up, Buttercup,' she said, two chapped hands on my cheeks. 'You're a woman now. You should be proud. I sure am.'

At this time of my life, as I reckoned with the dispiriting frigidity of my parents, I discovered how liberating it could be to assign my lived experiences to a fictional protagonist, placing them at a safe remove within the confines of fiction. I became so good at transforming my circumstances into poetics that my teachers lauded my creativity, and in so doing failed to recognize my coded cries for help:

In a bath of bluest blood she was born
A girl, unwanted, from her mother's loins torn

There you have it, Molly. You've been introduced to dear Mrs Mead and to your great-grandparents – the patriarch and matriarch of our tale. You'll come to know them all better as I continue my story. I swear to you that no matter what treatment I endured at the hands of my parents, I loved them with every fiber of my being, a blind devotion like no other. I emulated them and believed in their righteous superiority. I wanted nothing but to make them proud, yet in the end, I achieved the opposite of every youthful intention.

But let's begin at the beginning rather than portend the end. Let us return to a very important day when your gran, seventeen-year-old Flora, was a carefree young student, filled with nervous anticipation as she posed an important question to her parents. You see, the great gift of being an only child with a distracted mother and a father on the cusp of financial ruin was that I was free to do as I pleased. And what I pleased was so different from what other girls my age were interested in. All they dreamed of was dancing and dates, marriage and mates. I, on the other hand, wanted to learn. And learn I did. I was a brilliant student, Molly, with a voracious appetite for history, languages, arts, and my favorite subject of all – literature.

My father had an impressive library at Gray Manor, completely for show, a glorious room with floor-to-ceiling bookshelves, filled with leather-bound volumes organized according to subject and sometimes by author name: Antiquities, Art History, Charles Dickens, Economics, Egyptian Civilization, English Literature, Shakespeare. I swore to myself that I would one day read every volume in that room.

I loved learning so much that at the age of eight, I convinced my father to hire a tutor to teach me French, which I could converse in quite fluently after a year or two of lessons. At my private girls' school, I sat in the front row of class, and not even the girls calling me 'teacher's pet' could dissuade me from giving my full attention to the lecture. The world grew bigger and brighter every day. Suddenly, I had proof there was more to living than the rigid, cloistered ways of Gray Manor, with its affected austerity and flagrant worship of wealth, class, and rank. I longed to suck the marrow of life through education, and I dreamed of higher academic pursuits. Maybe I could be anything – a teacher, a professor, perhaps even a writer?

I was the only girl in my school with marks high enough to pursue arts and literature rather than home economics and coiffure. Two roads diverged, and I longed to take the one less traveled. But doing so meant leaving the girls' school and sitting crucial exams that would, if I passed, allow me to apply to university. My dreams rested not just on the results of those exams but on whether I'd be allowed to take them at all.

At my behest, the headmaster of my school arranged a meeting with my mother and father, and on a cold, rainy Monday, he ventured to Gray Manor to petition my parents on my behalf.

Never before had I seen the headmaster look so meek as he did on that rainy morning in the grand foyer of my father's mansion, wet from head to toe, slack-jawed as he took in the majesty of his surroundings. Uncle Willy, my father's butler, escorted him through the corridors and up the grand staircase to Papa's well-appointed office, where the poor man's knees were shaking as he knocked with a clammy hand on Papa's mahogany door.

'What do you want?' my father growled when the headmaster entered. 'I don't have much time.' Papa said all of this without so much as glancing up from his papers.

My mother was standing behind him, wearing a navy silk blouse and fashionable beige culottes she'd bought in Paris a few months before.

'Sir, madam,' said the headmaster. 'Your daughter asked me to come. You're very lucky. Rarely have I had a student as gifted as Flora – if ever.'

My father drew a deep breath and stood from his chair. It was a tactic of his, to stand and assume his full, imposing height, towering over everyone. His mouth shaped itself into a mirthless grin, a smile in name but not in spirit.

'Bit of a waste, no?' Papa said. 'To have a daughter with brains.'

'I . . . I don't see it that way, sir,' the headmaster countered. 'Do you, madam?' The headmaster turned to my mother, expecting agreement.

'What I would say,' drawled Mama, 'is that with a girl, it's best to invest in her looks if you're seeking long-term gains.'

'Beauty above brains,' my father quipped as he offered a hand to my mother, inviting her to stand by his side.

'I'm not here to dispute Flora's beauty,' said the headmaster. 'And she comports herself with grace at school. But you see, Flora has a chance to enter courses that will allow her to sit entrance exams for university. She has the aptitude for it, and the will, too. It would be a shame for someone so clever to eschew academics. It's a gateway to any profession of her choice.'

'A gateway,' my father repeated. He slow-marched to where I silently stood in the threshold of his office. He appraised me with his hawkish eyes, then came to a halt in front of me.

'Headmaster, look at her. Take her in,' he said, putting a finger to my chin, pushing my bowed head up so my embarrassed eyes met those of my equally embarrassed headmaster.

'Is she not a fine specimen?' my father asked. 'If Flora were a horse, she'd be a thoroughbred, don't you think? Who am I to withhold such a gift from mankind?'

I know these words will sound harsh to your ears, Molly, but these were different times, and believe it or not, it wasn't unusual for women to have their physical attributes assessed as if they were prizewinning livestock at a county fair. At the time, I found such appraisals either laughably silly or worse, complimentary, for I was too young to fear idolatry.

'What my husband is trying to say,' my mother offered, 'is that our daughter should attend a finishing school for girls, where she will be trained in home economics and other womanly arts and where she will learn, if we're lucky, to find herself a husband appropriate to her station.'

My father smiled at his wife, a real smile this time, with all his warmth shining upon her.

Despite my fears, I found the strength to speak up. 'Papa, Mama,' I said. 'Please excuse me for speaking out of turn, but I wish to take the prep course and the exams. I'd like the opportunity to prove myself.'

'To prove yourself,' my father echoed.

'To whom?' my mother asked.

'To myself, I suppose,' I said. 'I want to know if I have what it takes to succeed.'

'What it takes, Flora,' said my father as he hiked up his trousers, 'is something you weren't born with. I'm a businessman descended from a long line of businessmen. I know how the world works. A woman with a sharp mind is like a fish on a bicycle.'

My mother brought a mannered hand to her mouth to conceal her tittering laughter.

'Still,' said my father, 'if you're set on writing your silly exams, be my guest. Just don't get too far ahead of yourself. As your father, it's my job to decide your future. And there are better pursuits for a girl than university.'

'Thank you, Papa!' I said, hearing only approval and ignoring the cautions that came with it.

That was all I wanted – a chance. It was a step that would move me closer to my goal. Surely, if I passed my exams with flying colors, I'd be allowed to stream toward higher education rather than finishing school? Surely, if I was granted admission to a good university, my parents would support me? And surely, if one day I made something of myself as a professional, Mama and Papa would be proud of me for bringing glory to our family name? Surely, anything was possible, even for a girl?

I met the eyes of my headmaster, expecting to see excitement writ there. But all I saw was the grim line of his upturned mouth – another smile that wasn't quite a smile. And again, I chose to ignore it.

CHAPTER 5

'Molly, *mi amor*, please, wake up!'

I feel two gentle hands on the sides of my face. I recognize his voice – my beloved Juan Manuel rousing me from slumber. I open my eyes, expecting to find myself snuggled beside him in bed, but instead, I'm greeted by a swarm of strange faces. Amongst them is a giant camera so close my breath fogs the lens.

An arm pushes the camera away, and I focus on him – Juan, gazing down at me, his eyes two dark pools of concern.

It all comes back to me, where I am – the tearoom at the Regency Grand – and why I'm laid out on the stage floor. The golden *huevo* was supposed to be a trinket, but Brown and Beagle just confirmed otherwise, which means I'm in possession of a treasure worth millions.

'Step back!'

'Give her space!'

Mr Snow and my gran-dad are suddenly on the stage, helping Juan pick me up and bring me to the guest throne where I was seated moments ago.

The camera tracks us, then lands on me. Brown and Beagle, looking jubilant and expectant, return to their thrones, adjusting earpieces and smoothing their TV-perfect hair as Juan and my gran-dad are reluctantly ushered offstage.

'Looks like the maid could use a stiff drink,' Brown says, as he crosses his long legs and snaps his fingers.

'Tea,' I manage to croak, and Angela magically appears at the lip of the stage with a warm cup – orange pekoe, just the way I like it.

'Molly, you ready to roll?' Ironic Steve asks as he grabs the cup from Angela and hands it to me. 'You're okay now, right?' His assistant holds a black-and-white clapboard, ready to drop the arm.

'I'm better,' I reply, 'but I—'

'Roll cameras. Action!'

'Welcome back to the land of the living, Molly Gray,' says Brown with a blue-eyed wink for the camera.

'Folks, we've had our share of mishaps on this show . . .' Beagle chimes in.

'. . . we sure have,' Brown adds. 'On season three, a guest peed herself from excitement.'

'Let's not forget the time a man threw a plaster bust at us after a low appraisal. Remember that, Bax?'

'I have the scar tissue to prove it,' says Brown as he tweaks his nose.

'But never before have we had a guest faint on set,' Beagle explains. 'Congratulations, Molly! You're our first. And you've just come to and learned you possess a treasure worth millions. How are you feeling?'

'I'm . . . shocked,' I say. 'And I want to apologize for scaring everyone. When consciousness becomes overwhelming, I tend to shut down.'

'Well, you're back with us now,' Beagle continues, 'and viewers are desperate to learn how you came to possess this one-of-a-kind Fabergé prototype.'

'It was given to me by a gardener,' I say. I explain the full story, how as a child, I worked for several weeks alongside my gran as a maid in the mansion of a famous writer, and how one object – a magnificent, bejeweled egg on the mantel in the writer's parlor – completely enchanted me.

'Fascinating,' says Brown. 'Now this writer, can we confirm this story with him?'

'That will prove difficult,' I reply.

'Why?' Beagle asks.

'Because the writer, J. D. Grimthorpe, is very dead.'

'Wait now,' says Brown as he scratches his perfect head of blond hair. 'Wasn't that the author who was poisoned in this tearoom a couple of years ago?'

'The very one,' I reply.

'The plot thickens,' says Beagle as he rubs his hands together. 'So how did Grimthorpe's egg make its way to you?'

'I had reason to visit the mansion after Grimthorpe's death,' I explain. 'And Jenkins, the gardener, whom I knew when I was a child, was cleaning out the parlor, throwing out some old things, including the egg, but knowing how much I'd loved it when I was young, he offered it to me.'

'Did you have any idea of its worth?' Brown asks as he points to the Fabergé glowing brightly on the table between us.

'No. The only person who suggested it might be valuable was J. D.'s wife, Mrs Grimthorpe, but I never really believed her.'

'And why not?' Beagle asks.

'She had a habit of overestimating her own worth while underestimating everyone else's,' I reply.

'We see that a lot in this biz. Don't we, Bax?'

'That we do,' says Brown as the camera catches his strong jawline.

'When Jenkins the gardener confirmed the egg was a bit of junk, I believed him. But my gran always said beauty is in the eye of the beholder. That's why I wanted to keep it.'

'Molly, I'm not quite sure you grasp the life change that has just occurred. Do you understand you're now worth millions?'

I hear the words, and I comprehend them, but I cannot fathom how what Beagle said could be true. 'But . . . I'm just a maid,' I say.

The cameras zoom in on my face and the crowd starts to laugh and coo.

'Molly, do you watch our show regularly?' Brown inquires.

'Oh, I do! I'm an avid fan. So is my husband-to-be, Juan Manuel.' I shade my eyes from the blinding lights and search for him in the crowd. 'There he is, front row.'

'That handsome fellow in chef whites?' Beagle asks, sitting up on his throne.

The cameras pan to Juan, who jumps to his feet and waves his arms in the air madly. 'I love you, Molly Gray!' he yells. 'In sickness and in health, for richer or poorer! But I'm pretty sure we just got a whole lot richer!' Juan throws his chef's hat in the air, and the crowd goes positively manic.

'My, my,' says Brown when the audience finally calms down. 'You've got good taste in men, Miss Molly. I do love a man in uniform.'

'Since you're such a fan of the show, you must have learned a thing or two about the provenance of an antiquity and how it impacts an item's worth,' says Beagle.

'Indeed I have,' I reply. 'Your show is quite educational.'

'Here's what we know about your golden egg,' Beagle explains. 'It left its homeland during the revolution in 1918, likely via Fabergé himself, but after that, the paper trail went cold . . . until now.'

'Do you have any idea who owned this egg before Grimthorpe?' Brown asks.

'No,' I reply.

'And I'm guessing you have no idea who owned it after Fabergé?' Beagle asks.

'No,' I reply.

'Do you hear that?' Brown asks as he cups a hand to his ear. 'That's the sound of a few million dollars circling down the drain.'

The crowd responds with a resounding boo.

'Hold on one minute. Are you Bee-lievers or not?' Beagle asks the crowd. The answer comes in the form of hoots and applause.

'Molly, you are now connected to a pair of appraisers from the most renowned auction house the entire world over. When it comes to the mystery of long-lost art, Beagle and I are master sleuths. But the question is: Do *you* Bee-lieve in us?' Brown asks as his blue eyes meet mine.

I have no idea what to believe, and all I really want is to get off this stage and out of the limelight as quickly as possible, but out of good grace, I repeat the familiar TV tagline I'm supposed to say: 'I Bee-lieve in you.'

'Then we'll start our provenance inquiry with Jenkins the gardener,' says Beagle.

'I do hope he isn't "very dead" like Grimthorpe and your gran,' Brown says, a quip met with guffaws from the crowd.

'He's very much alive,' I reply.

'Then we'll get cracking.'

'Literally or figuratively?' I ask as the crowd cheers me on.

'Bless your little black bob,' says Brown. 'Bee-lievers, you've just met Molly Gray – maid, marvel, and millionaire. I promise you haven't seen the last of her. Let's give Molly a hearty round of applause!'

The crowd rises to their feet, clapping and whistling so loudly I block my ears to quell the din. Steve bounds onto the platform, grabs my arm, and whisks me off, guiding me through the paneled door leading to the greenroom.

It isn't long before the two hosts are backstage with me,

Beagle cradling the egg in his two tiny hands. 'Molly, you were amazing!' he says.

Brown approaches, hovering over me. 'The crowd gobbled you up.'

'You're a star,' says Steve with a tip of his ironic ball cap. 'We just aired a quick clip on our socials, and it's going viral already. My AD is fielding calls from all over the country. People want more Molly – and fast.'

'What?' I say. 'What does that mean?'

'You're made for TV,' says Steve. 'We'll edit the show overnight and air it tomorrow.'

'But don't we have more to appraise?' asks Beagle.

'No one brought anything nearly as good as Molly did, so we'll shoot the b-roll letdowns, then start researching the Fabergé's provenance ASAP.'

Beagle and Brown nod as Steve exits through the paneled door, letting Juan Manuel, Mr Preston, and Angela in as he goes. I can't recall a time I've been more relieved to see the faces of my loved ones.

Juan rushes over, pulling me into a warm hug.

'Molly!' says Gran-dad when Juan releases me. 'Are you all right?'

'You've got it made, maid! Get it?' Angela squeals as she grabs my arms.

'I get it,' I say. 'A pun. But what I don't get is what happens now. Am I truly . . . you know . . .'

'Wealthy beyond your wildest dreams?' Angela suggests.

'Yes,' I say. 'That.'

Beagle draws nearer, still holding the treasure in his palms. 'Molly, much will depend on the provenance of this piece and what you want to do with it. But I assure you this egg is incredibly valuable.'

'Most people sell their works,' says Brown, 'and if you opt for that, I assure you that Brown & Beagle Auction House will get the highest price possible.'

'But don't I have to prove the egg is mine?' I ask.

'If you can,' says Beagle.

'I don't have any paperwork. It was a gift,' I say.

'You have witnesses,' Brown replies. 'And, Molly, that egg of yours has been lost for over a century. Never once in all that time has anyone surfaced a document that references it.'

'Which suggests the finders keepers law applies,' Beagle adds.

'Meaning?' asks my gran-dad.

'When the original and true owner of a found item is unknown, it rightfully belongs to the finder. Molly, you're the finder,' Brown says, beaming down at us. 'In other words, the egg is yours.'

My knees go weak as I gaze at the priceless *objet* in Beagle's little hands. Is the egg twinkling or am I seeing stars?

'Oh, no. You're not going down again,' says Juan as he wraps a protective arm around my waist.

'Deep breaths,' Angela instructs, and I breathe until my vision returns.

'I'm okay,' I reassure everyone.

'Molly,' says Brown. 'Your life is about to change.'

'*Mi amor*, we won't have to struggle anymore,' says Juan. 'And we can have a big, fancy wedding – the marriage of our dreams!'

'If, and only if, you sell the egg,' says Brown.

'Of course she'll sell the egg,' Juan says. 'Right, Molly?'

I look at the expectant faces gathered around me – friends, family, and two shiny reality TV stars.

'Why wouldn't I sell the egg?' I say. 'After all, what could go wrong?'

CHAPTER 6

Dear Molly,

One of the great perils of youth is the false confidence that comes with it, but with each passing year, bravado erodes, taking the chip off and leaving something new in its place: humility.

When I was young – seventeen years of age, to be precise – I was elated that Papa granted me permission to take a prep course to sit university entrance exams. I was on top of the world – invincible. I ignored all of Papa's caveats and warnings. I was practically skipping as I escorted the headmaster out of my father's office, down the grand staircase, and all the way to the front foyer of Gray Manor. At the entrance, the headmaster handed me a long reading list, advising me to begin studying on my own before prep classes began.

'You'll be the only girl in the class, Flora. Are you prepared for that?' he asked.

'Of course,' I replied. 'What could go wrong?'

The headmaster's Adam's apple bobbed, but whatever he wanted to say, he swallowed it.

Uncle Willy, my father's butler, was standing sentry in the foyer. Strong, broad-shouldered, with silver hair and a distinguished mustache, he seemed to me an old man, though he probably wasn't even sixty at the time. I was forbidden from calling him Uncle Willy, a term of endearment that he loved but that both my parents found questionable. If you looked at his hands, you could tell he hadn't always been a butler, for they were as large as bear paws, the skin weathered and callused from physical labor.

Uncle Willy had once worked as a caretaker on the acreage bordering Gray Manor. A man more comfortable in stables than in mansions, he became our long-serving butler when I was but a babe in arms, an unorthodox hiring decision on my father's part, one that raised eyebrows amongst the trained serving staff, who suddenly found themselves led by a worker from the farm next door. Uncle Willy carried himself with great dignity, though, and could spot trouble a mile away. For that reason, Papa trusted him.

All of this flashed through my mind as Uncle Willy saw the headmaster out, then closed the door behind him. He turned to me expectantly. 'Well?' he said. 'Am I looking at a potential university scholar?'

My ear-to-ear smile was the only reply he needed, and

after a quick look to make sure my parents weren't about, Uncle Willy threw open his arms and I ran into them eagerly.

'You've always had gumption, ever since you were a wee girl. You do me and Maggie proud,' he said.

Maggie, a.k.a. my nursemaid, Mrs Mead, was Uncle Willy's sister. All the warmth I lacked from my own parents I found in excess quantities in those two beings. They doted on me hand and foot, celebrating my successes – my first steps, my first words, my first time riding a bicycle. They worried themselves silly over any setback I experienced, so much so that I sometimes felt they were my true parents, though there was not a drop of common blood between us. Despite the constancy of their love, I didn't always treat them well, for my parents drilled it into me that servants were lesser than.

Mrs Mead kept a small, thatched-roof cottage on the estate, given to her by my father when her husband, Franklin, a pilot in the war, was shot down by enemy fire. After Franklin was killed, Uncle Willy became his sister's chief protector. He'd lost his own wife, Prudence, to tuberculosis a year earlier, leaving him with a young son to raise on his own. I can see now the burden of grief Uncle Willy must have carried, but I had no sense of it when I was a child. He'd lost his wife so young, and his brother-in-law. He'd been left with a child to rear by himself.

Uncle Willy kept a room in town, but on his days off, he could be found at Mrs Mead's cottage, tending to her garden or her chickens, picking apples in the orchard or sitting down to a homemade shepherd's pie with his son and sister by his side. He never seemed more comfortable than when he removed his butler's uniform – a crisp black suit with a neat bow tie – to don his weathered overalls. It was as though he'd shed a disguise to reveal his natural skin.

As for Uncle Willy's son, who was about my age, I thought little of him when I was a child, didn't even care enough to recall his name. He was a brooding brown-eyed boy with broad shoulders like his father's. That lad lurked in the shadows of the estate and barely said a word. The truth of the matter, which I can see now, is that I ignored the boy out of petty jealousy. I wanted to be the only child Mrs Mead and Uncle Willy fawned over, the only child they loved. Early on, I convinced myself there was something about that boy I didn't like – the way he carried himself without apology, as if he had every right to visit the manor when in fact his presence was a special privilege granted by my father.

It is a sad truth that as children we take on the prejudices of our parents without even realizing we are doing so, and I internalized Mama and Papa's belief that the children of domestics were below my station, so unremarkable they were easily forgotten.

I despised seeing the boy loitering about the grounds while at the same time believing it was my God-given prerogative to go wherever I wanted and do as I pleased. Though strictly speaking I wasn't supposed to, I would visit Mrs Mead's cottage almost every day, finding in its rubblestone walls a comfort I never felt within the confines of my parents' posh manor house. Mrs Mead let me read or do schoolwork on her worn kitchen table. It was there, in her kitchen, that I learned to embroider and quilt, to bake bread and pies, and to brew a perfect cup of tea.

On rare occasions, after running out of the manor to the lawns and through the garden gate, then ambling down the stone paths, past the pond and farm fields, I would arrive at the squat, arched door of Mead Cottage and let myself in without so much as knocking.

'What's for tea?' I'd demand of Mrs Mead, who was usually toiling away at the stove or huddled under a lamp with her embroidery ring.

'Fresh biscuits and clotted cream,' she would reply, her green eye and blue eye crinkling with joy at the sight of me. 'Hot out of the oven for the little missus in ten minutes' time.'

Never once did Mrs Mead make me feel unwelcome, nor did she ever order me back to the manor house, where I belonged. It was her job to tend to me all day long, and then, after her shift was done, she found herself looking after me again in her very own home. I still recall the times when I'd swing the cottage door open to find that tousle-haired intruder occupying *my* chair at the kitchen table. Mrs Mead would take the boy by the hand and lead him out the door.

'Go find your father in the garden. Tell him we've got a visitor again,' she'd say, and lickety-split, the brooding boy would be gone. I'd gloat the second Mrs Mead closed the door on his back and she'd lavish attention on me once more.

What became of that boy I didn't know for several years. At some point, he simply vanished, rarely to be seen on the estate grounds. So all-consuming was my selfishness that it never occurred to me to ask Uncle Willy or Mrs Mead where he was or even to consider they might be capable of loving this child even more than they loved me.

When I was seventeen, sharing the good news with Uncle Willy about my admittance to prep school, I learned where his son had been all those years.

'You may very well find yourself in classes with him soon,' Uncle Willy revealed. 'My boy's back from boarding school, and he's about to attend your class.'

At first, I was confused. How could the butler's son be attending a private prep school for the wealthy and privileged?

Uncle Willy explained without me having to ask. 'Your father granted him another scholarship,' he said. 'So you'll see him at school.'

'I'm not sure I'd recognize him after all these years,' I replied. 'And besides, I doubt we'll run in the same circles.'

Molly, it hurts my soul to commit those words to paper, and it hurts even more to remember the pained look that crossed Uncle Willy's face when this classist quip so casually spilled from my mouth. But I was a parrot echoing whatever I heard at home, repeating it ad infinitum, lest anyone forget my family's God-given superiority.

'I'm happy you'll be studying, Flora,' Uncle Willy said, ignoring my callous remark. 'And I know you will achieve great things one day. Just don't forget your ol' Uncle Willy and Mrs Mead.'

'I won't,' I replied. 'I promise.'

Just then, I heard my name, a familiar voice calling me from somewhere deep within the manor. 'Yoo-hoo, Flora!'

'That's my sister,' said Uncle Willy. 'She's been looking for you. Your gown arrived, and she needs you for a fitting.'

'Right,' I replied. 'I better get to it. Thank you, Uncle Willy.'

'For what?'

'For everything,' I answered.

I made my way through the graceful front corridor filled with gilded portraits of Papa's noble ancestors – gloomy men holding fountain pens or cocked rifles and pale-faced women in corsets so tight they appeared on the verge of fainting. I walked past the banquet room, with its long claw-foot table, and then past the parlor, with its brocade settees and the ominous grandfather clock ticking time in one corner. Up the grand staircase I went, hearing the creak and groan of the antique oak under my feet as I climbed each perfectly polished step.

Once upstairs, I passed my father's office, then the library (my favorite room in the mansion), two lush and roomy bathrooms, and several guest rooms. I kept walking until I passed through the glass French doors leading to the west wing of the manor, which was mine and mine alone. I pushed through the ornately carved double doors to my vast bedroom, with its Queen Anne four-poster bed and throw pillows plumped perfectly by some hardworking, invisible maid.

'Mrs Mead?' I called out. 'Are you here?'

I found her in my en suite vestibule, lined with floor-to-ceiling mirrors on one wall and an antique vanity handed down to me through generations on my paternal line.

'There you are,' Mrs Mead said the moment I crossed the threshold. 'I've been calling you. Your father got cross and dressed me down for yelling in the hallway. Your mother will be here any minute. She wants to see you in the gown. Is it true what she said? Am I a step closer to calling you a scholar?'

I nodded. Mrs Mead smiled and pinched my cheeks with her dry hands.

'You were always a clever one, Flora. When you were a wee lass, you used to school everyone on vocabulary. I used to laugh and laugh – all those big words coming out of such a tiny mouth. You do us proud. You really do.'

'If only they would see it that way,' I said.

'See it what way?'

I turned to find my mother behind me, a manicured hand on one hip of her Parisian culottes.

'Never mind, Mama,' I said. 'The gown is here.'

'It's about bloody time,' Mama replied as she marched over to the clothes rack by Mrs Mead and began surveying the dress from all angles. 'Honestly, that couture house is a complete disappointment. This gown is one week late, no explanations.'

'Well, it's here now,' said Mrs Mead. 'And we've still got time before the Workers' Ball. Your daughter is such a natural beauty, she could wear a paper bag and still be the prettiest girl at the party.'

'I doubt that,' said my mother. 'Your father has worked all year long to court the right families, Flora, and the RSVP list is a veritable who's who of the nation's best and brightest. There's even a baron and baroness coming this year. I'm not saying you're unattractive. I'm just saying you'll have stiff competition.'

'I didn't realize the ball was a beauty contest,' I replied.

'Please don't start, Flora. You'll give me a headache.' Mama dabbed at her forehead with the back of her hand.

The Workers' Ball was a special event my parents held once a year. It was the one social engagement that mixed the workers in the region with the well-heeled owners of the estates they served. My father had held the ball for a decade and counting, and I don't know who dreaded it more – the workers or us. Still, it was a necessary evil, and for my parents, it was a chance to gossip with the other elites while sizing up the generation to come.

'That dress is fit for a princess,' said Mrs Mead as she took the gown off its hanger and gingerly passed it to me.

I ducked behind my Venetian dressing screen and put it on. I barely recognized the reflection looking back at me in the mirror. In an instant, I'd transformed from a studious, bookish girl into the belle of the ball. A light pink, the color of a damask rose, the fitted satin bodice hugged my torso and waist. Billowing skirts fell in a blushing cascade all the way to the floor. I secured the tulle straps on my arms, covering my shoulders as much as possible before stepping out from behind the screen.

Mrs Mead began to cry the second she laid eyes on me. 'My little girl. My wee babe, all grown up. And to think I once changed your nappies.' She pulled a hankie from her bosom and honked her nose.

Meanwhile, my mother surveyed me like a lioness sizing up prey. 'It fits,' she said, 'and the color is right. If only you knew how to wear it properly.'

She pulled the tulle straps down my arms.

'There,' she said, once my shoulders were bare. 'Never cover your best assets. Remember that.' She tugged at the bodice until my chest was practically heaving out of the heart-shaped corset.

'Mama,' I said. 'Do I have to show everything?'

'Accentuate the positive, eliminate the negative,' she replied. She stood back to appraise me again. 'With good makeup and the right shoes, you might turn a head or two.'

'Goodness gracious, she'll have the boys fighting for a chance to dance with her. Just you wait!' said Mrs Mead.

'That's not really the goal, is it? To make boys fight over me?' I asked.

'Of course it is,' Mama replied. 'Courting these days takes forever. It's not like in my time. Back then, your parents decided for you, and you were married within a month. Now there's the dating, the family meetings, the engagement, the financial arrangements behind the scenes. Marrying off a girl is worse than going through a merger.'

'Who says I want to get married?' I replied.

Mrs Mead and my mother exchanged an amused look.

'Always hold on to your dreams,' said Mrs Mead as she patted my bare arm.

'As long as you hold on to your husband,' my mother added.

'You're a relic, Mama,' I said. 'Nowadays, women can dare to be so much more than wives.'

'Oh, here we go with your "women's liberation" and "equal rights." Honestly, Flora, I'm on your side. I do wear pants, you know,' my mother retorted, as she strutted in her recently acquired culottes. 'Women these days have it better than ever, so why does this young generation insist on rocking the boat?'

I looked at my mother, so full of false bluster. All I could think about was how a month earlier, I consoled her when I found her lying in her bed with the curtains drawn, drunk on vodka, mascara and tears staining her cheeks. I didn't ask her what had happened because it was always the same – my father, caught in some dalliance with a woman half my mother's age.

'Are we sorted?' Mrs Mead asked. 'Is our Cinderella ready?'

'Can I take this gown off now?' I asked.

'As long as you wear it *exactly* as I showed you on the day of the ball,' my mother demanded.

'Fine,' I said, then I disappeared behind the Venetian screen to change back into my comfortable clothes. Once done, I popped out and announced, 'I'll be in the library. I've got books to read before classes begin.'

'Don't study too hard or you'll need glasses,' my mother called out, 'and what boy on earth will want you then?'

*

I can tell you, Molly, that it was a relief to leave my mother and enter my father's hallowed library, surrounded by perfect, cloistered silence and custom-made shelves of leather-bound volumes that reached from the floor all the way to the pudgy cherubs frolicking on the frescoed Renaissance-style ceiling. There was even a sturdy ladder on wheels that could be moved along an interior brass track, giving access to books on the highest shelves. And the scent of that room, Molly, I'll never forget it – old ink and parchment paper; worn leather; polished, lemony brass.

I removed the headmaster's reading list from my pocket and began searching for the tomes I required. But no matter what the category, no title listed could be found. I was certain I'd put *Great Expectations* back on the Dickens shelf just a few weeks earlier, and most definitely *Romeo and Juliet* had been amongst the other Shakespearean tragedies not long ago, so where was it now?

A galling thought occurred to me. Was my father behind this? Had he granted me permission to study only to then remove all the books I'd need to be successful? Was this some sort of cruel joke? A fiery dragon awoke in my belly, and youthful rage propelled me down the corridor to my father's office.

The door was open a crack, and through it I saw Mama perched on the side of his sprawling banker's desk while Papa, clearly distressed, paced the room, raking his hands through his salt-and-pepper hair.

'You can't just let that man walk all over you,' my mother hissed.

'What choice do I have, Audrey?' my father spat back. 'It's bend backward or lose it all.'

I slowly opened the door and stood in the entrance. 'What are you talking about?' I asked, looking back and forth between them. 'Is something wrong with Gray Investments?'

'Since when are my business affairs your purview?' my father replied. He then took a seat on his Capital Throne and drilled me with his judgmental eyes. 'Don't worry your pretty little head, Flora. What is it you want now?'

All of my boldness suddenly left me. I could barely gather strength to pose my question. 'Did either of you remove books from the library?' I asked as gently as I could.

'Do you really think your father and I swan about on settees immersed in *Pride and Prejudice*?' my mother retorted. 'It's bad enough *you* fill your head with that literary rot.'

'I just granted you permission to study whatever you want,' said Papa, 'and now you accuse me of stealing books from my own library?'

'I'm not accusing you,' I replied. 'I merely asked where they were. And if you haven't touched the books, someone has. Many are missing, the very ones I need,' I said.

My mother looked at my father. 'That boy,' she commented.

'What boy?' I asked, already perturbed.

'The butler's son,' said my father.

'You mean Uncle Willy's boy?' I asked.

'I beg your pardon,' Papa said. 'How many times do I have to remind you: you will call my butler "sir" or nothing at all.'

My mother shook her head in dismay. 'Flora, you know

it's dangerous to get too familiar with the servants. It confuses them. They forget their station.'

'If you're concerned about them forgetting their station,' I said, 'you should have the boy arrested for stealing books.'

'God help us all,' my father muttered as he cradled his head in his hands. 'Before you draw and quarter the lad, you should know I gave him permission to borrow whatever he wanted from *my* library.'

'You what?' I asked. 'Why?'

'Because he's this year's Gray Scholarship recipient, Flora,' my mother said.

Suddenly, what Uncle Willy had told me earlier became clear. His son had been awarded the Gray Scholarship, a yearly bursary my parents offered to a child of one of the servants working for us. Between the scholarship and the Workers' Ball, my parents believed themselves to be the greatest benefactors on earth.

'Flora, I've been financing that boy's schooling for years,' Papa said as he smoothed his lapels. 'Quite generous of me, I'd say.'

'Quite clever is what it is,' said Mama. 'The headmaster of that boarding school owed you a favor. And in return, your butler dropped his ludicrous petition for staff raises.'

'So you've supported his education all this time,' I said as my face colored with outrage. How was it that a servant's son could be granted privileges I always had to fight for?

'Tuition is a small price to pay to keep the staff from agitating,' Mama explained.

'But why would you give that boy access to the library when you know I need those books myself?' I asked.

'You see?' my mother said to Papa. 'She's already taking this school business too seriously.'

My father sighed. 'I'll speak to the boy's father and have him return the books. Now may I kindly get back to work? Neither of you women seems to have any understanding of the pressure I'm under – here you are, nattering on about nothing!' He punctuated this by slapping both palms on his desk, which made me and my mother flinch in unison.

'Yes, Papa,' I said quietly. The last thing I wanted was to cause an eruption of my father's red-hot anger. 'I'm sorry for disturbing you,' I added with a curtsy. My head bowed, I backed out of the office and closed my father's door behind me.

CHAPTER 7

It's curious, how a person can be there and not there at the very same time – that's what I'm experiencing in this moment. In the greenroom, Brown and Beagle are conversing amicably with Juan, my gran-dad, and Angela.

Everyone is so excited about the Fabergé, they're practically buzzing, but I'm feeling quite numb. It's only when Beagle addresses me directly that I snap to attention.

'Really, Molly. You won't regret your decision to sell the egg,' he says, still cradling the precious Fabergé in the nest of his hands.

'Auctioning it is definitely the right thing to do,' says Brown, 'and we'll guide you through all of the steps.'

'I still can't believe it,' Gran-dad says with a shake of his head.

'Molly, is it sinking in? We're going to be rich!' exclaims Juan.

I try to smile, but the sentiment won't reach my face

because all I can hear in my head is Gran – *All that glitters isn't gold.*

There's a knock on the greenroom door, and Mr Snow pokes his head in. 'I'm sorry to interrupt, but might I have a moment with Molly?' he asks.

I hurry to him. Mr Snow's forehead is furrowed with concern. Beads of sweat are threatening to unleash a torrent down his face.

'Molly,' Mr Snow says, sotto voce, 'I realize the news you've just received may change how you think about your employment at this hotel. You and Juan Manuel might think working here is now beneath you. Still, I'm wondering if I can count on you to at least finish today's shift.'

Instantly, I feel unsteady again. I can't believe what I'm hearing. 'What on earth would make you think I'd quit my job?' I ask in a voice so pinched it sounds foreign to my ears. 'I'm not going anywhere except upstairs to clean rooms. Did you really think this egg would change that?'

'I wasn't sure,' Mr Snow answers as he wipes his forehead with his pocket square. 'Money changes people, and I thought it might change you.'

'I can assure you it won't, Mr Snow. I am the same Molly I was a few hours ago. You can count on me.'

'What about them?' he asks, pointing to Juan Manuel, Angela, and my gran-dad, who are laughing heartily at whatever joke the Bees just told them.

I march over to their tight circle. 'Excuse me,' I say, 'it's time to get back to work. Mr Preston, since you're here, would you mind helping Angela wrangle the Bee-lievers?'

'No trouble at all,' he replies.

'And, Juan, can you direct your staff back to the kitchens to prepare for lunch service?'

'With pleasure,' he says, tipping his chef's hat.

'That's that. We're off,' I say, as I open the greenroom door.

'Wait!' Beagle exclaims. 'You're just going to leave the egg behind?' He holds out the precious heirloom, a look on his face that, unless I'm mistaken, suggests I've completely lost my mind.

'I'll put the egg in my locker, and then Juan and I will take it back home at the end of our shift.'

Beagle stares up at his husband, aghast at what I've just said. Then he turns to me and says, 'Molly the Maid, you are in possession of a valuable object that makes you a target. You could be robbed. Or worse.'

Juan's mouth falls open.

'I hadn't considered that,' I say.

'Remember – not everyone is a good egg,' Gran-dad adds.

'There's a safe in my office,' Mr Snow replies. 'Shall I place the egg in there for safekeeping?'

'Who else knows about this safe?' Brown asks.

'No one but me,' Mr Snow responds as he straightens his cravat.

'Until now,' Angela replies under her breath.

'We're off,' I say to Brown and Beagle. 'Thank you for the appraisal,' I add, curtsying before I leave.

Mr Snow opens the greenroom door, and I follow him out, with Juan by my side and Mr Preston and Angela behind us. The second we're in the corridor, we're accosted.

'Look, it's her!'

'Molly the Maid! Can I get a photo?'

'Where is it, Molly? Where's the egg?'

In an instant, I'm surrounded by a crowd of hotel guests, Bee-lievers, and miscellaneous lookie-loos.

'Step back!' Mr Preston demands.

'Give her space,' Mr Snow orders as he blazes a trail through the masses.

'Molly, you're becoming a celebrity – fast,' Angela says.

'Everyone wants a piece of you,' Juan adds as he puts a protective arm around me.

'There's no need for fuss,' I call to the crowd as I pass. 'I'm just a maid!'

Everyone bursts into a confusing round of applause.

Angela and Mr Preston head back to the tearoom while Mr Snow and Juan guide me to the front lobby. The crowds here are thinner, and we have a bit more space to breathe as we stand by the stairs to the basement.

'This is so strange,' Juan says. 'Molly, I don't want to leave you.'

'We'll talk everything through tonight. For now, we've got jobs to do,' I say.

'If you insist,' Juan replies.

'Don't worry,' Mr Snow counters. 'I'll make sure she gets upstairs safely. I'm sure all the fuss will die down momentarily.'

Juan grabs both of my hands. '*Mi amor*, you're sure you're okay?'

'Of course,' I say with a confidence I don't quite feel.

'That's my Molly,' he replies with a smile, then he starts down the stairs and disappears from sight.

'I'll escort you to the elevator,' says Mr Snow. We make our way to the lift relatively unencumbered, but as he presses the button, guests stare at me, exchanging whispers behind cupped hands. For the first time in a long time, I feel exposed rather than invisible. Every eye in the hotel is trained on me.

Ding – the elevator arrives. The guests part and allow me to step on alone, something that never happens. When I arrive on the third floor, I find Lily, one of our best maids, and Cheryl, one of our worst, cleaning rooms together. I often pair responsible Lily with problematic Cheryl, since Cheryl can't be trusted to get any work done by herself.

I grab a dustcloth from the trolley outside of Room 403, then join Lily and Cheryl inside. They're putting fresh sheets on a king-size bed, but Cheryl isn't paying attention. Instead, she's watching the TV, which is blasting *Chatter Box,* an entertainment news show.

Both maids turn when I enter the room.

'Molly!' says Lily. 'We heard!'

'When are you quitting?' asks Cheryl. 'Soon, I hope.'

'Don't count your chickens,' I reply. 'And turn that TV off right this second.'

Both Lily and Cheryl eye me curiously.

'Molly,' says Lily. 'You were just on *Chatter Box*. They ran a clip of you and the Bees.'

Slack-jawed, I stare at Lily exactly the way she's staring at me. 'You're going viral,' she says.

'Just like a plague,' Cheryl says. 'Hey, can I get a picture of you for my 'gram?' Cheryl removes her phone from her pocket and before I can even protest, she snaps a photo of me holding out my dustcloth.

'What on earth do you want my picture for, Cheryl?' I ask. 'Put your phone away and tuck that sheet in properly.'

Cheryl reluctantly obeys, but Lily remains frozen in place, staring at me with her saucerlike eyes.

'Lily,' I say, 'if you have something to say, say it.'

'Just don't forget the little people,' she replies, 'when you're rich and famous.'

Lily's words hit like an arrow. Without warning, tears spring to my eyes.

'Lily,' I say, waving my dustcloth in front of her face. 'It's me, Molly. I'm the same person I was yesterday, so why is everyone suddenly treating me differently?'

As Lily and I face each other, Cheryl, having abandoned the bedsheets yet again, punches at her phone with both thumbs. 'Done,' she says as she looks up, a Cheshire cat grin claiming her face.

'What did you just do?' I ask her.

'I messaged some friends,' she replies.

'Can I leave you to it?' I ask Lily. 'I need to check in on Sunitha and Sunshine.'

'Yes,' Lily replies. 'And, Molly, I'm sorry. I didn't mean to hurt your feelings.'

'My gran used to say to err is human, but to apologize is divine. Thank you, Lily,' I say.

We offer each other a curtsy while Cheryl rolls her eyes.

I leave them both and take the stairs to the third floor, where Sunitha and Sunshine are standing in the hall beside a short, bearded man in a trench coat.

Sunshine waves me over. 'Molly! This man has been asking for you. He says you know him.'

The man in front of me adjusts his trench coat, but he doesn't say a word.

'Do I know you?' I ask, trying to place him.

'I've stayed here before,' he replies. 'So you're Molly – spitting image. You're the maid with the golden egg?'

'I am,' I say. 'Which room are you staying in?'

The man stares at me and says nothing.

'Now before I alert security to an intruder in the corridor, what did you want to ask me?'

The man scurries down the hall without so much as a word.

'Wait!' I yell.

He disappears through the stairwell exit. I turn to Sunshine.

'He was asking us for your address,' she says. 'And your phone number, too.'

'What did you tell him?'

'Nothing,' says Sunshine.

'I have a sneaking suspicion he was up to no good,' I say.

'I'll tell Mr Snow about him,' she says. 'Molly, we heard

about the appraisal. We're so excited for you. This is going to change your life!'

Sunitha and Sunshine grab my hands, their faces beaming vicarious joy.

'Yes,' I say. 'That's exactly what I'm afraid of.'

The rest of the workday passes in a confusing blur. For the first time ever, I find myself the very epicenter of attention at the hotel. I try not to think about what happened this morning and what the news of the Fabergé egg will mean to my life in the future, but no matter how hard I wipe the slate of my mind clean, my environs find a way to remind me.

Normally, at least half of the rooms on any floor of the hotel have the 'Shh – please do not disturb' door hanger placed on the knobs, but today, when I arrived on the third floor, the hangers on every room read, DEAR MAID, PLEASE CLEAN!

Worse, every time I knocked on a guest's door and called out, 'Housekeeping! Is this a good time to return your room to a state of perfection?' the door swung open and smiling guests invited me in. One woman took the vacuum right out of my hands and sat me down in her guest chair to make me a cup of tea. Another guest offered me caviar. In summary, the guests in this hotel are *non compos mentis* – ergo, they've gone completely and utterly batty.

But the worst happened just moments ago, when I was cleaning my final room before the end of my shift. I looked up from my bottle of air freshener to find a group of Bee-lievers peeking their heads around my trolley, which was propping open the door.

'It's her!' they exclaimed as they rushed into the room.

'Can we have your autograph?' they asked while proffering Regency Grand pens and stationery.

'You want my signature? What for?'

'Do you realize that over three million people have watched that *Hidden Treasures* clip since this morning? You should see the memes. You're all over TikTok.'

I stared at the faces in front of me, sparkling like the very egg that got me into this situation.

'Is this your room?' I asked the Bee-lievers, who looked at each other with shifty eyes. 'Are you the occupants?' I asked more firmly.

'We're on the second floor. Hey, if you want to swing by after your shift, we'll open a bottle to celebrate. What do you say?'

'I say no,' I replied. 'Please leave this suite *tout de suite*. Guest privacy is paramount at the Regency Grand.'

A few minutes ago, shift complete, I changed into my civilian clothes, then rushed out the lobby's revolving doors carrying my shoebox, this time sans egg. Now, I'm catching my breath on the red-carpeted stairs.

'Yo, there she is! It's Molly the Maid!' Speedy yells to some guests the instant he spots me. 'Juan should be out soon, too.'

'Speedy, what are you doing?' I hiss as he lumbers my way.

'They've been waiting for you all day,' he says.

The little gang bounds up the stairs and surrounds me,

pushing flyers and business cards at me, making me offers for real estate and media appearances and trips to far-flung places I've seen only on postcards. Just as I'm getting weak at the knees, Mr Snow emerges through the revolving doors with Juan behind him.

'We've gotta get out of here,' Juan says as he grabs my arm.

'I've ordered you black car service,' Mr Snow replies. 'Hop in that limo. It will take you straight home.'

Juan rushes me down the red-carpeted stairs and into the waiting vehicle. Only when we're two blocks from home do I dare draw a breath.

'Are you okay?' Juan asks. He's gripping my hand so tight I can barely feel my fingers.

'I'm okay,' I reply. 'You?'

'A reporter came into the kitchen asking weird questions.'

'A bearded man wearing a trench coat?' I ask.

'That's the one. He wanted to know where Mr Snow's office was.'

'Did you tell him?'

'No. I chased him up the stairs and out the revolving doors. But when I came back, all the Bee-lievers and guests in the lobby started clapping – at me! Mr Snow had to fend them off so I could get back to work. Molly, what's happening? The golden *huevo* has turned everything upside down.'

'I know,' I say. 'It's been the same for me. But surely everything will go back to normal tomorrow?'

'Of course it will,' says Juan. 'And besides, we'll be rich beyond our wildest dreams!'

'We're here,' says the driver as he circles to the front door of our decrepit old building.

'What do we owe you?' I ask.

'Taken care of by the hotel manager,' says the driver.

Juan and I thank him, then head inside to our fourth-floor apartment. When the door is locked behind us and our shoes are stowed, I head to our threadbare sofa and collapse. 'Home sweet home,' I say.

'I've never been more relieved to be here,' Juan adds as he perches beside me. His beautiful chocolate eyes meet mine. 'Molly, are you sure you still want to marry me?'

'Why are you asking such a question?'

'It's just that if you're rich, you can do what you please, have whoever you want.'

I sit bolt upright and grab Juan's clammy hand. 'I don't want anyone else. For richer or poorer, right?'

'Yes,' Juan replies. 'I'm glad you won't toss me to the curb. Molly, we're going to have money for the first time in our lives. I was thinking maybe we can have a bigger wedding instead of just Angela and Mr Preston at city hall. And maybe we can have a real party afterward, with a catered meal, too? What about a brand-new wedding dress for you? And a diamond ring? It'll be better than your engagement ring, that's for sure.'

He points to Gran's old Claddagh ring on my hand. Try as I might to imagine something better, I can't. I love this ring with all my heart.

'I don't want a fancy ring,' I say. 'And my only dream, Juan, is not living paycheck to paycheck. Maybe now we can send a bit more money home to your family.'

'You would do that?' Juan asks.

'Of course,' I reply.

Just then, my phone rings. I remove it from my pocket and check the screen – unknown caller.

'Will you take this?' I ask Juan. 'I can't bear to speak to anyone right now.'

'Sure,' he replies as I pass him the phone. 'Hello? She's not available. . . . Wait, how did you get her number? . . . She's not interested. Goodbye.'

Juan puts my phone on the side table. 'Weird,' he says. 'That was a financial adviser. He got your number from a link on Instagram.'

'I'm not on Instagram,' I say.

'Don't worry. He's gone now. I hung up on him.'

'I'm exhausted,' I say.

'Molly, rest. I'll make dinner. It's Taco Tuesday, *mi favorito*!'

'Can I help?'

'No. I'll let you know when dinner's ready.'

I'm greatly relieved to head off to our bedroom and lie in the dark by myself, listening to Juan jangling pots and pans in the kitchen, the evening news on TV in the background.

I close my eyes and let my mind drift. I'm remembering a time, long ago, when Gran told me a story about a maid who walked a mile in the shoes of three different people. It's as though she's right here with me, sharing the moral of the story: be grateful for what you have, especially if you're loved.

'Molly? Molly, wake up. You have to see this.' Juan is standing by my bedside, gently shaking me awake.

I pull the covers back and groggily follow him to the living room. We sit side by side on the old, threadbare sofa.

'Look,' he says, pointing to the evening airing of *Chatter Box* on TV.

'. . . and she's taking social media by storm,' the anchor says. 'Here's the adorable clip from the hit TV show *Hidden Treasures,* featuring Molly Gray, a maid at the Regency Grand Hotel, finding out she's the owner of a Fabergé egg worth millions.'

The clip runs. Brown, tall and gallant, and Beagle, small and regal, share the news. I tell them I'm just a maid, then soon after, I faint and fall off my chair as the tearoom audience goes wild.

The anchor laughs as the clip ends. 'Normally, we'd call this a "rags-to-riches" story, but as you can see . . . it's *rag*-to-riches in Molly's case.'

The camera cuts to a photo of me in my maid's uniform holding up my dustcloth. It's the photo Cheryl took earlier today!

'There you have it, folks – Molly, the Millionaire Maid. We'll get her on our show as soon as we can, but first, we managed to track down two people who not only know her but also know about her multimillion-dollar egg. Mr Jenkins, Serena Sharpe, welcome to *Chatter Box.*'

'It's them!' I say, pointing to the familiar faces I see on the screen.

'Happy to be here,' says Jenkins, the Grimthorpes' old gardener.

'A pleasure,' says Serena Sharpe, J. D.'s former secretary.

'Let's start with you, Mr Jenkins,' says the anchor. 'I understand you were the long-serving gardener at J. D. Grimthorpe's mansion and that you knew Molly.'

'Indeed I did. I knew her when she was just a little mite. Mind as sharp as a tack, and she loved to clean, oh yes. When she spotted that egg in the parlor, she fell in love with it, even tried to polish it once and got in a spot of trouble.' Jenkins chuckles at the memory, and so do I.

'And was it really you who gave her the priceless egg?' the anchor asks.

'Guilty as charged,' he replies. 'Molly came to the mansion after the Grimthorpes both passed, and I'd been given instructions to clear out all their old things. I had that old egg in a box, ready to pitch to the curb, but I offered it to her, and she took it.'

'And you, Serena Sharpe,' the anchor says. 'You're the daughter of Abigail Sharpe, who was revealed to be the true author of J. D. Grimthorpe's novels. You inherited much of his wealth as a result.'

'That's correct,' she says.

'And it was you who asked Mr Jenkins to clear the mansion of all trinkets. Tell me, did you have any idea that egg was valuable?'

'None whatsoever,' says Serena. 'So many things in the Grimthorpe mansion were fakes, starting with the occupants.'

'Now that you know the Fabergé is real, don't you want it back?' the anchor asks.

'No,' she replies. 'I know firsthand what it feels like to have something that's yours taken from you. My mother lived with that her entire life. The Fabergé is Molly's, fair and square.'

'We're still trying to get to Miss Molly, but in the meantime, do you have a message for her?'

'I do.' Ms. Sharpe turns to the camera, and it's as though she's looking straight into my soul. 'When you have something of value, there's always someone ready to take it from you. So, Molly – be careful.'

CHAPTER 8

Dear Molly,

Today I broke the bad news to you – that my cancer is terminal. I didn't say it quite like that, but I did tell you that I'm not long for this world. You immediately dove deep into denial, convinced there must be a medicine to cure me, if only I saw the right doctor, if only I went to a different hospital, if only we had the funds to access better care.

Oh, Molly, how often I had similar thoughts about you when you were young, though for different reasons. What if I'd had access to specialized schooling for you? What if you'd received early education tailored to your needs? Try as I might, I couldn't afford to pay out of pocket for private classes, and I failed whenever I tried to navigate the system to get you specialized care. My dream of appropriate schooling for you eluded me then, just as better healthcare for myself eludes me now.

Molly, I don't have much time left, so while I have the strength, I'll carry on with my story. Let's continue from the moment my father's chauffeur dropped me in front of the esteemed private college and I galloped apace to my very first prep class in the school's hallowed halls. It was a joy to leave Gray Manor that morning, because with each passing day, tensions were growing at home. Something was wrong with the family firm, but what it was I didn't quite know. I caught snippets here and there – my father going on about looming threats and the interlopers who wanted to ruin us, but when pressed for details Papa would either rage or disappear into his office.

He began taking meals at his desk instead of at the giant banquet table with me and Mama. He became vitriolic and even more unpredictable than usual. Every day, he would yell at someone for something – the cook for burning the beef; the chauffeur for scratching the bumper; the maid for the mess in his office. Even unflappable Uncle Willy was on tenterhooks as my father wandered the manor, spewing venom wherever he went.

But on a bright sunny day, dressed in my pleated gray skirt and a clean white shirt emblazoned with my prep school's insignia, I walked through its corridors and never felt prouder. It's interesting, Molly, how a uniform provides a sense of belonging, and yet, as I was soon to learn, its protection did not extend to me.

After some searching through the hallways, I found the correct classroom on the second floor of the austere Gothic building. Most of my classmates – all of them boys – were already inside, roughhousing and paying no attention to the girl in their midst or to the headmaster writing notes on the board. The bell rang, and everyone rushed to find seats. I took the desk no one else wanted – front row, center, closest to the blackboard.

The headmaster welcomed us to the class, explaining that the weeks to come would be devoted entirely to preparations for sitting our exams on the classics of literature. As I looked around, I recognized some of the boys, though I'd never been in classes with them before. These were the heirs apparent of all my father's friends – the anointed aristocrats, the prodigal sons and captains of industry who would one day inherit the earth. It was immediately clear the boys had been classmates for years, whereas I was an intruder and the only girl in sight.

'Let me introduce some newcomers to our group,' said the headmaster as he addressed me with a nod. 'Come to the front of the class, tell us your name and one interesting fact about yourself.'

I walked to the front of the classroom, knees knocking. 'Hello,' I said as I looked out at the rows of young male faces. 'My name is Flora, and one interesting fact about me is that my name means flower in Latin.' I stepped one foot behind the other to perform a clipped curtsy. No sooner was my curtsy complete than the room erupted into guffaws.

'Hothouse flower!' a redheaded boy called out.

'Bloom off the rose yet? Can I help?' another boy yelled.

'That's *enough*!' the headmaster boomed as he eagle-eyed the class into submission.

Paralyzed in my place, I stared at the wooden planks at my feet.

'Flora is to be treated with the same respect you accord each other. He who disobeys will live to regret it. Understood?' the headmaster warned.

I looked out at the boys, only to be greeted by a sea of smirks and curled lips. But one boy in the back stood out from the rest, his brown eyes wide with fear, his broad shoulders rounded as though he was trying to take up as little space as possible though he was bigger and stronger than any other boy in the room. He looked vaguely familiar, but I couldn't place him.

'We have another new student joining us. He's been away at boarding school, but he's a local lad. He'll be sitting university entrance exams as well. Come, introduce yourself and share a fact,' said the headmaster.

The brawny young man at the back got up, nearly toppling his chair. He walked my way, then stood awkwardly beside me as he faced the class.

'Hello,' he said, his voice unapologetic and deep. 'I'm John.'

The penny dropped. I swiveled my head for another look at him. Broad-shouldered, that same brooding expression and confidence, the brown, tousled hair – this was the audacious usurper who'd once taken my spot at Mrs Mead's kitchen table. This was Uncle Willy's son.

'One fact about me,' he announced, 'is that I'm the recipient of this year's Gray Scholarship.'

'This year's pity case!' the redheaded boy quipped loudly.

'Round of applause for Poor John!' said another boy as he clapped limply while the others roared with laughter.

John turned to me. 'It's *your* family name on that scholarship. Aren't you going to say something?'

All the blood in my body rushed to my cheeks. I looked up at the hulking young man beside me. 'I wouldn't think a burly lad like you would need a girl to defend him.' I said it so loudly and caustically, it's a wonder my own tongue didn't burn right off.

In return, I got what I'd hoped for – the boys now jeered at John instead of me.

'Good one, Flora!' one of them called out.

'Zinger!' said another.

The headmaster put an end to the antics with the smack of a ruler against his desk. 'Silence! If I hear so much as an eye roll out of anyone, you're going to wish you never showed up today, understood?'

Just like that, order was restored. I hurried to my seat as Uncle Willy's irksome son followed me to claim his own.

The rest of the class passed without disturbance, and as the headmaster lectured on the classics and what we might expect from our exams, I took copious notes. Before I knew it, three hours had gone by. And when the headmaster announced, 'Class dismissed,' I raced out of the room.

In the echoing hallways, I jostled against exuberant teenage boys, all on their way to the cafeteria, as was I. I pushed my skirt down my thighs, wishing it covered my whole legs and not just my knees.

I felt a hand grab my arm. 'Hey,' I heard.

I turned to find the redheaded, catcalling boy from class standing in front of me. His pale eyes were skittish and twitchy, and he was short, not even my height. Away from his classmates, he suddenly seemed much less intimidating.

'Are you really Flora Gray, daughter of Reginald Gray, head of Gray Investments?' he asked.

I nodded.

I watched as a new esteem for me colored his expression. I was used to this. My father's name engendered awe in most circles, young and old. I will admit that I enjoyed it a little too much and even puffed up a bit.

'I . . . had no idea who you were. I'm Percival Peterson.' He held out a thin, pasty hand. 'I've heard about you from my folks.'

'And I've heard not a word about you,' I replied, 'which suggests my parents believe you're beneath me.'

This is how I was at the time, Molly. When wronged, I leapt for revenge.

'For a flower, you're sure no shrinking violet,' said Percival.

'Correct,' I replied.

He grinned as the tides of students swam around us. 'Walk with me?' he said. 'The cafeteria's hard to find. I'll show you the way.'

We strode through the labyrinthine hallways, turning this way and that, Percival telling me all about his professor parents and how they had holdings with Gray Investments. He talked about his two golden-boy brothers, both older than he was, and both acing statistics at university.

'How come you're not streaming toward math like they did?' I asked.

'I suck at numbers,' Percival replied. 'I'm not good at lit either, but I figure I can watch the movies of some of the books and pass if I'm lucky. We're here,' he said, pointing to a set of heavy doors and the sign above them that read MESS HALL.

'Sorry for what I said about you in class,' Percival offered. 'I was a jerk. Forgiven?' he asked, holding out his meek hand.

'Forgiven,' I said as I shook it firmly, glad to leave the classroom antics behind us.

'Hey, you were taking lots of notes in class. Can I see them?' he asked, his skittish eyes meeting mine.

All I could think about was a mouse Mrs Mead once cornered in her cottage, how it looked up at her broom, hoping beyond hope to survive her wrath.

'I will grant you that privilege,' I said, taking my notes from my binder and handing them to Percival. 'But I'll need them back.'

'Thanks,' he replied. 'Get ready, Flora. The mess hall is madness.' He pushed through the heavy doors as I followed.

The shrieks and roars of hundreds of hungry, unruly teenage boys assaulted my ears. Four headmasters stood sentry like points on a compass, alert to signs of impending food fights. Not far from us was a long table of boys from my class. They were shoveling food into their mouths from fresh cafeteria trays. They spotted us, waving and yelling, 'Percy! Percy!'

I looked around, trying to find a spot to sit, but the only

empty seats were at a table at the back of the hall. Alone, sitting on one end, was Uncle Willy's son, John. Beside him was an open lunch box, the only lunch box in sight. He took out a small parcel wrapped in wax paper. His eyes met mine, and I looked away.

Percival ambled over to the boys from our class, and I followed, but right before we arrived at their table, he turned to face me.

'I showed you the way here, but that's all I can do,' he said. 'You have to understand, you'll never be one of the boys.'

He dashed to the table, where his classmates made space for him.

At the back of the room, I could feel eyes on me – John, watching from afar. He bit into a roast beef and cucumber sandwich, Mrs Mead's specialty. He held out a hand, inviting me to take the empty place next to him. A red fury flared up my neck and cheeks. I turned my back on him and marched out of the mess hall.

CHAPTER 9

When I was young, I was exuberantly curious. I wanted to know everything there was to know. I used to pepper Gran with pressing questions as we sat at our kitchen table eating breakfast. One morning I asked what she would spend her money on if she suddenly became rich.

'A private school for you with good and kind teachers,' she said, 'and a little place to call our own.'

Now, years later, as I sit with Juan in our living room and he turns off *Chatter Box*, this memory of Gran returns. But before I can think on it further, there's a knock on the door.

'Are you expecting anyone?' I ask Juan.

'No,' he replies.

We make our way to the entrance, where I check the peephole, a habit drilled into me long ago.

'It's Mr Rosso,' I say.

'But we paid the rent in full just last week,' Juan says.

I open the door to our landlord. His crossed arms rest on his protuberant belly.

'To what do we owe the pleasure?' I ask.

Never one to mince words, Mr Rosso launches into it. 'I have some news. Your apartment is in poor condition. It's time to tackle the repairs,' he says as he wipes his nose with the back of his hand.

Juan and I exchange a baffled look, not because the poor condition of our apartment is any surprise to us – the faucets leak, the windows are drafty, and the old tub is so rusted we're afraid of falling through the ceiling onto the tenants below – but our copious complaints to Mr Rosso have been ignored for years.

'I'll be changing your appliances, putting in new windows, and renovating the kitchen and bath,' Mr Rosso announces.

I can hardly believe my ears. The very words I've longed to hear from him now spill out in a symphony of good news.

'This is wonderful!' I say. 'On behalf of all the tenants in the building, let me thank you for finally fulfilling your duties as our landlord. You won't regret—'

'Wait,' says Juan. 'What's the catch?'

'You have to buy the place,' Mr Rosso replies. 'I'm converting the units to condos. You can stay, of course, but only if you pay up.'

'*What?*' I say. 'We can't afford to buy this apartment.'

'Maybe not right this second, but we might be able to soon enough. What's the price?' Juan asks Mr Rosso.

'Your unit is a two-bedroom, so market value is about half a million.'

Juan's eyes threaten to pop right out of his head.

'That's ridiculous,' I say, stating the obvious.

Mr Rosso's mouth forms an expression that puts the grim in grimace. 'I thought you'd be happy about this. But if you don't want to own, plenty of others will.'

'How long do we have to decide?' I ask.

'Eight weeks,' he declares, then grunts.

'That's not enough,' I say. 'We need more time.'

'Eight weeks, max, or consider your place on the market.'

'We'll think on it and get back to you,' Juan replies.

Mr Rosso turns to leave but then swivels back. 'Oh, by the way, Molly, I just saw you on that show,' he says. 'You can't keep a priceless heirloom in this building. Last thing we need are thieves in these halls when I'm showing apartments. If you stay, the egg goes elsewhere.'

I'm about to give Mr Rosso a piece of my mind, but as I start to speak, Juan's hand squeezes mine.

'Goodbye,' Juan says as he closes the door on Mr Rosso.

Once he's gone, I stand in the entry, fuming. 'The nerve!' I say. 'He knows we're coming into money, so he's charging us a small fortune just to line his pockets. And he's suddenly decided to do renovations now?'

'It's called renoviction, Molly. It happens all the time,' says Juan.

'What can we do about it?'

Juan shrugs.

I look around the apartment, and despite the worn floors and the divots in every wall, all I see around me is home. I can't imagine not living here. Humble as it is, I love this apartment.

'We could buy it, you know,' Juan says.

'For half a million dollars? It's certainly not worth that much in its current condition.'

'You can dare to dream a little now, you know. What is it you really want, Molly?'

'A little place we can call our own,' I answer. 'Other than that, I have what I want most – you.'

Juan puts an arm around me and plants a kiss on my cheek. '*Te adoro,* Molly Gray,' he says. 'But surely you can dream a little bigger?'

I think about it for a moment. 'I suppose, if we're really dreaming, it might be nice to own a small bed-and-breakfast,' I say, 'just a few rooms, tastefully decorated, nothing too extravagant.'

'Yes! I can see it now – Molly the Maid's Inn and Tearoom!'

'You could make marzipanimals and pastries, and run the café,' I suggest.

'And you could be in charge of bookings and housekeeping,' he says.

'Nothing would give me more pleasure than polishing to perfection a tearoom of our very own. But, Juan, let's be careful. Gran always warned of the dangers of counting chickens before they hatch.'

'If I'd known the golden *huevo* was worth millions,' says Juan, 'I would have cracked it ages ago!'

The mention of the egg makes my stomach twist and turn, so much so that Juan actually hears it growling.

'*Mi amor,* you're hungry. I'll get the tacos started.'

I don't have the heart to tell him my stomach is responding to anxiety rather than hunger.

Juan starts cooking in the kitchen while I breathe my way back to stasis. Still, when he eventually calls me to the dinner table, there's little crunch in my munch. I'm discombobulated by Mr Rosso's threats, and even though I should be happy that our financial picture will change for the better, I still can't get my head around it. Also, my phone has been ringing nonstop – requests for interviews, offers to purchase the Fabergé, and various attempts to sell me duct-cleaning services. I asked one caller how she got my number and was told to look up @GossypGyrl on Instagram. Lo and behold, there was my dustcloth photo on Cheryl's latest post, with a write-up that said, 'I'm besties with the maid who made it big! Now you can be, too! Reply MOLLY for details.'

As it turns out, Cheryl is selling my phone number on KultureVulture.com, an online website hawking celebrity memorabilia and anything else that will make her a buck. It's not the first time she's profiteered from her employment at the Regency Grand. A few years ago, she was caught selling a rock star's underwear and other items pilfered right from the hotel. I should have fired her when I had the chance. Now, I regret my clemency. I phone Mr Snow to tell him what Cheryl is up to, and he promises to make her delete the posts immediately. Still, the damage is done. My phone is now ringing off the hook, so I turn it off.

All of this has resulted in a profound lack of appetite, for both me and Juan. We move our tacos around on our plates.

'I don't understand,' I say. 'The news about the Fabergé is supposed to be a good thing. Our lives are supposed to get easier.'

'They will,' says Juan as he reaches across the table to take my hand. 'Everything will be okay in the end.'

'If it's not okay, it's not the end,' I say.

After dinner, we read for a while in the living room. I clean the front closet – deep cleaning to give life meaning – then I put all the objects from my shoebox, including the old skeleton key, back in Gran's curio cabinet. Though it's been deemed worthless, it still intrigues me.

'Done and dusted,' I say once my cleaning is complete. 'Juan, I'm turning in. I can barely keep my eyes open.'

'Me, too,' he says from under Gran's lone-star quilt.

Together, we head to bed, and I fall asleep in the crook of his arm. But at 4:00 A.M. I wake with a start, and try as I might, rest eludes me. Long ago, Gran taught me to count my blessings rather than sheep when I can't sleep, and that's what I do in the quiet dark. The list of blessings is long – my husband-to-be, my gran-dad, my job at the Regency Grand, my home, my health . . . my wealth? But no sooner do I have the thought than I begin to fear the loss of all of the aforementioned. Just this morning, Mr Snow was about to take my job out from under me when he learned about the egg, and this evening, Mr Rosso all but kicked us out of the only home I've ever known. Is it my imagination, or have the cracks in our bedroom ceiling opened wider? Is everything about to fall on our heads?

When Juan's alarm goes off at 7:00 A.M., I wake with a start, panicked and breathless.

'Rise and shine, *mi amor*!' he chimes as he pulls the covers back and plants kisses on my forehead. 'Today's an exciting, brand-new day!'

I attach myself to his positive energy, letting it propel me to my feet, but the moment I turn on my phone, it vibrates like a rattlesnake.

'Juan,' I say, as I take the phone to the kitchen. He's bare-chested, wearing Gran's old paisley apron and scrambling eggs for two as he does most mornings. 'Look,' I say.

He sets his spatula down and takes my phone. My voicemail has filled to capacity, and there are hundreds of text messages from total strangers, not to mention more emails than I've ever received in my life.

'*Madre mía*,' says Juan. 'Molly, you're the It Girl.'

'What do we do?' I ask him.

'Keep calm and carry on,' he says.

'Right,' I say. But my response sounds hollow even to my own ears.

Juan and I get ready for work and are out the door before 8:00 A.M. As we leave our building, we spot my gran-dad standing in the parking lot by his car. He waves us over.

'Mr Preston?' Juan says. 'What are you doing here?'

'Is everything okay?' I ask.

'Everything's fine,' he replies. 'Molly, I tried to call you.'

'Let me guess, my voicemail was full.'

'Precisely. I saw you on the TV last night. And Mr Snow called to tell me what Cheryl did. That woman really is lower to the ground than a squirrel's behind. Mr Snow and I thought it best if I drove you both to work today rather than you walking.'

'Nonsense,' I say. 'Juan and I walk to work every day. Why should today be any different?'

But the moment I say it, a local news van pulls into the parking lot. Juan sees it, too, and his eyes go wide.

'Car's open,' says Mr Preston. 'Hop in.'

I jump in the front while Juan gets in the back. Gran-dad peels out of the parking lot before our belts are even buckled.

'I don't understand,' I say once we're halfway down the street. 'Why does everyone want to talk to me so badly?'

'You're a bit like the Fabergé,' my gran-dad says. 'Suddenly, people see your value.'

'Wait till the *Hidden Treasures* episode airs,' Juan says.

'They moved it forward to ten A.M. today. The network's been running ads nonstop,' Gran-dad says. 'It's bound to draw more attention to both of you, so be vigilant.'

'I have a funny feeling about all of this,' I say. It's like an alarm in my belly, an unsettling agitation that won't be ignored.

'Me, too,' says Juan.

'Listen, Molly,' Gran-dad says as we near the hotel, 'I was watching you onstage yesterday when you opened your shoebox. And I meant to tell you I recognized some of your gran's old things. I can shed light on them if you'd like.'

Leave it to Mr Preston to detect my anxiety and attempt to distract me from it. 'That's very kind,' I say. 'Maybe another time?'

'Of course,' my gran-dad replies. 'Only when you're ready.'

As we pull up to the hotel, Speedy lopes down the stairs and opens my door.

'Look who's here! It's Eminem-inem.'

I don't have the bandwidth today for Speedy's newfangled gibberish. 'Do me a favor and speak English?' I plead.

'Molly the Millionaire Maid! Three m's. Get it?' Speedy holds up a palm for a high five, which I limply deliver.

'Today's the day you slay, Molly,' Speedy says. 'The show's going to air!'

'Today's the day for extra care, Speedy,' Mr Preston says from the driver's seat. 'No letting guests through the hotel doors unless they have a good reason to enter. And no directing guests to Molly. Understood?'

'*Oui* and *sí,* Mr P,' says Speedy.

'Thanks for the ride, Mr Preston,' Juan says as we hop out of the car.

'Call if you need anything. And stay safe.'

Juan and I sail through the revolving doors and enter the hotel lobby. It's bustling with activity – Bee-lievers checking out, porters carting luggage, grips and assistants ferrying yesterday's camera equipment out the revolving doors. As I watch the commotion, Juan eyes me curiously.

'Why are you staring at me?' I ask.

'Molly, no one but me is paying you any attention. How does it feel?'

'Delightful,' I reply.

Juan and I take the stairs to the basement, then part ways. He heads to the kitchens and I go to the housekeeping quarters. In the change room, a few maids, including Lily and Sunshine, are surrounding someone, engaged in a heated discussion.

'It's wrong!' Lily says.

'They're not yours to sell,' Sunshine barks as the other maids chime in with a chorus of agreement.

'What's going on?' I ask, my voice cutting sharply through the mayhem.

When the maids turn my way, I see who they're circling – Cheryl. She's holding photos in her hands.

'Finally,' Cheryl says. 'I've been texting you since last night, Molly. You never got back to me.'

'Because I'm flooded with messages,' I say as I push my way into the middle of the huddle.

'Molly,' says Sunshine. 'Cheryl's at it again.'

'She's been selling pictures of you online, and to Bee-lievers and hotel guests in the lobby,' Sunitha adds.

'She claims they're autographed,' says another maid.

'They *are* autographed,' says Cheryl.

'Not by me!' I reply.

'A technicality,' Cheryl says with a shrug.

'Give me those.' I grab the photos from her hands, the same horrible shot she took yesterday of me holding my dustcloth like I'm waving goodbye to the navy. I rip the pictures in half and dump them in the trash bin. 'Please tell me you removed my phone number from that terrible website,' I say.

'Mr Snow made me, even after I offered him a cut of the proceeds.'

'You didn't actually,' I say.

'I would have offered you a cut, too,' Cheryl says, 'if only you'd texted me back. Fair and square, the maids all share, right?'

She's quoting from *A Maid's Guide & Handbook,* a manual I wrote a few years ago to codify proper moral conduct amongst maids at the hotel. I see now that no matter how many regulations one puts to paper, there will always be those who find their way around them.

'You know what, Molly?' Cheryl says. 'You wouldn't recognize a business opportunity if it slapped you in the face.'

'Can I take that as my cue?' Sunshine asks as she raises a flat palm toward Cheryl's cheek.

'That's enough!' I shout, which gets everyone's attention. 'We've got a dirty hotel to clean, and no time for bickering. Get uniformed and get to work, posthaste. Cheryl, if I hear so much as a whisper from any of these maids about you slacking off today, I will file a report to Mr Snow that's so damning, you may regret the day you gained employment here. Do you understand?'

Her mouth puckers like she's just sucked a lemon.

'Let's all head upstairs and polish to perfection,' I say.

*

On the third floor, Lily and I tackle guest rooms together. I saddled Sunshine and Sunitha with Cheryl, since they'll throttle her if she dares step out of line. Today, Lily's more silent than usual.

At one minute to ten, she asks, 'Should I turn on the TV? *Hidden Treasures* is about to air.'

'I lived it yesterday,' I say. 'I'm not keen to relive it again today.'

Lily nods and we continue cleaning in silence. But after we finish six rooms in record time, Lily remains strangely distant. 'Are you all right?' I ask as she rips soiled sheets off another bed.

She pauses. 'I'm just tired of the Cheryls in the world. Every time a good thing happens – like you learning you're about to become rich – there's a Cheryl who sours everything.'

I grab some fresh sheets from Lily's trolley and smooth them onto the bed. 'My gran used to say, "Keep good eggs close and bad ones even closer."'

'You think keeping Cheryl close means we'll rub off on her one day?' Lily asks.

'I live in hope,' I reply.

Just as we've finished the room and are about to leave, some guests buzz in. It's an elderly couple sporting Bee-liever pins on their lapels.

'We were just leaving,' I say. 'Your room is polished to perfection.'

'You're Molly,' the man replies. 'Molly the Maid.'

'We just saw you on TV,' says the woman.

'There's no need for fanfare,' I reply. 'I'm just a maid, a regular person like both of you.'

'We could tell that by watching,' says the man. 'Usually good things happen to the wrong people, but not this time,' he says. A smile breaks across his face that is so genuine, it makes me smile, too.

'My husband's a detectorist,' the woman explains. 'We came all the way from the countryside yesterday to share his finds with the Bees.'

'I thought I had a Viking burial hoard,' says the man, 'but I didn't.'

'Costume jewelry,' his wife explains. 'Circa 1960, buried in our backyard.'

'You win some, you lose some,' says the man with a shrug.

'You must be disappointed,' I say.

'Not in the least!' the woman replies. 'And we have you to thank for that.'

'Me?' I say. 'How so?'

'You proved the little people actually win sometimes,' the man says. 'To see a hardworking maid hitting the jackpot – it was incredible. You're a beacon of hope, Miss Molly, that's what you are.'

'Also, we made the b-roll,' says the man's wife. 'We were on TV just now! Our grandkids are thrilled, and our neighbors are throwing us a party at the pub tonight. We're checking out right away and heading home.'

I stare at the elderly couple, trying to grasp what it is they're telling me. From my maid's trolley, I grab a handful of turn-down chocolates. 'Take these for the road,' I say.

'Really?' the man asks as he holds out his hands. 'Thank you.'

'Do you want some soap?' Lily asks the woman. 'As a souvenir of your stay?'

'I've never felt so pampered in all my life,' says the woman. 'First stay at a five-star hotel and likely our last.'

'But the splurge was worth it,' the man adds.

'It was lovely to meet you,' Lily says as she guides her trolley out the door.

'Keep shining for us little folks, Molly,' says the man.

I curtsy deeply to the couple, then close their hotel room door behind me.

I leave Lily and take my trolley down to housekeeping laden with bags of soiled towels and sheets, but the moment the elevator opens to the lobby, heads turn my way.

'It's her!' someone calls out.

'Molly the Maid!'

'Can I have your autograph?'

'Come say hi to my mom!'

'We loved you on the show!'

I stab at the basement button, hoping the elevator doors will close, but the guests hold them open and pull me and my trolley out. I spot Mr Snow by the reception desk. He rushes over.

'Stand back!' he says. 'Give her space.'

I grip my trolley as the swarm of Bee-lievers proffers hands, pens, and cards.

'Molly will answer one or two questions,' Mr Snow says. 'Then she must get back to work.'

'Are you quitting your job?' someone calls out.

'Of course not,' I say. 'I've got rooms to clean.'

'When you sell the egg, will you splurge on something big?' another guest asks.

'Maybe a small wedding reception? It would be nice to throw a party,' I say.

'Can I come? Please?'

'I'll be your maid of honor!'

'I want an invitation, too!'

'We love you, Molly Gray! You're more than "just a maid"!'

Just then, a man standing near me snatches my name tag, ripping it right off my uniform, then runs down the hall.

'Hey!' Mr Snow calls out. 'What are you doing?'

'Leave it. It doesn't matter,' I say, even though it does matter, a lot in fact.

'Let's get you out of here,' Mr Snow says as he commandeers my trolley. I'm relieved when he buzzes us into a staff-only corridor. I lean on my trolley to catch my breath.

'Molly, I'm so sorry,' Mr Snow says. 'A fever spread through this hotel the second that show aired. Everyone wants a piece of you.'

'My gran used to say that money and fame make people behave badly.'

'The hotel phones are ringing off the hook. We've got months of requested bookings, but on one condition.'

'What's that?' I ask.

'That *you* are assigned as their room maid. If things keep going like this, we'll just rebrand the hotel as a Molly theme park.'

'That would be awful,' I say.

'I was joking. Molly, listen. Some VIPs are in my office. They need to talk to you.'

'I don't want to meet anyone else. It's too much.'

'These aren't strangers. It's Brown and Beagle, and their showrunner, Steve. They've got news to share.'

Mr Snow leads the way as I follow behind him. In his office, the Bees are seated on leather armchairs, drinking cocktails out of highball glasses and looking as dapper today as they did for the cameras yesterday. Steve, sans ironic baseball cap, finishes a phone call, then comes my way.

'Here she is!' he says, holding open his arms.

'Our shining star!' Brown exclaims as he holds up his cocktail glass.

'What happened to you?' Beagle asks, eyeing the rip in my uniform where my name tag was pinned.

'Everyone wants a piece of me,' I say.

Steve laughs. 'That's so great! Hey, our ratings are already through the roof. And since yesterday, we've had our best research crew working nonstop on the egg's provenance. They've talked to that Serena woman and Jenkins the gardener. You saw them on *Chatter Box*?'

'I did,' I say.

'Our researchers are making inquiries far and wide. Molly, not a single person has come forward with a credible claim on the Fabergé.'

'And we don't believe anyone will come forward,' Brown adds.

'So?' I ask. 'What does that mean?'

'Finders keepers, Molly. The egg is yours.'

'But what if someone comes out of the woodwork later?' I ask. 'I've seen that happen on your show.'

'Death and taxes,' says Steve. 'Those are the only certainties in this life.'

'We want to set an auction date fast – for next week,' says Beagle as he smooths his dark, shiny curls. 'And Mr Snow says we can hold it right here in the hotel.'

I turn to Mr Snow. 'Is this what you want?' I ask.

'What is it that *you* want, Molly?' he counters.

When I don't answer immediately, Steve jumps in. 'We need to sell while interest in the Fabergé is at its peak,' he says. 'The price is soaring. We're fielding offers from collectors all over the world. If you don't get more than fifteen million, I'll be shocked.'

The news sends me reeling. It's a number so large it doesn't even compute. With money like that, Juan and I could buy an inn, our apartment, and a lot more besides.

'You're the luckiest maid in the world,' says Brown, with a blue-eyed wink.

'Am I?' I ask.

'What do you want to do, Molly?' Mr Snow inquires.

I consider for a moment. 'I want this over with. I want my regular life back.'

'Perfect!' says Steve.

'Consider it done,' says Beagle.

'One week from today, we auction the egg,' Brown says, 'and, Molly the Maid, in a week's time, you begin a whole new life.'

CHAPTER 10

Dear Molly,

If you've been reading along, I imagine you're shocked by the version of your gran you're meeting in these pages. When I was a girl, I could be insensitive and cruel. I simply didn't know any better, and my parents served as terrible role models. Because I lacked a sense of belonging, I often tried to steal self-worth from those who possessed it naturally, such as Uncle Willy's son. But we reap what we sow, and if we do not cultivate kindness, malice springs from the soil and poisons everything. I did not learn this lesson easily, and I did not learn it on my own. For every loss I've suffered in this life, I've gained compassion, comprehension, and empathy. And if I had to do it all again, I wouldn't exchange these riches for all the gold in the world.

Molly, you're about to begin a chapter full of surprises, not all of them concerning me. Let's open a week after the start of my prep courses as I returned home from a day of intense but fulfilling lectures. I was surviving the trials and tribulations of the classroom, and though my classmates made me keenly aware of my gender every single day, I refused to let it hinder me. I studied with relentless resolve, ignoring taunts and provocations from other students. And as each day passed, I thrived on acquired knowledge, finding within myself deep reserves of tenacity I never knew I had.

Meanwhile, at Gray Manor, tensions continued to mount, and the susurrations about Gray Investments turned from vapor to a solid mass. My father's business was in grave jeopardy. Some foolhardy financial decisions coupled with a market crash had left his firm vulnerable to attack for the very first time in generations. There was talk of liquifying assets, selling stocks, dissolving trusts. Never before had I seen my father – a lion of a man with the soul of a conqueror – so weakened as to be mistaken for a lamb.

In the corridors of Gray Manor, Papa mumbled to himself. Dark circles found permanent refuge beneath his eyes, and when I saw a button hanging by a thread on his normally perfect Savile Row suit jacket, I found Uncle Willy right away. He was washing the cathedral windows in the foyer. 'You're Papa's butler,' I said. 'Do something. He's falling apart at the seams.'

Uncle Willy put down his spray bottle and cloth. 'Flora,' he said, 'I'm doing the best I can. Please recall that your father, in his infinite wisdom, fired half the manor staff some time ago. I've been filling in the gaps ever since, but he just put me in charge of the Braun Summit to be held at the manor in one week's time. How much more can one man take on?'

'The Braun Summit?' I repeated, uncomprehending. I knew about the upcoming Workers' Ball, but I had not heard mention of any other event taking place within the manor walls. I had, however, heard the name Braun bandied about by both of my parents, a name always voiced with fear and trepidation. Magnus Braun was the CEO of Braun Wealth, an up-and-coming investment firm that rivaled my father's. The way my parents spoke of him, you'd think Magnus was Zeus himself, able to smite his foes with a single bolt of lightning unleashed from his all-powerful hand.

'Flora, next week, Magnus and his board of directors will descend upon the manor for a key meeting,' Uncle Willy revealed, 'and if I'm not mistaken, your father intends to make one last-ditch attempt to convince them not to gobble up the family firm entirely. I've been given orders to create an illusion of grandeur, as though this estate weren't running on fumes and a skeleton staff. I've hired anyone with a pulse – just for one week. I'm to dress them in service uniforms for jobs they've never done in their lives. So can you see how a button on your father's jacket is not at this moment my foremost concern?'

Never before had I seen Uncle Willy so unnerved. This prompted me to make a rare and immediate apology. 'I'm sorry,' I said as I stared at my feet. 'I didn't know any of this.'

He sighed and softened. 'I'm sorry, too,' he said. 'Things aren't looking good.'

'But what does this mean?' I asked. 'Could we really lose everything, even the estate?'

'It seems so,' Uncle Willy replied.

I heard his words, but young as I was, I didn't really understand them. I'd been born into wealth, took it as a given. I could hardly comprehend that fortunes can shift unexpectedly, that pedigree and privilege can wither as quickly as a rose plucked from its stem.

'But don't you worry yourself, Flora,' Uncle Willy said. 'It isn't over until it's over. And in the meantime, you keep studying. Education opens doors. It's the one thing no one can take from you. Remember that.'

I surveyed the foyer to make sure no one was around, then I threw my arms around Uncle Willy and hugged him tight. 'Thank you,' I said.

I made my way deeper into the manor, walking through the corridor of family portraits, past the cavernous, lonely banquet room. I veered away from the entrance to the kitchen, with its stainless-steel work surfaces and Italian-tiled walls. A maid was on her hands and knees by the oven, scrubbing the checkerboard floor.

I looked away as I passed the main parlor, then rushed up the grand oak staircase toward my destination – the library. As I went, the idea of losing Gray Manor lingered in my mind. I tried to imagine what life would be like beyond the palatial manor walls. Having experienced nothing else, I assumed the estate would always be there for me, as would Mama and Papa. But as you know, Molly, it's perilous to assume.

In my father's magnificent library, I found distraction from the mood of doom and gloom in the manor by ensconcing myself in books, but for the first time ever, when I walked through the heavy walnut door, I was not alone. Halfway up the ladder, placing a leather-bound volume back on a high shelf, was a young man I never expected to find on *my* sacred ground – John.

'What exactly are you doing here?' I snapped at the lad, who, startled, nearly toppled off the ladder on wheels.

I stood imperiously, hands on my hips, staring up at him, to where his unruly head looked down at me from between the faces of two chubby-cheeked cherubs frescoed onto the ceiling. He gingerly stepped down the ladder to the safety of the herringbone-patterned floor.

'Hi,' he said as he wiped his hands on his worker's trousers. 'Don't worry about me, I'm fine.'

I huffed out loud at the presumption – that *I* should be worried about him when in fact *he* should be worried about explaining what in heavens he was doing in Papa's library. I glowered at him, directing laser beams of ire into his brooding brown eyes, until at long last he broke the silence and said, 'So you're desperate to know what I'm doing here.'

'Indeed,' I said.

'Your father talked to my father. And my father talked to me. Apparently, *someone*' – he said this mockingly, mimicking the same death stare I'd directed at him moments ago –

'accused me of stealing books from this library, even though I was given permission by your father to borrow whatever I liked.' He paused then, and I watched as his jaw clenched. He walked over to an antique brass book trolley on which various leatherbound volumes were stacked haphazardly. He placed his hand on the top tome as though he were swearing on a Bible. 'Think whatever you like about me,' he said, 'but know one thing: I'm not a thief.'

'Really?' I replied. 'And I should know that how?'

'I always give books back,' he replied. 'You don't remember?'

'I'm sorry?' I said, completely at a loss.

'Really? When we were kids?'

Truly, in that moment, I had no idea what he was talking about.

'So let me get this straight,' I said, barreling on. 'After taking all the books you knew I would need in advance of our classes, you decide to put the books back out of the kindness of your heart?'

'Not exactly,' he said with a galling smirk that looked out of place on such a handsome face. 'I needed a bit of convincing, but I think you'll find the volumes returned to their proper shelves – most of them, anyhow.'

'My father will be greatly relieved,' I said.

'Oh, you remember your father now?' he replied. 'The other day in class, it was like you completely forgot who he was. And I think you forgot who you are, too.' He smiled then, and his face filled with mirth, his cockiness making me irate.

The dragon in my belly awoke, flailing and raging until its fire colored my cheeks. Had he really expected me to use my father's good name to save him from the wrath of the boys in class?

'It must be tough for you,' I said, 'being the only son of a servant in the entire school.'

His head bowed and his broad shoulders slumped – my arrow had hit its mark. But a moment later, he recovered, and his eyes met mine once more. 'It must be tough for you, too,' he countered, 'being the only girl in class and being an even worse snob than her parents.'

I was wounded and furious all at once. This is the problem in love and war, Molly. All is fair, but the end result is the same – everyone gets hurt. I bit my lip hard, not caring if I drew blood so long as my hot tears did not spill humiliation down my cheeks right in front of him.

John studied me closely, taking in the minutiae of my expression. I was certain he was enjoying my pain, but as it turned out, I was wrong. 'I'm sorry,' he said. 'I don't know why I said that. It was a cruel thing to say.'

His voice was still prideful, but there was a catch in it now that I hadn't heard before, a sincerity that rang true as a clarion bell.

'You know it's us against them, right?' he continued. He took a step toward me. His eyes were warm and gentle. 'All those boys in our class, they're just jealous because they're not very bright. That's why they treat us like they do.'

He smiled, and I noticed his mouth for the very first time

– his ruby lips generous and full. I hated him for those lips, for his mouth that could be alluring and caustic at the same time.

I knew I should follow his lead and apologize, too, for the callous remarks I'd made, and for using him as a scapegoat in class. Here was my moment to take it all back, but I couldn't bring the words forth. Rather than apologize, I took the coward's route and changed the subject. 'There's something I don't follow,' I said.

'What's that?' he asked, curious head cocked to one side.

'Today in class, the headmaster said something about *Romeo and Juliet* being both a comedy and a tragedy. You just shelved Shakespeare's play in tragedy, where it belongs,' I said, pointing to where he'd placed the volume on a high shelf, 'which means I don't quite understand what the headmaster was getting at.'

'Love,' John replied simply, the word tripping off his tongue with such unabashed ease. In my family, the word was never said, but in his, it was everything. 'Two star-crossed lovers race toward their doom, and yet they have no idea,' he remarked. 'It's all fun and games for them, at least at first, then *bang* – someone dies and the party's over.'

I looked at him, seeing him for the first time – this working-class boy far beneath my station who was mature beyond his years, more nuanced and honest and forgiving than anyone I'd ever met. I didn't know what to think, what to say.

'I realize your parents would hate this idea, but we could study together if you want,' John said, picking up a volume from the stack of leatherbacks on the trolley. 'We could partner up, show those boys at school a thing or two about who takes the top of the class. Anything's possible: a girl can earn top grade; so can a lowly worker's son. If we team up, we won't have to fight over books. And though I don't like to admit it, I suppose I could learn a little something from a girl as smart as you.'

Blushing, I gobbled up the compliment, so starving was I for praise. Still, I was inexperienced in generosity – I offered none in return. 'Why do you think I would help you?' I asked.

His eyes grew two sizes. 'Why wouldn't you, Flora?' he replied.

'Excuse me?' I said. 'Are we that familiar now? It's Miss Gray to you.'

I watched as a look of abject shock claimed his face. He began to pace in front of me, his head shaking back and forth. 'Right,' he said, coming to a sharp stop in front of me. 'Clearly, I've forgotten my place again. How dare I call Her Ladyship by her given name. Listen, if that's how you want it to be, fine. But you're acting like a spoiled brat. For a while there, I thought there was more to you, but I see I got that wrong.'

'You did,' I said, crossing my arms against my chest. 'You got that, and much else, entirely wrong.'

He stomped toward the door, about to leave, but before he did, he turned back. 'Assuming I have to talk to you again – and I assure you, I'll go to great lengths to avoid it – I'll do as you wish and call you Miss Gray. But I expect the same from you.'

'Meaning?' I asked.

'Don't call me John. Call me by my father's family name, a name I am proud to bear and one I respect with every fiber of my being. From now on, to you, I'm Mr Preston.'

And so it was, Molly, that the man who you know by the very same name became on that day my heart's desire and my sworn enemy.

CHAPTER 11

My gran always said, 'Be careful what you wish for.' She was wary of excess in all its forms, and her dreams were small and simple. Whenever I'd dream bigger, imagining if we owned a mansion like the Grimthorpes' or could take a vacation to a far-flung locale, she'd issue her warning – a reminder that fate rarely gives without taking something away.

It's been a week since the moment I stumbled onto the tearoom stage and learned that the Fabergé was real. My life has changed so dramatically since then and in ways that defy all comprehension. Before my appearance on *Hidden Treasures,* I really was 'just a maid,' but since then I've become many things, including a meme, a dance, a party costume, and an array of comedy sketches. A quick scroll through social media reveals babies, celebrities, dogs, cats, and one bearded lizard dressed in my maid's uniform. The dance in my homage is done on a chair and ends with a move now known as 'the

Fabergé faint.' And yesterday, a late-night comedy sketch aired with a well-known comedian wearing a black wig, sitting on top of a giant golden egg while clucking, 'I'm just a maid!' until the egg exploded into a cloud of fresh bills.

I phoned Angela the second I saw it. 'What was that all about?' I asked.

'You haven't stopped trending,' she said. '"I'm just a maid" is the country's top catchphrase. You're outpacing "That's what she said."'

'Who is she?' I asked. 'And what did she say?' But Angela insisted I was missing the point as usual. Honestly, I don't want to be trending or in the spotlight at all. These past few days, my only stability has been Juan, who is trying to maintain normalcy though there's nothing remotely normal about our situation.

After I agreed to auction the egg, Juan and I learned via Steve that a *Hidden Treasures* film crew was going to follow us around to shoot something called a 'sizzle reel.'

'Is a frying pan required?' I asked.

'You're punking me, right?' Steve replied, but when I stared at him, confused, he said, 'It's a short documentary. Think of it as "a day in the life of Molly." It'll air during the live auction episode of *Hidden Treasures* next week.'

'But what if we don't want our private lives publicized?' I asked. 'It's already impossible to do our jobs. We're being followed everywhere.'

'Bit late to back out now,' Steve informed us. 'Plus, you signed the waiver, remember? You're an instant reality TV star, Molly. Aren't you happy? You're living the dream.'

Were we living the dream? If we were, neither of us was aware. I glanced over at Juan, who looked as dejected as I felt. Still, how dare we forget to count our blessings. I tried to think positively, to turn my frown upside down. 'It's just another week,' I said to Juan. 'We can manage, right?'

'Of course,' he said, grinning along with me. 'We'll make it fun. Like being movie stars.'

'Great,' said Steve as he adjusted his baseball cap. 'I'll get the crew. We'll start now.'

From that moment on, Steve's crew became part of our lives, coming and going as they pleased. A few days ago, I was vacuuming a guest room in the hotel when suddenly the crew entered.

'Don't mind us, Molly,' the assistant director yelled over the high-pitched whir of my vacuum. 'Just forget we're here.'

But it's hard to forget an entire TV crew when you're cleaning around their lights and booms and extension cords with hotel guests cheering you on from the doorway. I finished the job only to be told, 'We're going to do another take. Can you do that all again, Molly?'

'I'm going to have to,' I replied, 'since you just trampled the perfectly plumped carpet pile.'

Why the crew and lookie-loos laughed at that, I have no idea, but I'm getting used to laughter and baffling comments like 'She's so funny!' and 'I just love her!' and 'I can't get enough of Molly the Maid!'

At home, Juan and I have no privacy. On our one day off, when Gran-dad came over for dinner, the three of us had retired to the living room to watch a nature documentary when there was a knock on the door. Juan answered, only to find Steve and the film crew yet again.

'We want to capture a regular day at your apartment,' Steve said. 'We'll be in and out, split.'

Suddenly, the entire crew was in our living room, running cables and setting up cameras.

'Molly, you sit in the middle of the sofa. Mr Preston, take the spot to her left, Juan to her right. Okay, that's good. Now, turn on the TV and watch *Hidden Treasures.* Everyone act normal. And, action!'

Packed like sardines on Gran's old sofa, we were stiff and catatonic. We tried to 'act normal,' but there has been no normal since the discovery of the Fabergé's worth.

But this was not even the worst of it. Yesterday, Juan and Angela decided to surprise me. 'After work,' Juan announced, 'you've been invited to a very special boutique. Angela's going with you.'

'A boutique? For what?' I asked.

'Wedding dresses, Molly,' Juan said. 'A fancy shop wants to sponsor your dress! Isn't that amazing?'

'Meaning we don't have to pay for it?'

'Exactly. You can stop searching charity shops for hand-me-downs.'

'What's wrong with hand-me-downs? Also, what's the catch?' I asked.

'There is no catch,' said Juan. 'At least none that I can see.'

After work, Angela met me at the Social, and we sneaked

out the back door so as not to be spotted by any Bee-lievers or other guests desperate for a selfie with Molly the Maid. The walk to the bridal shop was such a simple pleasure, ambling down the sidewalk with my friend, being hassled by no one, watched by no one, being relevant to no one.

'There it is,' said Angela when we arrived at Tears of Joy Bridal Shop.

Wedding bells jingle-jangled as Angela held the door open for me. Inside was a pretty shopkeeper in a lovely pink suit, carrying a tray of champagne glasses.

'Molly! Or should we call you *Mrs* Molly. We're so glad you're here. I'm Carmen,' said the shopkeeper as she passed Angela and me flutes filled with bubbly. 'We've chosen three dresses that are just right for you. And we've got a private room for your fitting.'

'Well, butter me and call me a biscuit,' said Angela as she took in the high-end shop. 'Free champagne service? I could get used to this.'

Carmen escorted us to a large room filled with mirrors and floral bouquets. Three gorgeous white gowns hung from a rack by the change room.

'Those gowns can't possibly be for me,' I said. 'They're fit for a princess.'

'We take pride in every bride,' said Carmen. 'The first gown is a mermaid-modern cut, the second is a strapless trumpet style, and the last, a classic bridal ball gown.'

As Angela guzzled champagne on a white satin bench, I ducked into the change room and tried the first gown on. I popped out and presented myself to Angela and Carmen.

'It's giving Ariel vibes,' Carmen said.

'Exactly. A bit fishy,' said Angela.

I agreed. I ducked back into the change room and put on the strapless gown. Feeling quite self-conscious, I tiptoed out and stood before Angela and Carmen again.

'I love it!' said Carmen. 'Sleek and modern, a bit daring and sexy.'

'In other words, not Molly,' Angela said as she crinkled her nose.

'Agreed,' I replied.

'There's still one more gown,' said Carmen. 'Give it a try.'

I returned to the change room and came out a few minutes later.

Angela gasped the second she laid eyes on me. As I looked in the mirror, I knew this was the one – a perfectly fitted, heart-shaped bodice with tulle straps that grazed my shoulders. The skirt was made of layers of billowing white chiffon that went all the way to the floor. It was classic and timeless, like Cinderella's at the ball, and for the first time in forever, I felt elegant and beautiful.

'Do you think Juan will like it?' I asked Angela.

'Oh, Molly, he'll love it as much as he loves you. It's perfect!'

'Are you saying yes to the dress?' Carmen asked.

'I am!' I replied.

In that moment, Carmen pulled a white ribbon hanging from the ceiling. Suddenly, confetti fell upon us while

Pachelbel's Canon in D blared from hidden speakers. Then, out of nowhere, Steve and his film crew spilled into the room.

'What the hell?' said Angela as she leapt to her feet. 'What are you doing here?'

'Capturing Molly's special moment,' said Steve as a camera was shoved in my face. 'Molly, did you just say yes to the dress?'

'I . . . I did,' I said.

A handful of young ladies – strangers, all of them – entered the room, oohing and cooing at me.

'Pretend they're your bridesmaids,' Steve instructed as the ladies hugged me, jumping up and down for joy.

I stood stiffly, not knowing what to do.

'More champagne!' Carmen announced as she passed around flutes, shoving one into my reluctant hand.

'Clink glasses with your BFFs!' Steve ordered. I did what I was told, all while looking past the strangers to where Angela sat on the white satin bench.

'Aren't you happy?' Carmen asked as she put an arm around me and squealed. 'You're overjoyed, right? A blushing bride?'

I could find no words. Not a single one.

'Oh, look! She's crying!' one of the ladies said as she pointed at my watery eyes.

'This is Tears of Joy Bridal Shop, where we put the pride in bride,' said Carmen as she smiled at the camera.

I looked back at Angela. She was crying, too, her head shaking back and forth in disbelief. 'I didn't know this would happen,' she mouthed from across the room. 'Molly, I'm so sorry.'

CHAPTER 12

Dear Molly,

Long ago, a very wise woman offered me valuable advice: 'Be careful, for what at first you hate, you may come to love later.' I never paid much heed, not to this nor to anything else she tried to warn me about. It took me years to understand how right she was and how the heart can be so capricious.

As you read this diary, I expect you're experiencing no small measure of shock. And as you have now seen, the man you know as Mr Preston, the doorman of the Regency Grand, was in fact closer to me, more critical to my early life than I ever let on – and closer to you, too, but more on that later . . .

For the moment, I entreat you to accompany me to Gray Manor on the day of the Braun Summit, a day when one man – Magnus Braun – would decide the fate of my entire family and change the course of our lives. But fate is a trickster, as unpredictable as the heart, and though my father should have played the pivotal role in that day's events, I found myself cast as the unlikely lead – a part I was not prepared for and one I did not entirely understand.

In the days leading to the summit, Gray Manor became the seat of chaos. Uncle Willy had indeed found temporary staff to pose as full-time employees, so the house was teeming with servants who had no idea what it was they were supposed to be doing. These townspeople donned ill-fitting uniforms and tried to play their parts. There were maids with no notion of how to clean, chauffeurs with no cars to drive, and a sous-chef whose culinary prowess began and ended with the ability to butter bread. Mrs Mead soon found herself teaching a young maid how to polish silver, and Uncle Willy informed the shocked new footmen that their chief purpose was not shining shoes but serving meals.

In preparation for the summit, Papa, more gaunt and harried than ever, held arduous strategy sessions with his board of directors in the vast main-floor boardroom of the manor. Somber men dressed in suits carrying ominous black briefcases marched in and out of our home with their heads stoically bowed. If by accident I met one in a corridor, I would curtsy and say 'sir.' Distress was writ large on their faces. Like experienced physicians, they'd come with medicine, but they'd heard the death rattle and knew what was to come.

Meanwhile, my mother, smelling of vodka and lime, conveyed the truth of our situation in the plainest terms. 'Even if we could liquidate everything, Flora, there still isn't enough to save us from ruin.'

'Perhaps Magnus will take pity on us,' I suggested hopefully. 'If he takes over Gray Investments, maybe Papa can work for him.'

Mama laughed bitterly as she clinked the ice cubes in her glass. 'You don't understand men at all. Emasculation is a sport – one man's blood loss is another man's transfusion. If Magnus wants to swallow us whole, he will. It's that simple.'

'Then why hire all these servants to make it seem like we have endless means?' I asked. 'What's the point?'

'The point, Flora, is honor. The band must play as the *Titanic* sinks.'

If the threat of a sinking ship wasn't bad enough, there was also the fact that the young man I was no longer permitted to call John (a.k.a. Mr Self-Important Preston) was one of Uncle Willy's temporary hires. He'd pulled his son out of classes for a full week, and wherever Uncle Willy went in the manor, his son followed, copying his father's every move, bowing and scraping, opening and closing doors, passing serving dishes at meals, and generally acting like a pompous, lumbering baboon.

With each passing day, I despised that young man more. He lacked the poise of a proper footman, serving me from the right instead of the left at dinner, and deigning to ask me if I wanted bread instead of silently handing me the basket. I could not eat what he boorishly heaped onto my plate, nor could I bear to look at him, handsome though he was. When

I passed him in the corridors, the very scent of him – for he'd taken to dousing himself with excess quantities of his father's *eau de toilette* – made me retch. I didn't know then how love and hate exist in such close proximity, and when we fear love the most, we pretend to feel its opposite. Plus, I knew my parents would mock me for harboring feelings for a man below my station, so I convinced myself that what I felt was raging ire.

I was overcome with vicious thoughts about the young Mr Preston. Like Goneril in *King Lear* (which was on our syllabus), I longed to pluck out his eyes. Never once did I stop to ponder what exactly the young lad had done to deserve such an oversize serving of my vitriol or if perhaps there was some other emotion brewing beneath my extreme outrage. I relished pointing out his failings, especially in my parents' presence. Once, at dinner, I noticed the way he stood to one side, a smirk on his face, judging us all.

'A footman keeps his hands behind him, not in front of him like a jockstrap,' I remarked without so much as looking up from my plate.

Mama covered her smile with her napkin. 'Now, Flora, we can't expect the new help to know everything right away. Good service is learned over time.'

'Only a waiter in a bad restaurant places a napkin over his arm,' I muttered.

Mr Preston Junior removed the offending napkin and placed it on the sideboard. 'Please excuse my boorish ways,' he said to Mama and Papa. 'I'm grateful for your daughter's guidance, knowing her manners – and yours – are both nonpareil and anachronistic.'

Papa and Mama exchanged a perplexed look. 'Quite the vocabulary you have, young man,' Papa said, but neither he nor Mama had quite grasped that he'd just insulted us all.

The day of the much-anticipated summit, I was glad to leave the manor and go to school, for at least there I wouldn't run into John. In class, the headmaster gave out grades on our *Romeo and Juliet* essays and instructed me to go home and tell the fill-in footman on scholarship the 'delightful news' – that his essay had earned the highest mark in class.

A chauffeur rushed me back to the manor once classes were over, as I was expected to be on display once the Braun Summit began. Mama and Papa insisted I join the staff receiving line, greeting the heads of the firm as they entered our well-appointed boardroom.

The harrowing ride home left me nauseated. The chauffeur had never driven a luxury vehicle before, which, he helpfully explained, did not ride at all like a horse. To make matters worse, when we pulled up to the manor, a procession of black cars already lined the semicircular drive, each awaiting its turn to drop off one of Braun's corporate magnates, more dreaded men in black who, for better or for worse, were about to seal my family's fate.

When at last my driver arrived at the manor's stately entrance, Uncle Willy was not greeting guests at the door as usual. He'd been tasked with overseeing the boardroom procession, and in his place were two young footmen, one of them

Uncle Willy's son, looking exasperatingly dashing in a tailored black suit with a matching bow tie, his dark hair smoothed back, and for the first time ever wearing the appropriate amount of his father's *eau de toilette.*

As he helped me remove my coat, I begrudgingly delivered the headmaster's message. 'Your essay took top place,' I said.

'Really?' he replied. 'And how did you do?'

'Second place,' I said, 'not that it's any of your business.'

He smiled ear to ear as he held my coat on one arm. 'See? You should have studied with me when you had the chance. Us common folk are smarter than you think.'

If I'd had a scalpel in that moment, I would have taken swift pleasure in the surgical removal of his snarky, self-righteous grin. I rapidly changed the subject from his prize-worthy essay to the headmaster's reminder about the assignment due in a few days – a paper on the application of an Aesop fable to a true-to-life situation. This was a task I'd been dreading because I simply could not see in any of the fables a correlation to the real world.

'I noticed Aesop's book of fables was missing from Papa's library. Might you be so kind as to promptly return my father's book to its proper shelf so that *I* might have the benefit of perusing it?' I asked the obnoxious Mr Preston.

'Of course,' he said as he grabbed a hanger and eased my coat onto it. 'I don't need the book anymore because my essay's finished.' He eyed me smugly as he clanked the hanger onto a rack.

'And which fable did you choose, might I ask?'

'The lion and the mouse,' he replied. 'Do you know it?'

Indeed, I did. A tiny, insignificant mouse saves a fearsome lion by chewing through the hunter's net to free it. The moral of the story? Even the powerless are mighty in the right circumstances.

'My offer of a study date stands,' said John quietly. 'Who knows? I might be a mighty mouse who can free you from your academic tangle.'

Bile rose in my gorge. How dare he suggest I wasn't perfectly capable of freeing myself! 'That won't be necessary,' I replied as I turned on my heel and marched away, but I quickly swiveled to face him and added, 'Do remember to bow to your betters after taking their coats. I'm sure your father taught you that much.'

'Of course, Your Ladyship,' he replied. 'Thank you ever so much for the reminder.' He bowed then, so obsequiously he all but kissed the floor.

I huffed in disgust as I walked away.

Following behind a funereal procession of my father's men in black, I headed to the boardroom, which was at the very back of the manor, right across from the conservatory. It was a long, thin room, with wide-open double doors in front. The various directors from both firms were finding places at the table – Braun's board on one side, and my father's on the other. If you squinted, it would have been hard to tell the two sides apart, but there were subtle differences. Unlike Papa's men, Magnus Braun's men had removed their modern jackets and slung them on the backs of their chairs. They leaned back comfortably, whereas my father's employees were as rigid as dominoes in a row – ready to be toppled with the flick of a finger.

Papa's servants stood in a line on the Gray side of the room, an impressive show of strength and tradition. Uncle Willy was at the head, while Mrs Mead and her maids, looking jittery and uncomfortable, graced the tail.

My mother greeted every guest who entered the boardroom with an ersatz smile. She wore a green A-line Chanel dress that showed off the small waist she was so proud of. She kept touching the double row of diamonds on her necklace, a piece so heavy it called to mind the yoke of a draft animal. She welcomed Braun's men with all the false charm she could muster, but when I approached the double doors, her face fell.

'You're wearing your school uniform,' she whispered as she clutched my wrist. 'Get upstairs and change – quickly – then join the staff line.'

I heeded her command and hurried upstairs, changing into the dress Mrs Mead had laid out on my bed – green, like my mother's, with a low, scooped neckline. When I arrived back at the boardroom, the procession was over and my father was walking Magnus Braun to the head of the table. The servants held their places, and I joined the end of the line.

At the front of the boardroom, my father stood beside Magnus Braun, a man I'd heard so much about but had never laid eyes on. He was my father's age, with piercing blue eyes and blond hair streaked with gray. Like a falcon accustomed to its high perch, he carried himself with an easy grace. He was the only man in the room wearing a colored suit – indigo blue, contemporary and Italian, nothing like my father's traditional Savile Row.

Papa was just finishing a saccharine introduction, pontificating on the great glory of two powerful firms, alike in dignity, coming together for the good of all.

When he finished, Magnus spoke, his voice a precision blade. 'This matter doesn't require quite so much pomp and circumstance,' he said as he looked at the receiving line of servants standing awkwardly to one side. 'Reginald, as you know, my board of directors conducted a thorough review of your company assets. Given your debt load and liabilities, we're determined to purchase Gray Investments outright. In fact, the purchase was made this morning, which means the controlling interest now rests with Braun Financial, resulting in the official and immediate termination of your firm. All that's required are signatures, though that's a formality. Still,' he said, pulling out a Cartier pen from his breast pocket, 'let's get it done.'

My father's eyes grew wide, an expression of abject shock claiming his face. 'But this was avoidable,' he insisted. 'My men have worked for weeks to pave a path toward an amicable merger between our firms. Is there no other way?'

'You've valuated your company on its past, not on its present, and you're no longer worth what you say you are. We've given you ample time to produce further assets of value, and you've failed. Let me put it simply: you've got nothing I want,' Magnus said.

This elicited polite chortles from his men and coughs from my father's.

Just then, the boardroom doors creaked open, and the two footmen serving in the front foyer – one of them Mr Preston Junior – attempted to enter stealthily.

Magnus tracked them with his cold, predatory gaze. 'I must say, Reginald, this is an impressive parade of servants. I haven't seen anything like it since the last century.'

More chortles and guffaws.

Uncle Willy's annoying son took his place in line beside me. He touched my arm, trying hard to get my attention, then he shoved a book into my hands.

'Will you stop?' I hissed at him, as I snatched Aesop's fables, clutching it to my chest.

The commotion did not go unnoticed. Magnus Braun's raptorial eyes landed on me. 'You,' he said. 'What are you doing here? You're no servant.'

I didn't know what to say. What is the etiquette when your father's archrival announces he's gobbling up the family firm and then engages you in small talk?

I took a step forward. 'Sir, are you addressing me?' I asked.

'I *am* addressing you,' he replied. 'You clearly have no place in that line. So what are you doing here?'

'Flora, you heard the man,' said my father. 'Go to your room.' He said it as if I were a disobedient toddler staying up past my bedtime, when in fact my presence had been ordered by him and Mama.

'What's that book you're holding?' Magnus asked as he pointed at it with his Cartier pen.

'Aesop's fables,' I replied as I gripped the book tighter, my hands shaking.

'A scholar? And a girl?' Magnus said as he sauntered past my father, all the way to where I stood in line on the other side of the room. 'What do you think about . . . all of this?' he asked, gesturing to the men in black seated at the giant boardroom table.

'With all due respect,' I said, 'I know very little about business affairs and even less about the affairs of men.'

'The affairs of men!' He laughed then, as did most of the men gathered in the room.

'That being what it is,' I continued, 'I've been listening, and I can't help but think about the book I'm holding and how it applies to this particular situation.'

Magnus eyed me curiously. 'Explain,' he demanded.

'There's a parable in this book about a tiny mouse that chews through a hunter's net to save a mighty lion caught in it.'

'So?' said Magnus. 'What's your point?'

'That the mighty fall,' I said. 'And the mightier they are, the more they underestimate others.' I looked from my father to Magnus Braun. 'It's a peril for the lion, just as it's a peril in the world of business.'

Magnus tapped his Cartier pen on the palm of his hand,

a wide grin consuming his face. 'Flora Gray. If I'm not mistaken, that's your name.'

'It is,' I confirmed. I had no idea how he knew.

'It's a fitting name,' he replied.

'Her name was my choice,' said Papa from the other end of the room. 'The moment I laid eyes on her, I knew she was my precious flower, so I named her Flora.'

'How old are you?' Magnus asked, talking only to me.

'She's—'

'Seventeen,' I replied.

'What does your future hold?' Magnus asked.

'Studying at university, I hope,' I replied with a discreet curtsy.

'We haven't agreed to send her,' said my father. 'It's a matter of—'

'Your father and I are different in critical ways, but we have one thing in common,' said Magnus. 'We each have but one child. Mine is a son – Algernon. You should meet him. Would that be of interest to you?'

'Of course it would!' my mother screeched from her place by the boardroom doors. 'Flora would be delighted.'

'Would she?' Magnus asked, his fierce blue eyes meeting mine.

Knowing what was expected, I nodded.

'Now, Audrey. What's this ball you mentioned on my way in?' Magnus asked my mother.

'The Workers' Ball,' Mama replied. 'We would be honored to host you and your wife as our guests.'

'Shall I bring my son?' Magnus asked me.

'As you wish,' I replied, my head politely bowed.

'Then it's decided,' said Magnus as he held out his Cartier pen. 'A gift for the scholar,' he said, offering it to me.

'But you need it to sign the papers.'

'The papers can wait,' he said with a shrug.

I took the pen he held out to me and muttered my thanks.

Magnus Braun then clapped his hands once. 'We're done here. Let's go,' he said.

In unison, his men in black rose, grabbing their sartorial jackets and matching black briefcases.

'See you at the ball,' Magnus said as he followed his men out of the boardroom.

CHAPTER 13

The day has finally come – the day the Fabergé will be auctioned. The relief I feel in this moment is equal to the trepidation that lodges in the pit of my stomach. So much of my life has been lived in utmost invisibility, and in the last week, everything has turned upside down. Over the course of my career as a maid, guests have barely noticed me, walked by me without a second glance, but since I appeared on *Hidden Treasures,* my life – my very person – has become a public spectacle. I've felt entirely outside of myself, staging a performance instead of actually living day to day. Ironically, the more famous I become, the less I know about who I am . . . and the lonelier I feel.

But it will all be over soon. The egg will be sold, and Juan and I will have an excess of money for the first time in our lives. Juan, dreamer that he is, keeps talking about how our existence is going to change for the better, how all manner of things will become possible for us that weren't even imaginable before – the wedding of our dreams, a honeymoon in Paris, buying a house with our own backyard, endless date nights at the Olive Garden, which we will be able to drive to in our very own car. It's hard to even fathom. It still feels like a fantasy, and until this becomes real, I won't truly believe it. They say money changes people. Will it change us for the better or for the worse? Until our lives become our own again, I won't feel wholly myself.

Juan feels the same trepidation I do, though he's been putting on a good game face for an entire week as our privacy has been stripped from us. Last night, while the film crew completed another 'day in the life' shoot at our apartment, he kissed me very naturally as I entered the kitchen to help him with dinner.

'Do it again,' Steve ordered while the camera invaded our space.

'Do what again?' Juan asked.

'Kiss her as she walks into the kitchen.'

And so, I walked into the kitchen over and over, while Juan kissed me repeatedly only to be told it 'wasn't quite right.' With each repetition, the soul of the act was lost, and in the end, when Steve said, 'That's the winning take. Wrapped!' I could tell that Juan felt robbed, as if a very simple pleasure had been stolen from us, something we never even knew could be taken away.

Now, I'm sitting in the front seat of my gran-dad's car as he drives Juan and me to the Regency Grand, where the auction will take place at 10:00 A.M., live in the tearoom.

Juan and I are already uniformed, as Steve and the crew needed us 'camera ready' upon arrival. This is yet another film term I've added to my growing lexicon, alongside 'lavalier,' 'key light,' and 'over-the-shoulder shot.'

As Mr Preston pulls up to the Regency Grand, it's immediately clear this is no ordinary day. 'Molly, are you ready?' he asks.

'To be honest, I have no idea,' I reply.

On the front steps, a crowd has gathered, many of them dressed in imitations of my uniform, several wearing black wigs cut into perfectly blunt bobs like mine. Some hold posters saying, WE ♥ YOU, MOLLY! while others are clearly Bee-lievers, eager to meet Brown and Beagle.

'We can do this,' Juan says as he puts a steadying hand on my arm. 'A few autographs, a few photos, then we go inside, okay?'

'Okay,' I say.

'Good luck,' Mr Preston says. 'I'll be at the auction cheering you on.'

Juan and I step out of his car, and the second we do the crowd on the stairs races our way, proffering pens and snapping photos.

'Let them by!' Speedy orders as he cuts a path up the red-carpeted stairs. 'You'll both be ballin' soon. Can't say I'm not mad jelly,' Speedy says to Juan as we slip past him and through the gold revolving doors.

'What's he blathering on about?' I ask Juan once we're delivered into the lobby.

'Nothing important,' says Juan.

I'm relieved we're now inside, where at least I can catch my breath. Mr Snow has corralled guests behind a maroon cordon to await entry into the tearoom. The guests are wearing bright lanyards that say BEE & BEE VIP. Some sport *Hidden Treasures* buttons or have photos of the Bees in hand, ready for signing. But others don't look like typical fans. They're serious men and women in expensive dress suits, carrying sleek portfolios. One gentleman, who's wearing loafers with no socks and glasses I can only describe as Picassoesque, paces back and forth as he speaks on his phone. 'It's looking high. Big bidders all over the place. I'll give you fair warning before close of bid, but if you want it, act fast.'

'Her shoes,' Juan says as he eyes a willowy woman wearing a sack-like orange muumuu and impossibly high heels. 'Why are the bottoms red?' Juan asks.

'I have no idea,' I say.

Soon enough, all eyes turn our way, and there's an audible gasp as we're recognized. Mr Snow, who's been attempting to maintain order, says, 'If anybody steps one foot past this cordon, say goodbye to your coveted spot in the auction room. Is that clear?'

Much to my relief, the crowd takes a step backward, and Juan and I are safe, at least for the moment. Mr Snow dabs at his forehead with his pocket square as he walks our way.

'Mayhem,' he says by way of greeting. 'Molly, I'm very happy you're about to become a millionaire, but this event has proven extremely challenging, especially without your help.'

When plans for the auction were put in place, a week ago, Mr Snow delegated Angela to be in charge, a decision that, I'll admit, was a bitter pill to swallow.

'But I'm head of special events,' I said when he broke the news.

'You can't be the star of the show *and* its organizer. Please, Molly. Just this once.'

I followed Mr Snow's logic, and as I stand in front of the 'mayhem,' I realize I may have dodged a figurative bullet.

'They're waiting for you in the tearoom,' Mr Snow says. 'The egg will be transported there shortly. It'll be onstage during the auction.'

'We can grab it from your office,' I say. 'You're obviously busy.'

'Molly, it will be escorted by armed guards,' Mr Snow explains.

'Oh,' I reply – yet another reality I had not considered.

Juan and I make our way to the tearoom in silence. At the entrance, I survey the room in all its glory. The layout is a bit different today, the tables clothed in white linens as usual but no tea service in sight. Instead, each place setting comprises a paddle, every one numbered uniquely. At the back of the room is a raised platform, on which three rows of desks are neatly set, each with a black rotary phone on top. The crew is setting up lights and cameras. At the front of the room, Brown's and Beagle's thrones are on stage right, along with an extra throne featuring a monogram I've not seen before – a curlicue *M*.

Angela appears in front of us, her fiery hair in a tizzy. For once, she's not wearing her bartender's apron. 'Molly!' she says. 'I'm gonna bust a gasket. I don't know what I'm doing. I'm a bartender, not an events planner.'

'The room looks lovely,' I say.

'What's with the desks and phones?' Juan asks, pointing to the rows at the back.

'Call-in bidders,' Angela explains. 'That's how dealers communicate with their buyers. I'm told we've got some heavy hitters tuning in. Do you know how long it took me to source twenty-five black rotary phones? I had Sunshine and Lily working overtime on eBay.'

The second she mentions the maids, I feel a pang of guilt. 'Are they okay?' I ask. 'I've left them short-staffed.'

'Molly,' Angela says as she puts a hand on my shoulder. 'Stop worrying about everyone else for a second. Enjoy the moment.'

'She's right, *mi amor*,' says Juan. 'This is a once-in-a-lifetime experience. Let's savor it.'

Just then, Steve and the Bees emerge from the hidden paneled door to the greenroom. As usual, Steve's irony is advertised on his baseball cap. Baxley Brown and Thomas Beagle are dressed in their debonair velvet jackets – scarlet and blue, respectively. More than a head taller than Beagle, Baxley bends to whisper something in his husband's ear. Then both stars and the show producer make their way over to us.

'Welcome, Molly. Hello, Juan,' Beagle says.

'Nervous?' Brown asks.

'Yes,' I say. 'I don't know what to expect.'

'First off, this isn't a regular art auction,' says Brown.

'Think of it as televised theater,' says Beagle as he waves jazz hands at me, his ringed fingers glinting under the lights.

'This is my first auction,' says Juan.

'You never forget your first, am I right?' Beagle quips as he pokes Juan in the ribs.

Juan doesn't reply.

'Coming through!' we hear. We move out of the way as a glass display case containing the Fabergé egg is wheeled into the room by guards in bulletproof vests. 'Where do you want it?' one of them asks Steve.

'In my bank account,' says Steve, and everyone but Juan and I laugh. 'Put it on the spike marks onstage between the podium and the Bees' thrones,' he instructs.

Once the display case is set, Steve calls out, 'Lights!' and as if by magic, a spotlight illuminates the Fabergé as it sits on its golden pedestal, safe under glass.

'Are you going to miss it, the Fabergé?' Beagle asks me.

'My gran taught me not to covet material things,' I say. '*The only loss worth mourning is love.* That's what she used to say.'

'It's a shame Granny's dead – "very dead," as I recall,' says Brown.

'I lost my grandfather a few months ago,' says Beagle. 'It was hard.'

'He was a good man,' Brown adds as he puts a loving hand on his husband's arm. 'Dearly missed by us both.'

'I'm sorry for your loss,' I reply.

'We have just enough time for a quick run of show,' says Steve. 'Juan, sit in that audience chair. If we cut to you, wave like crazy and jump around like you did last time, okay?'

'Okay,' says Juan as he sits in his spot.

'Molly, that's your throne – with the monogrammed *M*. We had it specially made to commemorate our most popular guest ever,' Steve says.

'And our highest ratings to date,' Brown adds.

'Molly, you'll join the Bees onstage for an intro, then we'll cut to the sizzle reel,' says Steve. 'After that, the auction begins. Baxley is our auctioneer, so he'll take the podium. Expect lots of paddles in the air, Bax, and pay close attention to the dealers at the back. They're on the line with art collectors all over the world. Got it?'

Steve looks from face to face, and I realize I'm the only one who still has questions.

'But how does it end?' I ask.

'Highest bidder wins. When that gavel comes down, Molly, it's done. And you're rich.' Steve claps his hands together. 'Okay, let's get everyone in here. Where's the hotel manager? What's his name? Mr Sweaty?'

'Mr Snow,' I say, my voice cutting over the crew's guffaws.

'I'll get him,' Angela volunteers, but before she leaves, she turns to me. 'Don't pass out this time, okay?'

'A live Fabergé faint!' says Steve. 'Camera Two – zoom in close if it happens.'

Angela gives my hand a squeeze, then rushes off to find Mr Snow.

'Let's retire to the greenroom, Molly,' says Beagle as he takes my arm. 'It's almost showtime.'

'And three, two, one . . . and we're live to air!'

'Hi, everyone. Welcome to this special edition of *Hidden Treasures,* where I, Baxley Brown . . .'

'. . . and I, Thomas Beagle, appraise your long-lost works of art, taking the mystery out of history!'

'We're thrilled to have you here today for this rare live auction show, where we will change the life of one very special person. After last week's episode, you've come to know her well and to love her, too. She's trending, she's an It Girl, she's the woman of the week and maybe even the woman of the year! She's entrusted us today with the sale of something almost as precious as she is – her priceless Fabergé egg. She's Molly the Maid, but I know she's so much more than that to all of you. Come on out here, Molly, and lap up the love!'

I push through the greenroom door and take the stairs to the stage. The lights blind me, and the tearoom audience is whooping so loudly it takes all my willpower not to stop my ears with my hands. Beagle guides me to my throne. I perch shakily on the edge.

'Give the audience a wave, Molly,' Beagle instructs, and I do.

'She waves just like a queen,' says Brown as the audience laughs.

'Molly, we're thrilled to have you here today, and even more thrilled to be selling your egg on live TV!' Beagle says.

'In one week, as a result of *Hidden Treasures,* wouldn't you say your life has completely changed?'

'If you mean it's been turned upside down, absolutely,' I reply.

'Have you splurged? Have you gone out and bought something amazing to celebrate?' asks Brown.

'Some fancy tea towels. Very absorbent.'

The crowd laughs and laughs.

'Now before you ask, I'll tell you plainly, Molly, that the whole wide world is laughing *with* you not at you. Over the past week, you've become a media darling, the world's favorite girl next door . . .'

'So beyond buying tea towels,' says Beagle, 'what else will you do when you get your millions?'

'I'm not entirely sure,' I say. 'I'm still thinking it through.'

'Surely there's something exciting you'll spend the money on. After all, wedding bells are in your future.'

'Yes,' I say. 'Juan Manuel and I are getting married in just a few weeks.'

The camera cuts to Juan in his chef whites, grinning and waving in the front row, but his smile looks forced and strange. I'm reminded of how Gran once taught me that a smile does not always mean someone is happy. Juan's face is living proof.

'We hear you've been making preparations for your special day. The *Hidden Treasures* film crew has been following you all week. What do you think, folks – would you like to see a day in the life of Molly the Maid?'

The crowd hoots and hollers as a screen drops behind us,

and suddenly, the reel begins to sizzle. There I am, in a guest's room at the hotel, vacuuming the carpet into Zen-garden lines. When I turn off the machine, someone off camera asks if I'd ever run for office. 'I'm just a maid,' I reply. The live audience laughs and claps.

Next, I'm at home on the sofa squished between Juan and my gran-dad as we watch TV. The crowd giggles as we pass a bowl of popcorn between us. Cut to the bridal shop with Angela, where I'm emerging from the change room in a beautiful wedding gown. Women are suddenly jumping all around me, and while I know they're strangers, everyone watching thinks they're my bridesmaids.

Cut to Angela sitting on a white satin bench, tears in her eyes. 'You're beautiful,' Angela mouths. 'You're more than a maid!'

What? I can't believe what I'm watching. Those aren't the words Angela said at all. And the tears she shed at that moment had nothing to do with joy.

The reel ends and silence descends upon the room. The audience is sniffing and sniveling. The Bees have removed their pocket squares from their jackets and are making a big show of dabbing their eyes.

'Does everyone in this room need a tissue for their issue?' I ask.

More laughter.

'We love you, Molly!' someone calls out from the crowd.

'I don't know why,' I reply. 'I'm not sure what you all see in me.'

'We see that you're adorable,' Brown says as he crosses his long legs.

'Molly, how does it feel to watch your life on the big screen?' Beagle asks.

'Things didn't happen quite like that,' I say. 'In reality, it was different.'

'Reality is always different. And speaking of reality, the time has come, Molly, for us to address the reason we're here: to auction your exquisite Fabergé,' says Brown.

'Are you ready?' Beagle asks.

'It's been a fixture in my life for a long time. My gran and I used to have a savings account we called our Fabergé – a joke, since we had so little money in it.'

'I suspect your savings account will soon be worthy of the name,' says Beagle. 'Bax, your gavel.'

Beagle passes his partner a small wooden hammer that fits in the palm of his hand.

Brown assumes his imposing height and strides across to the podium as the lights overhead shift, illuminating for the first time the glorious Fabergé in its protective glass case in the middle of the stage. The crowd gasps as it comes into view.

'Ladies and gentlemen,' says Brown as he gestures to the egg. 'I'm thrilled to present an *objet d'art* unique in all the world, the likes of which has not been seen or catalogued in art literature for over a hundred years. Featuring gold trelliswork and a cabriolet base, encrusted in quatrefoils comprising ten rubies, twenty rose-cut diamonds, and over thirty Russian emeralds, this singular prototype egg is the original design upon which all the famous imperial Romanov Easter eggs were based. The house that created it is well known to art aficionados, jewel collectors, historians, academics, and *Hidden Treasures* fans the world over. That house is Fabergé.'

Quiet whispers travel around the room. The lights change again, plummeting the egg into darkness and illuminating Brown's tall form at the podium. He squares his shoulders to match his jaw, speaking with grave authority. 'We'll begin today's bidding at a cool five million dollars, offered from a call-in client at the back. Do I have five million five? Five point five million dollars?' Brown scans the paddles flinging up all over the room.

'No shy bidders today. We have five-five, going up to six, do we have six million – yes!' says Brown as he points to a caller at the back. 'Six million to Madame Orange on the phone, welcome, madam. Do I have seven? Seven million? Seven million to Mr Wigham at table five – nice to see you, sir. Eight, eight-five from our bidder in black. Do we have nine, nine million dollars? Yes, we do at table two. Let's jump to nine-five, nine million five hundred thousand dollars . . .'

As Brown repeats his banter, the bidders at the back consult with the clients on the phone lines, covering their mouths as they talk so no one can read their lips.

Brown natters on as the active bidders thin to just three. The tension mounts, but Brown maintains composure, enticing the bids higher and higher until he says, 'Nine million nine hundred thousand dollars to our audacious bidder in black. Thank you, sir.' He pauses, then places both hands on the podium. 'Ladies and gentlemen, as we approach a seven-zero bid, I want to remind you that not only is the work of art on auction today unique in all the world, but its current owner, Molly Gray, is a pop culture phenom and the maid of the moment. Do I have ten million dollars?'

The air in the room feels dense. The silence is deafening.

'Ten million! To Madame Orange, with her client on the line. Ten million one. Ten million, one hundred thousand dollars. Anyone?'

Brown eyes the crowd with his piercing blue stare. 'This is fair warning,' he says as he holds his gavel high in the air.

'And sold!' he proclaims, pounding the gavel down, the sound ricocheting throughout the room. 'Ten million dollars even. Thank you very much to your client, madam, and thanks to all of you who've joined us today.'

The lights go up and the *Hidden Treasures* theme music starts to play as polite applause issues from the crowd. Brown and Beagle unite at the front of the stage – one tall, one small – and both of them wave and shake hands with bidders as the cameras zoom in to close out the show.

It's then I hear a shout from the crowd.

'Wait!'

There's a cacophony of sound – music and chatter and gasps – but above it all, that voice again, so familiar.

'*El huevo!*'

In the front row, Juan is standing, waving his arms and pointing at the glass case at center stage.

It's then that I realize why he's clamoring for attention.

The display case is still there, a spotlight now shining gently down on it, but the precious egg that was inside it when the auction began has vanished.

CHAPTER 14

Dear Molly,

Life is a mystery. Try as we might to solve it, a new puzzle always presents itself.

The Braun Summit marked a colossal change in my life, a moment when fate pointed its sharp arrow at me. Before that strange day, I was but a burden to be borne by my parents, a costly problem that plagued them, but the second Magnus noticed me in Papa's oppressive boardroom, everything changed. It was as if both my parents recognized my value for the very first time, saw in me a pathway to a secure future.

Once Magnus and his men were out the front door of the manor on summit day, I was free to ponder what on earth had just transpired in that boardroom. I knew I'd achieved something significant, earning my father a reprieve from losing the family firm. But at what cost? Had I missed something, yet another subtlety of the world of men my mother was always reminding me I failed to comprehend?

My father said goodbye to Braun, seeing him off with a proper handshake and clap to the back. Then he locked the formidable manor doors behind his archrival. As Mama and I watched alongside the staff gathered in the front foyer, Papa paused and took a breath, his hand still clenched on the ornate brass door handle. 'You're all dismissed,' he eventually said, sending the servants away. 'William, take the workers to the housekeeping quarters and pay them what's owed.'

'Yes, sir,' Uncle Willy replied with a curt bow.

Soon enough, it was just me, Papa, and Mama at the entrance. Light streamed through the tall cathedral windows, catching me obliquely where I stood. My parents were gazing at me as if they'd never seen me before, as if the answer to a problem thcy'd been trying to solve for months had been right in their faces all along.

'What?' I asked them. 'Why are you looking at me like that?'

'My little Flora, my beautiful blossom,' said Papa. 'You did us proud.'

'A blessing in disguise,' said Mama. 'And maybe a wolf in sheep's clothing.'

'A wolf?' I said. 'Me?'

'Doesn't your book have that story in it?' Mama asked as she tapped my copy of Aesop's fables, which, along with the Cartier pen, I still clutched to my chest.

'That's a different book entirely,' I said.

'The point is, you saved the day,' said Papa.

Mama shook her head in disbelief. 'It feels like a miracle, like a fairy tale. You caught the eye of the king, Flora.'

'You made Magnus change his mind,' said Papa. He put a hand on my shoulder. 'I've harbored doubts about you since the moment you were born, but you just proved yourself an asset to this family.'

'You did,' said Mama. 'But make no mistake, this isn't the end. It's just the beginning. Keep your eye on the prize, Flora, do you understand?'

I did not understand, not a thing, but I nodded anyway.

'My daughter charmed Magnus Braun,' said Papa in disbelief. 'The wheel of fortune has spun, and it has landed on my precious girl.'

'Careful, Reginald,' said Mama. 'Men like Magnus are flighty. What takes their fancy one day bores them the next.'

My father ignored her and turned to me. 'May I see the pen he gave you?' he asked.

I handed the Cartier to him. Papa inspected the gold details and the glossy black enamel. 'It's authentic, the real thing, Flora,' he said. 'I wouldn't want you to lose it.' He popped the pen into his breast pocket. 'Good work today. You can go now,' he said. 'You're dismissed.'

The Workers' Ball was but a week and a half away, and there were endless preparations before the big event. Mama pleaded with my father to keep some of the temporary workers on staff, which he did. Soon enough, the manor was teeming with servants yet again. Only Mrs Mead and Uncle Willy knew the run of show from having worked the ball for so many years, but with the higher stakes of the Brauns in attendance, Mama was more invested in a display of grandeur than ever before.

In the past, the ball was a dance event featuring a live band and simple hors d'oeuvres. But this year, beyond the dance and band, Mama insisted on a full buffet dinner to be offered in the guest parlor just off the ballroom. She also insisted on reorganizing each room that guests would pass on their way to the ballroom so as to show off our family's precious heirlooms.

The front foyer now featured an intimidating medieval knight in shining armor, complete with a sword and a shield emblazoned with the family coat of arms. In the portrait corridor, Mama added ancestral busts and sculptures, their dead eyes staring at passersby as if assessing their worth and finding it lacking. She took Chinese porcelain vases and Grecian urns from other rooms, emptying those quarters entirely so that walking through that front corridor was like touring a private museum.

But the *pièce de résistance* was her lavish display of silver, usually kept in a large pantry in the basement of the manor – engraved utensils and platters, heavy chargers and chafing dishes, monogrammed candelabra and serving spoons – all of which graced the table and sideboards in the banquet room by the ballroom. I learned of my mother's plan to show off the family's extensive silver collection when a sheepish temporary maid named Penelope crossed me in a hallway and asked me where the silver pantry was.

'How would I know?' I replied. 'Ask Mrs Mead.'

No sooner had I said it than Mrs Mead appeared from the kitchen, huffing and puffing, and wiping her hands on her apron.

'Do you know where the silver pantry is?' I asked her.

'Ay. And the glassware rooms and the bedrooms and the laundry rooms, and much more besides. I was hired as your nursemaid, and somehow, I've become head maid of this household. Rest assured I'm not paid to be in charge, but yes, I do know where the silver pantry is.'

Mrs Mead then muttered something under her breath. I'll admit I never took any of her complaints seriously, but now I realize how overworked she was and that if she wanted to keep living in the cottage on the estate, there wasn't a thing she could do about it.

'Can you show this maid the way?' I asked Mrs Mead.

'Come,' she said to the shy girl in the hallway.

'Mrs Mead,' I called out as they were leaving. 'There's something I wanted to discuss with you.'

She cocked her head to one side, hand on her hefty hip. 'Does it look like I have time for a wee chat? Follow me downstairs and we'll talk as I set Penelope up to polish. Or is the little miss too posh to venture into the basement with us common folk?'

For the first time in ages, I soon found myself in the manor's subterranean lair – a labyrinth of low-ceilinged rooms filled with antique furniture, banker's boxes, filing cabinets, and all manner of sundry goods for the running of the household.

'The silver pantry,' Mrs Mead announced as she switched on the bare bulb in a room that looked very much like a dragon's hoard, filled floor to ceiling with cobwebs and filthy, tarnished silver.

Mrs Mead pulled out a basin, a jug, rubber gloves, and some rags from a cupboard. She set Penelope to work in an adjoining room. Then in the room filled with silver, she passed identical cleaning supplies to me.

'What's all this for?' I asked.

'If you're seeking my counsel, you might as well lend a hand,' she replied.

Though it was far below my station, I needed Mrs Mead's guidance, so I donned rubber gloves and polished an ornate silver spoon with a rag doused in some sort of lye solution, something I would never have deigned to do for anyone except Mrs Mead. I wasn't happy about it, not at first, but before long, something about the task became almost enjoyable. With a bit of elbow grease, the tarnish was eradicated. Real life is never that easy – the filth is much harder to wipe away.

'You see?' said Mrs Mead as she held up a gleaming silver platter. 'Silver teaches you things. Never judge by appearances. A tarnished piece might be a hidden treasure. Now what was it you wanted to talk about?'

It had been a week since the Braun Summit, and I still didn't know exactly what would happen when I met Magnus Braun's son, Algernon, at the Workers' Ball. Papa refused to discuss the matter, and Mama would broach the subjects of my jewelry and makeup but little else besides. I tried to ask Uncle Willy about it, but he muttered something about this being Mrs Mead's territory, not his. And so here I was with my nursemaid, in the dungeon-like basement, trying to get some clarity on why a man like Magnus was so set on me meeting his son.

'What it means, child, is that Mr Braun Senior is considering a match between you and his boy.'

I stopped polishing, caught my reflection upside down in the bowl of the silver spoon. 'What kind of match?' I asked. Fool that I was, I refused to see what was entirely obvious.

'Marriage. Did you not even understand that much? How can you be so clever at school and so daft at real life?'

I had no answer to her question, but I did know one thing. 'I'm far too young to wed.'

'Men like Magnus Braun browse early to buy later,' Mrs Mead said as she rubbed a round charger, bringing out a high and mighty shine.

'I want to go to university. I have no interest in boys,' I said.

'Is that right?' said Mrs Mead. 'Not even my nephew?'

I could not believe my ears. Her nephew? Though mildly handsome and passably intelligent for a servant's boy, his righteous arrogance grated on my every nerve. Still, I refused to acknowledge the truth that Mrs Mead had spotted beneath my thin patina of disdain. 'Your nephew thinks himself a gentleman because he's wearing his father's shiny shoes. But a pig wearing lipstick is still a pig,' I said petulantly.

Mrs Mead was adding lye to her cloth, and when a drop landed on her arm, she winced.

'Did that sting?' I asked.

'Not as much as your comment,' she replied as she wiped away the drop.

I know now that Mrs Mead expected more of me, that by keeping me close all those years, she believed I would one day wake up and see my parents' entitlement for what it was – privilege and prejudice that kept others in a state of perpetual servitude. But at the time, in my foolish, young mind, I believed Mrs Mead and Uncle Willy were rare exceptions, the only blue-collar specimens of real worth. It pains me to write this down, but it is the truth.

In that moment, by attacking Mrs Mead's nephew, I knew I'd insulted her terribly, and I tried to make things right. 'This isn't about your nephew,' I said. 'It's about me. I'm just not interested in boys.'

My nursemaid huffed dramatically. 'That will change,' she said as she fixed her blue-eyed-green-eyed gaze at me. 'In my estimation, the changes have already begun. There's a lot riding on this meeting with Algernon. But you never know. Maybe you'll fall for the young prince.'

'Impossible,' I said emphatically.

'Is it?' she said.

As I've come to learn, Molly, when you're young, you can be very certain of something, but too often, that doesn't mean you're right.

*

As the fateful day of the Workers' Ball approached, preparations at the manor ramped up even more. The entire household vibrated with nervous energy.

The day before the ball, my mother ordered the staff to fill the house with daffodils, which were in full bloom in the fields by Mrs Mead's cottage. Vases of the yellow flowers decorated every horizontal surface. Meanwhile, my father, having learned of Magnus's love of whiskey, set out to procure the finest bottles money could buy, displaying them on the bar in the banquet room.

At school, the headmaster returned our papers on Aesop's fables, calling me to the front of the class.

'Flora, you took top grade this time around,' he announced. 'I very much applaud your creative application of the lion and mouse fable to the business world. Well done.'

He shook my hand, and I felt a swell of pride. I walked back to my desk, eager to catch Mr Preston Junior's eye, fully expecting him to be peeved, but contrary to my expectations, he was smiling so genuinely it was as if he'd earned top place, not me.

I took my seat, turning my back on him. For the rest of class, I focused on the headmaster, who was offering pointers on how best to tackle comparative questions on our upcoming exams.

When we were dismissed, I was surprised to find myself surrounded by classmates, boys who were starting to see me as perhaps not so worthy of their disdain. Moreover, many of these young corporate heirs had been invited to the ball for the very first time. Redheaded Percival and his mess hall mates hoped to glean from me some clues about what to expect and how to behave at the ball.

'So there's dancing?' Percival asked.

'Of course there's dancing. What do you think a ball is?' I replied.

His mates chortled and knocked elbows.

'Will you wear a dress?' Percival asked.

'Not a dress, a gown,' I corrected.

'I can't picture you in a gown,' Percival replied.

'Good,' I said. 'I wouldn't want you to.'

His retinue of friends hooted at my witty rejoinder. I'd discovered that caustic humor offered the best protection against their jabs and barbs. I didn't care whom I hurt with my 'humor,' provided my ego remained intact.

Percival slunk away without another word, and his band of brothers followed.

Uncle Willy's son was now the only other student left in the classroom. He made his way over to my desk. He was close enough that I could smell his father's scent on him. 'Congratulations on your paper,' he said. 'I'm happy for you.'

'Thank you, Mr Preston,' I curtly replied.

He sighed and ran a casual hand through his tousled brown hair. 'Please, can we stop that?' he pleaded. 'Just call me John like you did when we first met, remember?'

His brown eyes were shiny and bright. There was a look of forgiveness and longing in them that made my heart clamor in my chest, though I did my best to deny it. Still, I found myself unable to tear my eyes from his. As I stared at him, a memory returned with such force it gave me vertigo. How I could have forgotten, I don't know, but sometimes, Molly, we bury deepest that which is too painful to remember.

When I was but a child, no older than five years of age, my mother held a ladies' tea party on the manor lawn. She invited all the bourgeois wives, who in turn brought their bratty little bourgeois girls. While the ladies enjoyed tea, I was to entertain the girls and host my own parallel tea party, sharing my books and dolls with them. Things turned sour when I demanded they listen to me read a story from my favorite picture book. The girls grabbed the book and crumpled the pages.

Irate, I grabbed it back, scolded them, then ran away from the party, past the lawns, through the garden gate, down the path toward the orchards until I was safe behind the Mead cottage, standing by the pond with my ruined book in the mud at my feet.

Only then did I allow myself to cry. Why were girls so mean? Why was it such a struggle to make friends? Why did I always feel left out? I imagined jumping into the pond and disappearing into the muck to live amongst the frogs. No one would miss me. But as I stared at my despondent reflection in the water, I felt a disturbing pull that made me back away from the water's edge.

I walked along the pathway to the knotty old oak tree on the edge of the estate. I sat against the massive trunk, and I wept. That's when I heard a voice behind me.

'Are you okay?'

I turned and saw a boy my age standing there. He was

wearing short pants, his brown hair tousled, his head cocked to one side.

'Go away,' I said as I wiped my tears.

'Are you the fairy?' he replied.

'I'm not a fairy,' I said. 'I'm just a girl.'

He moved closer. 'They come here sometimes. Fairies,' he explained. 'They put things in the knothole of that tree for kids like us to find.' He came closer and pointed to an oval hollow above me in the tree trunk.

'I once found a cat's-eye marble in there. And some skipping stones another time.' He smiled then, that same generous smile. 'I'm John.'

'John,' I said, trying his name on for the first time.

'Who are you?' he asked.

'Flora,' I replied.

'Flora!' I heard, but not from the boy beside me. It was my mother, shrieking, running down the pathway in her party dress and heels, her legs splattered in mud. She scooped me up in her arms and hugged me so tight I could barely draw a breath.

'She's here!' she yelled out to the trail of ladies following behind her.

Her grip released, and she put me down. She stayed at my eye level, looking me in the face. 'Your book,' she said. 'I saw it by the edge of the pond. I thought you'd drowned!' she cried as tears streamed down her cheeks.

I placed a hand on her hair. 'Don't cry, Mama,' I said.

It was then that she slapped my face. 'How dare you scare me like that!' she growled. 'You're a very bad girl. Come. Now.'

She grabbed my hand and marched me up the path, away from the little boy and all the grim-faced ladies who'd borne witness to the entire spectacle.

Back at the manor lawn, I was made to apologize to the little girls for ruining their tea party. Mrs Mead was instructed to take me to my room, where I was banished for the rest of the afternoon.

The next day, when no one was watching, I sneaked out of the manor and made my way back to that old oak tree. The boy wasn't there anymore, but in the knotty hollow of the trunk was my storybook, the mud cleaned off, the pages smoothed, the ripped ones taped up neatly.

From that point onward, I wholeheartedly believed in fairies, but what I should have believed in all along was John.

'You really don't remember?' John asked as we stood there, the only two left in the classroom.

He looked at me with the same glassy brown eyes he'd had as a child, the eyes of an old soul.

I shook my head and looked away, pretending I had no recollection.

'I wanted to tell you something,' John said. 'The other day, at the Braun Summit, what you did in that boardroom . . . It was brave. It was remarkable.'

'I did nothing,' I replied.

'That's not true,' said John. 'There's nothing more important than family, and you saved yours. Don't you see that?'

Was that what I'd done? I could give myself no credit, for

it had been by accident or instinct, but as John looked at me, it was as though he was seeing me in a whole new light.

'As your auntie would say,' I replied, 'don't count your chickens before they hatch.'

He laughed. 'Aunt Maggie would say that,' he said. 'Please. Will you call me John from now on? I promise not to be an idiot. And I promise not to hate you for being a rich kid. Truce?'

He held out his hand, and I took it. I felt a tremor run through me then, as if nothing else mattered except his hand in mine, soft and warm, a perfect fit. 'Truce,' I said as I held it tight.

'May I ask a favor?' he said. 'Tomorrow night, will you reserve a dance for me at the ball? I have a feeling you're going to be very popular.'

'Of course,' I replied, still holding his hand. 'As long as you don't step on my feet.'

'I think I've made enough graceless missteps lately. The next one won't be mine.'

'You're sure about that?' I asked.

Those lips, that disarming smile. I tell you, Molly, that man could light up the entire world. As I watched, he raised our conjoined hands and planted a delicate kiss on the back of mine.

'See you tomorrow night, Flora,' he said.

'Until then . . . John,' I replied.

CHAPTER 15

I'm sitting on the edge of the stage in the tearoom as my vision starts to clear. I didn't faint, not this time. Beside me is Juan, a protective arm around my shoulders, and on my other side is Angela.

'It's going to be okay, Molly,' she says.

'Just breathe,' says Juan.

I was sitting on my guest throne onstage when the auction ended and Juan yelled out, '*El huevo!*' I looked to the display case where the Fabergé had been, having just sold for ten million dollars, but it was gone.

Pandemonium took hold, and the crowd rushed forward. Mr Snow raced out of the room, and Steve ordered everyone to 'sit down!' Cameras and lighting equipment were tipped over, auction paddles flung to the floor. Brown and Beagle stood at center stage, staring wide-eyed at the empty display case. I took a few unsteady steps, then felt faint and sat on the edge of the stage. It's where I now find myself as bidders and buyers, collectors and crew members rush in and out of the room, everyone shouting contradictory orders.

At long last, Mr Snow appears at the tearoom entrance, someone following close behind him – a uniformed woman flanked by two male officers. The familiar, imposing woman marches in and calls out, 'I'm Detective Stark. No one else leaves this room until I say so! Got it?'

Her two officers block the doorway as the remaining onlookers head to wherever they were before the egg disappeared.

Detective Stark's steely eyes take in the film equipment and paddles on the floor, the Bees by the podium, the empty display case at center stage, and me, sitting on the edge, with Juan and Angela at my sides. I haven't seen the detective since the investigation into J. D. Grimthorpe's sudden death at the hotel. As always, Stark's presence elicits visceral butterflies.

The detective strides over. 'Molly,' she says. 'We've got to stop meeting like this.'

'I would say it's nice to see you,' I reply, 'but lying to an officer is a criminal offense.'

Stark's lips curl into what I believe is an amused smirk. 'Angela,' she says with a tip of her cap. 'Always good to see you. Still hoping to join the force one day?'

'Um, yeah,' she says. 'I'm saving for college. I hope to join the academy someday.' She glances at Mr Snow, who does not seem surprised by the revelation.

'And you, Molly? Any chance I'll see you on the force one day?'

'Unlikely,' I say. 'In fact, I'd rather avoid criminal activity than seek it out.'

'And yet somehow, it seems to follow you.'

'Unfortunately,' I reply.

'You were here when the egg disappeared?' Stark asks Angela and me.

'We were,' Angela answers.

'And you're Molly's fiancé,' Detective Stark says to Juan.

'I didn't do anything, I swear! I'm just a chef, and Molly's just a maid,' Juan pleads.

'Calm down,' Stark replies. 'No one's accusing you of anything.'

'Juan and I get nervous around police,' I say by way of explanation.

'I understand,' Detective Stark replies. 'But you're the victims of this crime, no? What was stolen was yours?'

'That's right,' says a voice behind me. Beagle moves to the front of the stage with Brown beside him. 'My husband was conducting the auction,' Beagle explains. 'He'd just brought down the gavel to close the bidding. When the lights went up on the display case, the Fabergé was gone.'

'We were both shocked,' says Brown as he stares down at his husband, his blue eyes wide.

Stark squints at the two dapper men before her. 'Did I ask for a play-by-play?'

'I should have introduced myself,' says Beagle. 'I'm—'

'I know who you are,' she replies. 'I've seen your show.'

'Always good to meet a fan,' says Brown.

'Who says I'm a fan?' Detective Stark responds. 'Now, Molly, did anyone unexpectedly come onstage during the shoot?'

'No one,' I say.

'We were all watching,' Mr Snow adds.

'That's right,' says Steve as he introduces himself to Stark. 'I can't believe the Fabergé was stolen right in front of our eyes. How can that be?'

'You tell me,' says Stark as she eyes Steve suspiciously. 'You're the showrunner, so you've got footage, right?'

'I do,' says Steve with a tip of his ball cap. 'I can make you a copy.'

'Not a copy. The original. I'll be leaving with it today.'

'If you insist,' says Steve.

Detective Stark addresses the others in the room. 'Is there anyone here who can shed light on what the hell just happened?' she asks.

The bidders and buyers, crew members and hotel staff look at her wordlessly, shaking their heads.

'A room full of bystanders and nobody saw a thing?'

She walks up the stage stairs, pacing around the display case twice, peering through the glass at the emptiness within. The bottom of the case, where the egg was sitting, is slightly displaced, but other than that, there are no signs of tampering.

She searches her pockets, puts on a pair of latex gloves, and nudges the case. As she shifts it, what's underneath comes into view – a round, brass outlet on the stage floor.

'Holy moly! And I mean that literally,' Angela says as she takes in the familiar hole in the stage floor.

'The vacuum port,' I say. 'The display case was centered on top of it.'

'Is that what this hole is?' Stark asks. 'A central vacuum outlet?'

'We had it installed during our first-floor renovation a few years ago,' Mr Snow explains.

'The Silent Sucker 2000,' I explain. 'It makes cleaning a dream.'

'Where does the vent lead?' Stark asks.

'To the greenroom,' I reply. 'There's another port in there.'

'Show me,' says Stark.

I lead her through the hidden paneled door to the greenroom, pointing to the outlet on the adjacent stage wall. Angela and Mr Snow soon file in behind us, leaving Juan by the stage.

'I vacuumed in here just last night, and I vacuumed the stage, too,' says Angela.

'Wait, aren't you a bartender?' Stark says.

'I was put in charge of events when Molly became a superstar. The job sucks, and if I'm not mistaken, so does what happened here,' she says, pointing to the vacuum outlet.

'I'm not following,' Mr Snow says as he adjusts his glasses on his nose.

'Someone – not me – left that vacuum port onstage open on purpose,' Angela explains.

'Bingo,' Stark says as she looks at the hole more closely.

'When the lights went down and the auction started, they attached the hose in the greenroom to suction the egg out of the display case,' Angela explains.

'So where's the collection canister?' Stark asks. 'The dirt's gotta go somewhere, right?'

'The utility closet,' I reply.

Angela's eyes light up. 'Maybe the egg's in there!'

Angela, Mr Snow, and I lead Detective Stark to the utility closet in the corridor outside the tearoom.

I open the door and point to the round canister in which all the grime vacuumed from the main floor collects. 'The belly of the beast,' I say, for that is how Angela and I refer to the container I emptied daily until she took over my job.

The detective pulls the hinged door with her gloved hands, but when the chamber opens, there's no Fabergé in sight. More disturbing is what is inside. Placed squarely on top of a pile of dust bunnies, miscellaneous crumbs, and a comingling of guests' hairs sits a small white card on which the following message is neatly typed:

Dear Molly,

Find the egg and you die.

CHAPTER 16

Dear Molly,

Do you recall the bedtime story I once told you about a princess and a frog? Once upon a time, a princess was drinking tea by a pond when she accidentally dropped her favorite teacup into the water. A frog retrieved the cup, confessing to the princess that he was always looking out for her and that he loved her. Moved, she was about to kiss the muddy creature when her betrothed, a prince, intervened, warning the princess that if she so much as touched that frog, he would abandon her forever.

I paused in the story at that point. I asked you who the princess should choose – the frog or the prince.

'The prince,' you replied with certainty, citing the frog's filth as the reason he was the worse choice.

'My dear girl,' I said. 'We should always look past the grime, for what lies beyond it may shine more brightly than anything imaginable.'

You nodded sagely, but did you actually understand? I suppose it doesn't matter, because even if you didn't understand then, when you read what I have to tell you now, you will.

The evening of the Workers' Ball was soon upon us, and for the first time in a long time, the mood at Gray Manor was giddy and buoyant. There had been so much doom and gloom about the house, so many threats of financial ruin, but on that night, all was forgotten, and as the moon shone high, the manor was bathed in shimmering magic.

Inside the house, the band had set up in the ballroom and had begun playing jaunty tunes, awaiting the arrival of guests. In the guest parlor, the catered buffet graced long, white-linened tables – freshly polished silver platters heaped with shrimp cocktails and caviar, French cheeses and foie gras.

Mama, Papa, and I took our places in the keyhole archway at the ballroom entrance, ready to greet guests. Papa looked gallant in his midnight-black tuxedo, with satin stripes down the trouser legs. Mama wore an hourglass Dior, black to match Papa, complete with satin gloves and a freshwater pearl choker featuring a cameo – her portrait in miniature on her own neck.

Mrs Mead had done my hair up, leaving a few tendrils falling gracefully and making up my face to accentuate my eyes and cheeks.

'My little girl is a young lady,' my father said the moment

he laid eyes on me. He kissed me on the cheek and fawned over me in a way he hadn't in ages. 'Doesn't she look elegant, Audrey?'

'At least she's wearing the gown properly this time,' Mama replied as she looked past me into the ballroom, displeased with the tiered champagne display. She barked sharp orders to the footmen standing by, but when she noticed a procession of guests coming our way, her tone sweetened instantly.

'Oh look, it's the Farquars! And the Petersons, too!' she enthused.

From that moment on, I greeted lawyers and litigators, brokers and bankers. I curtsied to CEOs and statesmen; I even bowed to a baron and a baroness who complimented my parents on their taste in furnishings.

'Your home is lovely,' the baroness offered as her tiara twinkled on her layered bouffant.

'Just a few family heirlooms,' said Mama.

'Was that a Limoges vase I spotted in the corridor?' the baron asked.

'Good eye,' said Papa.

The baroness followed her husband into the ballroom then, leaving us to greet the line of guests waiting patiently behind them. There were well-heeled matrons with sons and daughters debuting for the first time. There were the workers from our estate and from others nearby, too. Papa insisted we greet the workers with the same respect we afforded everyone else, a rule that applied but one night a year.

After a half hour, the procession of guests thinned as the

ballroom filled. Then, down the entry hall, arms linked, came Uncle Willy and Mrs Mead, with John walking tall between them. His wavy brown hair was combed neatly. He was wearing a black tuxedo with a straight bow tie. Even more arresting than his dapper outfit was the way he carried himself – without apology, always, shoulders back, face open, his smile inviting and real. I felt myself swoon a little as I watched him. I was glad we'd made amends and were no longer at war with each other.

'William, Mrs Mead,' Papa said as they approached. 'You both look dazzling.'

Uncle Willy was wearing his butler's best, but he'd accentuated his black jacket with a plaid pocket square. Mrs Mead fidgeted with the puffy organza sleeves on the gown she'd no doubt sewn herself out of old upholstery fabric.

'It chafes like the dickens,' she said, 'but if I pass as presentable, I'm pleased.'

'Presentable. That's the word,' said Mama.

Mrs Mead turned to John, staring up at him adoringly with her one blue eye and one green one. 'Don't just stand there gawking at the young lady. Say something, lad.'

Only then did I notice how quiet John had become, how his glassy brown eyes were fixed on me.

'You . . . you look . . .'

'Beautiful. Charming. Elegant,' Uncle Willy offered. 'Any of those will do, son.'

'You look . . . ravishing, Flora,' John said.

'Goodness,' said Papa. 'He's found his tongue.'

'And then some,' said Mama.

'How very kind, John,' I replied. He took my hand then, and for the second time in my life, he kissed it, lingering before letting go.

I could feel my knees weaken. I looked to Mama, her mouth a tight grimace.

'William,' she said, addressing the father rather than the son. 'It seems your boy doesn't know better than to kiss my daughter's hand. We'll overlook him taking such liberties.'

Uncle Willy flinched, but he didn't say a word as he bowed, then led his family into the ballroom.

'What did you say that for?' I hissed the moment they were out of earshot.

'Oh, Flora,' Mama hissed back. 'Don't lead the poor boy on. He hasn't a hope in hell of ever claiming you.'

'Claiming me? No one owns me, Mama.'

'Here she goes,' said Papa sotto voce.

'Not tonight, Flora. Behave,' said Mama.

I left them, going into the ballroom to find Uncle Willy, John, and Mrs Mead standing awkwardly in a corner.

'Apologies,' I said, looking from John to his father and aunt. 'Welcome to the ball. My family is grateful to you and yours, today and every day of the year, even if it doesn't always appear that way,' I said.

John's brow furrowed, but he responded with an elegant bow.

Before I could say anything else, Mama was at my side once more.

'Excuse me,' she said as she drew me away. 'The dance is starting, and they're not here yet.'

'Who?' I asked.

'The Brauns,' Papa said as he walked into our conversation.

'Reginald, what if they don't come?' Mama asked, her hands clutching the cameo at her neck. 'You know what that will mean.'

'Audrey, everyone's watching,' Papa said through a stiff grin as he met the eyes of the many guests glancing our way.

'Flora, entertain the young ladies,' Mama ordered as she pasted on a smile. 'When the band starts, dance with the boys from your class.'

For a moment, I wondered what she meant by 'class' – the boys from school or the wealthy young heirs gathered in the ballroom.

Just then, the band changed measure, from jazz preludes to a slow ballad – 'I've Got You Under My Skin' – sung by a dulcet-voiced crooner.

I wandered over to a group of boys from school, all of them standing in a corner, Percival in the middle. They looked uncomfortable in their tuxedos, like penguins awkward out of water.

'Welcome to Gray Manor,' I said by way of greeting. 'You're supposed to ask the girls to dance now.' I gestured to a group of young ladies on the other side of the room.

Percival stared at me. 'My friends don't know how to dance,' he said, pointing a thumb at his posse as if he himself were Fred Astaire.

'You all have feet, don't you?' I asked. 'And ears?'

'I'll show them how it's done,' I heard, and when I turned, John was behind me, a head taller than the other boys, hand extended. 'Flora, may I have this dance?'

I knew if my parents saw me opening the dance with the butler's son, they'd be less than pleased, but in that moment, I didn't care. I took John's hand and let him lead me to the middle of the ballroom floor. We put our arms around each other, and our feet fell into perfect rhythm for the very first time. It was so effortless and easy, Molly. We flowed as if his body was an extension of mine.

'Who taught you how to dance?' I asked, in awe that he was so fine-footed on the floor.

'My father,' he answered. 'He hasn't danced in ages, not since my mother died.' He looked down at his feet, and for a moment he lost his lead.

I gripped his hand tighter, and his head veered up, those brooding, deep eyes meeting mine. I tell you, Molly, that man was a marvel. Every step with him came easily. My arms fit into his like lock and key. And yet I took it all for granted.

'Are you nervous about the exams?' he asked as we whirled around the floor. The finals were fast approaching, and our fates hung in the balance.

'A little,' I admitted. 'I've been studying hard, but you heard the headmaster. The exams are tough. I may not pass.'

'Of course you'll pass,' he replied. 'You're the smartest person I've ever met. And the most beautiful, too . . . even if I get tongue-tied trying to tell you so.'

I was the one to look away then, fearing he might notice the blush rising up my chest and coloring my cheeks. 'You're very . . . smart yourself,' I replied as the ballad came to an end.

We stood still in the middle of the ballroom, and I felt him lean in, perhaps to whisper something in my ear, but then my mother's voice at the front of the room drew my attention.

'They're here!' she called out as several heads turned.

In the arched entry, my parents were greeting three late arrivals. One was Magnus Braun, in a daring white dinner jacket and black tuxedo trousers, a red rose boutonniere over his heart. As he shook my father's hand, he clapped Papa on the back so loudly, the sound ricocheted through the room.

Beside Magnus was a willowy blonde about my mother's age, wearing a royal blue empire gown – Mrs Braun, no doubt. She held the arm of a much younger man wearing a finely tailored, modern suit – metallic sharkskin – with no tie at all, and a white shirt, three buttons undone, revealing an expanse of tanned chest beneath. He, too, had an audacious red rose as a boutonniere. Blond hair in a pompadour quiff, the front left long like James Dean's; one errant lock fell in his face, and he swept it back casually with the palm of his hand. As he did, his eyes met mine – icy blue, like the eyes of a wolverine.

I watched as Magnus leaned in and whispered something to his son. Then the two of them were smiling and looking my way. Magnus waved. It took me a moment to wave back. Mama's black-gloved hand beckoned me over, her eyes conveying that I should make my way there urgently.

'Excuse me, John,' I said. 'My parents are calling.'

'So I see,' he said, then he looked down at his feet.

I made my way to the young man in the threshold. I'd never seen a man like him in real life. He looked like a movie star who'd just stepped off the silver screen into our staid manor home.

'There she is,' Magnus said as I approached.

So stricken was I by the sight of his son, I could barely peel my eyes off him.

'Flora, please welcome our special guests,' Papa said as he touched my elbow.

'Good evening, Mr Braun,' I managed to say.

'This is the rogue son I was telling you about, Algernon,' Magnus explained as if I hadn't already noticed his boy, as if the entire room hadn't noticed him.

I curtsied as I offered my hand.

'Don't bow too low or I might get used to it,' Algernon replied. He laughed then, and so did I. Then he pushed that churlish shock of long blond hair out of his eyes, grabbed my hand, and kissed it just as John had earlier, though he lingered longer. I was painfully aware that all eyes were on me.

'Aren't you going to scold him?' I whispered to Mama, 'just like you did with the last young man who kissed my hand?'

'Scold him?' she replied, fanning herself flirtatiously with one black-gloved hand. 'On the contrary, I was going to offer my hand next,' she said, and the guests in our midst laughed.

'Audrey,' said Papa. 'If you require a dashing gentleman to

fawn over you, all you had to do was ask.' Papa, in a gesture so unlike him, grabbed Mama's hand and dramatically kissed it as the Brauns clapped their approval.

A moment later, the woman on Algernon's arm addressed me. 'Aren't you just the prettiest little thing,' she said.

'Flora, meet my mother,' Algernon said.

'How do you do, Mrs Braun?'

'Oh, please. I'm not that old. Call me Priscilla. Even my son does.'

'Actually, I call you Prissy,' said Algernon with a gentle shove of her arm.

'Now, now. Behave,' his mother urged.

'Hardly my strong suit,' her son replied.

'Reginald, how would you feel if my son asked your daughter to dance?'

'Flora would be delighted!' my mother answered as she pushed me forward.

'Shall we?' said Algernon, releasing his mother's arm and taking mine. The crooner launched into 'Unforgettable' as the young Mr Braun led me onto the ballroom floor.

'So you're Flora,' Algernon said once we'd begun to dance. He drew me close, so close I could smell the bergamot on his neck. 'I've heard about you and your family from my dad. I'm relieved you don't live up to your name.'

I had no idea what he meant, so I asked.

'With a last name like Gray, I'd pictured plain and boring. I figured Mags was coupling me up with a brown bagger like those ones over there.'

He nodded to the clique of young ladies in the corner, all wearing pretty pastel gowns and staring at me with such envy that I ignored the insult Algernon had just hurled their way and found myself reveling in the fact that *I* had been deemed worthy, a cut above the rest, according to this alluring and daring young man.

'My dad says you're more than just pretty. He claims you're whip smart. I like whip smart,' he said, whispering the last part so close to my ear that the words seeped in like a sweet, hypnotic potion.

'I'm studying hard,' I said. 'I'm hoping to go to university, but I'm not sure I have what it takes.'

'You definitely have what it takes,' he said as his icy blue eyes looked me up and down. 'What are you studying?'

'Literature,' I answered. 'I love to read.'

'What a coincidence. I love to be read to. In fact, I think I could lie in your lap all day drinking wine and listening to your voice. You should come to Saint-Tropez later this summer. We can frolic on my dad's yacht. It's my last fling before Mags chains me to the family firm.'

Mags. Prissy. Everything about this young man was so modern and refreshing – exactly opposite my parents' stale and staid conventions. I looked over to where Mama and Papa stood on the edge of the dance floor with Algernon's parents. All of them now had drinks in their hands, and Papa was beaming as he watched us. Mama raised her champagne flute my way and gave me a discreet thumbs-up with her other hand. The look of pride in her eyes was one I'd seen only once and recently – on the day of the summit, right after Magnus Braun and his men left.

I turned to Algernon. 'You call your parents by their first names,' I said. 'And you didn't wear a tie to the ball.'

'A tie? They're nooses in disguise. Anyhow, this is how we swing in Saint-Tropez. The girls don't seem to mind. Do you like it?' he asked, getting so close to my mouth that if I moved an inch, his lips would have met mine.

'I do,' I said. 'I like it very much.'

And Molly, when I said that, I spoke the truth. In that moment, it was like I was suddenly possessed – mesmerized by Algernon's swagger and glamour, dazzled by his movie-star looks and emboldened by my parents' obvious approval. I felt overcome with a dizzying rapture for this stranger who'd just swept me off my feet.

As the song ended, Algernon closed the gap between us. My chest pressed against his, and our lips met. It was completely unheard of – to kiss a girl on the lips on the ballroom floor – but I knew my parents wouldn't dare disapprove. When Algernon drew away, all I wanted was more.

The band struck up a rock 'n' roll number by that Elvis fellow who my parents said was corrupting youth and the airwaves.

'Thanks for the dance,' Algernon said. 'If I don't take a turn with a few of them, there'll be hell to pay,' he added, pointing to the group of young ladies in the corner. 'But I'll be thinking of you the whole time, Flora. Catch you later?'

'I look forward to it,' I replied.

He strode away then, wordlessly taking the hand of a girl

in a lilac gown and leading her into a jive on the dance floor. Soon enough, the entire room filled with young couples gyrating to the beat. Magnus and Priscilla took to the floor and were twisting while my parents watched from the sidelines, my father grinning stoically and my mother clapping along awkwardly with her black-gloved hands.

Dance after dance, the mood in the room crescendoed. Buttons were undone and ties removed. Never had the Gray ballroom been worked into such a frenzy. A ruddy sheen blossomed on the women's faces. All decorum surrendered to the pure provocation of the new rock 'n' roll.

It got so warm that I downed two glasses of champagne, then headed to the ladies' powder room, where the window was cracked open and the air was not quite so charged. I ran my wrists under cool water and looked at myself in the mirror. My pupils were so large I barely recognized myself.

Just then, I heard sobbing, a girl's voice catching in her throat. I turned to see a young lady in a light blue gown sitting on a velvet settee in the corner. Beside her was Mrs Mead, an arm rubbing her back.

I dried my hands and made my way over. 'Is everything all right?' I asked Mrs Mead, for the girl's head was in her hands.

'Bring a tissue for her issue,' Mrs Mead whispered.

I spotted the uniformed attendant on the other side of the powder room and asked for a package, bringing it to my nursemaid.

'There, there,' Mrs Mead said as she offered the girl a tissue from the pack. 'Dry your eyes, my dear. Take a breath.'

'What's wrong with her?' I mouthed to Mrs Mead.

'We'll discuss this later,' she replied. 'I've sent John to look for you, Flora. Keep him close, you hear? Dance with him.'

'I danced with him already,' I said.

The girl broke down into a full chorus of sobs, and Mrs Mead rocked her back and forth while giving me the green-eye-blue-eye signal that I should be on my way.

I left the powder room and was heading back to the ballroom when I felt a hand on my arm.

It was John, his brow furrowed, his eyes wide. 'Flora,' he said. 'I've been looking for you everywhere.'

'Am I not allowed to go to the ladies' room?' I asked, withdrawing my arm.

'Of course you are,' he replied. 'Listen . . . just . . . be careful out there,' he said as his eyes traveled to the ballroom entrance and the frenzy within.

Oh, Molly, I don't relish admitting this, but in that moment, every fiber of my being suddenly revolted. In my deep state of youthful confusion, I found myself catapulted back to that place where love and hate exist in close proximity. And without realizing what I was doing, I turned a switch inside myself. All the hatred I'd once felt for John surged forth again, and I forgot the other feelings that had blossomed. Who did John think he was, trying to control me and tell me what to do? Why did he want to pin me down when all I wanted to do was fly?

'We dance once, and now you think you're the boss of me?' I said.

'What?' he replied. 'No, it's just that . . . people have been talking. I'm just saying you might want to be careful because—'

'You're jealous,' I said. 'And you can't admit it. Leave me be.'

'Flora, wait!'

But I didn't wait. Instead, I rushed to the ballroom like a moth drawn to a flame. Inside, I searched for him – Algernon – and found him with a highball in hand, holding court with Percival Peterson and the boys from class. He was telling them a story, and their heads were thrown back in laughter. While they celebrated Algernon, he glanced my way, and I felt my stomach flutter. I waved.

'There she is,' he said. 'Will you excuse me, boys?'

He sauntered over to me. 'Flora, how old are you?' he asked.

'Seventeen,' I replied.

'Old enough,' he said.

'And you?' I asked.

'Twenty-one,' he replied as he downed the rest of his drink. I'd figured he was a bit older than me, but I didn't realize by how much until that moment. 'What do you say?' he asked.

'What do I say to what?' He always spoke some youthful patois I didn't quite understand.

'Do you like convertibles?'

'The automobile?' I asked.

'Yeah,' he said, chuckling. 'The "automobile." What do you say to next Saturday night?'

'With you?' I was hoping beyond hope he was proposing a date.

'Pick you up at eight?' he asked.

'I would be delighted,' I said as I bowed my head.

He touched one finger to my chin, tipping it up so my eyes met his. He smiled, so casual, so free. Then he put both of his hands on my bare shoulders and kissed me deeply on the mouth. After a few moments, he drew away to look at me with those icy blue eyes.

'I don't know who's more taken by you – me or my father,' he said, 'but I think I'm the luckier one.'

'Luckier,' I said breathlessly. 'Why?'

'I get to kiss you,' he replied. 'He doesn't.'

He laughed and started to leave. But then he turned to me one more time, tossed that shock of blond hair out of his eyes, and said, 'See you Saturday, pretty little flower.'

CHAPTER 17

Be careful what you wish for.

It's been a week since the Fabergé disappeared right from under our noses, and Gran's refrain has repeated in my head the entire time. For a while there, I really thought Juan and I might be liberated from all financial constraints, free for the first time in our lives from worries about rent and soaring food prices and renoviction and the leaky kitchen sink. Maybe we could buy our apartment outright from Mr Rosso and become owners of our own home. Maybe we could afford the wedding of our dreams, surrounded by family and friends who would always remember our special day. But just as I dared to dream, the reverie became a nightmare. First, the egg disappeared. Then came the threat: *Find the egg and you die.*

I will admit all of this has rattled me to the core, though no one else seems as concerned as I am. And Juan – bless his heart – has tried to convince me that the note in the vacuum canister was not a credible threat and I'm not in any real peril.

The day after the heist, I had a Zoom call with Mr Snow and the Bees, who confirmed that the multimillion-dollar sale of the egg was nullified by our inability to produce the oeuvre for the buyer.

'What about insurance?' Mr Snow shrewdly asked. 'Certainly a reputable firm such Brown & Beagle Auction House has coverage for the priceless heirloom?'

'Of course,' said Brown.

'Absolutely,' echoed Beagle.

'But the insurance policy covers the last known purchase price of the work of art in question,' Brown explained.

'Which in this case is unknown,' added Beagle. 'The insurers will cough up something, but don't expect much unless you hire a lawyer, which, on a maid's salary seems . . .'

'Out of the question,' I offered.

This morning, Juan and I walked to work as usual, and when we arrived, he said, 'See? At least no one's looking for you. No one's waiting for you. No one wants to speak with you. You're not in any real danger, Molly.'

It was true. Not a single guest filing in or out of the hotel noted our arrival. And while the media had made the egg's disappearance a news story for the first couple of days, in the days since, people seemed to have lost all hope it would ever be recovered. As for interest in me, while the rags-to-riches story riveted public attention, the maid's return to rags had been met with a notable deficit in public fanfare. Even Speedy was nonplussed this morning when I asked him if any lookie-loos had inquired about me. He shrugged and uttered a typical Speedyism – 'No bling, no thing. You were really bussin' there for a minute, though.'

'Translation, please?'

'You were popular, Molls. Everyone wanted a piece of you. Some people would kill for that, you know.'

I studied Speedy's face – his doleful eyes and the way he always looked like a puppy dog about to jump up on you.

'You're so young, Speedy,' I said as I patted his arm. 'Be careful what you wish for.'

'I am careful,' he replied, before bounding down the stairs.

Despite the wallop of bad news lately, I've done as Gran would have wanted and am searching for the silver linings. First, *Hidden Treasures* won't be re-airing the auction because Stark classified the footage as evidence, meaning my days as a TV celebrity are, much to my relief, over. Juan and I can now go about our lives and our jobs again if not as usual then at least without being hounded. Second, while Mr Snow is moderately peeved that hotel reservations have dried up, the entire staff now has a chance to recover from the media circus of the last couple of weeks. Third, Detective Stark has committed to a proper investigation of the theft, which involves a wide-ranging review of possible suspects that for once does not include me. Last but far from least, beyond that dreadful note in the canister, no evidence has surfaced to suggest that anyone is actually plotting my untimely demise.

At lunch hour today, Angela accompanied me to the

precinct for an update on the investigation from Detective Stark. I can't say I was pleased to step foot in that building. My knees quivered as we made our way to the detective's office.

'Thanks for coming,' said Stark as she closed her door behind us and collapsed into her desk chair with an audible thud. 'I don't get it,' she continued. 'I've reviewed the footage; I've interviewed all the guests who attended the auction. I've talked to the hotel staff and interrogated the entire *Hidden Treasures* crew.'

'What did you learn?' Angela asked.

'That people in reality TV are as dim as blown bulbs. Apart from that, not much,' she said.

'I've been racking my brains to figure out what happened,' said Angela. 'I've rewatched every heist doc I've ever seen, and I still can't crack it.'

'Now listen, Molly,' Detective Stark said. 'Let's not give up hope just yet. I want you and Angela to be vigilant at the hotel. If you see something suspicious, report it to me right away – understood?'

'Certainly,' I replied.

'Yes, ma'am!' said Angela with a concerning amount of zeal.

'And, Molly? For what it's worth, I know it's a blow that the egg was stolen, but I doubt you're in real danger,' Stark reassured me. 'Whoever wrote that note was just trying to scare us all into giving up the search. But we're not going to let fear stop us, right?'

'Right,' Angela replied. 'We'll peer into every corner. We'll leave no stone unturned. We'll go over everything with a forensic fine-tooth comb!'

We left the precinct soon after Angela's litany of investigational metaphors, making our way back to the hotel. I expected to simply resume work, but Angela had other ideas. She convinced Mr Snow to put her in charge of a top-to-toe hotel search to uncover the egg or any clues to its whereabouts. To my surprise, Mr Snow agreed, putting the headwaiter in charge of the Social while Angela played amateur sleuth.

Angela asked that I be even more thorough than usual as I cleaned guest rooms, searching corners, closets, and drawers for 'hidden inculpatory evidence,' as she called it. I told her I would, then I headed upstairs to do my job as a maid, which, I can tell you, has given me great joy all week long. I worked alongside Cheryl, and remarkably, she tested my patience only once – when she used a guest's freshly cleaned toilet for her personal urinary purposes.

'It won't kill you to disinfect that toilet bowl again,' I said when she emerged from the bathroom.

'My death is not the one you should be worried about right now,' Cheryl shot back.

'What's that supposed to mean?' I asked.

'Someone threatened your life, Molly. Watch your back. There's no shortage of crazies out there, you know.'

'Thank you for your concern,' I said curtly.

For the rest of the afternoon, I tried to forget my fears – and Cheryl's not-so-veiled threat – but every time I opened a guest's closet or swept under a bed, I imagined a hidden culprit reaching out to grab me.

Now, my shift has finally come to an end, and I'm perfectly unharmed. I'm standing outside the gold revolving doors of the hotel, waiting for Juan so we can walk home together.

'There you are,' I hear behind me.

'Juan,' I say. 'How was your day?'

'I've had better,' he replies. 'A tornado hit this afternoon.'

'A tornado?'

Speedy bounds over and joins our conversation. 'You mean Angela, right?'

'Exactly,' says Juan. 'In her search for clues to the missing egg, which is now long gone, she made us clear out every cupboard, freezer, and drawer in the kitchen.'

'Did you find anything?' I ask.

'A long-lost carton of salt and pepper shakers, two spatulas, and your doorman's cap, Speedy.'

'Sick! I've been looking for it all week,' Speedy replies. 'For the record, Angela tornadoed me, too. She got up in my junk, searching my pockets and my podium. Didn't find nothing, cuz I'm mean and I'm clean.'

'Speaking of clean, Molly, the kitchen is a mess. I've still got to put everything back in the cupboards,' says Juan. 'It'll take me another hour. Do you want to wait?' He watches me, knowing that since the death threat, I've been worried about walking alone.

'I can make my own way home, thank you very much,' I say, full of bravado I don't actually feel.

'Are you sure?' Juan asks, staring at me with his kind brown eyes.

'One hundred percent. I'll see you later,' I say.

'See you, *mi amor*,' Juan says, squeezing my hand, then disappearing into the hotel.

I say goodbye to Speedy and make my way down the street, heading home to our apartment. It's a lovely afternoon, and as I stroll I forget all about the death threat and find myself enjoying the walk. I leave the posh downtown core and cross into my own decidedly unposh neighborhood. As I turn onto a side street, a black car slows beside me.

I try not to panic. *Only fools jump to conclusions.*

The car is merely slowing to avoid potholes, I tell myself. But when it flanks me for a full minute, I hasten my pace. So does the car. My heart starts to race. I glance at the vehicle, but the windows are tinted. I can't see inside. I break into a run, and instantly, the car picks up speed. There's no doubt now – the vehicle is following me.

I spot a dead-end alley up ahead with a pedestrian walkway at the end. I run full tilt into it, but a dumpster is blocking the pedestrian path. The car pushes toward me until my back is up against the dumpster, my hands held high in the air. 'Stop! Please!' I yell.

I close my eyes, expecting the car to hit me, but it doesn't. I hear a car door open, and when I look, a woman is standing by the driver's side.

'Don't be scared. I'd never hurt you, Molly. I swear,' she says.

She's about my height with straight black hair down to her shoulders, tinged with gray. Her face is porcelain pale. There's something so familiar about her, but try as I might, I cannot place her.

'I don't have much money on me, but whatever I have is yours,' I say in a tremulous voice.

'That's not why I'm here,' the woman replies. 'I need to tell you something. I know about the death threat. Molly, the danger is real,' she says.

I'm staring at the car, expecting someone to jump out and mob me, but that's not what happens.

'I'm alone,' the woman says, as if reading my thoughts. 'The car's not even mine. I stole it so I could warn you.'

'Stole it?' I say. 'Are you . . . the egg thief?'

'No,' she says instantly.

'But you know about it,' I reply.

'In more ways than you can imagine. I was watching *Hidden Treasures* when you found out the egg was worth millions. I couldn't believe it – you were right there in front of me, and so was the Fabergé. I watched that episode over and over again. I held my hand to the screen, wishing I could reach in and touch you. But someone else was watching along with me – a man I used to work for, and not a good one. Without thinking, I told him things I shouldn't have – about you, about Mom, and about the egg.'

Giant tears roll down the woman's cheeks. 'Molly, do you remember me? Not a day has gone by that I haven't thought about you. Not a single day.'

A memory returns with such force, vertigo sends me reeling. I lean on the dumpster, not caring if it's dirty, hoping beyond hope that I'll remain upright. 'The stranger at our door,' I say. 'The rent money.'

When I was barely ten years old, Gran was doing laundry downstairs when a woman showed up at our apartment claiming to be Gran's friend. I let her in. She sat with me at the kitchen table. The entire encounter was strange, and when giant tears rolled down the woman's cheeks, just as they do now, I knew something was terribly wrong. She left abruptly, swiping Gran's envelope with our rent money right off the table. It took me a long time to figure out who she was and why she'd come that day.

'You visited our apartment all those years ago. You came to see me,' I say now.

She nods, and more tears stream down her face.

'You're Maggie, my mother.'

'I am,' she whispers.

'She told me you were dead,' I say, but the truth is I was never quite sure if Gran meant it literally or figuratively. I look at my mother – her shaky hands, the tears running down her cheeks, the way she's leaning forward as if she wants to reach out and touch me. It's definitely her, and she seems genuine, but her sudden appearance in my life is unsettling, and my stomach clenches with fear.

'You stole rent money from your own mother. And from your own child,' I say. 'How could you?'

'I was sick, Molly,' she says. 'I wasn't clean.'

I remember the red marks up her arms, which in my innocence I thought were bedbug bites.

'Are you better?' I ask.

'Right now I am,' she says. 'When I saw you on TV, I couldn't believe it – my little girl, all grown up. And the Fabergé right there in front of you. It sat on the mantel in the Grimthorpe mansion when I worked there all those years ago.'

'So you really did work at the Grimthorpe mansion?' I ask.

'I did. Mom couldn't make the rent on just her maid's salary, so I dropped out of high school to help her. Things didn't go as planned. Grimthorpe was an awful man, Molly. Do you understand?'

'He took advantage of Gran,' I say.

'Not only her,' she replies. Her arms reach around her middle as if she needs them there to remain steady.

Something in me breaks. My tears spill with alarming force. I'm powerless to stop them.

'Your gran never knew,' my mother says. 'I never told her what happened. I just ran away. Then, in my stupidity, I shacked up with a man even worse than Grimthorpe. I came back, though.'

'To have me,' I say, putting the pieces together.

'Yeah. I stayed clean for a while, did my best to look after you. But I was so young, Molly, and so confused. I numbed myself any way I could.'

'A fly-by-night possessed you – that's what Gran always said.'

'She had a way with words, didn't she?' my mother replies.

'Fly-by-nights might just be my worst habit. It's like I can't see the truth until it's too late. The one who took your egg, Molly, he's a dangerous man. His gang was paid a lot of money to pull off that heist. I used to work for him, but when I found out what he'd done, how he stole your egg, I quit. Then I ran away. I've been in a safe house ever since. I've been trying to get to you.'

'Why?' I ask.

'Because I know those men, Molly. If you find that egg, they'll kill you. They really will. And if they hear I squealed to you, they'll kill me, too.'

'Why not tell the police?' I ask.

'The police? You think they're gonna help?'

'I don't know what to think,' I say. 'Why should I believe what you're telling me? You admit you're a thief.'

'Anyone can become a thief under the wrong circumstances, even your gran,' she says.

'Impossible,' I reply.

'Is it?' says my mother. 'It's because of your gran that the Grimthorpes got their hands on that Fabergé in the first place,' she says. 'My mother always said that egg represented her deepest regrets and that she ran away with it to start a new life.'

'But it was the Grimthorpes' treasure, not hers,' I say.

'At some point, it was hers. She basically admitted to having stolen it. Don't you see? All it takes is one moment of desperation to turn a good egg into a bad one. I'm not a bad egg, Molly. Neither was she.'

'If that's true, why didn't you come back for me? You should have returned to Gran and me long ago.'

'No,' she answers as she shakes her head. 'Leaving you with her was the best thing I ever did. Just look at you now.'

She smiles then. The look on her face is such a medley, but if I'm reading it correctly, it's sadness, tinged with pride. Something in me relents, and I suddenly feel the urge to reach out and hug her.

'Molly,' she says as she holds her trembling arms out toward me. 'Did you get any money when the egg disappeared? You got insurance cash, right? That's what I was hoping for – that you'd net out okay in the end.'

'No,' I say. 'It's not working out that way.'

'Oh,' she replies as her arms drop to her sides. 'But you're famous now. You must be raking it in from appearances, right? I hate to ask, but do you have a few hundred you can throw my way? I'm on the run here – for you. I can't go back now. I've risked life and limb to make sure you know the danger is real. You gotta help me out.'

I stare at her in disbelief. I can't believe my ears. Just when I was about to open myself to the possibility that my mother was actually doing something for me rather than for herself, she shows her true colors yet again.

'You want my money,' I say. 'That's why you're here.'

'Molly, honey. I'm your mom. I want the best for you. Please,' she says.

'I have nothing for you,' I reply. 'No money and certainly no feelings of warmth.'

Her face changes then, the softness mutating into cold, hard lines. 'After what I just did for you, this is the thanks I get?'

She awaits a response, but I have none to give.

'Have it your way then,' she says as she kicks a crumpled pop can by her feet. 'But watch your back. And beware of men in trench coats. You never know what they might do.'

She turns away from me then and gets back in her stolen car. A second later, the car squeals into reverse, and its driver, my long-lost mother, abandons me for the third time in my life.

CHAPTER 18

Dear Molly,

Everything can change in an instant. One chance meeting, one twist of fate is all it takes to change your path irrevocably. My entire life was different after the Workers' Ball. Suddenly, Algernon Braun became my sole focus. Nothing I'd experienced before prepared me for the free fall I found myself in after meeting him that night.

If this sounds confusing, Molly, I can understand why. It's true that I'd been allowing my heart to open to John Preston – a good man, a true and constant one, not to mention the fact that being near him made me feel safe and warm and complete. When we fell into lock step on the dance floor, I should have known. But, Molly, when you're young, the heart is so easily deceived, and it's common to mistake false love for the real thing. Innocent that I was, my girlish heart still belonged to my parents, and to my father most of all. I longed for their acceptance, and they'd made it clear that winning Algernon was the way to earn their love. I was desperate to please them, so when that daring young man with his outsize confidence and glamorous good looks strode into the ballroom, he swept my parents off their feet first, then me. Despite any rumblings and misgivings in my gut – that feeling like falling off a precipice, some impending danger just ahead – I followed my parents' lead blindly. I soon convinced myself that John was an illusion and that what I felt for Algernon was, like in a fairy tale, true love at first sight.

The feeling was heady and disorienting. After the ball, I was drunk with ecstasy at the notion that this boy – no, this man, for he was several years older than I was – might actually harbor feelings for me. It was as though something inside me had suddenly blossomed into being, unfurling into a longing I didn't know I held within. Visions of Algernon swirled in my head – us twirling on the ballroom floor, his open shirt revealing a V of sun-kissed chest, those eyes – provocative, beguiling, and deep – a girl could enter them like a labyrinth and lose herself forever.

Molly, I became sick with thoughts of him, smitten to the point of obsession. And the more girlish yearning I felt for this virtual stranger, the more revulsion surged in me toward the young man who'd long lingered in my periphery – John. I soon forgot the surge of warmth I'd felt when he kissed my hand, and the safety of his arms as he held me on the dance floor, not to mention the many moments of kindness and generosity he'd offered me over the years despite the fact that I'd so often treated him poorly.

The night of the ball, after all the guests left, I lay awake in my bed thinking only of Algernon. When at long last the dawn broke and I heard servants preparing breakfast downstairs, I made my way to the banquet table, still floating on a dream.

I was pleased to see Papa sitting next to Mama for once, taking a meal with her. Both of them looked different. It was as though some weight had been lifted overnight. Papa was pouring coffee into my mother's cup – a first, for certain – and when he finished, she touched his hand.

'Thank you, darling,' she said. 'Darling' – an endearment that rarely issued from her lips.

'There's my princess,' Papa said when I walked in. 'Our little Cinderella, our belle of the ball.'

He stood then, assuming his full height, walked over, and hugged me. He even planted a kiss on my forehead the way he had when I was a wide-eyed and obedient toddler. It was more affection than I'd received from him in ages. I froze in his arms. When he released me, I hurried to my seat across from Mama.

Mrs Mead appeared from the kitchen with a fresh coffee cup and added it to my place setting. 'Good morning, Flora,' she said, her tone sharp and clipped.

'Why are you serving breakfast?' I asked, since this was an anomaly.

'I'm asking myself that same question,' said Mrs Mead. 'I'm

not a cook and I'm definitely not a footman, but since the others have been dismissed, I'm left, as usual, to pick up the slack.'

'Mrs Mead,' said Mama. 'This egg isn't poached, it's boiled. Take it back to the kitchen and try again.' Mama held up her plate. Mrs Mead grabbed it without a word, disappearing to do Mama's bidding.

'Did you hear her?' Mama said the moment Mrs Mead was gone. 'She's getting stroppier by the day. How many families would keep a nursemaid for a girl who's turned seventeen? And to think we've been good enough to let her live in that old cottage, too. I'm this close to giving her a piece of my mind.'

'Leave it, Audrey,' said Papa. 'She's just tired from last night's festivities. You know how hard it is to get good help these days.'

'You're right, darling,' said Mama, patting his hand for a second time. She took a sip of coffee and smiled deviously at me from across the table. 'Someone made a good first impression last night,' she said.

Papa was decapitating his soft-boiled egg. 'Not only did you bait the hook, you got the fish to bite,' he said as he dipped his toast in the runny yolk.

'Let's not celebrate Flora's victory quite yet,' said Mama. 'Bigger fish have wriggled free.'

Mrs Mead returned to the breakfast room carrying two plates – Mama's poached eggs and my scrambled ones, which she knew were my favorite.

'Thank you,' I said as she set my plate in front of me.

'Madam, sir,' she said. 'Might I have a word after breakfast?'

It was a highly unorthodox request, so much so that Papa put down his fork and gaped at her.

'If there's something you need to say, just say it,' said Mama.

'It's not for sensitive ears,' Mrs Mead replied.

'If you're suggesting Flora's the issue, we do have eyes. We saw her last night, and while snogging on the dance floor is not exactly the norm at a Workers' Ball, we're going to let it lie,' said Mama.

Papa cleared his throat. 'Mrs Mead, it is my understanding that ladies – much like gentlemen – are not supposed to kiss and tell.'

'It's not that, not exactly,' said Mrs Mead as her hands worried her apron strings. 'It's about Algernon Braun. Last night, I met a girl who knew him from college.'

My heart stopped. 'She's not his girlfriend, is she?' I asked.

'Definitely not,' said Mrs Mead. 'In fact, she was surprised to see that boy at the ball. She claims she had an experience with him that was . . . unpleasant.'

'Unpleasant how?' asked Mama as she sliced into her perfectly poached egg.

'She didn't share the details,' said Mrs Mead.

'Oh, come on now,' said Papa. 'A handsome young lad like that can have any girl he pleases. He doesn't need to force it, if that's what you're suggesting.'

'Was she the girl crying in the ladies' room?' I asked.

'Aye, that's the one,' said Mrs Mead.

'Oh,' said Mama. 'That unfortunate wretch. My goodness,

Reginald, you should have seen how the girl was dressed. Her "gown" didn't even reach her knees. Mrs Mead,' said Mama as she swiveled to face my nursemaid, 'don't you think girls like that are asking for trouble? Maybe she egged him on and then changed her tune at the last second?'

'Hear, hear,' said Papa as he drained his coffee.

'It's not for me to say,' said Mrs Mead. 'What I do know is the shock of seeing Algernon undid that lass. And what she told me gave me pause. I thought you all should know. Flora, I heard you're seeing Algernon on Saturday night.'

'I am,' I confirmed, unable to control the smile that overtook my face.

'Well done,' said Mama. 'Be coy with the boy – inviting but not too much.'

Papa reached across the table to grab my hand. 'There is nothing that would make me prouder than if my daughter was the missing link that forged a bond between our two families. Can you imagine? The Grays and Brauns united? We'd be an unstoppable force.'

'Low and slow,' said Mama. 'The tortoise wins the race.'

'Am I the only one here with concerns?' Mrs Mead asked, her eyes wide.

'If people acted upon every unconfirmed rumor about young men, the population would plummet,' said Papa.

'Anyhow, it's not up to us. It's up to Flora,' said Mama. 'Flora, are you worried about Algernon?'

'Not in the least,' I replied, though something deep within me niggled.

'Good,' said Papa. 'Then it's settled.'

'Mrs Mead,' said Mama, 'after you clear our plates, please go upstairs and pick out some outfits for Flora's big date on Saturday.' Mama then turned to me. 'What do you say? Shall we have a think on outfits, darling?'

Darling. That's what she said – to me. So starving was I for my mother's affection that my eyes brimmed with tears.

'Dearest Mama,' I replied. 'I would greatly appreciate your help.'

Mrs Mead grabbed our plates. Then she turned her back on all of us and marched off to the kitchen.

It has always seemed to me that the good moments gallop apace, over too soon, whereas the dull ones extend into eternity. So it was that the Workers' Ball passed in the blink of an eye and my wait for the Saturday after, when I would see Algernon again, seemed interminable. I swooned about the manor, indulging in girlish daydreams about my upcoming date and the many exciting nights ahead that would be steeped in the dreamy magic of new love and starlit romance, all under the approving gaze of my parents' loving eyes.

On Monday morning, I trudged to class as usual, but very suddenly I lost interest in my studies. At long last I felt what so many girls my age had readily expressed in my presence, that school was tiresome, that it got in the way of what really mattered – thrilling romance and the stirrings of the heart.

I could barely concentrate in class. The only thing that captured my attention was the headmaster's lecture on *Romeo and Juliet* and the forces opposing the lovers' union. In my mind, I was Juliet and Algernon my daring young Romeo, but we were not star-crossed like they were. We were not doomed to tragic ends because no one stood between us. In fact, our two households wanted nothing more than to bring us together, so surely, love would triumph after all?

'There's less than a month to the exams,' said the headmaster. 'Your university admission depends on those results. I trust you will use these remaining weeks to study as much as you can.'

But I didn't, I couldn't. In class, my mind wandered, and one day after a lesson, John found me in the hallway.

'Flora,' he said, standing in front of me as I packed my books into my bag. I could ignore him no longer, and I looked up into those familiar, deep eyes. They were full of confusion, though I could see he was relieved that after evading him for several days, finally I was looking at him. Still, I couldn't hold his frank stare. I busied myself with my bag.

'Are you all right?' he asked, putting a hand on my shoulder.

'I'm perfectly fine,' I replied, though clearly I was not. Deep inside me, mixed emotions wrestled each other, manifesting in my complete inability to do something as simple as pack books in a bag. How was it I could be daydreaming incessantly about Algernon, yet the moment John stood in front of me, the allure of the Brauns and their son seemed a distant mirage, or even worse, a baited trap?

I looked up at John and wanted nothing more than to fall in his arms, to cry on his shoulder, to beg forgiveness, and then to kiss those inviting ruby lips. The contradictions in the pit of my stomach terrified me, and instead of examining them more closely, I pushed them down even deeper, denying them entirely. Then I dropped my books on the floor.

'Let me help you,' John offered, his hand never leaving my shoulder.

'Let me be!' I cried out. But I couldn't pull away from his touch.

John moved to face me. 'What happened at the ball,' he said, 'our dance. I've never felt anything like it before. Can you honestly say you don't feel what I feel?'

I couldn't. And I wouldn't. As I looked at him, I saw my parents' faces, imagined them jeering at me, my mother's curled lip, my father's dead-eyed disdain, as if I was not only a fool but a traitor to myself and them.

'Me with the butler's son,' I said, scoffing and shaking my head. 'My parents would never approve.'

I expected John to be outraged by my offhand dismissal, but he wasn't. To my utter surprise, his face lit up like a sun. 'So you do feel it,' he said. 'You just can't say it.'

'I never said that,' I replied.

'You didn't have to.' He took my bag from my shaking hands and placed the two fallen books inside. Then he passed it back to me, our fingers touching. 'Flora, be careful,' he said. 'There are rumors swirling about the Brauns. All that glitters isn't gold, you know. Workers talk. My aunt heard some things.'

'Your aunt is a busybody who shouldn't meddle,' I said. 'And my parents know best.'

'I'll have *you* know that your parents are—' He stopped himself.

'Are what?' I demanded, feeling heat surge from my belly and color my cheeks.

'My father and my aunt have always been their betters. And you know it.'

There it was, that same old arrogance. 'How dare you?' I hissed. 'You don't know the first thing about any of us. How could you? You're just a servant.'

His eyes widened and his mouth dropped open. 'Have it your way,' he said as he turned and walked away.

I watched him tread down the corridor, not quite disappearing into the crowd because he always stood head and shoulders above everyone. I longed to call him back, to tell him I was sorry and that I was wrong.

But I didn't. I let him go.

At home, for the first time ever, I basked in my parents' love. It was as thrilling to me as it was surprising that they saw me in a whole new light. To my great joy, as I awaited my date with Algernon, still a few days away, Mama and I became closer than ever. We had a meeting of the minds for the very first time.

'Honestly, I'd written you off. I never imagined your head would emerge from your books. My little late bloomer – I thought this day would never come,' she said.

Together, we ransacked my closet, and every day I tried on new outfits Mrs Mead had picked for my big date, but they were all so dowdy and plain. My mother agreed.

'I have an idea,' she said, as I slipped behind my Venetian screen, wiggling out of another shapeless frock. 'A shopping trip, darling. Just the two of us. I know you don't like shopping, but—'

'I'd love that, Mama!' I exclaimed.

And so I found myself linking arms with her, traversing high-end boutiques and fashionable downtown department stores in search of the perfect outfit. We enjoyed each other's company for the first time in memory, and that day Mama seemed almost happy.

After many change room visits and an equal number of insults hurled by Mama at various shopkeepers, we landed on a look that worked.

'Thoughts?' I asked Mama as I emerged from the fitting room in a poodle skirt and a cashmere sweater.

'Flirty and fresh,' said Mama. 'And my, my, how that V-neck becomes you.'

'Accentuate the positive, eliminate the negative. Isn't that what you always say?'

'Have you been listening to me all this time? Come, darling. Let's max out your father's store credit.'

At long last it was Saturday. Mama helped me pin-curl my hair and perfect my rouge. Then at 8:15 P.M., fashionably late, the doorbell rang. Algernon stood on the threshold in front of my parents, Uncle Willy, and me. He was wearing a leather bomber jacket, and true to his word, he'd driven his sky-blue convertible, complete with chrome tailfins, right to the manor door.

'It's customary to turn off the ignition upon arrival to a manor house,' Uncle Willy suggested as he approached the entry.

'Boys will be boys,' said Papa, offering Algernon a hearty handshake and a clap on the back.

Algernon greeted my parents, then turned to me.

'Wowzer,' he said to my mother. 'She looks good enough to eat.'

'Now, now. Just a nibble,' said Mama.

After a bit of small talk, Algernon agreed to have me home before midnight. 'I'd never let a girl this pretty turn into a pumpkin,' he said.

'We won't wait up. We know she's in good hands,' said Papa.

Algernon led me to his car as my parents and Uncle Willy stood vigil.

'Say hello to your folks for us!' Papa called out.

'Oh, I almost forgot,' said Algernon. 'They want you to drop by for a whiskey tasting next Tuesday. But beware – Prissy and Mags love to show off their art. My mother is a bona fide collector, and my father goes on and on about color and shadow. You'll need the whiskey to get through it!'

'Tell them we'd be delighted,' said Mama.

'We look forward to it!' Papa added.

And before I knew it, I was in the passenger seat of a blue convertible, driving down the highway with Algernon Braun by my side. Everything – every last detail – was just as I'd imagined it. Until it wasn't.

*

We were nearing the drive-in as the sun began to set. Algernon entertained me the entire ride over, telling me stories about his college friends and the high jinks they got up to in their dorm. He said he wasn't returning to school. 'Apparently, they don't want me back. Plus, I'm not cut out for it.' The wind tousled his blond hair.

'I know what you mean,' I replied, because for the first time in my life, education seemed dull in comparison to the young rebel beside me with only one hand on the steering wheel and the other poised between our seats just inches from my knee. Every now and again, Algernon's eyes would leave the road to drink me in.

'I can't get enough of you,' he said. 'If we don't park soon, I'll cause an accident.'

I couldn't help but blush. Every word that spilled from his mouth was a tantalizing elixir designed to make me feel special and wanted and beautiful. By the time we pulled into the drive-in, I was giddy and lightheaded.

'Where should we park?' he asked.

'Up front?' I suggested. 'I'm one of those girls who sits close to the blackboard.'

'Of course you are,' he said. 'But this isn't class, Miss Flora. And anyway, how much of the movie are you planning to watch?'

He pulled into a spot at the back of the lot and jumped out of the car to put the top up on the convertible.

'Come on,' he said once he was done. 'Let's hit the concession stand.'

He took me by the hand and led me through rows of cars

to the front of the lot. Several times, I jumped at the sound of a car horn honking – yet another friend of Algernon's trying to get his attention. We stopped a total of six times to say hi to this couple or that one, all of them asking who his cute new girlfriend was while inside I secretly screamed with joy.

At the concession stand, he bought me chocolate caramels, and on our way out the door, we bumped into the last person I expected to see at the drive-in.

'Hi, Flora,' he said. He was holding two tubs of popcorn in one hand and a Coke in the other.

'John? What are you doing here?' I inquired.

'Am I not allowed to watch a movie?'

'Who's this?' Algernon asked.

'John Preston. We met at the ball,' John said in a tone sharper than a knife.

'Did we?' said Algernon. 'Sorry, I've forgotten. The bartender had a heavy pour, and the company was too distracting,' he said as he casually flung his arm around my shoulders.

John's jaw clenched.

'Who are you here with?' I asked, but John just stared at me mutely.

'I get it,' said Algernon. 'Ol' Johnny boy here isn't the type to kiss and tell. Am I right? Listen, we'll let you get back to her, whoever she is. Nice to meet you.'

'Wish I could say the same,' John muttered under his breath.

Algernon pulled me away, and the second we were out of earshot, he asked, 'What the hell was that all about?'

'No idea,' I replied.

I could feel John's eyes on our backs without even having to turn.

I was relieved when we were back inside the safe haven of Algernon's convertible. We talked for a while as darkness descended. Soon enough, the film began. Algernon opened the chocolate caramels and we both partook as we watched. Before long, he put his hand on my knee, and I'm sure he could feel me trembling. The chocolates fell by the wayside, and he came closer.

'Sweeter than candy,' he said, then kissed me deeply. I drank in the scent of him, the caramel from his mouth, and before long, he was kissing my neck. I lost all sense of time and all sense of decorum, too. It would be a lie to say I didn't like what was happening, for at first I did. I was flattered he found me at all attractive. After a while, the windows fogged up and I could barely see out. On the movie screen, two blurry actors were talking about love, but what the plot of the movie was, I couldn't say. Suddenly, Algernon's hand was on my inner thigh, traveling up and up. It was happening so fast. I felt claustrophobic. I needed to think, to breathe.

I held a hand to his chest. 'Can we crack a window?' I asked. 'It's getting warm.'

Wordlessly, he rolled down his window a bit, then picked up where he'd left off.

Oh, Molly, these were different times, and I was so young and naïve. I was out of my element, delighted to have wooed Algernon but terrified of all that lay beyond the realm of his kiss. I wanted to slow down, maybe even to halt entirely. I hoped his hands would take my cues and relent. What I felt was no longer pleasant, and when he undid the top button on his jeans, I didn't know what I would say to make him stop. I could hear my mother's voice echoing in my head – *Girls like that are looking for trouble.* Was I one of those girls, the kind who teased, then let a boy down?

'Please,' I said, finding my voice at last. 'Can you slow down?'

That's when I heard it – a sharp rap on the foggy driver's side window.

Algernon pulled his hand away and adjusted his jeans. 'What the hell?' he said.

He rolled the window down to reveal Mrs Mead standing there with a tub of popcorn. 'Hello, Flora,' she said cheerily, just as she did every morning when she pulled back the curtains to let the daylight stream into my bedroom. 'John bought too much popcorn. We were wondering if you'd like the rest.'

'Who the hell are you?' Algernon asked.

'Mrs Mead, Flora's nursemaid, at your service,' she said and didn't she even curtsy.

'And that there is my brother, butler to Flora's father. I hear you've already met my nephew, John?'

Algernon looked into the shadows, where both Uncle Willy and John were standing by my father's old car – John holding a Coke and Uncle Willy another tub of popcorn.

Mrs Mead pushed the popcorn through the window. Her

one blue eye and her one green eye pierced Algernon with the most withering look I have ever witnessed. 'On the house,' she said. 'Popcorn keeps the mouth and hands busy. Enjoy!'

When Algernon took the tub, she waddled away.

He rolled up the window, then passed me the popcorn.

I held it in my lap, not caring if the butter stained my new skirt. 'Shall we watch the film?' I asked as I settled into my seat.

'Not much else we can do with an entire family of proles watching,' he replied.

'I'm so sorry,' I said, venturing to take his hand, which he pulled away. 'Really, my apologies,' I added. But even as the words left my mouth, I knew I didn't mean them, for what I felt in my heart and soul was pure and utter relief.

CHAPTER 19

I run. I run as fast as I can, leaving the alleyway and racing home. I arrive in record time, bounding up the stairs to our apartment and turning the key in our door. Juan is pacing in the entrance, his eyes wide, phone in hand.

'*Madre mía,*' he exclaims the second I enter. He hugs me so tight I can feel his heart pounding in his chest. 'I called you and you didn't answer. Are you okay?' he asks.

I realize then that Juan has been as worried about the death threat as I've been. He's just been hiding it to make me feel safer.

'I'm fine,' I say between gasps for breath. 'I'm okay.'

'Where were you?' he asks. 'I came home expecting you to be here, and you weren't. Then you didn't answer your phone. I was so scared.' He takes me by the hand and leads me to Gran's threadbare sofa. He puts both of his palms on my cheeks. 'I don't know what I would do if . . . if something ever—'

'Juan, I'm okay,' I say. 'But I have some things to tell you.'

I recount the whole story about my walk home – how a black car sidled up to me, blocking me in an alley, how I thought I was going to die.

'We need to call the police – now!' he says, interrupting.

'Wait,' I say. 'There's more.' I tell him how my mother came out of the car and all the things she told me – how the egg was stolen by a gang of hired men who don't want it found, how it once belonged to Gran, and how, worst of all, not only did my mother ask me for money but her parting words to me were a threat.

As I deluge Juan with the shocking details, his phone on the coffee table rings.

'It's Mr Preston,' he says. 'I left him a panicked message.'

'Take the call. Tell him I'm okay,' I say.

Juan answers and relates what happened to me. Then he ends the call. 'He's on his way here. He wants to see you.'

'Now?' I say.

'Yes now,' Juan replies.

In the time it takes for me to answer Juan's copious questions and for Juan to brew tea and put together a plate of hors d'oeuvres à la Juan, there's a knock on the door. I open it, expecting only my gran-dad but am greeted by a twofer that includes a very anxious-looking Angela.

'Angela? Why are you here?' I ask.

'You went missing, Molly. Juan called Mr Preston. Mr Preston called me. Did you really think we wouldn't come running?'

Angela and Mr Preston launch themselves at me. They're hugging me so tight my spleen is about to burst.

'I'm okay,' I squeak from the middle of the sandwich, 'or at least I was until a second ago.'

Reluctantly they release me.

'Molly,' Angela says, 'there are days when you test my patience, but I can't stand the thought of a world without you in it.'

'My thoughts exactly,' says my gran-dad as he sets a bag on the floor.

Mr Preston and Angela remove their shoes, and because they know me so well, they wipe the bottoms and place them neatly in our front closet. It's then I notice Gran-dad's hands are shaking.

'You can relax. I'm fine. Please, sit.'

We gather in the living room, and as Juan serves tea, I repeat the entire alley ordeal.

Gran-dad eyes me darkly as he listens. 'So she's crawled out of the woodwork again – my daughter. Maggie.'

'She wanted to warn me,' I say.

'Warn you?' Gran-dad replies. 'Do you have any idea how many times I tried to help her over the years? Her mother – your gran – tried, too. But she always fell back into her old life. And now that dreadful life is edging closer and putting you in danger.'

There's a knock on the door.

'Now what?' I ask. 'Did someone order a clown?'

'Not exactly, but I did text someone,' says Angela as she jumps up to open the door.

Detective Stark stands in the threshold. She's wearing a baggy tracksuit, looking piqued and flushed. 'I was grocery shopping, but I came running the second I got Angela's message.'

'Clearly you weren't the only one,' I say, as I gesture to my living room, which is now so packed with guests that Juan has to bring in a chair from the kitchen so the detective has somewhere to sit.

With everyone jammed in, I sit on the sofa between Juan and my gran-dad, recounting one more time everything that happened from the moment the black car sidled up to me to when my mother drove away. When I finish speaking, everyone is silent.

'We have to find her,' says Detective Stark. 'We have to find this Maggie Gray.'

'No!' I reply vehemently. 'I don't want to find her. And I don't want to find the egg. Since I went on that TV show, the Fabergé has brought me nothing but anguish, and calling off the search is the only way I'll be safe. She said as much.'

'If Maggie's telling the truth,' says my gran-dad. 'But what if she's not? What if you're in danger regardless?'

Angela stands and starts to pace the only free spot of floor in the room. 'There's something that's bugged me ever since the egg disappeared – that note in the vacuum canister. Why was it addressed to Molly?'

'Because whoever wrote it knows I'm the one who cleans the canister,' I reply.

'Angela's right. It doesn't make sense,' says Stark. 'If the gang that pulled off this heist really wanted the search to stop, why not threaten the police instead of you? You're just a maid.'

'She's more than that to us,' says Juan. 'She's everything.'

'What I'm trying to say is that Molly might be connected to this egg in ways we don't quite fully understand,' Stark clarifies.

'Yet,' Angela adds.

'Gran is the missing link,' I explain. 'My mother all but said so. But what I can't believe is that she would ever steal anything from anyone.'

'Agreed. I knew Flora well,' says my gran-dad, 'and I can tell you, that woman was no thief.'

'Necessity can make a thief out of anyone. I've seen it before,' says Stark.

'Impossible,' my gran-dad replies. 'Flora was different.' He stands then and walks to the door, where he left his bag. He grabs it and brings it to the living room.

'Molly, when you were on *Hidden Treasures,* your shoebox contained many of your gran's things, and as I mentioned before, there was one item in that box that caught my eye, and it wasn't the Fabergé.'

'The key?' I ask.

'Yes,' he replies as he removes a book from his bag.

He hands me an old leather-bound diary with a heart-shaped lock on the front. 'She gave this to me for safekeeping before she died,' says Gran-dad. 'She told me to give it to you, but only when you were settled and ready to read it.'

'I'm decidedly unsettled at the moment,' I say. 'And far from ready.'

'But, Molly,' Angela says. 'What if she's left you a message? What if the diary contains clues about the egg?'

'Gran never talked about her past,' I say. 'She was very secretive and reluctant to reveal anything. *Let sleeping dogs lie.* That's what she always said. My guess is this book contains recipes or fairy tales. She loved to make up stories – the more fanciful, the better.'

Juan gets up from the sofa and walks over to Gran's curio cabinet. He picks up the skeleton key from the shelf where I used to keep the Fabergé. 'It can't hurt to try the key,' he says.

He returns to the sofa and passes it to me. I take it in one hand as I hold the diary in the other. I put the key in the lock – a perfect fit. I turn it once, and like magic, something clicks.

CHAPTER 20

Dear Molly,

It is said that the easiest way to solve a problem is to deny its existence. I know this because I've lived it. Over the years, I've often thought about that date with Algernon and what would have happened if Mrs Mead had not followed me to the drive-in, interrupting at just the right time. Would things have turned out differently? Would I have seen the truth about Algernon faster, averting all that came after?

I can almost hear your voice as you read this – *Denial isn't just a river in Egypt.* You like that saying a lot – a pun, your favorite. But denial *is* a river, and after that date with Algernon, I found myself carried away on it yet again, convinced that Mrs Mead, Uncle Willy, and John were busybodies and that Algernon's actions at the drive-in had been entirely justified. Of course he would have stopped if only I'd asked him more directly; of course it was my fault for not making my boundaries clear; of course I'd spent a week preparing my outfit just to lure him, so how could I feel anything other than flattered that he'd found me so irresistible?

These thoughts were driven home the morning after my date, when my mother pulled back the curtains on my bedroom window. 'Rise and shine, darling,' she said as she let the light in. 'How was your night with the most sought-after bachelor in the land?'

Mrs Mead stood in the threshold of my bedroom, her arms tightly crossed. She was the one who usually woke me and pulled back my curtains. 'I doubt Flora will be seeing that young man again. Am I right?' Mrs Mead asked, looking at me with such pity that it hit me like a tidal wave, flushing me further down the river.

'I can speak for myself,' I retorted. 'And for the record, Algernon is wonderful.'

I knew it was what my mother wanted to hear. She squealed loudly, then sat on the edge of my bed, hugging me. 'Oh, darling, this was meant to be. It's a dream come true for all of us. Just remember,' she said, pulling away to meet my eyes, 'men love the thrill of the chase. Give him a little, but not everything.'

'Yes, Mama,' I said.

In the doorway, Mrs Mead watched, slack-jawed. But she didn't dare say another word.

Things moved quickly after that. There were more dates with Algernon, and everything about him enchanted me. I set some boundaries, and I was relieved that he didn't try to cross them, though he got petulant when I held my ground.

My parents assured me everything between the two families was going splendidly, perfectly – 'exactly as it should,' said Papa – and because I'd never seen both Mama and Papa so happy and had never been lavished with so much of their affection, I remained in denial about any misgivings I had about Algernon.

All of us were caught up in the heady magic of the two families coming together – dinners at the manor or at the magnificent Braun mansion, with copious amounts of champagne and whiskey, and comments from both sets of parents about what a fine couple Algie and I made and how we were like thoroughbreds – a triumph of good breeding that would pay off in the future.

When we visited the Brauns, Magnus and Priscilla would lead us through vast white rooms filled with priceless art. They luxuriated in schooling my parents and me on the art world, referring to masterpieces as 'investments' and making sure we understood that Picasso and van Gogh were worth more dead than alive.

Meanwhile, John lurked in my periphery as he always had. He admitted overhearing me at that drive-in when I urged Algernon to stop. He was the one who sent Mrs Mead to the convertible. I was furious when he told me. I raged and accused him of jealousy.

'I *am* jealous,' he admitted. 'But that doesn't mean you're not making a terrible mistake.'

I didn't listen. Not to him. Not to Mrs Mead. Not even to Uncle Willy's oblique petitions – his sideways comments about men with agendas and his cagey reminders about the importance of education.

Education. Oh, Molly, I'm ashamed to say that when it was time to sit my exams, my father made it clear he forbade me from taking them. 'What's the point?' he asked. 'Your future is staring you right in the face. And university is a waste for a girl with your prospects.' And so, at the last moment, I told the headmaster I was backing out, and I stopped attending class.

And then one day, barely able to contain her excitement, Mrs Mead broke the news – 'My nephew,' she said, beaming, 'he's going to university!'

Not only had John passed the entrance exams but he was top of the class.

'Congratulations,' I said when next I saw him outside of Mrs Mead's cottage. 'You're going to be a scholar, likely one of the best.'

My compliment didn't even register. He just stood, scratching his head and staring at me. 'I don't get it, Flora,' he said. 'How is it possible that you didn't even try the exams?'

'I'm just a girl,' I said with a shrug. 'I don't have what it takes.'

John shook his head and walked away.

With my dream of education thoroughly quashed, I devoted myself to the full-time pursuit of Algernon. I took cues from my parents as they fell further under the Braun spell. My father worked hard to draw Magnus close. They shared post-dinner brandy and cigars in one man's den or the other's, swapped stories and histories, drew up private paperwork – a quiet backroom deal between gentlemen and fathers, one that would seal not only my fate and Algernon's but the fate of our two family firms.

When it happened – a marriage proposal – two short months after I had been swept off my feet by that boy in the ballroom, it did not go as I'd imagined it. We were at the Brauns' that night, and after dinner, instead of my father and Magnus smoking cigars in the parlor, Priscilla suggested we all retire to the art wing, where she was eager to show off a newly acquired oeuvre.

We made our way to a modern room with streamlined white divans, on which we sat, digestifs in hand. Algernon, wearing a dinner jacket for once, put his arm around me and kissed my cheek. In front of our parents, he was always the very picture of tenderness, though when we were alone he was either distracted or demanding.

Priscilla drew our attention to a waist-high white pillar in the middle of the room on which sat a marvelous, twinkling *objet*. It was an egg, jewel-encrusted, ornate, resting atop a gold pedestal base.

'Our latest acquisition,' she announced. 'You have no idea the trouble we went through to acquire this piece.'

'Nor will they ever,' added Magnus.

'It's a Fabergé,' Priscilla continued, 'a priceless heirloom, the only one of its kind in all the world.' She paused then as we admired the egg, shimmering on its pedestal. It looked almost alive.

'Algernon – it's time,' Priscilla said, and beside me, her son took his cue and kneeled, grabbing my hand.

'Flora Gray,' he began. 'I'm doing this with your parents and mine present,' he said, 'because if I didn't, they might all disown me.'

Both sets of parents laughed.

'I know this is quick, but it comes with your father's blessing and mine,' he said, his icy blue eyes staring into mine. 'We've all been scheming, and we'd like to set a date for a year from now, when you turn eighteen.'

He paused, waiting for me to say something, but I was completely and utterly dumbfounded. 'I'm sorry,' I said. 'I'm not quite sure what's happening.'

'Flora, I'm popping the question: Will you marry me?' he asked.

I looked from him to my parents, searching for some clue that might explain the one thing that was missing. 'But there's no ring,' I said.

Priscilla's sparkling laugh echoed through the cavernous room. 'The ring will come later, dear. First, we fill your trousseau. We offer this gift – the Fabergé. It's worth a fortune, and we give it as proof that we value you immensely . . .'

'. . . and as proof that our son adores you,' added Magnus as he raised his whiskey glass.

'Flora, you're leaving me hanging,' Algernon said. 'What do you say?'

'She says yes!' exclaimed my mother.

As I looked at Mama, I mirrored her nodding head and the word escaped my own lips, too – 'Yes,' I repeated just the way she'd said it. Something in the pit of my stomach twinged. I felt instantly sick, like I'd just made a terrible mistake. I thought of John, saw him in my mind's eye. Suddenly, I wanted to take my answer back, to withdraw my consent, but it was too late.

There were gasps of joy and rounds of applause. There were pats on backs and so many tears. My father stood, offering a hand to Algernon. 'Let's get this young man off his knee before it cramps,' he said, hauling his future son-in-law – the son he'd always wanted and had never had – to his feet. He embraced him in a bear hug, then toasted to his health.

They formed a neat little clique, all five of them, congratulating one another, pulling out hankies, clinking glasses. They didn't notice when I made my way to the white pillar in the middle of the room.

I looked closely at the Fabergé for the very first time – the rows of diamonds and emeralds and rubies, the glimmering gold base. And that's when it occurred to me that for the Brauns and my parents, there was only one thing of value in that room, and it most definitely wasn't me.

CHAPTER 21

As I sit on the sofa in my living room, all eyes – Juan's, Gran-dad's, Angela's, and Detective Stark's – are trained on me. The diary in my hands clicks open. The key is a perfect fit. The lock gives way, and whatever Gran wrote inside the diary is now accessible.

'Aren't you going to have a look?' Angela asks. I can't explain it, the tingling sensation in my palms, the charged feeling coursing up my arms and electrifying my entire being. I part the spine slightly, enough to glimpse the first page. As predicted, it's some kind of fairy-tale collection à la Gran. I slam the diary shut, because the sight of her handwriting threatens to undo me in front of everyone, as do the very first words I see, a salutation I immediately hear in her voice, resonant and clear as though she's right beside me – *Dear Molly.*

I look up from the diary. They're watching me expectantly.

'You don't have to read it now, only when you're ready,' says my gran-dad. 'Flora made that clear when she gave it to me.'

I lock the diary, then set it and the key on Gran's curio cabinet.

'It's pretty unlikely that your grandmother's diary will shed light on what's happening now with the egg,' says Detective Stark. 'At the moment, our biggest lead is Maggie Gray. I need to get back to the precinct and look her up. Maybe I'll find an address, see if she has a police record or any sketchy affiliations.'

'Her given name is Margaret,' says my gran-dad. 'She was named after my aunt.'

'Your aunt?' I say. 'You've never mentioned an aunt.'

'She's long gone, I'm sorry to say,' he replies. 'An excellent woman. Your gran knew her well.'

'Molly,' says Detective Stark, 'it's best you lie low for a bit, just until I get answers on this Maggie woman. I don't think you should go to work tomorrow. Maybe take a day off. Relax a little.'

'A day off?' I say, barely understanding the concept.

'Just stay home and put your feet up until I give you the all clear,' Stark says.

'Molly's not going anywhere,' Angela pronounces. 'Not if I can help it.'

'Since when do you decide my life for me?' I ask.

'Angela's right, *mi amor*,' says Juan. 'We've all just been scared half to death. Until we know more, you should stay home as the detective suggests.'

'It won't take long. A day, two max,' says Stark.

'But I have a job to do. Mr Snow counts on me,' I counter.

'I'll call Mr Snow myself and explain,' says my gran-dad. 'He'll understand.'

The truth is in times of trouble I prefer to work. I've always found it an excellent distraction. 'What will I do all day alone in the apartment?' I ask.

'Clean?' Juan suggests. 'The front closet could use a good tidy, and I did see a dust mote or two on your gran's curio cabinet.'

I know what he's doing – trying to get me to like the idea. It's only when I hear Gran's voice in my head – *Never look a gift horse in the mouth* – that I warm to the notion.

'If it makes everyone feel better for me to stay home, that's what I'll do,' I say.

'I'll bake you shortbread tonight, so you can have biscuits with your tea tomorrow,' Juan offers. 'And I'll call to check in during the day.'

'So will I,' says Angela.

'Me, too,' echoes Gran-dad.

And so, it's settled. Tomorrow, Juan will go to work, and I will stay in our apartment on my own. Thanks to the missing egg, I have become a prisoner in my own home.

'Rise and shine!' Those are the first words I hear the next morning, much like every morning, as Juan whisks back the curtains and lets the morning light shine into our bedroom. I'm about to get out of bed and hurry off to shower, but then I remember I'm not in any rush today since I'm not going anywhere. I watch as Juan putters around the room, picking out clothes and putting on his slippers.

'I don't see why I shouldn't go to work,' I say. 'Even Detective Stark admitted there's a low probability that I'm in real danger.'

'Molly,' says Juan as he turns to face me. 'What is it you always say about that Egyptian river?'

'Denial isn't just a river in Egypt?'

'That's the one,' he replies.

This clearly isn't a battle I'm going to win.

Juan readies himself for his workday. We have breakfast, and soon enough he's off to work.

'I'll call you later, *mi amor*,' he says, planting a kiss on my lips and hugging me tight. 'I'll miss you at the hotel and so will the staff, but there's always tomorrow.'

I say goodbye, then I lock the door behind him, leaning against it as I survey our apartment, wondering what I'll do with myself for the rest of the day.

No point weeping when you could be sweeping.

In Gran's honor, I'll give life meaning with deep cleaning, starting with her curio cabinet. I grab my supplies and begin with the middle shelf, polishing Gran's collection of souvenir spoons. Each one holds a memory of a precious moment we spent together. I'm burnishing one from Killarney, Ireland – pure silver with a green inlaid shamrock on the handle. I remember when we acquired this spoon, not in Ireland, because our travels were relegated to the armchair variety. We were walking past a mansion where Gran worked as a maid when I was about twelve years old.

At the end of a long, winding driveway was a cardboard

box outside the iron entry gate. It was filled with all manner of trinkets – a crystal vase, bamboo placemats, some dishes and teacups (much better than ours at home), and this silver souvenir spoon.

'Are they really getting rid of all these things?' I asked, shocked that such treasures could be abandoned outside a gate. 'Let's grab the whole box!'

'Not without checking first,' Gran insisted. 'We are not thieves. We take only what's rightfully ours, remember? You wait here.' She went through the iron gate, walked up the driveway, and rang the doorbell of the regal mansion. A man stepped out, and she spoke to him for a moment, then returned a few minutes later.

'We're free to take what we want,' she announced.

'The whole box!' I said immediately.

'No. We'll choose one item, and we'll leave the rest for others.'

'But why can't we take it all?'

'Because, Molly,' she said as she looked me in the eye, 'pride is taking less than you need. Generosity is leaving a gift for others.'

I nodded, taking in her words.

'What do you choose?' she asked.

I looked into the box again and held up the souvenir spoon from Ireland. 'This,' I said.

'But that's not the thing you most want,' she replied. It was true. Were I to choose for myself, I would have taken a teacup, but I knew Gran loved souvenir spoons. I knew she'd treasure it.

'Generosity,' I said, placing the spoon in her hand. 'Meaning: leaving a gift for others. I do listen, you know.'

Her eyes became glassy, then she held me tight. I could not understand why she was suddenly crying.

'Have I done something wrong?' I asked when she released me.

'No,' she said. 'You've done everything right.'

Now, as I polish the spoon, the memory shines. I think of my mother, Maggie, claiming that Gran was a thief, that she stole the Fabergé. How could such an honorable woman, good to a fault, do such a thing? I put the spoon back with the others, then turn my attention to the diary and key sitting on the top shelf of the cabinet.

Yesterday is history. Tomorrow is a mystery. There's no time like the present.

I take Gran's diary in my hands. I put the key in the lock and twist – click. It opens. I'm shaking as I make my way to the sofa, where I begin on page one – *Dear Molly.*

Just then my phone rings, and I jump. I put down the diary and answer my phone.

'Molly, it's Mr Snow. I'm sorry to bother you. I've asked Mr Preston to pick you up and bring you to the hotel right away.'

'Of course,' I say, 'I'd be happy to work today. I was worried about leaving you short-staffed.'

'It's not that, Molly,' he says. 'We've found something.'

'Found what?' I ask.

'The Fabergé egg.'

CHAPTER 22

Dear Molly,

I've always tried to impress upon you that your worth is not determined through the worldly goods you possess, nor will it ever decrease because someone refuses to see your value. Here's what I've learned over the years: you can't make people see what they don't want to see. And the most precious treasures are often overlooked.

Once I was engaged to Algernon, I became privy to the many behind-the-scenes negotiations that had led to my betrothal. Mama and Papa eagerly shared the details, so proud were they of the outcome. Instead of swallowing Papa's company whole, Magnus merged his firm with Papa's to create Braun-Gray Investments. The new business married contemporary and traditional investment philosophies under a singular banner. My father was now in charge of regular investments, whereas Magnus handled a new arm dedicated to the purchase and sale of high-end artifacts.

It was my father who insisted that as part of the deal I be offered an engagement ring of immense value. 'It must be worthy of my daughter's hand,' he'd said during negotiations.

But when neither side could agree upon the value of the ring, Priscilla had proposed an alternative – 'a modern trousseau' is what she called it, one that would appreciate in the years to come 'much like the marriage between our children.'

'Your father is a brilliant negotiator, Flora,' Mama revealed at dinner one night a week after the engagement as she recounted the details. 'We've lost nothing, only gained in this arrangement.'

'What do you mean?' I asked.

'You have the Fabergé,' said Papa as he cracked his lobster tail.

'But what did the Brauns get in exchange?'

'You,' said Mama as though I were a fool.

Papa was so bullish about the merger that he hired more staff at the manor to show off his rising fortunes. Shy Penelope became a full-time maid-in-training, a helper for Mrs Mead. She now served our meals and waited on us hand and foot while Mrs Mead cooked and did everything else my parents demanded of her.

'Penelope,' said Mama at dinner, 'take this butter dish back to Mrs Mead. It's not warm enough.' The girl grabbed the dish and rushed off.

'Flora, in case you're wondering,' said Papa, 'if for any reason Algernon gets cold feet, you still get to keep the egg.'

'It's an insurance policy for the rest of your life,' said Mama. 'Its value is truly significant.'

'Is it?' I asked. 'Do we have proof?'

'*Proof?*' said Mama as she laughed out loud.

'Proof is in possession,' said Papa, 'and possession is nine-tenths of the law.'

'What about the other tenth?' I asked.

'Don't worry your pretty little head over such things,' Papa advised. Any misgivings I had about being itemized on a balance sheet were quelled as I basked in the warmth of his gaze.

'Here you are,' said Mrs Mead as she emerged from the kitchen and plunked my mother's steaming butter dish in front of her. 'Is it to your liking now, madam?'

'It will do,' Mama replied.

'Does anyone else wish to lodge a complaint about their dinner?' Mrs Mead asked.

'That'll be all, Mrs Mead,' said Papa.

She disappeared back into the kitchen.

'Now that the merger's complete, it's time to celebrate,' said Mama. 'Both families will host private festivities in honor of the impending marriage. The Brauns invited us to their yacht in Saint-Tropez in a couple months' time.'

'And I'm taking Magnus and Algernon deer hunting on our grounds. We're set for this weekend. Remember how I bagged a twelve-pointer after winning your hand, Audrey?'

'That stag's head is in the basement somewhere – macabre thing,' remarked Mama, and Papa chuckled.

'I don't want a deer to die just because I got engaged,' I said.

'Darling, it's not about what you want. Let the men wear camouflage and shoot at things if it makes them feel virile.'

'We'll need assistants,' Papa said. 'William and his son will have to do.'

'Why them?' I asked. 'I doubt they've shot guns in their lives.'

'Good,' said Papa. 'They won't show up Magnus and Algie.'

And so it was that the next Saturday, the Brauns showed up at the manor and Uncle Willy let them in.

'There's my girl,' Magnus said as he kissed both my cheeks. 'Pretty as a picture, isn't she, Algie?'

'Sure,' he replied, looking at me briefly before turning his attention to the two rifle cases slung over his shoulder.

'It's torrential out there,' said Priscilla as she wordlessly passed her umbrella and overcoat to Uncle Willy. 'I can't believe you silly boys want to hunt in this atrocious weather.'

'The call of the wild, Prissy,' said Algernon. 'You wouldn't understand.'

'I suggested swapping the hunt for a gentlemanly poker game in the drawing room, but Reginald's having none of it,' said Mama. 'Oh, here he is now.'

Papa strode into the foyer dressed in a tweed plaid jacket and matching hat, waterproof breeches, and tall black boots.

Magnus and Algernon suppressed a laugh, though Papa failed to notice.

'There's tea and delectables,' said Mama, 'to warm you before you set out.'

We made our way to the banquet room, where the table was laid with fine white linen. Silver serving trays were filled with dainty sandwiches, macarons, and scones, all of which Mrs Mead and Penelope had been preparing for days.

'Take a seat,' said Papa. The Brauns drew up chairs, and Algernon reached for a scone, heaping it with jam and devouring it in two quick bites.

'A healthy appetite, I see,' Mrs Mead said, bringing the scones closer to him.

'Always,' Algie replied.

'Speaking of appetites,' said Mrs Mead. 'Do you know the Farquars?'

The Brauns stiffened at the mention of the name. It was so unthinkable for Mrs Mead, a maid, to initiate conversation with guests that Mama and Papa swiveled to face her.

'We don't know them,' said Algernon in a monotone drawl.

'Well, we do,' his mother corrected. 'But we're not close.'

'Oh? You must have run into them at the ball,' Mrs Mead said. 'I understand their daughter went to college with your son, until—'

Magnus now turned to Mrs Mead. 'How do you know that?' he demanded.

'Oh, you know how maids talk,' said Mrs Mead. 'People think we're invisible, but we do have eyes and ears.' She managed to say all of this in that same singsong voice, a tone that made the words sound almost benign.

'Mrs Mead,' said Mama. 'Shouldn't you be in the kitchen?'

She curtsied and left the room without another word.

'Penelope, tea,' Mama ordered, pointing to the empty cups on the table.

'I apologize,' said Mama once Mrs Mead was gone. 'Honestly, I'd wash her mouth out with soap if I wouldn't get arrested.'

'Is this one as fresh as the other?' said Algernon, pointing to Penelope as she filled his teacup. But as he watched her, his face changed. 'Do I know you?' he asked.

Penelope turned and began to fill Magnus's cup. 'No, sir,' she said, but as she pulled the spout away, it caught on the fine porcelain rim, sending the cup crashing loudly against the hard herringbone floor.

'Penelope!' my mother screeched.

'I'm sorry!' said Penelope as she retreated to the sideboard.

Mrs Mead appeared at the entrance. 'What's all the ruckus?'

'That fool of a girl just poured tea all over me,' said Magnus as he dabbed at his trousers.

'It was an accident. I'm sorry,' said Penelope.

'Not to worry,' said Mrs Mead. 'I'll clean this up. Penelope, make a start on the laundry downstairs.'

Penelope rushed out of the room as Mrs Mead got on all fours and began retrieving the shards on the floor.

'Well, that was more commotion than necessary,' said Papa.

'Please, everyone. Help yourselves to the spread. I think you'll find the food better than the service,' said Mama.

'I've had my fill,' Algernon announced as he stood and threw his napkin on the table. 'Plus, I've never actually seen the whole manor. Flora, why not give me a tour?'

'Certainly,' I replied, grateful to leave the tension-filled room and pleased that I might have a moment alone with him. He'd been avoiding me since the engagement, and I thought I knew why.

'No closed doors until after the wedding,' said Mama.

'My son knows the rules, Audrey,' Magnus replied with a chuckle.

My cheeks now fully crimson, I led Algernon out of the room and through the first floor, then up the main staircase to my wing of the manor.

'Where's your father's office?' he asked as we reached the second floor.

I led him to Papa's office, and when I opened the door, he waltzed right in and sat in Papa's chair, leaning back as if he owned the place.

'My mother calls that the Capital Throne,' I said.

He began rifling through the papers on my father's desk.

'I wouldn't do that. Papa likes his things just so.'

'Does he?' Algernon said as he got to his feet and came my way. He rested his arms on my shoulders, and his cold blue eyes met mine.

I was grateful to have his attention. Now was my chance to make things right.

'I want to apologize for not saying yes to you right away when you proposed,' I said. 'In the absence of an engagement ring, I didn't fully understand what was happening. I'm an utter fool.'

'Do you like the Fabergé?' he asked.

'Yes.'

'Good, because it's worth more than any ring. Mags and I went to great lengths to acquire it,' he said.

'How so?' I asked.

'It belonged to a baron with deep connections in the art world.'

'I met a baron at the Workers' Ball. Was he the former owner?'

'Maybe. My father had plans to go into business with that man, but he backed out at the last minute, claimed he didn't like my father's business style. Can you believe it? That's why Mags got into bed with your father. Your family's our fallback plan.'

Fallback plan? The words hit hard, but I tried not to show it. 'If the baron and your father had a falling-out, why did he sell your father the egg?' I asked.

'He didn't,' Algernon replied.

'I'm sorry?'

'Look, Flora. My father and I have one thing in common – what we want, we take.'

He let go of me then and paced the room, stopping by my father's filing cabinet to open one of the drawers.

'Are you suggesting the Fabergé is stolen?' I asked.

'What I'm saying,' he said as he slammed the filing cabinet shut, 'is that to be my wife, you can't ask so many questions. Your job is to keep your mouth shut and look pretty on my arm. Can you manage that?'

I felt as though I'd been slapped. His words were so shocking I lost the ability to produce my own.

'Good,' he said. 'We have an agreement. Let sleeping dogs lie, Flora.' He opened another drawer. 'You can go now,' he said as he rifled through it. 'I'll be down when I'm good and ready.'

I backed out of Papa's office and hurried down the stairs to my parents.

'Ah, there she is,' said Papa as I entered the banquet room.

'Where's Algie?' Priscilla asked.

'In the powder room,' I replied. 'I expect he'll be down shortly.' Why I lied for him, I can't quite say, but somehow I knew that was my duty as his wife-to-be. I took my seat at the table.

As Algernon's parents and mine chatted, I pretended to eat a scone, but my stomach had curdled.

Mrs Mead appeared at my side. 'Are you all right, dear?' she whispered as she filled my teacup.

'I . . . don't know,' I replied.

After what felt like an eternity, Algernon strode into the room, flopping down in a dining chair. 'Now I'm hungry,' he announced as he filled his plate with sandwiches.

'What on earth were you up to?' Priscilla asked.

'I was admiring the manor,' he replied as he waved for Mrs Mead to fill his cup. 'I hope you don't mind, but I had a look around your office,' he told Papa.

'Mind? Of course I don't mind,' my father replied. 'One day that desk will be yours, son. But not yet. I've still got some juice in me.'

Just then Uncle Willy and John appeared at the threshold

looking somber and uncomfortable, dressed head to toe in camouflage.

'We should leave soon,' Uncle Willy urged. 'The weather's only going to get worse.'

'Well, look who it is. I remember you,' said Algernon as he rose from his seat and sidled over to John. 'What do you have there?' he asked, pointing to the well-worn rifle in his hand.

'A .22,' John answered.

'I didn't know you hunted,' I said, confused by the incongruous sight of John with a weapon.

'Only when necessary,' Uncle Willy replied. 'We've both had occasion over the years to rid Mrs Mead's gardens of groundhogs.'

'That rifle's far too weak for what we're bagging today,' Algernon said. 'I brought two rifles. You can use one of mine – silver-tipped bullets for a cleaner kill.'

'Big game hunting isn't my thing,' John said.

'You haven't lived until you've watched a stag die,' said Magnus. 'It's invigorating.'

'We'd better go,' Uncle Willy urged.

The men stood and made their way out of the banquet room. 'John, Willy, keep your wits about you,' said Mrs Mead from the doorway.

The men gathered their gear and were soon heading out of the conservatory, marching past the manicured lawn toward the garden gate. My mother, Priscilla, and I watched until they disappeared into the dark, dank forest.

'Let's hope the deer gets lucky,' said Mama as she turned from the windows.

'My thought exactly,' said Priscilla.

'Shall we retire to the parlor for a ladies' chat?' Mama proposed.

In the parlor my mother and Priscilla gossiped and name-dropped while I feigned interest and occasionally forced a laugh. The talk turned to the wedding, which was nearly a year off, but to hear them discuss it, you'd have thought it was a week away.

Papa's antique grandfather clock ticked in the corner, time crawling at a snail's pace. And then, in the doorway, pale as a bedsheet, Penelope appeared.

Mama ignored her until she could no longer. 'What is it you want, Penelope?' she snapped.

'Mrs Mead,' the girl answered, her voice tremulous and weak.

'She's in the kitchen,' said Mama.

The girl floated away as if in a trance.

Once she was gone, my mother whispered to Priscilla, 'She's *not* working out.'

'Good help is so hard to find,' Priscilla replied.

A few minutes later, Mrs Mead ran past the parlor, moving so quickly she was barely recognizable. As Mama and Priscilla ignored her in favor of a discussion on the importance of wedding favors, I poked my head into the corridor. Mrs Mead was heading toward the conservatory. I heard the glass door slam as she exited the manor.

I returned to my spot on the settee.

'What do you think, Flora?' Mama asked.

I was so tuned out I had no idea what they were discussing. 'I leave that to you. Mothers know best,' I said.

'You see? She's become much more pliant since meeting your son.'

'I'm glad he could be of service,' said Priscilla.

It wasn't long after, maybe thirty minutes, that a great crashing sound was heard down the hall.

'My goodness, what's the commotion?' said Mama.

She headed to the conservatory, and Priscilla and I followed, halting in the doorway of the glass room because what we saw before us was a vision from a nightmare.

All five men had returned from the hunt, their faces muddy, their bodies drenched. Papa's tweed cap had vanished; his hand was trembling. Both he and Magnus held their rifles stiffly. Algernon stood beside them, rifle gone, eyes wide with shock. Uncle Willy was moaning something about a deer in the forest. In front of them all stood John, his face streaked not only with mud and tears but with fresh blood. In his arms he held Mrs Mead, her head lolling, blood spreading across her chest like a rose blooming in fast motion. It was a portrait of terror, Molly, as fresh in my mind today as the day I witnessed it.

'Don't just stand there!' my mother screamed. 'Do something!'

But only Uncle Willy and John moved. They gently lowered Mrs Mead to the floor, where they held her blue hands and wept over her.

Despite my mother's protest, there was nothing to do, for the truth was clear to everyone. Mrs Mead was dead, and no power on earth could bring her back to life.

CHAPTER 23

The egg has reappeared. I can't quite believe it. It doesn't make sense. But that's what Mr Snow told me just now on the phone. He's sent someone to pick me up from home and bring me to the hotel, so I head out of my building and wait on the sidewalk for a car to appear. I'm expecting a taxi, but what arrives is a police cruiser.

Detective Stark rolls down her window. 'Hop in,' she says. 'I'm going where you are.'

And so, not for the first time, I find myself heading to the Regency Grand in Detective Stark's police car.

'Why would the egg suddenly reappear?' I ask the detective as she drives.

'I have no idea,' says Stark, 'but we'll find out more once we get there.'

When we arrive at the hotel, Mr Snow is pacing anxiously on the red-carpeted stairs.

Speedy lopes over and opens my car door. 'Molly! Your egg's got legs. It ran back to you,' he says with a strange grin on his face.

'Speedy,' says Mr Snow. 'Are you the doorman or the town crier?'

'Is it really true?' I ask as I exit the car and head into the hotel with the detective.

'It's true,' says Mr Snow.

'Where was it found?' Detective Stark asks. 'And who found it?'

'It was . . . a team effort. You're about to hear the entire story.'

Mr Snow escorts us to his office, where I'm surprised to see several of my colleagues gathered. Angela, Sunshine, Lily, Cheryl, and even Juan are standing in a row, looking very much like a police lineup of usual suspects. On Mr Snow's desk, twinkling mischievously, is the object that has caused me both great elation and immense consternation – the Fabergé egg. Perplexingly, next to Mr Snow's desk is my maid's trolley.

'Why is my trolley in here? And what is everyone doing in this office?' I ask, since no one has volunteered a word.

'Your answer is on the desk,' Angela says as she points to the elephant in the room, which in this case is egg shaped.

'*Mi amor*,' says Juan. 'I think you should sit down.'

'I think *I* should sit down,' says Detective Stark as she saunters over to Mr Snow's desk, removes a notebook from her pocket, and settles in. 'Let's start with who found it,' she suggests.

'It wasn't me!' Cheryl exclaims, hands in the air. 'I had nothing to do with this.'

'For the love of dill pickles,' Angela exclaims.

'If there wasn't a copper in this room,' Sunshine adds, 'I swear I'd—'

'For once, Cheryl's not lying,' Juan says. 'Technically, she didn't find the egg.'

'It's not about *who* found it,' says Lily.

'Exactly!' Angela replies. 'It's about who put it there in the first place.'

My head is swiveling so quickly amongst speakers I fear I might get whiplash. The more they bicker, the less I understand. I slide into one of Mr Snow's leather armchairs.

'Cheryl,' says Mr Snow. 'Let's start from this morning when you arrived at work.'

'Fine,' she says, crossing her arms. 'But let the record show that I ain't done nothing.'

'Double negative. We know what that means, right, Molly?' Angela says.

'Stop!' yells Detective Stark. 'You're wasting time.' She sighs and puts her elbows on Mr Snow's desk, which only heightens my anxiety. 'Cheryl, say something relevant – and fast,' the detective demands.

'When I got here this morning, I met Mr Snow in the hallway outside of the housekeeping quarters,' Cheryl says. 'He told me Molly wasn't coming in, and I was thrilled to be Head Maid for the day.'

'I never said you were Head Maid,' Mr Snow clarifies. 'You assumed.'

'At least we know who puts the a-s-s in that word,' says Sunshine.

'Cheryl, please continue,' says Mr Snow.

'I grabbed Molly's trolley and made my way upstairs,' Cheryl says. 'Then I—'

'Wait, why did you take Molly's trolley instead of your own?' Stark asks.

'Molly wasn't coming to work,' Cheryl replies with a shrug.

'That's not why she took it,' says Lily. 'Molly replenishes her trolley at the end of every shift.'

'And if there's a shortcut,' Sunshine adds, 'you can be sure Cheryl will find it.'

'What's the big deal?' Cheryl says. 'Fair and square, the maids all share.'

As she quotes *A Maid's Guide & Handbook,* I officially want to join the bandwagon of colleagues lining up to throttle her.

'Can we get to the point?' Stark asks.

'I'm trying to, but this lot keeps chirping me,' says Cheryl. 'I went upstairs and started cleaning rooms. I took off a bunch of sheets, and my laundry bags were full by the time Sunshine found me.'

'Correction: I didn't find *you.* I found Molly's trolley blocking the hallway, and you'd disappeared.'

'Let me guess, "taking a load off"?' I say.

'It was break time,' Cheryl replies.

'When I spotted Molly's trolley,' says Sunshine, 'I thought I'd lend a hand by taking it downstairs. I left the bags at the laundry, then spotted Cheryl "taking a load off" in the change room. She told me Molly wasn't coming to work, which means I'd just inadvertently done Cheryl a favor by bringing her back the trolley.'

'Why did the chicken cross the road?' Detective Stark asks out of nowhere.

Everyone shrugs.

'To find out *where the hell the egg was*!' she yells as she slams a hand on Mr Snow's desk. 'Can we *please* get to the point?'

'I realize this story is taking a circuitous route,' says Mr Snow as he adjusts his crooked glasses, 'but you'll see why once we get there. Sunshine, continue.'

'I told Cheryl to get back upstairs, then left the change room,' says Sunshine.

'And I took Molly's trolley to the kitchen,' says Cheryl, 'leaving it in the hallway while I dropped off a bin of dirty dishes I'd collected from guests' rooms.'

'Aren't you forgetting something?' Juan asks. 'You took a little something on your way out of the kitchen.'

'Oh yeah. Some sweets on a tray,' says Cheryl. 'They looked like crap, but I scarfed one down and it wasn't half bad.'

'That wasn't crap. That was a prototype marzipanimal!' Juan says. 'You have no idea how hard it is to make a giraffe out of marzipan! And here's where my part comes in, Detective,' Juan continues. 'I stopped mixing icing and went out to the hallway to give Cheryl a piece of my mind, but then I saw

Molly's trolley there. I knew it was hers the same way everyone else did: no one stacks toilet paper like Molly does – a perfect pyramid. Then Lily appeared in the hall, so I asked her why Molly's trolley was outside the kitchen when Molly herself was at home.'

'And I said not to worry,' Lily interjects. 'I told Juan I'd take care of Molly's trolley. I was planning to bring it back to the housekeeping quarters, but first I went to the Social, because Angela needed tea towels.'

'I can corroborate that,' Angela replies. 'I was behind the bar, but Lily has this way of sneaking up on you, stealthy as a ninja. I was pouring a cranberry soda, and bam, she spooked me, and the drink went flying, making a big pink mess of Molly's toilet paper pyramid. "Shite on a kite!" I said to Lily. And together we started pitching the soggy rolls into the trash.'

'When we got to the middle row, we both saw it,' says Lily. 'The egg was nestled right in there. I screamed. I couldn't help it.'

'I swore,' Angela says. 'Do you wanna know what I said?'

'Some things are best left to the imagination,' Mr Snow suggests.

'We were both in shock,' says Angela. 'We covered the egg with a tea towel, then I picked up the phone and called Snow right away.'

'And shortly after, I called you, Detective, and then I called Molly,' says Mr Snow.

The detective removes her cap and rubs her forehead. 'You could have just said the egg was found in Molly's trolley.'

'No, we couldn't,' Angela replies. 'You needed to hear the whole trajectory. Because the Fabergé was either in that trolley from the very beginning of the day or someone along the way put it in amongst the toilet paper rolls. Those suspects are all here in this room.'

Detective Stark nods slowly, making a note on her pad.

'I didn't do nothing,' says Cheryl. 'You can't arrest me just because my co-workers hate my guts. You gotta have proof.'

'Thanks for the legal lesson,' says Detective Stark, though her tone seems to suggest a lack of sincere gratitude.

'If I were the thief,' Cheryl offers, 'why would I go to all the trouble of stealing the egg just to return it?'

'Don't know, Cheryl,' says Angela. 'Why don't *you* tell *us*?'

'*I never took it in the first place!*' she snaps.

'But you ate my giraffe,' says Juan, 'and these maids can probably fill the detective's notebook with tales of your creative pilfering.'

'True,' says Sunshine, 'but this doesn't have Cheryl's signature paw prints on it. Her swindles are always sloppy and self-serving. This one isn't her style.'

Amazingly, everyone nods along to this, including Cheryl. There's nothing about the heist or the egg's curious return that seems remotely Cherylesque. In fact, no one in this room seems at all suspect to me.

'It's a plant,' says Stark. 'Whoever put the egg in Molly's trolley did it last night. The heist was a professional job, and for whatever reason, so was the return of the egg. It was Molly who was supposed to find it.'

'Look on the bright side,' Angela offers. 'At least you've got it back, Molly. Now you can sell it and get rich!'

I suppose she's right, but everything about the Fabergé now terrifies me. My mother warned me about the egg being found, and now, here it is.

'What happens next, Detective?' Mr Snow asks. 'Since there's no longer a crime?'

'The crime of theft remains, but it becomes harder to prove when stolen goods are returned, not to mention harder to understand,' says Stark. 'I'm guessing you checked the trolley to see if there was a note this time?' She directs the question to Angela.

'I didn't think of that,' says Angela. 'I didn't want fingerprints all over things.'

'Bit late for that,' says Stark as she walks over to the trolley. She looks down into the middle row of the pyramid I built just last night. There's a hole in the center where the egg must have been. She reaches for something, picking it up gingerly between two fingers. It's a single square of two-ply toilet paper with writing on it.

Detective Stark reads aloud:

Dear Molly,

Sell the egg or you die.

CHAPTER 24

Dear Molly,

It's one thing to lose someone in the natural order of things but another entirely for someone to die before their time. I could not believe what I was seeing on the conservatory floor because it was so completely unnatural – Mrs Mead, my beloved nursemaid, a kinder mother to me than my own had ever been, who just over an hour earlier had been serving me tea in the banquet room. Now, she lay lifeless at our feet.

What happened next is a blur, a series of tragic tableaux. Someone must have called the police – my father, perhaps, or John? Uncle Willy let them in. The officers were known to the Brauns, greeted Magnus and Priscilla with respectful tips of their caps. Notes were taken, details and stories logged. A coroner arrived, officially declaring what was obvious to everyone – Mrs Mead was dead.

In the tumult that followed, no one seemed clear on how many shots had been fired. Was it one as Magnus and Algernon insisted or two as John and Uncle Willy had claimed? When questioned in the parlor, Uncle Willy revealed that he and Magnus had gone one way in the forest in pursuit of a noise in the underbrush. John and Algernon had each gone their own separate ways. Uncle Willy said he never fired a shot; neither had Magnus or Papa. But when John and Algernon were asked if they'd fired, only one of them nodded.

'I shot into the air,' said John. 'Why kill a harmless animal? I wanted to scare it away.'

'And you, son?' an officer asked Algernon. 'Did you shoot your weapon?'

'No,' said Algernon. 'I . . . I don't recall.'

The men explained what happened, each of their stories dovetailing. John heard a cry that sounded not at all like a deer but like a woman's scream, and he ran toward it. When he arrived, he found Mrs Mead collapsed and bleeding out in the underbrush. He dropped the rifle he'd borrowed from Algernon and knelt beside his aunt. Algernon arrived soon after, and Uncle Willy, Papa, and Magnus just after that. John and Uncle Willy tried to stanch the wound in Mrs Mead's chest, but it was too late. She was already gone.

After hearing everything, caps in hand, the officers asked the men to take them back to the forest. They ventured once more into the violent downpour, leading the police to the clearing in the underbrush where Mrs Mead had fallen. They recovered two identical firearms in the vicinity – each missing one bullet. The truth of whose rifle was whose had been washed away by the rain.

Once the men returned to the manor, we gathered in the parlor. The officers again asked Algernon if he'd fired a shot, and this time, his answer changed.

'I think I fired, but earlier – way before the maid came running out of the woods.'

'This maid, Mrs Mead,' one officer said. 'Why would she run out like that? What on earth made her rush outside during a storm?' He surveyed the faces before him.

John and Uncle Willy were sitting side by side on a settee, shaking their heads, their faces pale and drawn.

'Heaven knows what she was thinking,' my mother said in an unsteady voice. 'We have no idea what made her run off like that.'

'We were chatting with Flora right in this parlor,' Priscilla offered. 'I didn't even notice the woman run past.'

'I did,' I said. 'But I don't know why she was running.'

Algernon was seated across from me, between Priscilla and Magnus. His parents held protective hands on his back. He was mute throughout the conversation. He never looked up from his feet.

Only later did it dawn on me that someone had been absent during the officers' interrogation. We thought so little of her that we forgot about her entirely. Had she been there, she could have answered the officer's question, for she was one of only two people who knew exactly why Mrs Mead had run.

*

We were all in shock in the days that followed, and I was in deep mourning for the very first time in my life. I'd never lost anyone massively important to me. Death before that had been remote and romantic – something in plays and fairy tales.

The grief I experienced upon losing Mrs Mead was more than emotional. It was physical. It was hard to walk, hard to talk, to wake, to sleep. But my grief was nothing compared to whatever John and Uncle Willy must have felt upon losing this woman who was like a living hearth, bringing warmth and comfort to everyone who approached, and to her family most of all.

As the days passed, it became clear what the police were thinking. They'd returned to the manor several times with follow-up questions, mostly about John. Did he have a history of violence? Was there any reason he might have wanted his aunt dispatched? How long had he been a hunter?

Uncle Willy endured this line of questioning stoically. John wasn't violent. His aunt was like a mother to him. Apart from the odd groundhog, he wasn't a hunter at all.

'We all make mistakes,' the officer said when questioning John directly. 'If it was an accident, you might as well say so.'

John never wavered from his initial statement – 'I shot that rifle into the air. I didn't kill her.'

I wanted so much to comfort him, for he seemed a husk of his former self. His brown eyes were red-rimmed and downcast, his shoulders slumped, and whenever I tried to speak to him, it was as if he didn't hear me at all. Like a specter, he simply drifted away.

Meanwhile, Uncle Willy allowed me to hug him and to cry on his shoulder, but his embrace felt distant and weak. He was so bereft, he lacked the energy to console me and I was so accustomed to the constancy of his generosity, the sudden loss of it compounded my grief. For the first time in my life, I realized that what I valued most in this world I could lose in a heartbeat.

Still, Uncle Willy never missed so much as an hour of work at the manor. He stood sentry at the door and did my father's bidding. When he wasn't there, he was at the cottage, wandering the grounds aimlessly or sitting at Mrs Mead's kitchen table, staring off into space.

My parents responded to Mrs Mead's death with their usual lack of tact. 'We've talked with the Brauns,' my father announced two days after Mrs Mead died. 'Algernon's fine, just a bit shaken. And they know the police well, so you needn't worry, Flora. We'll wear black for a few more days in honor of Mrs Mead, but after the funeral, life will go back to normal. You understand,' he said.

But I didn't understand. There was no going back. There was no normal to return to.

'It's an awful bit of business, darling, a terrible shame,' my mother said, 'but it could have been worse.'

When I asked her what she meant, she merely shrugged, but I knew. It was only a servant who'd died, not one of us. We weren't equal in life, so why would we be equal in death?

In the days that followed, I spent as much time as possible away from my parents. The sight of them now revolted me, and yet I couldn't have said why. I holed myself up in my room, crying in my bed, day and night. I half expected Mrs Mead to walk through the door, to sit on the edge of my mattress and comfort me as she'd done so often in the past.

There, there, child. All will be well. Mrs Mead's here now.

But she wasn't. She'd never be there again.

When the autopsy report arrived a week after her demise, the cause of death was no surprise – a bullet through the heart. But no bullet was found in her body, and subsequent searches of the forest turned up two shells but no clues.

The day of the funeral arrived, and for the first time in my life, I picked my outfit all by myself, weeping as I did so.

We met the Brauns outside the small chapel in town where many of the workers from the surrounding estates lived. It was the first time I was seeing Algernon since the accident, and somewhere in my heart of hearts, I suppose I'd hoped he would offer me some kindness, some comfort, some sympathy. But my hope was dashed when he could barely look me in the eye, as though the raw sight of my grief appalled him.

As we awaited our turn to enter the chapel, he wrestled with his black tie. 'It's strangling me,' he said. 'I'll wait outside.'

'You'll do no such thing,' his father growled. 'You will appear in that chapel as will we all. The whole town is watching, Algernon, including the police. You will show you're grieving alongside everyone else.'

'But you already spoke to—'

'Grab Flora's hand, Algie,' Priscilla ordered. 'Offer her your handkerchief if she weeps. Do you understand?'

He took my hand as our families entered the church, and we sat in a pew at the back.

The small chapel was soon filled to bursting. It could barely contain all the people who'd been touched by Mrs Mead and who felt compelled to honor her in death as she had honored them in life. There were maids and gardeners, farmers and grocery store clerks, chauffeurs and chefs. None of my parents' associates were there – no captains of industry, no barons and baronesses, no lawyers, doctors, or real estate tycoons.

But everyone seemed to know Mrs Mead. The ladies' auxiliary enumerated her contributions – establishing a soup kitchen for the needy and a knitting circle that sold their wares to raise funds for the local children's charity. The choir lauded Mrs Mead for founding their quarterly concert series, and several adults stepped forward claiming she had raised them as her own. How was it that Mrs Mead had known so many, touched so many, loved so many? How was it she'd made such an impact, sowing kindness and goodness wherever she went, and yet somehow I'd been woefully oblivious to her life beyond loving me?

There were eulogies by the various townsfolk, and the last person to speak was her beloved nephew, John. He walked up to the podium and looked out at the crowd. The ladies fanned themselves and dabbed their eyes with handkerchiefs. Something he saw gave him strength, and his shoulders drew back. He became the proud, tousle-haired boy I'd first encountered long ago outside his aunt's cottage. He summoned a smile for the congregation, and when his eyes landed on me, I held them, sending all the love I had left in me his way.

'You knew her as well as I did,' he began. 'Aunt Maggie was a walking heart. She was capable of one thing only – giving of herself. She asked for so little in return, apparently fueled by vapors or whatever mysterious energy she received in exchange for so much giving. She was no withering daisy, though. She railed against injustice of all kinds, reserving her blistering tongue for those who deserved a dressing-down. Most of you never saw that side of her, but a few of you did.' He glanced at my parents, and they shifted in their seats.

'My aunt Mead defended the working class. She believed wholeheartedly in education, something she never had. When her husband died in the war, she made a dwelling out of an abandoned stone shed in the woods, proving that a home can be forged from anything. She knew that no matter how grand a lodging might be, if it has no heart, it is nothing.

'But perhaps the quality that made Margaret Mead so remarkable was her ability to see the suffering of others. She was drawn to it, and she was called to ease it. There was no pain that Aunt Maggie couldn't make better or sometimes heal entirely. It was as though she was brought into this world to comfort all who sought solace.

'She wasn't my mother, and yet she became that. From the heads nodding, I know I wasn't alone in feeling this way. I ask you now to keep a corner of your heart for Margaret Mead's spirit. Let it lodge there, for in that humble dwelling, generosity will take root and provide hope to many. Thank you.'

John left the podium and went straight to Uncle Willy, holding him tight. I felt myself rise from the pew, every instinct in me propelling me toward them.

'Sit down,' said Algernon gruffly as he gripped my wrist and held me back.

'They're not your family,' Mama hissed between gritted teeth.

I sat back down in our pew, doing as I was told, obeying as I always did. To this day I regret it.

After the funeral and the burial, the Brauns escorted us back to the manor. Uncle Willy and John arrived as we were seated in the parlor, excusing themselves to go to the cottage.

I intercepted John in the conservatory. Uncle Willy was already out the door and heading to the garden gate. I grabbed John's hand before he could leave. 'Thank you,' I said as I looked into his gentle brown eyes.

'For what?' he replied.

'For knowing exactly what to say and how to say it. And for sharing Mrs Mead with me for all these years. I never deserved her. And I never deserved you. I'm so sorry,' I said, erupting into tears.

Something in him shifted then. It was like he suddenly saw me again. He drew me to his chest, and I wrapped my arms around him. He nestled his face into my hair, his mouth so close to my ear. 'Of course you deserved her, Flora,' he whispered. 'And she had enough love for the both of us and for many others besides.'

Crying, we held each other for a long time, and I sensed that feeling return – the feeling I'd felt on the ballroom floor, of John and me falling into lock step, as though not everything between us had to be expressed out loud, for so much could be said without words.

Eventually, I pulled away. 'You should be with your father,' I said.

He put his hands to my cheeks. He wiped away my tears and planted a single, warm kiss on my forehead.

He walked out the door and headed toward Mrs Mead's cottage. Everything in me told me to follow, but still, I let him go.

When I returned to the parlor, drinks were being served by Penelope, who'd suddenly found herself catapulted into Mrs Mead's role. Without a head maid's guidance, she had very little idea of how to do the job. Her hands were shaking as she set glasses on a tray.

'Where's the ice, Penelope?' my mother asked. 'We can't have whiskey without ice.'

'Apologies,' Penelope said as she ran from the room.

Algernon wrestled his tie off and threw it on a sofa, then plopped himself down. 'That funeral service was unbearable,' he said. 'I thought it would never end.'

'Audrey, if you're looking for a new maid, I have a few names,' said Priscilla.

'Ideally, I'd like to hire a chef and a general maid,' said Mama, 'and get rid of you-know-who.' She whispered the last part as she pointed to the doorway through which Penelope had disappeared.

'I'm going to check on her,' I said. 'Penelope's struggling without Mrs Mead. We all are.'

Mama merely shrugged.

I looked at all of them – my parents, my fiancé, and my in-laws-to-be, and a bitterness rose in my gorge. I couldn't leave the room fast enough.

In the kitchen, Penelope was removing ice from the freezer.

'Can I help?' I asked, startling her so much that she jumped.

'I . . . I can't go back in there,' she said.

'Of course you can,' I said. 'All you need to do is put the ice in a bowl along with silver tongs, and then leave the rest to me.'

She was wide-eyed, trembling, her eyes filling with tears. 'You don't understand.'

I felt it then, a jolt in the pit of my stomach.

'Mrs Mead tried to warn you,' Penelope whispered. 'And she tried to warn me, too. About him.'

Him. At first, I thought she meant my father. But as I looked in her eyes, realization dawned.

'By him, you mean . . . my fiancé,' I said.

She nodded.

'I know why Mrs Mead was running,' she said quietly.

'What are you saying?' I asked as I laid a hand on her quivering arm.

'I told her my secret,' she said.

'What secret?' I asked.

'If I tell you, you'll blame me. But it wasn't my fault.'

'Please, tell me,' I said. 'I won't blame you.'

Penelope then revealed everything that had happened in the leadup to Mrs Mead being shot. On Mrs Mead's orders, Penelope had gone to the basement laundry room, where she was sorting clothes when someone came into the room. She had her back turned when he entered, but she knew his voice. He told her to keep her back turned and to stay quiet and still.

'I should have screamed, but I was too scared,' Penelope said. 'I swear to you, I didn't provoke him,' she said through tears. 'I shouldn't be telling you this. You won't believe me.'

'I believe you,' I replied. I remembered how Algernon had recognized her at tea that day, how she'd dropped a cup on the floor.

'Do you know him? Algernon?' I asked her.

She nodded. 'I didn't realize until the day of the hunt, but yes. Before I took this job, I used to work for a baron and baroness. I did their laundry, cleaned their floors. But things went missing from the estate, and they accused the staff.'

'Did they dismiss you?' I asked.

'They dismissed everyone,' she replied. 'The entire work-force.'

Everything fell into place then, all the puzzle pieces aligning to form a terrible picture, and the focal point was the Fabergé. 'Penelope, did the baron own an egg,' I asked, 'a bejeweled egg on a gold pedestal? Was it one of the items that went missing?'

'I don't know,' said Penelope. 'They had so many fine things, so much art, it was like their home was a museum. But I remember him being there.'

'Algernon?' I asked.

'Yes. I found him alone in the art wing, all by himself in a grand room. He yelled and ordered me away.'

My mind and my belly churned. I couldn't keep up with my thoughts. 'When you took the job here, did Mrs Mead know you'd been dismissed?'

'I'm ashamed to say I kept that from her. I was afraid she'd never hire me if she knew.' She looked down at her feet. 'The other day, in the basement, when he grabbed me, he kept repeating, "You don't know me." He said it over and over again – "Squeal and you'll pay."'

Her round, terrified eyes searched mine for solace. I held her hands and asked her what happened next.

'I don't remember. I'm afraid it's a bit of a blur. Eventually, he left, and I got myself together. I went upstairs looking for the only person I thought might help me – Mrs Mead. She was in the kitchen. I told her everything. All of it.'

I recalled Penelope's pale face in the doorway of the parlor. I thought she'd seen a ghost, but I was wrong – she *was* a ghost.

'Mrs Mead was so angry. "My brother and nephew won't let this happen," she said. "He won't get away with any of this, not again." That was the last time I saw her alive. The next time I laid eyes on her was when they brought her into the conservatory and placed her body on the floor. And then, at the funeral, after I paid respects to Mr Preston and his son, young Mr Braun drew me aside. He knew I'd told Mrs Mead everything. He said if a deer keeps quiet in the forest, it won't get shot. Only the noisy ones get the bullet. That's what he said.'

It's hard to explain what I felt in that moment – the shock, the horror, the impotence, the outrage. And there was something else, too. It was as if a spell had been broken, as if some veil of enchantment had been fully cast aside. I saw everything clearly for the first time – who the Brauns really were, the lengths to which they'd go to protect themselves and their abominable son. I was a hair's breadth away from being Algernon's long-term partner and CEO of alibis. Marrying him would mean condemning myself to a lifetime of cleaning up after his crimes.

'Mrs Mead was right,' I said. 'He won't get away with this.'

'But he's your . . . your . . .'

'My fiancé?' I said. 'No, he's not. Not anymore.'

CHAPTER
25

Dear Molly,
Sell the egg or you die.

Detective Stark holds up the two-ply on which the message is written in block letters, the words formed in black marker, the intent crystal clear.

'Who writes a death threat on toilet paper?' Sunshine asks.

'I can't decide if it's ominous or hilarious,' Angela replies.

'First you're dead if you find the egg; now you're dead if you don't sell it?' says Juan. 'Detective Stark, is this serious?'

'It's flushable. How serious can it be?' Angela says.

'My hope is that both threats are bluffs, but until we find the thief, we won't know for sure,' Detective Stark replies.

'Did anyone see a man in a trench coat last night?' I ask. My mother had warned me to be on the lookout for such a man, one of her fly-by-night associates.

'Nope. We saw a guy like that once, on the day the egg was appraised, but never again,' says Sunshine.

'Describe him to the doorman and see if he entered the hotel last night,' Detective Stark suggests.

'Good idea,' says Mr Snow. 'Sunshine, Juan, let's talk to Speedy now.'

'Before you go,' says Stark, 'be sure not mention the return of the egg to anyone. The last thing we need is for the media to descend on this hotel again and draw more attention to everything – and everyone,' she says, looking at me.

'Understood,' says Mr Snow. 'Molly, shall I stow the egg in the safe?'

'Please do,' I answer.

'And we'll all stay quiet about it, right, Cheryl?' Mr Snow suggests.

Cheryl nods, reluctantly. Mr Snow picks up the egg and puts it in the wall safe behind his desk. He checks it's secure before he walks away, the others following after him.

Once they're gone, Angela collapses in the leather armchair opposite me.

'What now?' I ask her and the detective.

'I looked into Maggie, your mother, and so far, there's no police record for a Margaret Gray. And we can't find an address for her either.'

'I don't get it,' says Angela. 'If this was a professional heist, why return the egg?'

'The only thing I can think of is the thieves were worried they'd be caught. We need to consult experts in the art world.'

'The Bees,' I say. 'They might understand what makes a thief return a work of art. Should we call them?'

'They'll want you to put the egg up for sale again,' says Angela. 'And they'll want you on their show.'

'No show,' I say. 'My fifteen minutes of fame were more than I ever wanted.'

'I'll call them, make the boundaries clear. It's not a bad idea,' says Detective Stark. 'Molly, what do think? It's up to you.'

'Do it,' I say. 'Call in the Bees.'

For the second time in the same day, I find myself sitting in the passenger seat of a police cruiser with Detective Stark at the wheel. We're headed to Brown & Beagle Auction House in one of the highest new skyscrapers in midtown.

Before all of this, I could never have imagined meeting the stars of *Hidden Treasures,* and even now, I'm shocked that Detective Stark secured a meeting with them so expeditiously.

'They're really going to see us right away?' I ask the detective as she pulls out of the Regency Grand.

'She's a detective, Molly. Who's going to say no?'

This last statement comes from the backseat of the cruiser, where Angela is talking through a small window in the bullet-proof glass separating her from us. She begged Mr Snow to give her the afternoon off, and rather than enter a battle of wits with a notoriously stubborn redhead, he relented when the detective said it was fine for her to tag along. There was no way I was sitting in the backseat like a criminal, but Angela was thrilled by the prospect – 'a learning opportunity,' she called it.

Now, she launches a verbal tirade through the small window, peppering the detective with questions about organized crime, unsolved murders, and the various ways serial killers have successfully made bodies disappear.

The detective delights in sharing her expertise, none of which is doing anything to quell my jittery nerves. By the time we arrive at our destination, I have learned that cyber criminals are the new mafia, that cold cases are on the rise in the downtown core, and that hydrochloric acid is a surefire way to dissolve bones.

After a short drive that feels eternal, we arrive at the Bees' headquarters, entering a gleaming modern building with a concierge who directs us to the elevators. 'Top floor,' he says. 'The boys are expecting you.'

As we ride up, Angela pontificates on the predilections of infamous cannibals while I lean against the elevator wall, hoping not to faint. When the doors open, the Bees – and fresher air – greet us.

'Molly!' Beagle says the second I step into the glowing white lobby.

'We're so glad you've come. It's quite the ride up, isn't it?' Brown says.

'One more second in that elevator and I would have arrived horizontally,' I reply.

'A Fabergé faint, right in our elevator!' Brown says as he towers over me, his blue eyes sparkling.

'Made for TV,' Beagle quips as he waves his small, bejeweled hands.

'No,' I say. 'No TV.'

'I made that clear during my call,' says Detective Stark. 'The details of this conversation are to remain confidential. Understood?'

'Mum's the word,' says Beagle.

'It's Angela, right? The bartender turned events manager?' Brown asks.

'That's me,' Angela replies.

'And . . . why are you here?' asks Beagle, his eagle eyes drilling into hers.

It's a question I've been asking myself since the moment Angela hopped into Detective Stark's cruiser.

'I've got the eye of the tiger,' Angela explains. '"Criminal radar" is what they call it in policing. Isn't that right, Detective?'

'Angela aspires to join the force one day,' Detective Stark says. 'I've allowed her to come with us to support Molly as a friend. Let's hope I don't regret it.'

'We'll retire to our office,' says Brown.

The Bees lead us out of the sleek reception area into the rooms beyond. The first is high-ceilinged, with massive modern artworks on every wall, many of which remind me of an abstract piece that used to hang on a wall in the Grimthorpe mansion when I was a child. Gran nicknamed it the 'bourgeois blobs.'

We file through another room full of life-size marble statues depicting Greco-Roman gods in various states of undress.

'It's like walking through a museum,' I say. 'Are they real?'

'We deal only in originals,' Beagle explains. 'Fakes, facsimiles, and copycats need not apply.'

'We both descend from art-dealing families,' says Brown. 'To maintain excellence over generations requires preserving not only the art but a sterling reputation.'

'Please,' says Beagle. 'Step into our office.'

We enter a massive room with a magnificent crystal chandelier hanging from the ceiling. Paintings in ornate gold-leaf frames grace every wall – portraits of ladies in corsets hiding coy glances behind silk fans, scenes of English hunts in the countryside with foxes and dogs on the run, and still lifes of bowls replete with overripe fruit. Matching desks sit side by side, a small one with an indigo desk mat and a much larger one with a scarlet mat. Brown seats himself at the large desk and Beagle at the smaller one.

'Please,' Brown says, gesturing to the gilded Queen Anne's chairs in front of them, which I can't believe we're allowed to even go near, never mind grace with our backsides.

'So tell us,' Brown says once we're settled. 'What is so revelatory you couldn't even say it on the phone? I presume you have a lead in the case of the stolen Fabergé?'

'Much more than that,' I say.

'The egg was found,' Detective Stark reveals.

'Found?' Brown echoes, his eyebrows shooting up to his perfect golden hairline. 'Where?'

'In Molly's trolley, of all places,' Angela volunteers.

'Well, congratulations, Molly! This news is most auspicious,' says Beagle. 'This means we can start the sale right away.'

'We can,' says Brown. 'And don't worry about the price. Reappearances do wonders for art values.'

'So reappearances like this do happen,' says Stark. 'You've seen stolen art re-emerge like this before?'

'It's not entirely uncommon,' says Brown. 'There are famous cases – the *Mona Lisa* stolen by a workman at the Louvre and returned a couple of years later . . .'

'. . . the Goya stolen by a bus driver from a major gallery and returned to a left-luggage office,' adds Beagle.

'There was a note with the egg,' says Stark.

'A ransom note?' Brown asks. 'Is this an art-napping?'

'It can't be,' says Beagle.

'What's art-napping?' I ask.

'It's when high-end thieves demand ransom in exchange for returning the art, but no professional pilferer returns the piece *before* getting paid,' Brown explains.

'I'll show you the note,' says Stark, taking out her phone and sharing a photo she took at the scene.

Brown and Beagle study the close-up. 'Is that . . . parchment paper?' Brown asks.

'More like two-ply,' Angela offers.

'The egg was found amongst rolls of toilet paper,' the detective explains.

Beagle hands the detective her phone.

Brown is shaking his head. 'It doesn't make sense. Organized thieves steal art as black-market collateral, and individual thieves are motivated by private possession. But this return? It doesn't fit any pattern I've ever seen. Thomas, do you get it?'

'I'm as baffled as you are, Bax,' his husband replies. 'But what I can say is any serious blackmailer would have upped the ante by now. And the good news is the egg is back, which means you can actually follow the advice on this note.'

'Meaning?' I ask.

'You can auction the egg,' says Brown.

'If I sell it, will the threats disappear?' I ask.

'It's hard to say,' Brown replies as he massages his chiseled jawline.

'I can't see why they wouldn't,' says Beagle.

'Plus, you'll be a multimillionaire. You can hire a private security detail to protect you for the rest of your life,' Brown reasons.

The very thought sounds horrific. 'All I want is for my life to return to normal, to marry Juan in peace and get back to our simple, happy existence.'

'Do not underestimate the power of money. With money, anything's possible,' says Beagle as he smooths his dark curls.

'This has been helpful,' Stark says as she stands. 'If you think of anything else that might help this investigation, call me right away.'

'Certainly,' says Brown, standing and assuming his full height.

We are about to make our way out of the office when a painting by the exit catches my eye.

'Who is that?' I ask as I stare at the remarkable portrait of a man in uniform awash in a purple backdrop, his face almost glowing, his eyes meeting mine as if he's about to step off the canvas and proffer a ring for kissing.

'Ah,' says Beagle. 'That's my grandfather, the late Baron Beagle.'

'He looks just like you,' Angela replies.

'The spitting image,' I say. Underneath his portrait, written in oil, is a line in Latin – '*Ars longa, vita brevis,*' I say, reading it out loud.

'Art is long, life is short,' says Beagle. 'My grandfather was a true connoisseur, an aficionado of priceless pieces. He taught me everything I know about art. I miss him terribly,' says Beagle, as he snatches his pocket square from his indigo jacket and wipes his watery eyes.

'He passed about a year ago,' Brown explains as he puts a consoling arm around his grieving husband. 'We're far from over it. We both loved that man dearly.'

'I'm sure you did,' I say. 'Have you considered doing an episode in his honor on *Hidden Treasures*? Your fans would love to hear your family's backstory.'

'My grandfather wouldn't have liked that,' says Beagle. 'He suffered several losses over his career, and he worked hard to claw his way back to success. He didn't like the spotlight.'

'Proving that the progeny doesn't always match the blood,' Brown quips as he playfully nudges his husband's arm. 'Am I right, Thomas?'

They both laugh.

'We'll leave you now,' says Stark.

'Thank you for your help,' I say.

'Think about it, Molly. Consider selling the egg,' says Brown. 'Life is short, but art is long.'

'I'll think about it,' I say as Baron Beagle's eagle eyes follow me out of the room.

CHAPTER 26

Dear Molly,

Faith is a wonderful thing. And being a believer is a virtue, provided what you believe in is the truth rather than lies. When faith is used for good, it can move mountains, but when it fuels injustice, it's a terrorizing force. Be careful what you believe in, Molly. And listen when your instincts speak.

When Penelope told me what Algernon had done to her, there was no question in my mind – I believed her. In my heart of hearts, I knew that man was capable of terrible things, and yet I'd ignored everything and everyone who'd tried to warn me. How I managed to deceive myself for as long as I did, I do not know, but when I heard Penelope, my foolish delusions evaporated along with any girlish dreams I'd had about marrying a prince of a man.

The second the Brauns left our house the day of Mrs Mead's

funeral, I petitioned my parents for a moment of their time. 'It's urgent,' I said. 'You need to hear this.'

We retired to Papa's office, where he sat in his Capital Throne and Mama perched on his desk beside him.

I launched into my story, reminding them of how on the day of the hunt, Algernon had requested that I take him on a tour of the manor.

'I recall,' said Papa. 'He complimented my office.'

'At some point, I left him to explore on his own,' I said. 'He all but ordered me away.'

'Neither your father nor I am inclined to stop a man's explorations, am I right, Reginald?' Mama prompted.

'I couldn't have put it better myself,' Papa replied.

'You don't understand. He went downstairs to the laundry room. He searched out Penelope. He . . . he—'

'Penelope? The maid-in-training?' my mother said.

'She must have called Algernon downstairs,' Papa surmised as he leaned back in his chair.

'Why would she do such a thing?' I asked. 'What had she to gain from that?'

My mother laughed out loud. 'What had she to gain from an illicit dalliance with one of the richest heir incumbents in the land? Reginald, why is our daughter as green as a bean?'

I hadn't even told them what happened, but they were acting like they already knew, as if they'd seen this play out so many times they didn't require the actual details. I told them how Penelope had once worked for the baron and baroness, how she'd seen Algernon there and how shortly thereafter, the entire staff was dismissed because some art disappeared.

'Oh, Flora. She's protecting herself,' said Papa. 'If I've learned anything in my years as an estate owner, it's that the help is often to blame.'

I couldn't believe my ears. Nothing I said seemed to matter. Next, I told them that Algernon had very likely stolen the egg and that he'd assaulted Penelope, then threatened her at Mrs Mead's funeral.

'That hardly sounds like a threat,' said Papa. 'He was merely warning the new maid of the dangers of wandering in the woods on her own. If Mrs Mead had heeded such a warning, maybe she'd still be alive today.'

'Mrs Mead was running to warn *all of us* about the Brauns,' I said, my voice cracking. 'She was trying to save me and she was trying to get justice for Penelope. None of us have been listening. We didn't want to accept the truth.'

My father stood then, his chair scraping loudly against the floor. 'What that young maid said proves nothing,' he pronounced. 'And instead of casting aspersions on Algernon, you should look closer to home. It's clear the police suspect John shot his own aunt. Maybe it was an accident, but what if it wasn't? Or what if his father is covering it up?'

'Uncle Willy?' I said in utter disbelief. 'He has been nothing but loyal to his sister and to this family. He's devoted his entire life to us. And that's how you treat him?'

'I told you before, Flora. You will call the butler "sir" or you will call him nothing at all. Do you understand?' My father said it quietly, but through the guise of tranquility, a storm was brewing.

'You're such a foolish girl,' said Mama, with a woeful shake of her head. 'You're not seeing straight.'

'You're wrong,' I said. 'I'm seeing for the first time. And if you don't want to acknowledge the truth about Algernon – and his parents, who'll defend him no matter what he does – there's nothing I can do about it.'

'This case is closed,' said Papa.

'You're not a judge,' I shot back.

'Maybe not, but I am your—'

'I'm not marrying him,' I said, cutting him off. 'I won't do it. I've made a terrible mistake. I won't marry Algernon.'

'Take it back,' said Mama, 'quickly.' Her voice was pinched, her hands worrying the pearls at her neck. She stood, bracing herself against the back wall of Papa's office.

Papa lunged at me, grabbing my wrist with one hand and shaking his closed fist in my face.

'I am your father,' he spat at me, his eyes like those of an angry god. 'You will do as I say. And mark my words, you will wed Algernon Braun.'

I don't know how I did it, but I escaped my father's grasp. I wriggled free and I ran from his office. I hurried down the grand staircase and out the glass doors of the conservatory. I ran without thinking, over the lawns, through the garden gate, down the pathway, past Mrs Mead's cottage to the knotty oak tree that bordered the property next to Papa's.

When I arrived, I wasn't alone. John was sitting under the tree. He'd changed out of his funeral clothes and was wearing a work shirt and overalls. He was holding something in his hands. It glinted in the fading light.

'Flora?' he said, surprised to see me.

I was bent over, catching my breath.

'Are you okay?' he asked.

'Yes,' I replied. 'No,' I said, changing my mind. 'I have no idea.'

He patted the long grass beside him. I sat down, leaning against the massive trunk, my shoulder touching his.

'Where's your father?' I asked.

'In town,' he replied. 'He's staying there tonight. He couldn't take it – the cottage. Too many memories.' As he said this, he turned over the shiny object in his hands. It was a gold Claddagh ring, with a heart in the middle held by two tiny hands.

'Your aunt's?' I asked.

'Her wedding ring,' he replied. 'When her husband died, she took it off and never wore it again. But I know she cherished it. It reminds me of her.'

I took John's hand and slipped the ring on his pinkie finger. 'There,' I said. 'A perfect fit. You should wear it for her.'

He nodded, his Adam's apple bobbing as he tried to keep the emotion down. 'Where were you running off to?' he asked.

'I don't know,' I replied. 'All I know is what I'm running from.'

I told him then – about Penelope's assault in the laundry

room, about how she suspected Algernon had stolen art from the baron, and about Algernon threatening her at the funeral. I watched as his jaw clenched.

'So that's why my aunt was running – to tell us everything Algernon had done.'

'She didn't want him to get away with it.'

John was speechless for some time. At last, he said, 'He shot her, but we'll never be able to prove it. He saw her coming, that's for sure. Maybe she confronted him in the woods. Somehow, he knew she was about to spill all his dirty secrets. My aunt always knew more than she let on, Flora. Maids take care of one another. There's a whisper network among them. The Farquars' maid told her Algernon had made unwanted advances on the Farquars' daughter. He was kicked out of college for that. The girl's parents went to the police, but the Brauns paid them off to make it all go away. People like the Brauns can weasel out of anything.' John's shoulders slumped. He picked at blades of grass in the small space between us.

'You tried to warn me, John. So did your aunt. This is all my fault,' I said as I broke down in tears.

He took my hands in his. 'No,' he said. 'The blame rests on the Brauns, not on you. My aunt loved you like her own daughter. She would have done anything for you, and there's nothing you could have done to stop her. There was something she wanted to give you, but she didn't quite know how.'

'What?' I asked.

He stood. 'I'll go get it,' he said.

He walked to the cottage, appearing a minute later with a leather-bound book under his arm. He sat down beside me, his back against the tree, his shoulder touching mine again. 'It's a diary,' he said, 'with a lock and key. She wanted to give this to you as a gift for passing your exams, but when you . . .'

'When I blew my education entirely,' I offered.

John smiled meekly. 'She didn't know what to do with this after. But I know she wanted you to have it. She told me so.'

He passed me the diary. I turned the key in the lock, and the book clicked open, revealing page after enticing blank page. 'I will cherish this always,' I said. 'Whatever will I write in it?'

'Your life story, maybe?' John suggested.

'As if anyone would be interested in that,' I replied.

'I would be,' he said, turning his beautiful brown eyes to me. 'Except I'd rather be in it than read about it.'

I stared at him for a good, long time, drinking in the sight of him. There he was, my beautiful John. How was it I had not seen earlier the vast difference between a frog and a prince? All that glitters isn't gold, Molly, and I learned that from John. He'd always been there, steadfast and true, not ostentatious or showy like Algernon and his kin. I'd mistaken the replica for the real thing, but in that moment I knew the difference. John was nothing like the Brauns, and he was most certainly nothing like Algernon. The man under that tree, even in mourning, was my heart's true desire, the love of my life. The light was fading, dusk on the edge of night.

'I have something to tell you,' John said. 'I got into university, on full scholarship, too. I leave this fall.'

'She told me, your aunt,' I said. 'She was so proud of you. But why didn't you tell me?'

'Well, we weren't really speaking. And I wasn't sure you wanted to know. Flora, it should have been you. You should be going away to school.'

'There's no one more deserving than you. You're going to be a university scholar,' I said. My joy for him was genuine. 'I have something to tell you, too,' I said. 'I'm not marrying him. Algernon Braun is a liar and a cheat, and other things so much worse I can't bear to name them. I just told my parents I'm not going through with it, but they refuse to accept the truth. My guess is that Algernon's parents paid off the police to stop all the investigations against him. What kind of people would do that?'

It was a question neither of us could answer.

'I've been living in a fog,' I said, 'bewitched by his family and my own. It took your aunt's death for me to snap out of it. I'm so ashamed.' I started to cry again.

John wrapped me in his arms, and I fell against his comforting chest. 'It's okay,' he said. 'She wouldn't want you to feel ashamed. She was so proud of you. If she was here, do you know what she'd say?'

'Everything will be okay in the end. If it's not okay, it's not the end,' I said, quoting one of Mrs Mead's favorites.

'Exactly.'

'John,' I said, drawing away to meet his eyes. 'There's another reason I can't marry Algernon.'

'What is it?' he asked.

'You. You're the reason. I love you, and I'm a fool for not always realizing.'

His eyes were searching mine, incredulous. 'Are you sure?' he asked. 'Is what you're saying really true?'

'I've never been more certain of anything in all my life,' I said.

'I may need you to repeat that. You might need to say it over and over for me to really believe you. Can you do that, Flora?'

'I can,' I said. 'And I will. It would be my pleasure.'

'Flora Gray, I love you. I always have.'

John's lips met mine, and our kiss was blissful. At long last, I had something I'd always wanted but thought I could never have. It felt warm and safe, thrilling and real. I don't know how long that kiss lasted, but eventually one of us pulled away. I leaned against him, feeling his heart beating, proof that life goes on despite the sorrow and loss.

'Do you remember at school when you asked me if I remembered this tree and the knothole when we were kids?' I asked him.

'You said you didn't remember.'

'I lied,' I replied. 'I do remember – that kind little boy with tousled brown hair and those eyes that belonged to a much older soul. You've always been you, John. You've always looked out for me. You cleaned up my storybook and you left it in the knothole for me to find,' I said, pointing to the hollow right above our heads.

'Must have been the fairies,' he said with a sly grin.

'No,' I replied. 'The only real magic is you.'

I won't go into details about what happened next, Molly, not because I'm hiding anything from you but because it was a moment so sacred that I struggle to capture it in words. Suffice it to say that what I learned that night as the sun set upon us is that love and loss, life and death exist in such close proximity. Sometimes the biggest losses lead to the greatest gains. Sometimes the darkest days end in the brightest nights.

We lay in each other's arms all night long, with the moon full overhead and the grass dewy beneath our skin. It was tender and fulfilling; it was familiar yet entirely new. It was everything my heart had ever desired. *He* was everything my heart desired. It was as if we were picking up where we'd left off on the dance floor – falling into perfect step. We fit each other like lock and key. It had always been that way, and it will always be. I'd found it at last. This, Molly. This was love.

CHAPTER 27

After meeting with the Bees, Detective Stark drops me off at home, and I spend the rest of the afternoon cleaning the apartment. I wash and wax the old parquet floors until they gleam and shine. I scour the rusty bathtub until I'm certain there's not a germ in it. In the living room, I consider dusting Gran's curio cabinet, but when my eyes land on her diary – the key lying beside it – I feel a sudden pang that hits me right in the heart, and I need to lie down.

I head to the bedroom, where I'm about to collapse in bed, but my feet have other ideas. They lead me to the closed door of the room I rarely enter, the space that Juan has been good enough to never suggest we turn into anything else than the shrine it has always been – Gran's bedroom. The door squeaks as I enter. The room is just as she left it years ago – her ruffled blue bedspread perfectly smoothed across her mattress, two plump pillows on top. On her bedside table the brass, heart-shaped jewelry box I bought her for Christmas years ago shines brightly, a beacon in the dark.

A wave of grief rolls over me. 'Oh, Gran,' I say out loud. I lie on her bed, hugging one of her pillows tight to my chest. 'Gran, what should I do? Should I sell the egg or not?' I ask out loud. 'What if someone really is out to get me? What if I'm in danger?'

Loud and clear, I hear Gran's answer as though she were perched right next to me – *Turn the page. Start a new chapter.*

I close my eyes, ruminating on her words, letting them soothe me. The next thing I know, I hear a key in the front door and Juan's tremulous voice calling, 'Molly? Where are you?'

I jump off the bed, rearranging the pillows and spread. I hurry out of the room, closing the door behind me.

Juan is standing in the living room, his shoulders tense. '*Dios mío,*' he says the second he lays eyes on me. 'What were you doing in there? Are you all right?' he asks as he gathers me in his arms.

'I'm perfectly well,' I say. 'I was going to clean Gran's room. Then I lay down for a moment, and I must have fallen asleep.'

'Good,' says Juan as he showers me with kisses.

'How was your shift at the hotel?' I ask.

'Regular. Nothing to report, except that Lily, Sunshine, Angela, and Sunitha all miss you. They told me to tell you that.'

'Thanks,' I say. 'I missed them today, too. And you,' I say.

Juan smiles, then goes to the door and locks it. 'Molly, I'm glad you're home safe.'

'Me, too,' I reply. 'Detective Stark took me to see the Bees. Turns out, it's not uncommon for stolen art to reappear. They don't think I have anything to worry about. Maybe the thieves got cold feet.'

'As long as *you* don't get cold feet,' says Juan as he takes my hand and leads me to the sofa in the living room.

'I'm afraid you're stuck with me, for better or for worse,' I say.

'Always for better,' he replies, 'but I'm concerned that with everything going on, we can't concentrate on our wedding. You still need a dress, and we need to figure out the reception.'

'Not to mention where we'll live after we're married,' I say. 'If Mr Rosso sells our apartment out from under us, where will we go?'

'I don't know,' says Juan. 'But let's not focus on that right now. Accentuate the positive, eliminate the negative, right?'

'Right,' I say.

'And speaking of positives, you're not going to believe this, but Cheryl apologized today.'

'Cheryl?' I say.

'She came to the kitchen this afternoon acting even shiftier than usual. I expected her to try to sell me swampland on the moon, but then she suddenly apologized for eating my giraffe marzipanimal in the morning.'

'I can't believe it,' I reply. 'She must want something. The question is: What?'

'Exactly,' he says.

'I have a funny feeling about all of this. The egg's disappearance and its return. It's like there's a puzzle piece right in front of me, but I can't quite see it. If I could just place it in its spot, the entire picture would be complete.'

'The *huevo* has always been a mystery.'

'Hard to crack,' I add, waiting for Juan to smile at my pun, which he does. 'The Bees want me to sell it. Should I?'

'You'd be rich,' he says, 'like they promised before.'

'A promise that failed to materialize,' I say.

'What will you do?' Juan asks.

'I don't know. I need to think it through. All I want is my life back, for things to return to normal for both of us.'

'All I want is to marry you,' says Juan, 'and for us to live happily ever after for the rest of our lives.'

'A fairy-tale ending,' I say.

'Just that.'

Juan gets up from the sofa to start dinner, and in an hour or so, we're eating a delicious stew that tastes so much like Gran's that when I close my eyes, I imagine she's sitting at the table with us. After we clean up, Juan and I watch a David Attenborough documentary about apex predators. Despite the high drama, Juan keeps nodding off, his head landing on my shoulder.

'I'm going to bed,' he announces when a shark attack startles him awake. 'Are you coming?'

'I think I'll read for a while,' I say.

'Okay, *mi amor.*' He kisses my forehead, then stands. 'Don't stay up too late. We have work tomorrow.'

'I'll be in bed soon,' I say.

He shuffles off to our bedroom, and I finish the documentary.

When it ends, I turn off the TV and sit quietly on the sofa, my mind churning. I look over at Gran's curio cabinet, where her diary sits on top. I take a deep breath, then grab it. I settle on the sofa, pulling Gran's lone-star quilt around me. I turn the key in the lock and begin reading.

Dear Molly,

I read one entry, then the next, then the next. Once I start, I can't stop. The pages turn, and her life, her history, unfurls before my eyes. It's as though I'm seeing her clearly for the very first time, this woman who was my everything and yet a mystery in many ways. All of the pieces fall into place – every choice she made, every decision, all the wisdom she imparted to me, lessons learned from her own mistakes.

To err once is human. To err twice is idiotic.

By 2:00 A.M., I've learned all about her parents and about the manor where she grew up. With each new entry, Gran comes more alive, more fully fleshed in the afterlife than she was when we sat on this sofa together, watching *Columbo.* And behind her I see another ghost taking shape, the outline of the formidable woman who helped Gran become who she was – not her birth mother but my great-aunt, Mrs Mead.

We had more in common than I ever realized – Gran and me. We both had mothers who failed us. Mrs Mead stepped in to care for Gran, and Gran stepped in to care for me.

There's a generosity to both decisions that moves me to my core. I have to stop reading because I can't see through my tears.

I go to the kitchen, where I make tea in Gran's favorite cup – the one with the cottage scene on it, a modest stone dwelling with a thatched roof and gardens all around. Oh my goodness. It wasn't just a teacup to her – it was a memory of hearth and home, of Mrs Mead standing by the stove while Gran did homework at her kitchen table.

With Gran's warm cup in hand, I nestle under her quilt in the living room, and I pick up reading where I left off.

Mr Preston – John. My gran-dad. He was always there in the background of her life, and yet she didn't always see him clearly. Oh, this man, the love of her life and her greatest loss. Frogs and princes, maids and butlers, barons and tycoons.

The pages turn and turn, the hours pass, but I cannot stop reading. I hear the birds stirring outside, dawn creeps up the sky, but I'm riveted to the page – Gran speaking to me from the great beyond.

Be careful what you wish for.
All that glitters isn't gold.
Love is the only gift that lasts.

I turn the last page, and I can't stop the tears that flow from my eyes. Never have I felt as close to Gran as I do in this moment. I clutch the diary to my chest, and I say *thank you* over and over and over.

This is how Juan finds me at 5:00 A.M., hugging an old leather-bound diary and talking to it as if it were alive.

'Molly, are you okay?' he asks.

'Never better,' I reply as I wipe my eyes.

He appears unconvinced. 'Did you stay up all night?'

'I did,' I reply.

'You read her diary?'

'Every last word,' I say. 'I know everything now.'

'Everything?' he asks.

'About me, about her, about who we really are and where we came from. It's all there between the lines,' I say. 'And I know who took it.'

'Who took what?' he asks.

'The Fabergé,' I say. 'And I might just know who returned it, too.'

CHAPTER 28

Dear Molly,

It is the prerogative of the young to rail against injustice, and it is the fate of the old to endure it. When you were a child, you railed against anything you perceived as unfair, wanting so much for the wrongs of this world to be righted. You had no notion that justice comes at a cost, one that is too often paid by those who can least afford it.

It will hurt you to know that Algernon never paid the price for anything he did. There was no further investigation into Mrs Mead's death. It was deemed an accident, and he escaped justice. As for everything else he did, it was swept under the carpet by his parents, who greased many a palm so their golden boy could slip through the loopholes they'd opened wide for him. I suspect Algernon Braun plundered and pillaged for the rest of his days.

When I asked Papa about everything I'd told him and what

the consequences would be, he said three words – 'Let it go.' And so I did, but I refused to let go of everything.

A few days after Mrs Mead's funeral, the Brauns were invited to the manor yet again – life going on as usual, as if Mrs Mead hadn't died, as if a girl in our retinue had not been egregiously wronged, as if I was going to marry Algernon and enact my parents' wishes.

I waited until after dinner, and when Penelope disappeared into the kitchen, I stood. 'I have an announcement,' I said in front of both families. 'Algernon, I'm not marrying you. Our engagement is off.'

'Is this a joke?' Algernon said, laughing. But he saw from my face that this was no laughing matter.

'I'm refusing a life with you. This marriage was my parents' will, not my own, and I'm not going through with it.'

There were few words after that. My mother stuttered and stammered. She even begged for the Brauns' forgiveness, claiming that I was out of my wits and would soon apologize. My father remained statue still, saying nothing. Priscilla and Magnus rose from the table and silently marched their son out of the banquet room, past the parlor, through the portrait corridor of our long-lost relatives, and out the front door of Gray Manor, which Uncle Willy held wide open.

My parents watched as Magnus and his family turned their backs on us. Once outside, Magnus stopped between two imposing Roman columns. He turned around, to address not me but my father. 'You won't get away with this,' he said. And with that, all three of them left for good.

The moment Uncle Willy closed the manor door behind them, I ran to my bedroom, for I knew if I didn't move fast, I'd suffer the full wrath of Papa's rage.

Uncle Willy and John had known ahead of time what I was planning to announce, and they were primed for the aftermath. Papa rushed up the grand staircase after me, and Uncle Willy followed, stopping my father before he entered the heavy double doors to my bedroom. Buried under my quilts, I heard words exchanged, but Uncle Willy, who'd always been a gatekeeper, now forbade his employer from entering his own daughter's room.

My father's heavy footsteps retreated down the hallway. Next, I heard the slamming of his office door. Then came the bellowing roar as whatever rage he'd reserved for me no doubt befell my mother.

My bedroom door opened, and Uncle Willy's face appeared. He nodded, and I got out of bed. He accompanied me down the servants' back staircase, and I ran out of the conservatory, over the lawns, and through the garden gate to where John was waiting to take me to the safety of Mrs Mead's cottage. That night, I slept in her bed while my beloved John and dear Uncle Willy kept vigil by the cottage door.

The next day the sun rose, though in truth I had doubted it would. Uncle Willy went to work at the manor, and around noon, he returned to tell me it was safe for me to go home. Whatever he said to my parents I was not privy to it, but Papa ceased to be a physical threat. Still, when I walked into the manor, Mama and Papa were as cold as ice. They could barely look at me, said not a word to me, no matter how I tried to make amends. I'd lost my golden sheen; I was no longer their darling girl, and while my presence was tolerated, it was clear I was an impediment to their aspirations, living proof that a girl is but a burden.

As the days passed, when I wasn't sneaking to the cottage to visit my beloved John, taking refuge in his arms and his love, I holed myself up in the library and read book after book. I knew Papa kept the Fabergé hidden in the filing cabinet in his office, and one day when he wasn't around, before the Brauns could ask for it back, I took what was mine. I hid the egg behind a stack of my favorite novels in the library, and my parents, so distraught about losing the Brauns' favor, failed to notice the egg was gone. Sometimes, I would shift the stack just to look at the beautiful, shiny object. At the height of my despair, I even talked to it. 'Beware,' I warned it. 'You may be a coveted treasure one day and pitched to the curb the next. I would know.'

It wasn't long after that the men in black – Magnus's henchmen, his corporate fixers – came knocking on the manor door. They brought back the original divestment papers to be signed by Papa with a deadline of under a week. The merger between the Brauns and the Grays was officially dead, and my father's firm would soon be dissolved, his assets stripped away.

Papa paced the hallways, rarely coming to the banquet room for meals. Mama perpetually smelled of vodka and lime.

She stumbled about the manor, ordering staff around, except they were figments of her imagination – ghosts from a bygone era. Not even Penelope worked for us anymore. She simply failed to show up one day, and as for the other servants, Papa couldn't afford them without the merger, so all but Uncle Willy left, with no thanks or pay.

I soon learned to cook my own meals, simple fare – egg on toast, or crumpets with tea. For the first time in my life, there was no one to serve me, and so I re-created from memory dishes that Mrs Mead had made as I'd watched, my little legs swinging back and forth under her cottage kitchen table. Sometimes, I would sneak out to eat with John and Uncle Willy at the cottage, and on those occasions, there was something so sustaining about Mrs Mead's hearth, a pot of stew simmering on it, though it would never taste as good as hers.

I wasn't very hungry in those weeks when everything fell apart. In fact, I had trouble keeping food down. At first, I chocked it up to stress – to being undone by grief and uncertainty about what my future would hold. It was as if a pox had descended on our household, a curse on the entire Gray family.

But it wasn't this curse that soon concerned me most, for there was another causing great apprehension. In those days, that's what we called a woman's monthlies, Molly – the curse. It had been weeks since I'd bled, and at first, I'd ignored this lapse, until I could ignore it no longer.

One afternoon, when Uncle Willy was helping movers cart off antiques from the manor, I went to the cottage to break the news to John.

'I'm late,' I said.

'You're early. Dinner's at six.'

'You're not following,' I replied.

He looked at me, reading the meaning in my eyes.

'Are you sure?' he asked. 'Really?'

'Yes,' I said. 'I don't know what to do. I'm so ashamed.'

I expected him to rage and fume, to call me loose and blame me for our indiscretions, but of course, I was confusing him with other men I'd known.

'There is no reason for shame,' he said. 'I'm overjoyed, Flora! I can't believe my luck.' He picked me up and spun me around in his arms. He held me tight, spilling tears of joy on my shoulders. I felt fortunate and doomed at the same time.

We visited a doctor, who confirmed what I already knew. And next, we told Uncle Willy. He took it stoically, his feelings clearly mixed, but he, too, spilled tears of joy for us all.

He held my hand and John's on Mrs Mead's kitchen table. 'If only she'd lived to see the day. It was her biggest dream, you know, that the two of you would find each other one day, a hope lodged in her heart, one that I dashed regularly, thinking it too preposterous to imagine. And now, here it is, as though she willed it into being.' He went quiet for a moment. 'But what about university, John?'

'I'll defer. I'll go some other year. I'll find us all a place to live. I'll get a job. We'll get away from this cursed manor, all of us. Life will finally begin.'

Life will end, I thought to myself, and I wonder if Uncle Willy had the same thought but was too good to voice it.

'Where there's a will, there's a way,' he said. 'That's what my sister used to say. We'll figure everything out in good time.'

The next day, Uncle Willy found me in Papa's library and told me to go to the cottage right away. 'John's waiting for you,' he said.

When I sneaked out the back and made my way to the cottage, John wasn't there, but a trail of wild rose petals plucked from their blooms marked a path to the old oak tree. Standing beside it was the love of my life. He got down on one knee and proposed to me right there. I said yes, and he took the Claddagh ring from his pinkie and put it on my ring finger – a perfect fit.

There was only one thing to do after that – tell my parents. I begged them for a moment of their time, and we assembled in Papa's office. His desk and Capital Throne were gone, sold to the highest bidder and replaced with an old folding card table and chair from the basement.

'I am with child,' I said simply, expecting to be disowned on the spot.

Mama looked at Papa, her face filled with an emotion I could hardly comprehend given what I'd just said. Her eyes were bright with hope. 'But this is a miracle,' she said. 'This is fate ordained!'

'My dear girl,' said Papa as he rose to his full height and gently placed his hands on my cheeks. 'This is wonderful news.'

'He'll have to marry you now,' said Mama.

Only then did I realize what they'd both assumed. 'It's John,' I said. 'John is the father.'

A storm cloud came over Papa, a great darkness enveloping him. He grabbed both of my arms. 'That's a lie. Tell me it's a lie!' he growled.

'It's the truth,' I said, as I tried in vain to pull away.

'The butler's boy had his way with you? Under my roof?' Papa boomed.

'He won't get away with this!' said Mama.

'John is not to blame,' I explained. 'I love him, and we're engaged.'

Papa looked down at the ring on my finger, and for a minute I thought he would spit on it, but he unhanded me then and stormed out of his office.

'Where are you going?' I asked as I rushed down the stairs after him.

He marched all the way to the front of the manor, where Uncle Willy stood vigil by the door.

'You're fired,' he said. 'Leave the manor immediately – you and your wretched son. He raped my daughter. If you don't leave now, I'll skin him alive.'

Uncle Willy merely bowed his head, as though he'd been expecting this and only this. He strode past my father and took my hand in his, about to march out the stately front door with me in tow.

'Leave her,' my father snarled as he broke our connected hands. 'Be gone!' he roared; then he pushed Uncle Willy out, slamming and locking the door behind him.

Papa turned to me, gripping my jaw in his viselike hands. 'You're a disgraced woman. You're good for nothing now. Go!'

he yelled. Then he landed a strong and sudden blow to my face.

Cradling my stinging cheek, I ran to my room, and I hid in my bed, quaking.

Mama came in a few minutes later. She sat on the edge of my mattress, and I wished it was Mrs Mead perched there, not her. 'You had it coming,' Mama pronounced. 'Let me see?'

She drew the covers away, examining my swollen cheek.

'I've seen worse,' she said.

So had I, on her face.

'You're not the first girl to disgrace herself, Flora, and you won't be the last. Once he calms down, I'll talk to him. No one has to know. There are ways out of this, you know.'

What she then proposed was a nightmare vision, a visit to a secret kind of doctor I vaguely knew existed.

'I can't do that,' I said. 'I won't.'

'Then we'll send you to a birth house. This is what's done, Flora. If you weren't so naïve, you'd know that. You'll have the baby, and no one will be the wiser. You'll go for "a stint in the countryside, a finishing school for girls," then you'll return in ten months or so as though nothing ever happened.'

'But what about my baby?' I asked.

'What does it matter so long as it disappears? After the birth, you and the bastard child will both get a fresh start. Your father will keep quiet if he thinks he can use you to leverage getting close to a family of stature. We need that now more than ever.'

So many thoughts swirled in my head. Two roads diverged.

John and Uncle Willy were banned from the manor, and I was certain John would want me to leave with them, but where would we go? John was willing to give up everything, to surrender his only chance at education and bettering himself, all for me and his unborn child. I could go with him, or I could do what my mother had proposed – disappear into a birth house, where I would have the baby, then return to Mama and Papa, and to this life, as though none of it had ever happened.

I considered the two possibilities, my mind racing. I decided on the spot. I came up with the plan.

'Take me to a birth house,' I told Mama. 'Make it all disappear.'

'I'll make arrangements. You'll leave in a few days. You'll come back a new woman, Flora, refreshed and reborn. Your father and I won't say a word. We'll find the right family for you to marry into.'

She brought me ice for my face, and when she left to find my father, I tiptoed down the corridor to the servants' staircase. I scurried out the conservatory door, making my way to the cottage. Uncle Willy was packing in the bedroom. John was emptying the kitchen cupboards.

'Oh, Flora,' John said the second he saw my face.

'It's just a bruise,' I said. 'It's not so bad.'

'Did he . . . Please tell me he didn't . . .'

I knew what he was asking. 'He hit only my face,' I said.

'Thank heavens,' he said as he drew me close. 'He fired my father,' John said. 'We have to leave right away. You're coming with us. He's a maniac and a tyrant. You'll be safe with us, Flora.'

'Where will you go?' I asked.

'In town for the night. After that, we don't know.'

'You're coming, Flora, right?' John begged.

'Have you deferred your university enrollment?' I asked.

'Not yet, but I will. That doesn't matter right now.'

'There's no rush deferring,' I said. 'And, John, I don't think I should go with you just yet, not in my condition. I'll slow you and Uncle Willy down. I can hardly keep anything down these days. I can't just sleep anywhere the way you and he can. In my state, I need to be careful.'

'But I can't leave you behind,' he said. 'Look what he did to you.'

'Papa's had his rage. The worst is over. I'll find you soon.'

'When?' he asked, confused.

'Come back for me in a week's time, once you're more settled. I'll have my suitcase ready. We'll meet at noon at the old oak tree, and you can take me with you to wherever you are. I'll be waiting for you,' I said.

'We'll start our lives over. We'll be a perfect little family, just the four of us.'

I nodded, my tears obscuring my sight. 'What will Uncle Willy do for work now?' I asked.

'I have no idea,' said John. 'Nobody even knows what a butler is these days. At his age, he may not find another job. He's worried, but he won't say it.' He put his hands on my shoulders. 'So we have a plan? You'll meet me at the oak tree in a week's time? I'll have a room ready for you, Flora. I can't promise it'll be posh, but I'll take care of you, no matter what.'

'I know,' I said. 'I have to go. They can't catch me here.'

'I love you, Flora,' he said.

I held him tight, and I told him I loved him more than anyone in the world. Then I turned my back on him and ran toward the only life I'd ever known.

True to her word, my mother took care of all the details, and a few days later, I was shipped to a birth house far from the manor. There was no way I was going to let John ruin his future the way I had, his only chance at freedom from a life of servitude.

A week later, John would show up at noon at the old oak tree, expecting to find me there, suitcase in hand. But I would be long gone. He would look in the knothole, and there, to his great disappointment, he would discover what the fairies had left for him – a gold treasure, the Claddagh ring, a heart held in two tiny hands.

This is what you do, Molly, for those you love. You make sacrifices, and when you have no other choice, you set them free.

CHAPTER 29

'Molly, your eyes are open and you're speaking, but I think you're asleep. You're not making sense, that's for sure,' says Juan as he stands in the living room, looking down at me at 5:00 A.M.

I'm wrapped in Gran's quilt on the sofa, cradling her diary like a baby. My eyes are puffy, and I haven't slept a wink. I know I sound like a lunatic. 'I'm wide awake, Juan. I promise you,' I say. 'I've read every word that Gran wrote. This diary is the answer to everything.'

'Okay,' says Juan. 'Explain.'

He sits down beside me. He scratches his bedhead, which is crested like a rooster's coxcomb. I recount in short form everything I've just read about Gran's early life – how she grew up surrounded by wealth and privilege, yet the opulent manor she lived in was never a warm home. I tell him about her parents, how cruel they could be, how love meant so little to them that they'd even sacrifice their own daughter for financial gain. I introduce him to dear Mrs Mead, my great-gran-dad's sister, a mother to so many, a woman who died too young. And I tell him about my gran-dad, too, who appears on almost every page.

'It's a love story like no other,' I say. 'When you read this, you'll see Mr Preston in a different light. He loved Flora with his whole heart, and she loved him with all of hers.'

'Molly, that's nice,' says Juan. 'But what does any of that have to do with the Fabergé?'

'Gran was never a thief,' I say. 'Anything she took was hers by right. I know that for a fact.'

'Molly,' Juan says as he grabs my hand. 'What about the golden *huevo*?'

I tell him about the Fabergé, how it was given to Gran as an engagement gift, hers and hers alone. I reveal all the pressure put on her to marry Algernon – a fly-by-night, a thief, a wolf in sheep's clothing, and many things even worse. I explain the intricacies, the complications, the dropped clues that Gran wouldn't have known she was dropping, for she had no idea that the egg would one day find its way back to me, that I would hold it in my hands and keep it on a shelf in her curio cabinet – her history twinkling before my very eyes.

Juan is looking at me like I've truly lost the thread. '*Café*?' he offers. 'I think you need some.'

'Please,' I say. 'Hear me out.'

He nods and refocuses, trying to put the pieces together.

I recount Gran's journey after she left the manor, connecting the dots to what must have transpired, leading all the way to her curio cabinet in this apartment.

'Sometimes, it's not what's on the page that tells you the most, it's the blank space in the margins – like the outline at the scene of a crime that proves a body was once there even well after it's gone.'

I reach for my phone on the side table. I dial a number.

'Who on earth are you calling?' Juan asks. 'It's just after 5:00 A.M.'

'Detective Stark,' I reply. 'She has to hear this.'

'Now?' says Juan.

'As Gran would say, *there's no time like the present.*'

Juan makes some coffee and brings out a tray with crumpets, honey, and jam. He puts the spread on the living room table beside Gran's diary. 'The detective should be here any minute,' he says.

'Yes,' I say. 'And the others.'

After trying – and failing – to explain to Juan everything I learned from Gran's diary, I made a series of calls, first to Detective Stark, then to my gran-dad, and finally, to Angela.

As usual, Angela's was the most colorful response. 'For the love of ducks, it's still dark out, Molly. You need me to come over *now*?'

'You don't have to,' I said. 'But the detective's on her way. She was very interested in what I told her on the phone.'

'I'll be there. But there better be coffee.'

Now, I'm pacing in the living room, thinking about how I'll explain it to everyone when they arrive.

There's a knock on the door. I rush to the peephole and see my gran-dad looking as bleary-eyed as I feel. The second he enters, I rush at him, hugging him as tight as I can.

'Good heavens, Molly,' he says from the midst of my full-body grip. 'What's all this?'

'You loved her so much,' I say, squeezing him even harder.

'Your gran? Of course I did,' he says as he tries, unsuccessfully, to free himself from my grip. 'But you knew that.'

'Not the way I do now,' I say. 'Her diary. It's a tell-all. And you – you kept so many secrets!'

'I did not,' he says.

'You and Gran came from totally different worlds. You were set to go to university. Your father was a butler.'

'But I've told you those things before,' he says.

He's right. He has. And yet that only proves you can know something – it can be staring you right in the face – and the deeper meaning can escape you entirely.

'Your aunt, Mrs Mead, she died a tragic death. This Claddagh ring,' I say, pointing to it on my finger, 'it was hers before it was Gran's. Your father, William Preston – a.k.a. Uncle Willy – he was my great-grandfather's butler!'

'All true,' says my gran-dad. 'I suppose I never shared those particular details. Didn't see the point. Like your gran used to say, *it's all water under the bridge.*'

'She loved you with her entire being,' I say. 'She really did.'

'Molly,' Juan says, 'If you don't let go of Mr Preston soon, he's going to lose circulation.'

'Sorry,' I say, releasing him. 'I've had quite a night. I feel like I'm seeing for the very first time.'

'Molly, you said on the phone that you know more about the egg,' says Gran-dad.

'Yes,' I say. 'I do.'

'Hello? Can we come in? And if you hug me like that, I swear I'll scream blue murder,' Angela warns. She and Detective Stark are standing behind my gran-dad. Angela looks like the Bride of Frankenstein, her red hair in statically charged disarray. Detective Stark is wearing a tracksuit, her hoodie pulled over her head. They both appear barely conscious, though they've certainly had more sleep than I have.

'Come in,' I say. 'I know it's early.'

'This better be good, Molly,' says Stark.

'Have a seat,' says Juan after he wipes down everyone's shoes and stores them neatly in the front closet.

We gather in the living room, and I wait until everyone has coffee before speaking. 'Thanks to Gran's diary,' I say, as I hold it in my hands, 'I've deduced a string of crucial clues that connects us to the culprits who stole the egg,' I say.

'And who are they?' Stark asks.

'To figure that out, you have to follow the trail.'

'Great,' says Stark. 'A six A.M. treasure hunt.'

'The Bees are connected,' I say. 'But the question is how and to what end. When she was young, my gran was about to marry into a wealthy family firm. The husband and wife,

Magnus and Priscilla Braun, dealt in art,' I say. 'Isn't that right, Gran-dad?'

'Not exactly,' he replies. 'They were certainly wealthy, but theirs was an investment firm.'

'At first,' I say, 'but at some point, that changed. They were definitely art collectors.' I find the entry in Gran's diary where she talks about visiting the Braun household, going from room to room full of priceless antiquities. I pass the diary to Gran-dad.

'I never stepped foot in the Braun mansion. I had no idea Priscilla Braun was an art collector,' he says as he passes the diary to Detective Stark.

'And their last name – Braun,' I say. 'Gran-dad, did you never connect it to the Bees?'

'Why would I?' he asks.

'Braun means Brown,' I say. 'It's the same name.'

'And the easiest thing for a family of pedigree to modify their last name – especially if they were trying to hide something,' says Stark.

'Now look at this,' I say as I take back the diary in my shaking hands. I flip through it to find the entry where Algernon admits to Gran that the egg was stolen by father and son. I read Algernon's chilling words out loud – '"What we want, we take." And see here?' I add. 'Gran asked her fiancé about a baron who Magnus Braun was about to go into business with before getting cozy with us Grays. A *baron*,' I say, waiting for someone to connect the dots.

'Beagle's grandfather was a baron,' Juan says.

'That portrait in their office. The baron died a year ago,' Angela adds.

'Touché,' I reply.

'Show me where Baron Beagle is named,' Detective Stark says, putting down her coffee for the first time.

'I can't,' I say. 'Because Gran doesn't name him, not specifically, but a couple of times, she references a baron who was an art dealer. Her parents knew him. The baron and baroness came to a ball at Gray Manor.'

'Goodness,' says my gran-dad. 'They did. The Workers' Ball was a big to-do that year, because Magnus Braun *and* a baron were in attendance.'

'But was the baron a Beagle?' Stark asks. 'Did you meet him, Mr Preston?'

'Me? Meet the baron?' Gran-dad says. 'I was a fill-in footman. The Grays would never have introduced me to someone of such high status. Plus, I had eyes for only one person that night.'

'My gran,' I say. 'You danced with her. You fell into lock step.'

'Did she say that?' Gran-dad asks, his eyes glassy when they meet mine.

'She did,' I reply.

'Mr Preston, I didn't know you danced,' says Juan.

'Another well-kept secret,' I reply.

'Please, can we keep this moving?' Stark asks. 'Molly, what you're saying is that your grandmother was connected to both the Braun *and* Beagle families via the egg. And, Mr Preston, you never knew about that?'

'I had no idea. The Brauns were dubious, though,' he replies. 'And years ago, when I worked as a gatekeeper for the Grimthorpes, I never saw the egg because I was never allowed in the mansion. The first time I laid eyes on the thing was in that curio cabinet after Molly brought it here one day. And the only Fabergé Flora ever referenced was her bank account.'

'Our joint savings,' I say. 'She always called it the "Fabergé."'

'Coincidence?' Angela asks.

'Probably not,' says Stark.

'If the Bees have a legit claim on the egg, why didn't they just say so when it first appeared on their show?' Juan asks.

'Because they're hiding something,' says Angela as her fiery hair sways.

'We should let the Bees read the diary entries and hear what they have to say,' I suggest.

'That's exactly what we shouldn't do,' Stark replies. 'They may not deny the connection, but they won't reveal the truth either. If we want to get to the bottom of this, we have to ambush them.'

'But how?' asks Gran-dad.

'A sting,' says Angela as she suddenly pops to her feet.

'Tell me more,' says Stark as she puts her coffee down.

'The note. It's telling us what they want us to do,' says Angela. 'We need to follow their advice. Molly needs to sell the egg.'

'I don't understand,' Mr Preston says.

'If the Bees are really behind the egg's disappearance and

return,' Angela explains, 'we'll only know why once there's a winning bid on it. The second that egg is sold and the Bees are alone together, they'll discuss their motives and their plans. If we're listening in, we'll piece it all together. We'll know what they've been up to this whole time – and why.'

'Bingo,' says Juan.

'They know the hotel has no surveillance – "guest privacy is paramount at the Regency Grand,"' says Mr Preston. 'What if that's why they insisted the auction happen there in the first place?'

'So no cameras could catch anything going on outside of the tearoom,' I add.

'Remember,' Angela says. 'The Bees have no idea that we know they're connected to all of this, which is why the plan only works if we keep that diary a secret.'

'It's our ace in the hole,' says Stark.

'So we set up a ruse to make it appear that the egg has been bought by some big, rich collector,' says Angela.

'And we hold the auction at the hotel,' Stark adds, 'but this time, we have hidden eyes and ears and cameras everywhere.'

'Mark my words, the second that auction is over, if we're listening in and the Bees don't know it, we'll know what they've done,' Angela says.

'They won't see it coming,' I add.

'But to do that, doesn't Molly have to agree to sell the Fabergé?' asks Juan.

'Of course,' says Stark. 'Molly, do you agree?'

'Agree to what exactly?' I ask.

'To stinging the Bees,' says Angela.

'And to saying *hasta luego* to the golden *huevo*,' says Juan.

'Molly, it's worth a try,' says Detective Stark. 'The only way to crack this egg is to sell it.'

CHAPTER 30

Dear Molly,

Life is unpredictable. Like an episode of *Columbo,* it never turns out quite the way you think it will. Some hitch takes things in a new direction you could never have foreseen from the outset.

So it was for me when at the age of seventeen, pregnant, I left the only home I'd ever known. In my suitcase, I packed my roomiest clothes, the blank diary from Mrs Mead, a little bit of cash, and the Fabergé egg, which neither Papa nor Mama knew I'd taken with me.

There was no fanfare at my departure. I said a curt goodbye to Mama, but Papa refused to see me off. A black car arrived and a chauffeur I'd never met before drove me hours away to a sagging, unmarked farmhouse in the nondescript countryside, where I was greeted by Mrs Lynch, the stern-faced matron who ran the place. She had straight black hair and slits for eyes. Judgment was writ so large on her face that it was no surprise when her first words to me were, 'So you got yourself in trouble.'

Though I wasn't yet showing, she stared at my midriff as though the devil itself was lodged in my womb. I expected Mrs Lynch to take my suitcase and show me into the farmhouse, but she walked right past me to the chauffeur's window, where he handed her an envelope, which disappeared into her bosom.

The car drove away, and wordlessly she marched toward the house as I followed, suitcase in hand. The house was clean and spare, with wood finishings polished to a high shine, homemade white eyelet curtains on every window, and wooden floors that groaned as though the burden of feet upon them was too much to bear.

I was escorted to a room upstairs, Mrs Lynch pointing out the door and then turning on her heel to leave. But when I opened that door, the room was occupied.

'Mrs Lynch,' I said. 'This is the wrong room. There are three girls in here already.'

She looked at me wryly. 'Did you expect a private apartment complete with maid and room service?' She laughed, a sound bereft of all joy. 'Yours is the fourth bunk, farthest from the window. The girls don't bite – unless you deserve it.' She turned and walked away.

I crept into the room and stood there as three wide-eyed young ladies, their pregnancies much more advanced than mine, assessed me from head to toe.

'So you're the new one,' said a girl with a moon face and big blue eyes.

'Miss Moneybags the Turd,' said a short, curly-haired girl as she crossed her arms against her sizable belly.

'Look at her suitcase, all prissy and proper. Are you Mary Friggin' Poppins?' asked the third, an olive-skinned girl in a dress so worn, I could see the silhouette of her skinny legs clear through it.

'I'm Flora Gray,' I said, putting down my suitcase to curtsy. 'Pleased to meet you all.'

The moon-faced girl came to my side. 'Don't let them scare you,' she said. 'They've just never met a princess before.'

'Oh, I'm not a princess,' I said.

'The hell you aren't,' said the spindly girl, as she pointed at my silk blouse.

'I'm Amelia,' said the moon-faced girl by my side. 'That's Bridget,' she said, nodding toward the curly-haired girl, 'and that's Dolores,' she added, gesturing to the spindly one with olive skin. 'This is your bunk.' She picked up my suitcase and brought it over to a worn bunk bed, pointing to the mattress on top.

'Lovely,' I said, as I looked around for a closet or a chest of drawers, but there was none. The other girls didn't seem to have possessions, and I noticed that while clean, their shoes looked as worn out as the girls themselves. They'd all lost their sheen and shine.

I knew instantly that I didn't belong. I'd never met girls like these, or if I had, I'd ignored them, believed I was above them.

I soon learned that none of these girls could read. They hadn't even made it through primary school, forced by circumstance and necessity to work from an early age. Their families were nuclear only in the sense of combustion, and they'd been handed off to some relative or 'family friend' who'd shown them little care and who'd rendered them powerless and penniless.

I couldn't believe Mama had sent me to such a place. At first, I thought there must be some mistake.

Mrs Lynch greeted me at breakfast in the dining room the day after my arrival.

'How'd you sleep?' she asked. 'Everything up to snuff?'

'Actually,' I said sheepishly. 'The room is a tad drafty, and the mattress is quite worn. The springs are poking through. I don't suppose you could spare another blanket and pillow?'

'Of course!' she replied. 'While I'm at it, why don't I get you a free stay at the Ritz. I hear the staff check for peas under the mattresses so your beauty rest isn't disturbed,' she said, punctuating this with a mock curtsy that made all the girls laugh.

As you can guess, no extra blanket or pillow ever appeared, and I was not moved to the Ritz, or anywhere for that matter. In fact, my pillow soon vanished, and only a week later did I see it again, on top of the manure pile by the barn. I slept with my head on my suitcase, and when no one was watching, I stuffed the Fabergé and the diary into my mattress, safely hidden under the popped coils.

My only solace at the farmhouse was Amelia, the moon-faced girl. She was kind and gentle, clearly underprivileged, but a walking heart. She kept me safe from the others. And she truly believed I was a princess. Nothing I could say would convince her otherwise. She begged to hear about my life, and I shared with her.

'I lived in a manor house,' I said. 'With Mama and Papa.'

'Was there a butler?' she asked.

'Yes,' I replied.

'And a maid?'

'More than one,' I answered.

'Was there a ballroom?' she asked.

'Indeed,' I replied. 'And a parlor, and a library, and a conservatory.'

'See?' she said. 'You *are* a princess.'

She asked me question after question, demanding every detail, delighting in every nuance I shared.

'Tell me again about your father's library,' she'd say. 'How many shelves of books? And the volumes had gold writing on the spines?'

'Yes,' I replied.

'And the silver pantry in the basement. Describe it again.'

I would detail the rows and rows of platters and chargers, gravy dishes and silver spoons that Mrs Mead and Penelope polished to a high shine. As we folded clothes, scrubbed floors, or toiled over boiling pots in the kitchen, Amelia would listen to me describe every detail of Gray Manor, for this is how we whiled away the time in the farmhouse, not sprawled on lounge chairs while our bellies burgeoned, but put to hard labor as penance for our sins.

Mrs Lynch worked us to the bone. There was a laundry in the basement that serviced well-to-do households in town; a chicken coop that yielded eggs sold by Mrs Lynch at the back door; a garden we tended with vegetables sent to Sunday market; curtains, coverlets, and quilts all sewn by hand and sold to a high-end boutique in town. There was nothing Mrs Lynch didn't monetize, the money always going straight to her bosom. I swear there was a bank in there, filled with funds for her and her alone.

For my months at the farmhouse, I woke before dawn and went to bed just after dusk, exhausted and worn. I got used to my rusty mattress and learned to sleep through anything – springs digging into my side, snoring and nightmares, weeping in the dead of night (an altogether common sound). Every night, I prayed I'd done the right thing, reminded myself that I had chosen this for the sake of John, so that he would not have to suffer for my mistakes. It would only be a few months, and then I would go back home to the life I knew.

All the while, the baby in my belly grew, and one day, as I held my hand to it, I felt that little being ripple and move. Then, it was stronger, doing kicks and somersaults. At night, when I couldn't sleep, I felt the shift beneath my palms, and I swear I could feel that baby trying to reach for my hand. Molly, my unborn child became my best friend. In my mind, I spoke to it and reassured it. 'We'll get through this – you and me. Where there's a will, there's a way.'

One day, as Amelia and I were sweeping out the chicken coop, I decided to ask her a burning question. By that point, her belly was as round as her face, and I knew her time was coming soon. 'Amelia, who's the father?' I ventured, thinking we were close enough that I could ask.

She put down her broom, her big blue eyes wide with shock.

'Never, ever ask that,' she whispered. 'If you'd asked any of the other girls, they'd've scratched your eyes out.'

I was shocked and speechless. 'I'm sorry,' I said.

'We don't all live in manor houses, Flora. For us, there's no fairy-tale ending.'

I apologized again, and she picked up her broom, sweeping my comment out of the coop alongside the excrement.

Once a month, all of us girls were taken to what they called the 'giddyup room'. It was a small office on the main floor, where our feet were put in stirrups, and we were poked and prodded by a visiting physician. Mrs Lynch stood vigil in the room, and when the doctor pronounced his verdict, 'Fit as a fiddle,' in my case or 'Anemic. Needs more meat,' about Amelia, he spoke only to Mrs Lynch. It was as if we mothers-to-be were not even there.

Sometimes, well-dressed couples would visit the farmhouse, and as we toiled away in the laundry or stooped in the garden, Mrs Lynch would bring them around to look at us. They'd whisper and point like we were zoo animals, and we girls were instructed not to address them directly. These silent visits were reminders of what would happen to our babies once they were born, something none of us could bear to think about or even discuss amongst ourselves.

Two months went by, and I had no word from my parents. I asked Mrs Lynch every day if she'd received a call, a telegram, a letter – anything.

She shrugged and said, 'No.'

But one day when she was out of earshot, Amelia found me. 'She burns mail, you know. I've seen her. Takes the checks out, then burns the rest. Don't give up hope. Your parents are waiting for you.'

Whether that was true or not, I never found out, but her words lit a much-needed candle in the dark.

After three full months, I still had not experienced a birth in the farmhouse, and as it turned out, the first I witnessed was Amelia's. She went into labor in the middle of the night, waking me with her piercing scream. Mrs Lynch and the girls, myself included, led her to the giddyup room, where she lay on the examining table. Her moon face was ashen and covered in sweat. Mrs Lynch and some of the girls knew the drill, prompted her to push, offered her a hand to squeeze. I had no idea what to do and watched from the sidelines, flinching with every bloodcurdling cry.

I will save you from the details of what occurred next, Molly, but suffice it to say things did not go well. The doctor was called but far too late. When he arrived, he checked Amelia's pulse and shook his head. He looked around and diagnosed the patient in two sharp statements. 'Hemorrhage,' he said to Mrs Lynch. 'Nothing to be done.'

'Get a sheet from the laundry downstairs,' Mrs Lynch ordered, but my feet were stuck to the floor, my eyes glued to the savage scene on the table in front of me. 'Go! Make yourself useful.'

I rushed off, returning a few moments later with a sheet as thin as a shroud.

Dolores took it from me and laid it over Amelia's pale body, covering both her and the silent pink bundle one of the girls had placed in the crook of her lifeless arm. Eventually, a hearse arrived at the house, and Amelia was loaded into it, though the pink bundle remained behind on the giddyup table.

Everyone knew the next steps, had clearly been through this, either at the farmhouse or in their lives before. At dawn, while Mrs Lynch watched from a window, I followed the girls to the field beyond the garden, where crooked barn-board crosses nestled amongst tall, swaying grasses. I'd noticed them before, but in my naïveté, I thought they marked some farmer's pet cemetery, his tributes to old sheepdogs laid to rest. But when the shovels came out and we began to dig, I realized how daft I'd been, my mother's harsh words echoing in my head – *our daughter's as green as a bean.*

As I joined in the burial of Amelia's stillborn child, I made a vow to myself and to my unborn babe: *This won't happen – not to you, and not to me.* My child kicked in my belly, making its presence known. That little life was conceived out of love, and it would be born into love. I promised I would bring that baby into the world, and I would remain its mother for as long as I lived. All there was left to do was make it happen.

CHAPTER 31

It's been one week since I read Gran's diary, and these past few days Gran has felt even closer – her voice, her memories, her advice ringing in my mind. I know that will never change.

Once Detective Stark and Angela presented the plan of a sting, I knew they were onto something. I decided on the spot to sell the Fabergé at auction – again. Excitement buzzed through me, as though Gran herself was egging me on (pun intended). Her diary was our secret weapon – the proof that the Bees and the Grays were connected.

As we converged in the early morning, bleary-eyed in my living room, I told everyone I was ready to sell. Detective Stark suggested I call Brown and Beagle right away to set up the auction. With her, Juan, Angela, and my gran-dad watching, I practiced the message I would leave on their answering machine. When I felt ready, I dialed their number on speaker phone so everyone could listen in. Though it wasn't even 7:00 A.M., to my surprise, Brown answered.

'Molly? Is everything okay?' he asked.

'Perfectly fine,' I replied.

'Then why are you calling so early?'

'I want to sell the egg.'

'That's wonderful!' said Brown. 'Beagle's still asleep, but he'll be thrilled when I tell him. We'll get all the big bidders back. I'll ring Steve and set up a special *Hidden Treasures* show for the redux. You'll go viral again – Molly the Maid returns! Just you wait.'

Beside me, Juan shook his head.

'A private sale – no TV, no cameras, no publicity. We'll hold the auction at the Regency Grand,' I said, 'with proper security this time. Detective Stark can help with that.'

Beside me, the detective gave a thumbs-up.

'We'll set the date for a month from now,' said Brown.

'In a week,' I countered.

'A week? Okay. Is there anything else?'

'Just a question,' I said. 'Your grandfather. What was his name?'

Angela ran a finger across her neck as though I'd just made a grave error.

'Magnus,' said Brown. 'Why do you ask?'

'Yesterday, we learned so much about Beagle's grandfather, so I was curious about yours. And your father, what was his name?'

Juan's and my gran-dad's eyes went wide.

'Algernon,' Brown replied.

'Is he alive?'

'Deceased, or "very dead," as you might say, Molly – a boating accident in Saint-Tropez not long after I was born. He was with my mother, and he fell from the yacht without her even noticing. A real tragedy.'

'Pushed,' I said sotto voce.

'I'm sorry?'

'Ooouuff,' I said, correcting myself. 'What a loss.'

'Indeed,' he said. 'Beagle should be up soon. I'll tell him we're going to auction. Is there anything else?'

'That's plenty. Goodbye.'

It was that simple. The auction was set. And in the seven days since that call, we've madly prepared the Regency Grand for every eventuality. It was decided that we'd set up hidden cameras and sound equipment at crucial locations throughout the hotel so we could see and hear everything. We gathered in Mr Snow's office to discuss the matter. Mr Snow wasn't keen at first.

'We've never allowed this kind of surveillance at the hotel. Guest privacy is paramount to us. It's part of our appeal.'

'Part of your problem, too,' Stark observed. 'It's just for one day.'

Mr Snow reluctantly agreed, and he seems to have come to enjoy the elaborate secret preparations. 'The penthouse suite on the fourth floor can serve as our headquarters,' he offered. 'We can run the whole covert operation from there.'

'It'll need a name,' said Juan.

'What about the penthouse suite on the fourth floor?' I suggested.

'A short-form, a code,' Angela insisted, and I do believe I detected an eye roll.

'The Black Hole?' I offered. The name suggested the secrecy of the mission and the untimely death of a certain guest who died in that same suite a few years ago.

'Perfect!' said Stark.

'She has a way with words,' my gran-dad declared.

After that, we decided who else would be in on the sting, and Speedy's name came up. At first, I was against this idea. 'I'm not sure we can trust him,' I said. 'Besides, I don't understand a word he says.'

'You don't need to understand him,' said Angela. 'Just let him run the tech. He's a wizard, Molly. And he knows the hotel inside out.'

And so it was decided that Juan would bring Speedy to Mr Snow's office.

'Yo!' Speedy said as he entered. 'Is this a VIP party? Is there bottle service?'

I would have walked him out then and there had Angela not stopped me.

'Speedy, we need your help,' Mr Snow announced.

'What we're about to tell you must be kept in absolute secrecy,' Detective Stark added.

'Excretion is my middle name,' said Speedy.

'Good grief,' I exclaimed with a sigh.

Detective Stark then explained that she wanted Speedy to work with her officers to set up hidden surveillance cameras and microphones throughout the hotel on the day of the auction – in the lobby, in the tearoom, at the Social, in Mr Snow's office, on the front steps, and in the greenroom.

'Sick!' Speedy replied.

'If you're ill, we'll find someone else,' I said, relieved.

'He's fine, Molly. He's excited to help,' Angela explained.

Late last night, we completed the entire clandestine setup. Speedy made a list of the equipment needed, and Stark and her surveillance team provided it. While Angela and I prepared the tearoom with phones for call-in bidders and put auction paddles on the white-linened tables, Speedy and Stark's team ran wires and mics for sound, and hid cameras in key locations.

Now, the day is finally here. In a couple of hours the auction will take place and the Fabergé will be sold to the highest bidder – or to someone who appears to be the highest bidder. After, there will be a private reception at the Social so we can draw people away from the greenroom, where Baxley Brown and Thomas Beagle will be alone, and where, if we're right, we'll learn more about their motives and their connection to the egg.

It's seven in the morning, and Juan and I are waiting outside our building for Gran-dad, who will drive us to the hotel. I'm so nervous, I can't stay still.

'I've seen jumping beans less antsy,' Juan says.

'What if we're wrong? What if all these preparations are pointless? What if the Bees aren't the thieves?'

'We won't lose anything by trying, Molly. Plus, the sale isn't real, so in the end, you'll still have the egg.'

'If it doesn't disappear again,' I say.

'Over my dead body,' Juan replies.

Just then, Gran-dad drives up and we hop in his car. He's wearing his doorman's greatcoat and cap, his uniform out of retirement for today only, since he's filling in for Speedy. Speedy has officially called in 'sick,' but unofficially, he'll be upstairs, manning the Black Hole.

We drive in silence to the hotel, and Juan and I say goodbye to Mr Preston on the red-carpeted stairs.

'Everything will be okay in the end, Molly,' my gran-dad says.

'Let's hope that's true,' I reply.

Juan and I leave Gran-dad and make our way through the revolving doors, heading straight to the fourth floor, where Detective Stark lets us into the penthouse suite. It's now a high-tech hub, the furnishings pushed to the walls to make room for monitors, speakers, and keyboards. Speedy is working with Stark's surveillance team, checking the feeds as Detective Stark looks on.

Speedy looks up. 'You *maid* it!' he says when he sees me. 'Get it?'

Of course I did, as it was a pun.

'*Madre mía,*' Juan exclaims as he surveys the various cameras that let us watch what's happening all over the hotel. 'This is incredible.'

'Layer in the sound,' Detective Stark orders. One of her

officers slides a switch on the console, then Speedy directs us screen by screen so we suddenly hear what's happening in each surveillance location. There's Mr Preston on the red-carpeted stairs giving guests directions to a waffle house. And there's Cheryl in the housekeeping quarters mumbling about sore feet and taking a load off. Angela and Mr Snow are in the greenroom greeting the Bees, who are dapperly dressed as usual and who are asking for me. 'She'll be down soon,' says Angela, clear as a bell.

'Speedy,' I say. 'You really are a technical wizard.'

'Big ups to po-po here. She got us all this sick equipment,' Speedy says.

'And if we catch the thief,' Stark replies, 'I may forgive what you just called me.' She then turns to me. 'We're all set. Molly, Juan, Speedy, you know what to do?'

'Totes,' says Speedy.

'We're ready,' Juan and I reply.

We ran through everything the night before – how I will be in the tearoom with the Bees and Mr Snow, watching the auction unfold; Detective Stark will stay in the Black Hole with Speedy, overseeing the cameras and sound; Angela will be in the bedroom beside them, calling in her winning bid to a dealer in the tearoom who, thanks to Stark faking Angela's credentials and bank balance, is convinced she's a nouveau riche collector; Mr Preston will man the entrance and report any suspicious intruders; and two officers have been assigned 'hen duty' with Juan – protecting the egg not only when it will leave the safe in Mr Snow's office but when it is taken to the tearoom before the auction begins. There will also be several plainclothes police officers scattered through the hotel.

Last night, I'd insisted on no display case. 'Juan will hold the egg,' I demanded. I wanted the person I trusted most in all the world to hold it the palms of his hands. The detective agreed.

'Good luck, Molly,' says Stark now as she sees me and Juan out the penthouse door. 'If anything goes wrong, we're a text message away.'

Juan and I make our way downstairs to the front lobby, which is buzzing with expectation. The settee area is cordoned off, and within it are various dealers and art aficionados wearing Bee & Bee VIP lanyards, all of them waiting patiently to be let into the tearoom. It's certainly not as busy as it was the last time we attempted a sale of the Fabergé, but as I look at the crowd, I suddenly feel very nervous indeed.

'We'll get through this, Molly,' Juan says. He squeezes my hand, then we part ways.

I head to the tearoom and find my place at a table up front. Soon after, Mr Snow enters and takes the seat beside me.

'All good upstairs and everywhere else?' I ask.

'Affirmative,' he replies.

Soon, a valet enters and escorts the guests from the lobby into the room. They take their assigned seats and get comfortable. At the back, dealers pick up phones, making contact with buyers all around the world. I spot Madame Orange, the familiar buyer, amongst them; today she is wearing a different dress but it's as tangerine in shade as the one she wore the last time she was here. She gets on a call, talking with her 'foreign buyer,' who, little does she know, has hair that matches her dress and who is just four floors above us.

'It's starting,' Mr Snow announces a few minutes later.

Two burly officers make their way through the tearoom entrance, hands on their holsters. Behind them comes Juan. In his steady, white-gloved hands he holds Gran's egg, and the twinkling sight of it brings a frog to my throat. I don't know why, but it's like Gran herself is being carried into the room. I push the emotion down as Juan takes the stage, his eyes meeting mine.

Tall Baxley Brown and his diminutive husband, Thomas Beagle, emerge from the greenroom. They step up to the podium as a hush descends.

'Good morning, all. I'm Baxley Brown.'

'And I'm Thomas Beagle.'

'And together we represent Brown & Beagle Auction House . . .'

'. . . the most trusted purveyors of fine art in the world.'

'This auction is private rather than televised,' says Brown.

'Because the seller experienced certain . . . irregularities after the last auction, she wishes minimal fanfare this time around,' Beagle explains. 'Brown, your gavel. Let the auction begin.'

Beagle steps away from the podium, and Brown takes over.

'The Fabergé egg in question – displayed onstage in front of us by the current owner's fiancé – recently reached a selling price of ten million. Today, we expect to surpass that, so our bidding will begin at seven million. Do I have seven million?' Brown asks.

Paddles fly up all around the room.

'And seven point five . . . Eight to the man up front. Eight million is the leading bid. . . . Nine, from Madame Orange, no stranger to the art world. Ten to the gentleman at table four. Do I hear ten-five? Yes, noted, madam.'

I think of Angela upstairs, upping her bid, her hair in a tizzy.

'And I see you at table two. Eleven million. No, eleven-five, to the bidder beside you. Yes, Madame Orange, raising to twelve. Do I have twelve million five? Twelve million – and it's back to you at table two. And raising to thirteen million. Do I have thirteen?'

As I hold my breath, Brown surveys the crowd.

'High or low, there's Madame O. We're at thirteen million. Do I have thirteen-five? Anyone? . . . This is fair warning . . .'

Brown raises his gavel, then it thuds against the podium, the sound echoing throughout the room.

'Sold for a lucky thirteen million to an anonymous bidder on our phone lines, represented by Madame Orange.'

Polite applause breaks out in the room. Beside me, Mr Snow's shock at the selling price is evidenced by his eyebrows, which have shot up beyond the rims of his glasses.

'This concludes the auction,' says Beagle. 'And judging by our egg holder, not a moment too soon.'

Juan is sweating, his hands shaking as he tries to hold the egg steady in his palms. Officers flank him, and he's escorted out of the room with the egg. Mr Snow exits behind them.

Beagle and Brown step off the stage and come right to me.

'Congratulations, Molly,' says Brown.

'Thank you,' I say.

'I'll bet you're glad that's over,' Beagle adds.

'I will be,' I say.

'Listen, we're going to change in the greenroom. Then we'll meet you at the Social for the afterparty, okay?'

'Yes,' I say. 'Take your time, and we'll see you there.'

I watch as they head through the paneled door, disappearing from sight.

As everyone files out of the room, I excuse myself, then run up the back stairs to the fourth floor. Using my master keycard, I slip into the penthouse suite, securing the door behind me.

'It's done!' I say to Stark and Speedy as I lean against the door, catching my breath. 'They're in the greenroom.'

'Shh,' says Stark.

'Zip it,' says Angela.

At the console, Speedy turns up the sound in the greenroom. I hurry over to watch the screen.

Brown and Beagle are seated on a couch right below the hidden camera.

'Congrats, Bax. That's a very healthy commission you just scored us,' says Beagle as he squeezes his husband's hand.

'Goodbye, Molly. Goodbye, egg,' says Brown. 'Shall we order a bottle of Veuve to celebrate?'

'Not yet,' Beagle says, as he smooths his dark curls, then turns to face his partner. 'There's something we need to discuss.'

'Can't it wait?' says Brown as he reaches a long arm around Beagle's shoulders.

'Please, Bax. I have to tell you something,' Beagle pleads.

Both men are silent for a moment as Brown waits for his husband to speak.

'This is about me,' says Beagle as he crosses his slender legs. 'I was the one who—'

Beagle's lips are moving, but the sound has suddenly cut out.

'We can't hear him!' says Angela. 'Turn it up!'

'Speedy, what's going on?' Stark asks.

'The little dude's leg wigged out! He crossed it and popped the plug.' Speedy points on the screen to a cord on the floor.

'Cripes on a crutch, now what?' Angela asks.

I don't know how it comes to me or why, but a lightbulb goes off. 'Angela!' I say. 'Follow me. Now!' I grab her by the arm and head to the penthouse door.

'Where are we going?' she asks.

'To the tearoom,' I say.

'But we won't see a thing from there,' she replies.

'Irrelevant!' I say. 'We'll have our ears to the ground. And for the record, Angela, I mean that literally.'

CHAPTER 32

Dear Molly,

I hatched a plan – to escape the farmhouse. One day, when the laundry van came to take the bags of clean clothes to town and drop off dirty ones, I waited for Mrs Lynch to approach the driver for payment, and as she counted the bills, I jumped in the back of the van and hid behind the mountain of clean clothes. Fortunately, no one saw me, and when Mrs Lynch closed the van doors, I knew I had a chance.

As we bumped along the country road, I fumbled in the dark, holding on to my suitcase, which I'd slipped under one of the bags. When the van stopped, I was ready. The doors opened, and the driver grabbed two big bags, bringing them out to a lovely house on a pleasant street in town. I waited for my eyes to adjust to the light, and as the driver chatted with the woman who answered the front door, I made a run for it, suitcase in hand. At seven months pregnant, I was slow and clumsy, but I was determined to make my escape.

Soon enough, I was in the center of the bustling town, asking for the bus station and being eyed suspiciously by the locals, who clearly wondered why a pregnant young girl with a fancy suitcase was traveling by herself. With the little bit of money I still had hidden inside my case, I purchased a ticket that got me all the way to the town closest to home. The return trip took hours, and I gazed out the window, imagining what I would say to Mama and Papa when they opened the manor door.

After more than a half day of travel and a long, lonely walk from the bus station to where Gray Manor was situated on the outskirts of town, I arrived at the familiar front door, exhausted and hungry.

I rang the bell and waited, my speech prepared – *Mama, Papa, the farmhouse was a dangerous place. I know you'd never want harm to come my way. That's why I've returned. Please, take pity on me. I'll do whatever you ask, just let me come home and have this baby.*

But when the door swung open, a woman appeared who was most definitely not my mother. Smartly dressed, with a strand of pearls around her neck and her auburn hair in a neat chignon at her nape, she looked familiar and yet I couldn't quite place her.

'Flora?' she said. 'Flora Gray?'

It was then that I realized. 'Mrs Peterson,' I replied. 'You're Percival's mother. I went to school with your son . . . for a few months, anyhow.'

'Yes, of course. He told me all about you. He was quite besotted.'

Her eyes traveled to my belly, taking in my condition. My gaze went past her. I fully expected my mother to appear and explain that Mrs Peterson was there for a ladies' tea. But that didn't happen.

'Where's my mother?' I asked.

'Your mother?' Mrs Peterson echoed. 'I'm afraid no one really knows where your parents are.'

'But . . . this is Gray Manor,' I said, a certain learned righteousness creeping into my voice.

'Not anymore,' she replied. 'The Brauns put it up for sale months ago, and my husband and I were the winning bidders.'

I must have looked about to faint, for Mrs Peterson reached out a hand to steady me. 'You didn't know,' she said.

Tears threatened to spill from my eyes.

'Please,' she said. 'Come in.'

The next thing I knew, I was seated in the parlor of what was no longer my home learning that my parents had forfeited the manor and simply vanished. Rumors abounded about where they'd gone once their fortune was stripped from them. Questions were raised about me, and many of my parents' former acquaintances, the Petersons included, had heard Mama and Papa had gone to France to meet up with me.

'They said you were at a Parisian finishing school,' she revealed.

It was glaringly obvious that wasn't the case.

'And how's Percival?' I asked. 'Where is he?'

'At university,' she said. 'He went abroad. My son was never a great student, but somehow he passed his entry exams.'

I broke down entirely then, sobbing into my hands. Mrs Peterson rubbed my back. I confessed where I'd been sent, described the farmhouse and Mrs Lynch and the girls, how we were worked to the bone.

'I now know how to cook, clean, launder, and raise chickens – all skills I never in my life thought I'd learn.' I alluded to the horrors of the place and the fact that not all mothers and babies made it out alive.

She shook her head. 'I'm sorry to hear this,' she said.

'I don't believe my parents meant to abandon me. They must have sent word, but I never received their letters. Are you sure you don't know where they are?'

She looked at me with such pity when she said, 'Flora, I have no idea. There was a young lad who came by a few weeks ago,' she said. 'He said he used to work here. He was asking about you.'

'John Preston,' I said.

'Yes, that's the name. Is he the—'

'If he comes again, you never saw me,' I said.

She noticed my shaking hands. 'Tea?' she asked.

'Please,' I replied. She disappeared into the kitchen, returning with tea and scones. I was so famished I ate mine in two bites.

'Have another,' said Mrs Peterson, offering me the basket. 'I'm not great in the kitchen, but I try.'

'You have no cook?' I asked.

'No cook, no maid, no servants at all. It took everything we had to buy this manor,' she said, smiling tightly. 'Flora, what will you do now?'

I stared into my teacup and began to weep yet again. 'I don't know.'

'A girl in your condition doesn't have many options,' Mrs Peterson said, pointing out the obvious. 'I don't suppose you'd be interested in using your newfound skills.'

I had no idea what she was suggesting. I stared at her, dumbfounded.

'I could use the help,' she added, 'in exchange for free room and board.'

'Are you offering me . . . a job?' I asked.

'I can't offer you pay, but you said you can cook and clean. Listen, it would only be until the baby was born, but if I've offended you—'

'No,' I said. And knowing I had no other options I asked, 'How soon can I start?'

So it was that I went from being to the manor born to serving as a maid for the new owners. I cleaned and cooked and laundered for the Petersons. And I hid myself in their home as my belly grew and grew.

I had my own room off the kitchen – a spartan chamber that used to be Penelope's. My old wing upstairs now belonged to Percival, though I never did see him, as he was away at school. Papa's beautiful library was entirely empty – every last bookshelf bare. Only the main floor of the manor was furnished, for the Brauns had auctioned off all of my parents' things before selling the property. Mrs Peterson explained that my parents' former friends and colleagues had snapped up their antiques and heirlooms, proudly displaying them in their stately homes and relishing telling the tale of how the Grays fell from their high perch and ended in penury.

'It seems the only heirloom left from this estate is the one item I took with me – the Fabergé,' I said.

'The Fabergé?' Mrs Peterson repeated. 'You have it? Your parents made a ruckus about it before leaving. They accused the Brauns of stealing that egg from the manor,' she revealed.

'It was mine. I took it with me when I left. I kept it hidden in the farmhouse.' I then explained about Algernon and our failed engagement and the gift I was left with in the end.

'Would you ever sell it?' Mrs Peterson asked, her voice lilting on the last two words.

I saw my opportunity, and I took it.

'Of course I'd sell it,' I said. 'For the right price.'

'Great,' said Mrs Peterson. 'Give the egg to me, and my husband will find a buyer.'

Molly, I put that egg into Mrs Peterson's hands, and a few weeks later, just as my feet began to swell and my back was in pain much of the time, she interrupted my dusting and drew me aside.

'We sold it,' she announced as she pressed an envelope into my hands, 'to a writer my husband knows. We received a decent enough price, so the funds in the envelope are yours.'

It was an astonishing sum – a few thousand. I was so

desperate that it didn't even occur to me to ask how much the Petersons had kept for themselves, but I now suspect they made off with a fortune. At the time, it didn't matter, because that envelope was my lifeline, an answer to my prayers.

My due date was a month away. There was still no sign of my parents. I announced I'd depart in a week's time, and the Petersons did nothing to stop me. I filled my suitcase with my clothes and Mrs Mead's blank diary. I took my envelope of cash, and I left the manor for good. First, I went to town, and then I took a bus into the city, where I rented the cheapest apartment I could find, one that you know very well, Molly, for it is the one you call home to this very day. I deposited my money in a bank account I called the Fabergé for reasons that are probably now quite clear. And through the Petersons, I found a job in the city as a maid for the Astors, well-to-do friends of theirs who'd moved to the urban center.

I worked for a few short weeks; then one day, while I was scrubbing their marble floors, my water broke. They were good enough to take me to a hospital, where I gave birth in a room away from the other, married mothers. While birthing, I held the hand of a total stranger, a nurse who assured me everything would be okay, and in my delirium I would have sworn she was someone I knew.

And so it was that into the world came the most beautiful infant, with dark, tousled hair just like her father's and po-celain skin much like yours, Molly. And unlike my mother when I was born, I was overjoyed to learn my child was a hale and hearty girl.

'What will you name her?' the kind nurse asked.

'Margaret,' I said. 'Maggie for short.'

'A perfect name,' said the nurse, 'for a perfect little girl.'

She placed the bundle against my chest, and for the second time in my life, I fell madly in love.

CHAPTER 33

Keep calm and carry on.

This is what I tell myself as I rush down the stairs with Angela by my side.

'Trust me!' I say. 'Where there's a will, there's a way.'

We run through the lobby, past hordes of guests, and when we arrive at the tearoom, I tell the officers at the threshold, 'Let no one in unless I say so.'

'And you are?'

'Molly the Maid!' I bark.

I rush up the stage stairs and squat down, looking for something. 'There,' I say. 'That's it!'

'What's "it"?' Angela asks, struggling to catch up.

'The vacuum outlet. It leads to the greenroom. Now be quiet,' I say as I fish off the cover.

The moment I do, we hear two voices, clear as day – it's the Bees, conversing in the greenroom next door.

Angela's eyes go wide. She pulls out her phone to record. Then we both lie on the stage, ears to the boards.

'But why steal an egg we were about to sell?' Brown asks, his voice pure disbelief.

'I did it for you,' says Beagle.

'You're not making any sense,' says Brown.

'The Fabergé belonged to my grandfather, Baron Beagle.'

'The egg we just auctioned for thirteen million?' Brown asks, incredulous.

'Yes,' says Beagle. 'Years ago, he told me about a prototype that was stolen from him. He never said it was a Fabergé. And he never said who stole it. But when he got sick a couple of years ago, he confessed the thief's name – a man named Braun.'

Angela and I stay stock-still. Someone shifts on the unseen sofa in the other room.

'Wait. My grandfather?' Brown says.

'He was an art thief, Bax,' says Beagle. 'Granddad told me he was renowned for it even though he was never caught. He worked in tandem with his son.'

'You mean my father, Algernon Braun? So the rumors are true,' says Brown.

'I'm afraid so. But the baron adored you. He didn't want the sins of your grandfather to ruin us, so he kept the connection quiet. Plus, there was no egg. It hadn't been seen in decades.'

'But then it reappeared,' says Brown.

'On our show, no less. And the second I laid eyes on it, I

knew we had a problem – our reputation was at stake. If someone came forward and knew your grandfather was an art thief, we'd be ruined, our business up in smoke, our TV careers canceled.'

'So you stole the egg?' Brown asks.

'Let's just say I know some unsavory fellows with experience in making valuables disappear. I was about to sell the thing on the black market so it would never see the light of day.'

'The note in the vacuum canister,' says Brown. 'Did you put it there? Did you threaten the maid?'

'I wasn't going to hurt her,' says Beagle. 'I just wanted everyone to stop looking for it.'

We hear footsteps. One of the men has stood from the couch. We can hear him pacing the room. 'But why return the egg, Tom? What were you thinking?' Brown asks in disbelief.

'As I was settling my grandfather's papers, I came across an old bill of sale. Here. Look.'

The crumple of paper, the groan of the sofa as Brown sits back down. 'But this is for a piece of jewelry,' Brown says.

'Look closer,' Beagle replies.

'Gold trellis and a cabriolet base, ten rubies, twenty rose-cut diamonds, emeralds in quatrefoils. My god,' says Brown.

'There's no finders keepers law that trumps this. My grandfather bought the egg fair and square. Look at the letterhead and the signature,' says Beagle.

'The House of Fabergé,' says Brown. 'So you returned the egg when you found this bill of sale?'

'Yes, Bax. I did. And the egg is ours by right. This paper

is proof. It doesn't matter if your grandfather stole the egg because *my* grandfather was its last legal owner. And I've got the paper trail to prove it.'

'Why didn't you say something earlier?' Brown asks. 'Why let the maid auction it off?'

'The sale price, Bax. We just set its base worth without any provenance. If we lie low for a bit, then produce this bill of sale in a year or so, the price will skyrocket. We'll be rich beyond our wildest dreams.'

'An artful deception,' says Bax.

'I'm glad you agree,' Beagle replies.

'But how could you?' asks Brown, his tone sharp and accusatory. 'For my whole life, I've been running from my family's dirty dealings. I've always wanted to be different from them, to earn my way, to keep things clean. And now you do this?'

'No one ever has to know,' says Beagle. 'We can buy the villa in France. We can get a yacht in Saint-Tropez just like the one your mother had when you were a kid.'

'You're just like them – my father and my grandfather. You're a thief.'

'Please, all I want is for us to—'

Just then, Stark enters the tearoom. Angela and I pull away from our listening hole on the stage floor as Stark puts a finger to her lips. She saunters over, places the vacuum cover back on the port.

'You'll never believe what we just heard,' I whisper.

'Oh, I'll believe it,' says Stark. 'Speedy and I watched what you were doing in here. Brilliant. He got a battery backup mic working in the greenroom. We heard everything, but we couldn't record it.'

'I've got your back,' says Angela as she holds up her phone. 'Voice memo.'

'I can't quite fathom it,' I say. 'One good egg, one bad.'

'Two Bees, one sting,' says Angela. 'It hurts to hear what Beagle did.'

'It really does,' says Stark.

'What now?' I ask.

'Well,' says Stark. 'Would either of you be interested in watching a detective make a celebrity arrest?'

CHAPTER 34

Dear Molly,

The end is near. My time is nigh.

I have spent these last few weeks writing to you whenever I've felt well enough to do so, but it gets more difficult with each passing day. In the morning, you feed me my medicine with breakfast, and by the time you head to work, the pain abates enough for me to continue writing. But I know the truth: my time is running out. The pain overtakes me sooner every day, and I cannot keep my hand or my mind steady enough to write. Forgive me, Molly, if my penmanship isn't polished to perfection, and forgive me, too, for drawing this tale to a close so soon. I want to go on. I wish I could, but alas, few people get to choose their ending.

In my previous entry, I told you about my stroke of good fortune – how after amassing a nest egg from a literal one, I was able to rent a modest apartment on my own and soon after gave birth to the most beautiful baby girl – your mother, Maggie. Oh, Molly, how I loved that child. Everything about her enchanted me – her coal-black eyes and her dark hair, her chiming giggle, and her chubby little toes. The Astors allowed me to bring her with me to work in exchange for free overtime. I carried her from room to room in a laundry basket as I scrubbed, cooked, and cleaned. I spoke to her all day long, my maid-in-training, my little apprentice.

Most often, when I looked at her, I saw John, but sometimes traces of Mama or Papa, too. I thought of them often, half expected my parents to waltz into my apartment and rescue me from what my mother would have called 'a hovel.' Or maybe they'd ring the Astors' front doorbell someday and whisk me back to a glorious new estate and a life of privilege that now felt so remote it was like a dream.

But that never happened. Instead, with each passing day, I realized with more and more certainty that I was on my own, but my solace was that Maggie grew and thrived. Her first steps were taken on the marble floors of the Astors' parlor. And when she spoke her first word, it wasn't 'Mama' but 'spoon.' I'd started my little collection in the curio cabinet – thrift shop finds and hand-me-downs. She loved to play with those old silver spoons, admiring her reflection in the bowls.

Before long, my infant was a toddler, and then a little girl off to school. Time, Molly. It passes too quickly, and one day, you find yourself with so little of it left. Occasionally, life is marked by some unexpected occurrence, as was the case when a mystery guest walked into my life out of the blue, arriving at my apartment door when Maggie was five years old. While my daughter played tea party on the living room floor, I looked through the peephole and almost fainted on the spot.

There he was, the love of my life, the father of my child – John Preston. I was breathless. I didn't know what to think, what to feel. He was older – time had marked him as it had marked me – but he was the same. I opened the door and just stood there, staring at him.

'Flora,' he said, taking me in; then he noticed the little girl serving tea to her dolls on the floor.

'John,' I replied. 'Please, come in.'

As Maggie played, we sat on the sofa and talked. Over five years had gone by and yet my heart raced at the sight of him. He told me how disappointed he had been to arrive at the old oak tree on the day I was supposed to meet him and how he found nothing there except what the fairies had left in the knothole. I apologized, explained that I couldn't let him ruin his life, 'not for me, not for anyone – not even for her,' I said, gesturing to our beautiful little girl babbling to herself on the floor.

I asked him if he'd graduated from university. He had not, he said, because he never went. Uncle Willy couldn't find work, and so John had to move to the city with his father, taking on a job to support them both.

'So what do you do now?' I asked.

'I'm a bellhop at the Century Hotel downtown.'

I had to laugh. 'The top two students in our prep class – a bellhop and a maid. Life isn't fair.'

'No, it isn't,' he replied.

'How's Uncle Willy?' I asked.

He shook his head. 'He died two years ago.'

The news hit me like a blow to the chest. 'I'm so sorry,' I said. 'He was good man, like father like son.'

John stared at me. 'I looked for you everywhere, Flora,' he said. 'I asked about you. No one from back home knew where you'd gone. I thought you'd died.' His eyes filled with tears. 'And then not long ago at the hotel, I ran into that snivelly-faced redhead who was in our prep class. Percival. Do you remember him?'

'Of course,' I said.

'He's a politician now. Can you believe it? Couldn't write a sentence when we knew him, and now he's running for office.'

'The way of the world,' I replied.

'His parents got me your address.' He wrung his hands in his lap, and that's when I noticed the ring, not the Claddagh, but a simple gold band on his ring finger.

'I'm . . . married,' he said. 'Mary. She's a good woman, Flora. She reminds me of my aunt. You remember her?'

'How could I forget?'

I looked over at our little girl playing on the floor. 'Maggie,' I said. 'Will you serve our guest some tea?'

John's mouth fell open upon hearing the name. His daughter trotted over, offered him a plastic teacup, then curtsied and walked away.

'Thank you . . . Maggie,' he said, his voice cracking. He turned to me. 'You have to let me help you. And her,' he said.

'We're fine,' I said. 'We make our way.'

'If ever there's a problem, Flora, if you find yourself in need, I'm here. For you and for her.'

'Thank you,' I said, my voice constricted and meek.

'You should meet her, my Mary,' said John. 'She knows everything – about us, I mean. And she understands, too. She's a good woman with a big heart.'

'I would expect no less from a wife of your choosing,' I said.

John gave me his phone number and I gave him ours, but whenever he called, insisting on helping us, I declined. Months later, I received a call from a cheery woman with a voice like chimes tinkling in the wind. It was Mary Preston, inviting me to tea. I went because I didn't know what else to do, and I'm glad I did. John was right – she was a bighearted woman with so much love to give, it spilled everywhere. She became my lifelong friend. The moment I met her, I knew I'd done the right thing by letting John go. I'd spared him the travails of a harder life, and Mary loved him as well as I ever could, made him so happy, and eventually gave him a baby girl named Charlotte.

Mary visited me often after that. Knowing how hard it was to make ends meet on a maid's salary, she'd hide money in my house for me to find after she left, always refusing to take it back, saying with a wink it wasn't she who'd left it but the fairies. Mary and John were quietly there for us always, whenever we needed. Once, I asked her why she'd accepted me in her life, given the history between me and her husband.

'Because we're the same, you and me. There but for the grace of God go I. Besides, we have something important in common,' she said.

'And what's that?'

'All we've ever wanted is for John to be happy.'

But when your mother was a teen, Molly, the problems began, and John and Mary were desperate to help. We tried to guide Maggie back to the fold, but our tactics didn't work. And when you were born, you were a beacon of hope, lighting up our lives, but Maggie still struggled. Young as she was, she couldn't cope. She disappeared with a fly-by-night, leaving me to raise you as my own. Know this, Molly: I love you with every fiber of my being, and I will love you long after I'm gone. Others love you, too, more than you realize.

As time passed, Molly, you grew and you learned and thrived in your own way. And when you were of age to seek employment, it was John to whom I turned. He was working as a doorman at a posh hotel called the Regency Grand. I asked if he'd talk to the manager about getting you an interview as a room maid, and he did. Your interview didn't go well. Mr Snow felt you lacked the social skills required to be in a public position, but John begged him to give you a chance, said he'd look out for you. Mr Snow relented.

You proved all the naysayers wrong, Molly. I still remember your first day, how you came home so joyful and excited. I hadn't seen you so happy since those few weeks at the

Grimthorpe mansion when I pulled you out of school and you worked side by side with me, my maid-in-training, my little shadow.

You've excelled at the Regency Grand, and you've made me so proud. But then came my diagnosis, and when I told you, you went straight to the river, Molly – denial. I worry what will happen when I'm gone. How will you cope? Will you make it on your own?

A few weeks ago, while you were at work, John came to our apartment for a visit. I shared my concerns with him. 'She'll have no one to look out for her once I'm gone,' I said.

He was shocked, upset even, which for John is a rarity. He said something that relieved a burden weighing heavily on my shoulders.

'Flora, you couldn't be more wrong. Forever and always, Molly will have me.'

CHAPTER 35

'Detective! How lovely to see you,' Beagle says as Stark walks through the door and claims the greenroom while Angela and I stand in the threshold behind her.

'Bax and I are just finishing here. We'll be at the Social in a moment. By the way, congratulations,' says Beagle. 'The security today was flawless. Molly, Angela – I hope you kept some champagne chilled for us.'

Beagle invites us into the room.

'Mr Brown, you're free to leave,' says Stark to the tall blond man who looks entirely bereft despite his dapper scarlet jacket.

'Leave? Why would Bax leave?' Beagle asks. 'Where he goes, I go.'

'Not this time,' says Stark. She walks over to the tiny, dark-haired man with bejeweled fingers and eagle eyes. 'Thomas Beagle, you're under arrest,' she says. 'You have the right to remain silent. Anything you say can be used against you in a court of law.'

'Arrest? Is this some kind of joke? Where's the hidden camera?' Beagle says with a chuckle.

'They're pretty much everywhere,' Angela replies.

'There must be some kind of mistake. I've done nothing wrong,' Beagle says.

'A Bee-liever convinced of his own lies,' I say.

'You hired a criminal gang to steal the Fabergé, and you threatened Molly, twice,' Stark says.

'But this is ridiculous. Bax, say something.'

'What am I supposed to say, Tom?' says Brown. 'That I thought I knew you? Thought I could trust you? You're a wolf in designer clothing.'

'Don't say that,' says Beagle. 'You know me better than anyone.'

'I thought I did. But I don't. Not anymore.'

'That dog's delulu,' I hear from somewhere behind me.

I turn to see Speedy standing in the doorway, pointing to Beagle. Two police officers behind him enter the greenroom and head straight for Thomas.

'Will you kindly translate Speedy into English?' I ask Angela.

'He says Beagle is delusional,' she explains.

'Scammed by tech, bruh,' says Speedy as he shakes his head.

'We heard every word you said to Brown a few minutes ago,' says Stark. 'You admitted to stealing the egg. And to returning it for your own gain, so, Thomas Beagle, grandson of a baron, you're under arrest.'

Stark's two officers take Beagle by the arms, putting him in handcuffs.

'Do you know who I am? And do you have any idea who I know?' Beagle says, raising his voice.

'One more word and I'll raise your threat charges to three,' says Stark.

The detective and the officers lead Beagle out of the room as Speedy follows close behind.

Once they're gone, Brown approaches me, his face a mask of shock. 'Molly,' he says. 'I didn't know any of this. I had no idea my own husband could be capable of such a thing. All I wanted was for you to sell the egg so it would change your life for the better.'

'And for your commission,' says Angela.

'Yes, for that, too,' admits Brown. 'Is that a crime?'

I shake my head. 'No, it's not,' I say, 'but do you realize our families are connected?'

His eyebrows scrunch. 'What do you mean exactly?'

'Your father, Algernon Braun, was once my gran's fiancé, but the wedding was called off. And I can tell you that as far as eggs go, your father was a particularly rotten varietal.'

Brown looks down at his feet. 'I suspected as much,' he says. 'I don't know much about my father because he died so young. My mother avoids talking about him. And my grandfather, well, let's just say I never trusted his accounts of his own son. There are questions he would never answer about his biggest art acquisitions. He even made us change our family name from Braun to Brown after someone accused him of falsifying a certificate of authenticity to make a big sale. He was never charged, but those accusations made me wonder.'

'Your grandfather, Magnus, and your father, Algernon, stole the Fabergé from Baron Beagle. I have proof.'

'Proof?' Brown repeats, incredulous.

'Her gran's diary. Written testimony,' says Stark.

'Where's your grandfather now?' I ask.

'Six feet under,' Brown says. 'I'll admit I never looked into the allegations against him for fear of what I'd uncover. When Magnus died, the accusations died with him. Since the day I took over the firm, my dealings have been squeaky clean. Whatever my father and his father did, I was never a part of it.'

'So we have something in common,' I say, 'besides the Fabergé.'

'What's that?' he asks.

'We both come from a bad lot, and we want to do better.'

'Regrettably, it seems that way,' says Brown.

Just then, Juan rushes into the greenroom, breathless and shaky.

'Speedy told me what happened. Molly, are you okay?'

'I'm fine,' I say. 'We're all fine.'

'Thank goodness,' he replies as he hugs me tight. For once, I don't care if we're in the workplace and if we're breaking a contact rule.

'Where's Beagle?' Juan asks.

'In handcuffs, off to the precinct,' says Angela.

'We caught him in flagrante,' I say. 'Where's the egg?'

'In the safe. Mr Snow and two officers are keeping a close watch.'

I turn to Baxley Brown, who looks dejected. He's the only one who can answer my burning question. 'Mr Brown,' I say. 'What happens now, with the egg, I mean?'

'By rights, it belongs to my husband,' he says. 'The bill of sale proves his grandfather was the last legal owner, so whoever Madame Orange's wealthy buyer is, the egg won't be theirs for long.'

'Drat,' says Angela with a shrug. 'I guess I'm no gatrillionaire.'

'Wait, you're the wealthy buyer?' says Brown.

'Busted,' Angela replies. 'The sale was a fake-out.'

'I can't believe it,' I say. 'After all he's done, Beagle is still the legitimate owner of the egg.'

Brown gives me a look that doesn't fit any I've ever come across in my catalogue of human expressions. 'Never count your chickens before they hatch,' he says.

CHAPTER 36

Dear Molly,

Today, while you were at work, a special visitor came to see me. You know him as our friend Mr Preston, the doorman at the Regency Grand, and I know him as my beloved John.

He sat with me by my bedside, and we relived old times. He held my hand, and I couldn't help but notice how much we'd changed – maps of our lives written in crevices and age spots on our thinning skin. We talked about Mary and how much we both miss her. We reminisced about Uncle Willy and Mrs Mead and my long-lost parents . . . and our missing daughter, Maggie. We said a prayer for them all.

I told him, 'This will be the last time I see you in this life, and I want you to know that I will always love you.'

We wept together, and he knelt by my bed, his head of

silver, tousled hair resting on my bony shoulder.

He took something from his pocket. At first, through my tears I couldn't see what it was, but as he held it forth, the heart twinkled between two tiny golden hands – the Claddagh ring.

'It didn't work the first time, so I'm trying again now,' he said. 'Flora, I have always loved you, and I always will. Will you take this silly old man to be your loving husband for whatever time you have left?'

I couldn't believe it. He proposed to me right there, as I lay weak and dying in my bed. It was like turning back the hands of time, doing things over, doing things right. My answer was resounding and instant. 'Yes,' I said.

We exchanged marriage vows that shall remain the only secret I keep from you, Molly. And when he slipped that ring on my finger, though it once was a perfect fit, it was now too big for me. I slipped the ring off and put it in his palm, closing his fingers around it.

'Hold on to it,' I said. 'If ever Molly finds someone who she . . .'

I couldn't say the words. It was a dream so big I feared giving it voice.

'I understand,' said John. 'I'll keep it for her. And I'll give it to her if ever the time is right. I promise.'

'And one more thing,' I said, pointing to my bedside drawer. He opened it, taking out this diary.

'My stars,' he said. 'You kept it all these years?'

'I did,' I replied. 'And recently, I started writing in it. It's for Molly, and it's my story. She's not ready to read it yet, but I trust you'll know when it's time. When the moment is right, you give it to her. She'll know how to open it. The next time you visit, come in here and take it from that drawer. Keep it safe.'

He nodded, then tucked the locked diary back in the drawer.

'Will you lie with me awhile?' I asked.

'Just like the old days, underneath the oak tree?'

'Just like that,' I said.

He came around the bed and lay beside me, holding my hand. I was so content, I must have drifted into a deep sleep, for when I woke some time ago, he was gone.

Normally, the pain would have kicked in by now, but John took it away with him, leaving peace as his parting gift to me. I know it won't last long, but it's nice for now. And I'm using this time to finish my final chapter, my last letter to you.

My dear Molly,

Once upon a time, there was an old maid who lay dying in her bed. She'd once had everything and lost everything, only to find that anything of value came back to her in the end.

I have lived a perfect life, a charmed life, a fairy tale in reverse. I was born wealthy and I die poor, but it matters not a jot. Here is the moral of my story. There is only one, and it is this: Love cannot be stolen. Not by anyone. Those who do not know love place no value upon it. Often, they don't even know it's there. But people like us, who do know it, who see and feel it and cherish it, possess a treasure that can never be taken away.

Love endures. It lasts. It will endure beyond me, I promise. Love is what I leave behind so that every day of your life, you will know that I'm with you. And from you, I take the same – your love – as comfort into the night.

My heart is yours forever, as yours is mine,

Your gran

RGH

One month later

REGENCY GRAND HOTEL

CHAPTER 37

The day has finally come. For the longest time, I thought it never would or that some calamity would strike me down before I could enjoy this moment IRL, as Juan would say. But here I am, dressed in a beautiful used white gown that Angela and I found at a vintage shop and that Sunitha and Sunshine altered for me stitch by hand-sewn stitch.

It is my wedding day. I'm seated on the terrace of the Regency Grand, hidden behind a privacy screen so none of the guests in the lobby below can spot me. I've been hiding for over an hour, sneaking peeks through the slats and observing the bustle below as guests enter the hotel.

I've always loved the view from this terrace – the opulent lobby with bellhops click-clacking across the fine marble floors; the emerald love seats where guests whisper to each other, their secrets absorbed by the plush velvet. Today, the people entering the lobby are not strangers but invited guests, all known to me. They're dressed so elegantly, and I can tell they're excited to witness the ceremony that will join Juan and me in matrimony for the rest of our lives.

I should be nervous, but I'm strangely calm. So much has happened in the last two months. I was about to become a multimillionaire. Then I wasn't. I was popular. Then I wasn't. I was the victim of theft and threats. Then I wasn't. And just when all the commotion around the Fabergé seemed resolved, the upheaval at home intensified. Two weeks ago, Mr Rosso ordered us out of our apartment. Though it hasn't yet sold, he believes it will look better to potential buyers empty rather than with Juan and me in it. While planning our wedding, we've packed our lives into cardboard boxes. Our search for a new apartment has been fruitless – the cost of rent has skyrocketed in this city – but just when we thought we might become homeless, Gran-dad stepped in, offering us a room in his house. 'You'll always have me,' he said, 'and besides, it'll be nice to have two young lovebirds around. You can stay as long as you want.' And so it was decided that, a week after our wedding, we will move in with Gran-dad as we continue our search for a home of our own.

I don't know what the future holds, and despite so much uncertainty, generosity abounds wherever I look – in the dress I'm wearing, lovingly tailored by my friends; on the tables in the lobby below me, filled with delicious delectables, made by Juan's kitchen staff. The very fact that this wedding is taking place at the Regency Grand is thanks to Mr Snow's beneficence. He approached me a few weeks ago, his brow furrowed.

'Molly,' he said. 'I know you've always insisted on a small city hall wedding, but are you sure that's what you want? It's not too late to hold the wedding here.'

'That's very kind, but Juan and I can't afford it,' I said. 'The rental cost alone equals my yearly salary.'

'Goodness gracious, Molly. You're part of the Regency Grand family. I'd never make you pay. Did I not make that clear?'

'If you did, I'm afraid I missed the cue,' I replied.

'All fees will be waived, and the catering will be my gift to you and Juan. What do you say?'

Juan and I gratefully accepted, and just like that, our four-person, city hall wedding exploded into a full-blown ceremony to be held in the Regency Grand lobby, followed by a catered reception and dance in the tearoom.

Not long after today's date was set, I received a phone call from Baxley Brown. He wanted to update me, not only about the Fabergé but about his former partner in life and art, Thomas Beagle.

'Molly, he pleaded guilty to all the charges against him. Thomas wanted me to tell you how sorry he is for what he put you through. Sometimes good people do bad things,' he said.

'I know that,' I replied. 'And the good ones make amends. I'm glad to have his apology.'

'Speaking of amends,' said Baxley, 'he signed over full ownership of the egg.'

'To whom?' I asked.

'To me,' Brown replied, 'as compensation for the harm he's caused me. *Hidden Treasures* was canceled after his crimes became headline news. Our auction business will never recover. I thought long and hard about who to sell the Fabergé to, and in the end, I sold it to a museum. I took a lower price, but it was worth it to see history preserved.'

I was quiet as I took this in. How fitting that the egg would no longer be a hidden treasure, that it would be on public display to be enjoyed by one and all.

'You've done a good thing,' I told Baxley Brown. A thought occurred to me, about good deeds and how one begets the next. 'I wonder,' I said, 'if you'd join Juan and me on our wedding day. It's only two weeks away. We'd love to have you.'

There was silence on the line. 'You'd want me there? No hard feelings?'

'None whatsoever. We'd be honored to have you as our guest.'

'Count me in,' Brown replied.

Now, as I peek through a crack in the privacy screen, I spot Baxley Brown easily in the lobby since he's a head taller than everyone else, and he's wearing his trademark indigo velvet waistcoat. He's chatting with his former showrunner, Steve (sans ironic baseball cap, thank goodness), who he's brought along with him. Mr Snow welcomes them both, bowing in his dapper coattails. Nearby, Sunshine, Sunitha, and Lily – my radiant bridesmaids – are helping themselves to free champagne courtesy of Mr Snow. They're dressed in matching yellow satin gowns sourced from a discount store.

On my orders, they're making small talk with Cheryl, who came to me a week ago most distraught after Mr Snow had me put her on probation. She was given a week to shape up or be dismissed from her job.

When I shared the happy news that Juan and I were to be married at the Regency Grand, she was shocked, but not for the reason I suspected. 'I thought we were friends,' she said.

'Friends?' I said, dumbfounded. 'Whatever gave you that idea?'

She sniffed and crossed her arms. 'So that's what you think of me. I'm no good at my job, and it's clear I'm the only maid not invited to your wedding.' Her bottom lip began to quiver.

'Goodness gracious, are you really upset because of that?'

'Yeah,' she said, nodding vigorously.

'But why would you want to come? You don't even like me. You conspire against me at every turn. And at work, you do nothing to help the other maids.'

'Because I'm always left out,' she said as tears spilled down her cheeks.

I know that feeling – to be left out, to be shunned despite one's best intentions. I looked at Cheryl, and I suddenly saw her shirking behavior in a whole new light.

'You and the other maids,' she said between sobs, 'you're like neat little peas in a perfect freak pod. I'm always the odd one out. Makes doing a good job kinda pointless.'

'Cheryl,' I said. 'No one wants to leave you out. But we fear the consequences of including you.' I took a risk then.

'Juan and I would be honored if you'd attend our wedding, but you must lead with generosity and kindness on our special day and every day at work. You know the consequences if you don't. As for the maids, if you do your job well, they'll include you in the fold. Can you do that?'

She considered, then nodded. True to her word, since that conversation, Cheryl hasn't 'taken a load off' even once during a shift. Not only that, she's splitting tips fair and square with the other maids for the first time ever. Now, she clinks glasses with Sunitha and Sunshine, a picture I thought I'd never see.

Just then, all the maids turn toward the gold revolving doors as Speedy sails through them. Dressed in a frilly baby-blue tuxedo, he turns around to show off the back of his jacket – silver letters spelling out DJ SLAY. He lopes over to where Juan's kitchen crew is gathered by the champagne flutes and hors d'oeuvres, exchanging high fives with them. Speedy will DJ both our ceremony and our reception in the hotel's tearoom. He's promised his musical selection will be 'sick,' which I now understand to be a very good thing indeed. He's even rigged a webcam in the lobby so that Juan's family can watch the entire ceremony all the way from Mexico.

Angela, my maid of honor, is next to enter the lobby. She's dressed in the same style of yellow dress as my bridesmaids, her hair pinned in a neat chignon at her neck. For once, not a single red strand is in a tizzy. A brawny woman wanders over to greet her. At first, I don't recognize her, but then I realize it's Detective Stark in a cocktail dress, her hair falling in soft curls on her broad shoulders. Angela's lips move a mile a minute. She's no doubt sharing that she recently gave notice to Mr Snow after having been accepted into the local police academy, prerequisites waived on account of 'experience in the field.'

As I watch all of this from behind my privacy screen on the terrace, the last arrivals revolve through the hotel's gleaming gold doors. There's my gran-dad with Charlotte, his daughter, who's traveled from afar just for this. After them, in files my beloved groom, Juan Manuel, looking so handsome that my breath catches in my throat. It's the first time I'm seeing him in his white tuxedo. I was there when he found it at the thrift shop around the corner from our apartment. He tried it on in the change room, assuring me it was perfect, but when I begged for a peek, he said, 'Not a chance, Molly Gray! Not until our wedding day.'

Now, my impossibly gorgeous fiancé greets the gathered guests. I can tell he's nervous because he can't stand still. My gran-dad, dressed in a lovely black suit and bow tie, puts a hand on his shoulder and whispers something in his ear, which makes a smile break out on Juan's lovely face.

Charlotte finds Mr Snow, who's pointing to the second step of the grand staircase, which is where we've agreed she'll stand for the ceremony.

A few weeks ago, Gran-dad called me. He was so excited, he didn't even say hello. 'Molly, Charlotte was promoted. My daughter is now a judge! Can you believe it?' he announced.

'You must be so proud,' I replied.

'Indeed I am. Now that she's a judge, she wants to officiate your wedding. What do you think?'

'Really? She'd do that for us?'

'Of course. She'll fly in specially for it.'

I didn't need to ask Juan, because he was listening in and nodding vehemently.

'It would be our honor,' I replied.

Now, Charlotte takes her place on the grand staircase, and when Mr Snow taps a Regency Grand silver spoon against a champagne flute, all heads turn his way.

'Please make your way to the staircase. The ceremony is about to begin.'

Only then do my palms start to sweat. In the confines of my white, heart-shaped bodice, I struggle to breathe. *Don't faint, Molly,* I tell myself. *Not now.* I hear footsteps on the marble stairs and my gran-dad peeks around the privacy screen.

'Molly,' he says. 'It's time.'

I know he said the words, but I hear them in Gran's voice, not his. Oh, Gran, you said it in your diary – the good moments gallop apace, over too soon. I want this day to last forever. I want to remember everything.

'I'm ready,' I say to Gran-dad.

He takes my arm and holds me upright as he's done so many times before. Step by step, we descend the marble staircase as, courtesy of DJ Slay, Pachelbel's Canon in D echoes through the lobby.

I take in the sea of faces below – family, friends, colleagues, loved ones. I've never been very good at reading expressions, and I cannot quite believe what I see reflected back at me on every single face. If I had to name it, I'd say it was admiration – and maybe even love. What I have done to deserve so much of it, I'll never know, but I'm grateful beyond measure.

We make our way to the lower steps, and Gran-dad releases me. Juan steps up to take his place at my side – so dashing, so handsome. My lovely bridesmaids file in behind me, and behind Juan, his mates from the kitchen stand in a neat, black-tied row.

Charlotte speaks as the music dims. 'Welcome, one and all. We are here today to join this hardworking maid and this talented pastry chef in lifelong matrimony. At the request of Juan Manuel Morales and Molly Gray, I'm to keep this service short and sweet – why? Because they're both concerned that having so much of the Regency Grand staff gathered here leaves the rest of the workers shorthanded.'

Muffled laughter echoes through the lobby.

'If that doesn't tell you everything you need to know about this wonderful couple, I don't know what does,' says Charlotte. 'You have watched this relationship blossom right here in this hotel, proof that love can grow pretty much anywhere – and under the strangest circumstances.'

Charlotte reaches into a pocket of her skirt and takes out a ring. 'For many years, this ring graced my father's finger. You know him as Mr Preston, the former doorman of this hotel. This ring was given to him on his wedding day by my dear departed mother, Mary. He now offers it to Molly to give to Juan. Molly?'

I take a deep breath, then grasp the ring between my fingers. Juan is right beside me, his beautiful brown eyes brimming with tears. I take his warm hand in mine, and I place Gran-dad's ring on Juan's finger. Then I speak the vow I have practiced in front of the bathroom mirror so many times – 'Juan Manuel, in the hope that our love will shine forever,' I say, 'I have polished this ring to perfection. With it, I thee wed.'

I feel his hand grip mine.

My gran-dad steps forward. He takes a ring from his breast pocket, holding it up for the crowd to see. 'This ring may look familiar to you. Molly has been wearing it as her engagement ring for many months now. Juan was desperate to buy her a new ring, but she refused. She wants only this one. It once belonged to her beloved grandmother, Flora Gray, and it was Flora's dream that Molly would one day wear it on her finger, carrying her heart – and mine – with her wherever she goes.'

My gran-dad passes the ring to Juan.

'Molly Gray, *mi amor,*' Juan says, 'in every language, you are the love of my life, and I will cherish you to the end of my days. With this ring, I thee wed.'

He fits the familiar ring onto my finger, and as I look down at it, I'm certain it's shining more brightly than ever before. I look up into Juan's beaming face as Charlotte says, 'I now pronounce you husband and wife. You may kiss the bride.'

We've gone through all of this before, but it suddenly occurs to me that we're about to make a terrible faux pas, an unthinkable breach of etiquette and decorum.

'Wait!' I say, stopping Juan before his lips meet mine. I search out Mr Snow in the row of guests before me. 'I forgot to request your permission,' I say. 'Mr Snow, is this okay?'

'Is what okay?' he asks as his glasses slip down his nose.

'That we kiss,' I say. 'It's most certainly against hotel policy for workers to snog *en pleine vue* in the lobby.'

'For the love of ducks, Molly!' Angela calls out.

'Be a rebel! Break the rule!' Speedy calls out.

'Molly, of course it's okay,' says Mr Snow.

I look at Juan, and I nod. He leans in and kisses me, and I throw my arms around him with complete abandon.

A whoop of joy crescendos around us. Am I levitating or has my brand-new husband lifted me off the floor? When I open my eyes again, I'm on the bottom step of the grand staircase, held in the arms of a man who for richer or poorer, in sickness or in health, will love me for the rest of my days. Never in my life have I been happier than in this moment.

It is late. I'm sitting on the stage in the Regency Grand Tearoom. I've kicked off my white kitten heels, though no felines were harmed in their creation. I'm sitting in my beautiful white wedding dress, resting my feet after too much dancing. This night – it's been the most magical of my entire life. It's not over yet, though. I just need a little break to catch my breath.

The guests are still on the dance floor – maids and bellhops, waiters and cooks, valets and receptionists. The men have loosened their ties, and like me, the women are now mostly barefoot. True to his word, DJ Slay is 'killing it with the spins.' Song after song, the guests just keep on dancing. Even Mr Snow is in on it. He's removed his pocket square and is waving it as a flag as he leads a conga line around the room. Cheryl is between Sunitha and Sunshine, her face a tight grimace, but her feet do a little bunny hop that reveals more joy than I've ever seen her express before. Angela's hair has gone completely rogue, and Lily, who's in line behind her, squeals every time she's swatted by an unruly strand. My gran-dad sits at a table with Baxley Brown, Steve, and Detective Stark. They're all grinning at the antics on the floor. Angela grabs the detective, who tries to protest but eventually claims her natural role as the conga line's powerful tail.

Juan is walking toward me. He climbs the stairs to the stage and collapses in the seat beside mine.

'This is for you,' he says, offering me a Regency Grand plate with a slice of cake on it. It's not just any cake. It's the top layer of the Noah's ark wedding cake his staff baked specially for us, featuring two of every marzipanimal Juan has ever created. The literal *pièce de résistance* now stands on the slice in front of me – two giraffes, one in a black tuxedo, the other in a white wedding gown.

'We're giraffe marzipanimals,' I say.

'It's a marzi-miracle,' Juan replies.

'This whole night feels like a miracle, a dream come true.'

'The speeches,' Juan says. 'I'll never forget them.'

'Nor will I,' I say. First, Mr Snow gave a toast that turned into a long-winded discourse on a drone's duty to protect the queen bee. When Angela cut him off, Speedy took the floor, saying something I barely understood. Last, my gran-dad, a.k.a. Mr Preston, thanked all the guests for attending and spoke at length about the great mystery of love. 'If it's false, it never returns; if it's true, it comes back to you when you least expect it,' he said. He then reminded us that those who could not attend our wedding in person were there in spirit. At first, I thought he meant Juan's family, but when he looked at me and bowed his head, I knew exactly who he meant – Gran. And I also knew that he, like me, had accepted the fact that Maggie – his daughter, my mother – was never coming back again.

'Juan!' shouts a young sous-chef from the dance floor. 'Speedy's got a spin dilemma. He needs you in the booth.'

'Do you mind?' Juan asks me.

'Not at all,' I say. He kisses my cheek and heads to the DJ booth at the back of the tearoom as Baxley Brown walks up the stairs toward me.

'Molly,' he says. 'I'm leaving shortly, but I wanted to give you this.'

He passes me a pale blue envelope.

'That's very kind,' I say. 'There's a box by the exit that you can drop it in.'

'I'd rather this stayed in your hand,' he replies.

'Very well,' I say.

'I had a great night,' Baxley says, 'but Steve and I have an early start tomorrow. We've got a meeting with a network looking to launch a new show featuring long-lost art.'

'Sounds like a new start.'

'I hope so,' he says. 'For you, too. Congratulations, Molly. And please open that envelope sometime tonight. Don't wait too long.'

'As you wish,' I say. 'Thank you for coming.'

Baxley bows, and I stand and curtsy back.

Once he's left the room, I open the envelope as requested. It's a card to celebrate our wedding, and there's a check inside, which I place on the table as I read the message in the card:

Dear Molly,

I'm sorry your family suffered because of mine. Shall we change the course of history? To make amends, I offer this, no strings attached, on your wedding day. Have a wonderful life.

– Baxley Brown

At first, I have no idea what to make of this message, but when I pick up the check, I realize with a shock that it's for an astonishing sum – $500,000. For a second, I think I'm seeing things.

Juan bounds up the stairs.

'Molly, are you okay?' he asks as he takes in my slack-jawed face.

I show him the card and the check. 'Juan, Mr Brown gave us money – I think it's the proceeds from the museum that took the egg. We can buy our apartment now.'

Juan studies the check. 'No. Is this for real? Did he forget to place the decimal?'

'It's for real,' I say. 'That man's ancestors were rotten, but I tell you, Baxley Brown is a good egg.'

I take the check and put it back in the card, placing it in Juan's warm hands. 'Give this to Mr Snow. Tell him to put it in his safe, *tout de suite.* Tell him to treat it like the Fabergé.'

Juan nods, then runs down the stairs to find Mr Snow.

I sit in my chair again as the music changes tempo. 'Unforgettable' plays and couples take to the floor. For the first time all night, I'm alone at the head table, but no sooner do I have the thought than I see her, clear as day, take a seat in the chair beside me. This has never happened before. Up until now, she's only ever been a voice in my head, an echo from the past. But now, she is right here. And she's sitting beside me holding her favorite teacup, the one with the cottage scene on it. Her hair is silver-white, her crow's-feet crinkle as she smiles at me, her face a pure and golden glow. My gran.

She takes a sip of tea, then looks down at the ring on my finger. *Once upon a time,* she says, *I dreamt of this day.*

'So did I, Gran. So did I.'

I never knew my dream would come true.

'Nor did I,' I reply.

My dear Molly, life is a fairy tale.

Wonders never cease.

And love – love is the greatest gift of all.

ACKNOWLEDGEMENTS

Readers, the first thank-you goes to you. Thank you for all the letters and notes you've sent me over the years, for sharing your thoughts and personal stories about this series. You've reminded me that books have a magical power to bring people together. You've also been the most generous caretakers (as good as Gran!) – protecting Molly, rooting for her, and generally proving that you are, as Molly would say, very good eggs. Thank you for loving Molly.

Thanks also to the following people, all of whom have helped me find my way through the maze of story:

Madeleine Milburn. There are more things to thank you for than I can possibly enumerate here, but most of all, thank you for having such faith in my ability to find a new voice in this book and for always guiding me with such grace and intuitive wisdom.

The amazing team at Madeleine Milburn Literary Agency – Rachel Yeoh, Valentina Paulmichl, Hannah Kettles, Giles

Milburn, Saskia Arthur, Megan Capper, and Hannah Ladds. How is it that you're an ocean away, and yet I know you're cheering me on from afar? Your good spirit, your positive energy, your talent, and your endless hard work is such an inspiration. You are my people.

Massive thanks to the superb team at Ballantine, especially my editor, Hilary Teeman, who has been there from the very beginning and who has helped shaped Molly and the entire world of this series into what it has become. And to Kara Welsh, Kim Hovey, Taylor Noel, Megan Whalen, Karen Fink, Angie Campusano, Elsa Richardson-Bach, Diane McKiernan, Elena Giavaldi, Virginia Norey, Pamela Alders, Cindy Berman, Angela McNally, Sandra Sjursen – thank you for the big and small things you do every day to bring my books to life.

Also across an ocean are the endlessly creative folks at HarperFiction UK. My unfailingly poised editor Charlotte Brabbin always inspires me to give just that extra bit more, and her team – including Maddy Marshall, Frankie Gray, Holly Martin, Harriet Williams, Emily Scorer, Lynne Drew, Libby Haddock, Ellie Game, and Ruth Burrow – have made publishing such a pleasure.

To my beloved home team of Penguins, including Kristin Cochrane, Adria Iwasutiak, Bonnie Maitland, Meredith Pal, Beth Cockeram, Sara James, Catherine Knowles, Marion Garner, and Kelly Hill. Thank you for stepping up and leaning in when I needed it the most. I am so lucky to count you as colleagues and friends. You continue to teach me every day and to remind me what's so wonderful about this madcap business we're in.

To Josie Freedman, for helping me navigate the TV and film world.

To Arlyn Miller-Lachmann, for essential early reads.

To Nicole Winstanley, for her wisdom and brilliance.

To my dear friends, who know exactly when to make me laugh and how. Thanks to Sarah Fulton, Aileen Umali and Eric Rist, Martin Ortuzar and Ingrid Nasager, Roberto Verdecchia, Sue Trenholm, Clodine Sponagle, Sarah St. Pierre, Janie Yoon, Adria Iwasutiak, Sarah Gibson, Felicia Quon, Jess Scott, and Zoe Maslow.

To my family, always – Tony and Theo, Dan and Patty, Devin and Joane, Freddie and Pat. And to Jackie and Paul, forever in the margins and in the wide, blank spaces between the lines.

Discover more novels in the Molly the maid series by the *Sunday Times* bestseller, Nita Prose

There's a festive mystery unfolding at the Regency Grand Hotel . . .

Enjoy a seasonal novella featuring Molly the maid

Available now